MISSING EARTH

MISSING EARTH

C.H. BYART

Copyright © 2017 C.H. Byart
All rights reserved.

ISBN-13: 9781542662024
ISBN-10: 1542662028
Library of Congress Control Number: 2017901233
CreateSpace Independent Publishing Platform
North Charleston, South Carolina

*is dedicated, with love, to my wonderful boys:
Jonathan, Sean, William & Patrick.*

CONTENTS

Glossary · ix

Part I · 1
Chapter 1   Surveyors of Fate · 3
Chapter 2   The Potion · 7
Chapter 3   The Evil Demons · 14
Chapter 4   Good and Bad Virgins · 18
Chapter 5   Godless Ouroboros · 23
Chapter 6   The Greater Good · 27
Chapter 7   Idle Playfulness · 31
Chapter 8   Follow Yourself · 35
Chapter 9   Matthew · 40
Chapter 10   Bonds that Bind · 49
Chapter 11   I Feel Happy Here · 54
Chapter 12   Aperture Aberrations · 58
Chapter 13   Crucifixion · 60
Chapter 14   The Grace of God · 67
Chapter 15   Human Weakness · 71
Chapter 16   A Glimpse of Heaven · 74
Chapter 17   You Could Not Think Ahead or Behind · · · · · · · · · 81
Chapter 18   Struggling Optics · 86
Chapter 19   Madness · 92

Chapter 20	Picasso	97
Chapter 21	A New Contented Stillness	104
Chapter 22	The Need for Softness	107
Chapter 23	Immeasurable	110
Chapter 24	Staring Into Your Soul	113
Chapter 25	Soranus and Eolus	120
Chapter 26	Paranoia	127
Chapter 27	The Gift	130
Chapter 28	Pax Romana	135
Chapter 29	In Due Time	142
Chapter 30	Gaius Suetonius Paulinus	151
Chapter 31	Shalom, Aelius Galenus	157

Part II **163**

Chapter 32	The Light is Free	165
Chapter 33	The Well	167
Chapter 34	Travels with a Drui	171
Chapter 35	Orin	174
Chapter 36	The UnderWings	179
Chapter 37	Missing Earth	190
Chapter 38	Finding Yeshua	200
Chapter 39	Spirit of Man	228
Chapter 40	Becan	233

Part III **259**

Chapter 41	Dolphins	261
Chapter 42	Frozen Currents	272
Chapter 43	I Will Never Fly	291
Chapter 44	Yeshua's Nest	299
Chapter 45	The Dry Pond	310
Chapter 46	Innis and Aine	319
Chapter 47	Muriell	328

| Author's Note | 337 |
| About the Author | 341 |

GLOSSARY

Abrux	husband of Glenna, friend of Galen
Adonia	mother of Soranus and Eolus
Agricola	Roman Consul and Governor, responsible for the complete and final conquest of Britannia, late first century
Aine	loyal Briton, wife of Innis
Alana	adopted daughter of Orin and Tiernan
Anthousa	wife of Nicon Galenus, mother of Galen
Armaigen	first Drui on Earth who commands all earth spirits, friend of Tiernan and Yeshua
Asclepius	god of medicine in ancient Greek mythology
Becan	son of Elestrem and Nuada, adopted son of Yeshua
Barrius	Roman Legion Legate, IX Geminia Legion
Borvo	village liar and cheat
Brithomar	Chieftain and Briton warrior, Silures tribe
Caeoimhin	son of Orin and Tiernan
Cathal	Chieftain and Briton warrior, Deceangli tribe
Doros	bully and drunk of Pergamon

Egan	son of Orin and Tiernan
Eircheard	brother of Armaigen
Elestrem	wife of Nuada and Yeshua
Eolus	brother of Soranus and half-brother to Galen
Francoise	travelling American student in Europe
Gaius Suetonius Paulinus	Governor of Britannia, Roman Imperial Legate
Galen (Aelius Galenus)	Greek physician, friend of Armaigen, Tiernan and Yeshua
Glenna	wife of Abrux, friend of Galen
Hypatos	senior servant to Galen
Innis	loyal Briton, husband to Aine
Joseph	father of Yeshua
James	brother of Yeshua
Kiefer	Roman General, Batavian Amphibious Unit
Lazarus	friend and follower of Yeshua; was raised from the dead by Yeshua
Matthew	disciple of Yeshua
Morgana	wife of Brithomar
Muriell	sister of Armaigen
Nicon Galenus	husband of Anthousa, father of Galen
Nuada	husband of Elestrem
Orin	wife of Tiernan, Drui warrior
Picasso	artist, creator of cubism
Pilate	Pontius Pilate was the Prefect of the Roman province of Judaea, responsible for the execution of Yeshua
Pliny the Elder	Roman historian and philosopher who documented the ceremonies of the Druids.
Ronat	Briton warrior, Silures tribe
Rozenwyn	daughter of Elestrem and Nuada, adopted daughter of Yeshua

Salome	sister of Yeshua
Simon	brother of Yeshua
Slavious	Roman Legion Legate, XX Valeria Legion
Soranus	brother of Eolus, half-brother of Galen
Tiernan	apprentice to Armaigen, friend of Yeshua, Drui leader who commands all earth spirits
Taryn	Briton warrior, Silures tribe
Yeshua	spirit of man, friend of Armaigen and Tiernan
Ynys Mon	Welsh name for the island of Anglesey

MISSING EARTH

C.H. BYART

If the blades of warm grass had been allowed to grow,
The still heaven and earth were to freely flow,

All joyous singing, wet mouths praising never old,
Then this spirit story naught ever need be told.

C.H. Byart

PART I

Chapter 1

SURVEYORS OF FATE

Now I smile; that night, I was terrified.

I was afraid as I stared into the blue round hood of the old stranger. There was a storm outside, and the lamps flickered with the movement of many servants trying to light the dark room.

I could only see the dissimilar shadows of his face as he examined me. He seemed busy doing something, and I heard the muted sounds of many different voices. His tall body was hunched over, like a bird picking at a dead fish. I felt his hot, fresh breath as he looked at my skin and bones, pressing softly on my stomach, chest and shoulders. He sat beside me and held my wrist.

I felt trapped. I wanted to run away, but did not have the strength, for my fever controlled me.

The stranger pushed back his hood revealing an ordinary, dark-sunned face; blue eyes edged a comforting smile. He stroked my forehead brushing the hair from my face. He closed his eyes, as mine became wide as the sun. Then, as if on cue, I closed my eyes as he placed his cold hand over my face; I felt the slight trembling of his voice, as he mumbled something, it sounded like the language that was spoken to the poor or mad beggars in the street, I usually ignored.

There was a momentary silence and I wished that he was finished. I opened my eyes; he stared at me, stroking my cheek and said quietly,

"Not feeling well? We will fix that, my little spirit. It's not too late. You will soon be running around again."

My father blurted out, breaking the submissive silence, "We will pay anything. Do anything."

The hooded stranger continued looking at me as he held one hand up to stop my father from speaking. He kindly studied me, "My name is Armaigen." He pointed to the other man standing at our table, "That is Tiernan; he is my apprentice." And as he smiled, his long, grey beard curled up at the bend of his mouth. "In the corner behind me, is young Yeshua. He is making something special for you, something I have taught him."

Yeshua was busy and did not say anything at first. His head was down, busy at work with his hands; then he looked up and smiled. He was carving something? What was it? He looked not much older than I, with tangled, long hair and a full beard. He was seemingly full of strength and excitement, yet he looked young enough to be one of my friends. I felt that, soon, when he was older, he could be anyone's friend, for that matter.

This did not make sense to me at the time and I was happy to see someone nearly my age. I smiled, weakly, with my lips only. Yeshua stared at me, nodded and continued working, still smiling, concentrating with his head bowed. Both of our eyes had briefly met; his eyes almost appeared as two stars in the dimly lit room. I wanted to see his eyes again. Perhaps they had reflected off the lamps, for the room had a stillness, like we were in one of those huge Roman temples my father builds. They were hollowed-out places where you gave homage to something, and sensed an unspoken respect. I was not sure of myself; the exhausting symptoms of my fever caused many vague impressions and a careless vulnerability.

The other stranger, Tiernan, busied himself at the table; he appeared much younger than old Armaigen. Tiernan had a full, dark beard and a mischievous concentration while working. He had pushed his hood and sleeves back, and appeared occupied, as he gave a quick glance in my direction. He was madly scraping and crushing something in a bowl, taking other leaves or roots from his leather bag, muttering to himself, sorting different plants and breaking off certain quantities in the mixing bowl. He added and drained out the excess water onto the ground, until the right mixture was decided upon.

I was only an observer; I did not really understand exactly what he was doing, but I had the feeling that whatever he was making, I would have to put in my mouth.

Tiernan then stopped, looked closely at the bowl, smelling it, as he seemed suddenly pleased with himself. He passed the bowl to Armaigen. I thought he might be Armaigen's brother for they seemed related in some way. I was just a child; it had no meaning to me for all men with beards looked alike.

Maybe all three were brothers?

Armaigen dipped one finger into the bowl and tasted it. He also smelled it slowly, like savoring a hot drink, thinking carefully for a few moments. Tiernan went back to his table, wiping it clean.

Friendly Yeshua appeared beside me, holding my head up, as I cautiously gulped; Armaigen gently poured the entire contents, slowly down my throat. I could not breathe at first, choking, gasping for air, as Yeshua said, "Breathe. Slowly. Look at me." Then, afterwards, he gently laid my head back when finished. "Good."

I did not feel good. It was so hot and stale in the room. Armaigen patted my shoulder, smiling, "That will help you."

It tasted worse as I felt it drain into my stomach. I began coughing, wanting to sit up but Armaigen held me down as I struggled. I turned, "Father! I feel sick."

I even arched my back trying to escape, but I was too weak. Armaigen held me down, then let go, warning me, "Lay still. The taste will go soon."

Yeshua looked at Armaigen, "Perhaps more water?"

Armaigen agreed, "Just to wash the taste from his mouth."

"Yes." Yeshua poured a bowl of water; he studied the water, mixing it with his finger, almost playing with it, as a child like me would. As he brought it over, he smiled, "It's so clear, so cold."

Armaigen lifted my head up. He then cupped his fingers, filling his hand with water, as it slowly dripped into my mouth. "It will wash the bitter taste away. You will feel better. The first time it is always bitter and dry." He stroked my face. I nodded, trusting him. I knew I was safe and would not die that night.

Chapter 2

THE POTION

Armaigen stood upright and went over to Tiernan. "How much longer will you be?"

"Not long."

Yeshua wiped his hands on his clothing and sat on the bed beside me. He reached inside his cloak, "I have a gift for you, my little friend. I think I may have missed a spot." He showed me and I said nothing. He looked carefully at whatever he had made. "Yes, of course." He continued speaking as he applied blue paint from one of his fingers to the small, white chiton poderes figure, concentrating, "I believe the custom is blue stripes?"

He looked up at my confused father and held it up to him, "A physician?" My father looked puzzled, for he did not understand what was going on at the time. He came closer to look, as his voice trailed away, "A physician? What does this mean?"

Yeshua spoke quietly with a whisper to me, but everyone in the room could hear what he said, "Keep it close to you. Follow it. It is a refuge."

Armaigen and Tiernan nodded, not looking.

Armaigen came closer looking at me, then my father, "Much depends on this. Your son, Aelius Galenus will save the earth one day."

Yeshua placed the wooden figure in the palm of my hand. I saw that the figure was an older man. It was very detailed, not as old as my father, for the wooden figure had dark, brown hair, a beard and was taller. Yeshua wrapped my fingers tightly around it, held my hand, and looked deeply into my eyes. I was worried to look back into his eyes at first, and it took some moments to focus on his bright, happy eyes, as I felt a growing confidence and became inquisitive to stare back without interruption or fear.

Yeshua's eyes shimmered, like hot, glass stones on a beach. I even saw specks of gold or silver. It was not clear to me, for I was a boy and did not know how all eyes were supposed to look, but these eyes were different. Perhaps, it was the light in the room playing tricks with me. For how could anyone have pieces of colourful stones in their eyes that blushed like water?

"I will miss you, my little friend." He clasped his hand harder around my hand. "Take care of this."

Yeshua looked at the blue paint remaining on his fingers and then at me. He hesitated and seemed to think about wiping his hands on his clothing but stopped. He then drew a blue circle on my forehead and said to my father, "Do not wash this off, it will come off by itself in a few days. Allow the dye to sink in, to become a part of him. Show him what it looks like by drawing it many times, then he will remember it. It is life itself."

My father stuttered, agreeing, but not understanding, "Help him draw it? Yes, of course! I am an architect!"

Yeshua looked down at me, "Be like a ship's pilot in a storm. Can you do that for me?" I knew what a pilot did; the words that came to mind were 'smart' and 'brave'.

My father looked grateful and weak to the strangers. He did not understand too much at that moment. "Yes. Of course, we will. A ships pilot; I will help him, I think." He seemed confused and never did talk to me about the meaning of the pilot later, and I felt no need to ask. Sometimes, we all miss the obvious.

Armaigen looked slightly uncomfortable. He looked at Yeshua; he was expecting him to say something else. Apologetically, he looked at my father, then Yeshua again. "Yeshua's youthful enthusiasm for insights gets beyond even us and sometimes, too much talk is not good. Much has happened tonight." Armaigen looked at me, "You must rest."

Tiernan had cleared the table of bowls but he seemed bothered by something and hurried, stuffing the contents in the last of his bags. He muttered, "The Romans. We must go!" He seemed preoccupied, and in a hurry to leave.

Yeshua did not seem rushed, but at ease. He quietly smiled at me, raising an eyebrow about some good news he wanted to tell me, but he kept it to himself; it was his little secret.

Armaigen continued, "He will sleep soon. Leave the paint on. Do not wash it off for now. Let him sleep and gain his strength back. By tomorrow, you will notice a difference."

"Galenus will get the best care. This, I promise." My father looked around the room at the strangers. "How did you know to come? I did not expect anyone, especially tonight. The other physicians said they could not help anymore. It was up to the gods."

Tiernan did not look up, putting the last item back into the bag tying it tightly with a snap. He sounded sarcastic, speaking slowly, "The gods! You might as well say that men do not need to eat." He shook his head as he lifted some bags up and around his shoulder; waiting.

Armaigen paused and patiently looked at Tiernan. He turned his head back trying to make a final point, "What Yeshua was saying is that the blue circle has many meanings. It is a blessing. You must keep it to yourself, what happened here tonight. No one must know or your son will be in danger. We were not here; that is your story. Do not mention our names."

"Are the Romans looking for you?"

I held the carving of the physician flat on my chest, watching the faces of everyone in the room. The mood seemed to shift to one of uncertainty and tension. I was beginning to feel tired.

Armaigen, "Yes. They seek us."

"What is your crime?"

"Murder."

"What?" My father looked suddenly alarmed.

Armaigen, "Be not afraid of us, it is the Romans. You Greeks know what the Romans are like, the positions they get us into."

"You risked your life coming into our village? How did you know my boy was sick?"

"We travel. We all travel; the air floats us like ships." Armaigen moved his hands following the motion of the waves. He looked down at me and the figure I was holding.

I was nearly asleep; I tried so hard to stay awake.

"The carving will help him know what he is to do as he becomes a man." Then he made a circle in the air, "It is a route to follow."

"How?"

Armaigen, "We do not know all the answers. Life grows as any condition permits. We, all of us, hear and see the voices in the wind. That is what brought us here. We are all healers, speakers, restorers of the land. Our sole mission is to serve all that is seen and unseen. If we can cure a small boy, then we have done our job. Roman feet suffocate all land on this earth. Some call the Romans good fortune, but the spirits of the land are suffering. Your son is an important part of what is to come and you both must be silent about today, for the rest of your lives. Your boy has been blessed; accept the path I speak of."

There was a pause, as Armaigen continued, "Tell him that he will grow old, but not look old, and that he must search for us when he is a man."

"How will he know where to go? Or when?"

"It will just happen. That is all we know or can tell you."

I tried to keep my eyes open but the words were beginning to be a blur of smoky, jumbled letters, without any meaning to me. The fever, my seemingly miraculous cure by strangers, it was all too much and I don't remember falling asleep, like a contented cat.

My father later told me that Tiernan gave him five leather bags full of the medicine I had just taken. The instructions of what it was, and how to make it, were fortunately written by Yeshua in Greek, the only written language my father knew. When I was young, my father would mix it every week, always making sure there was a good supply of it in the house.

As I got older, I learned from my father, the right blend of plants while following the correct sequence of the recipe and other necessary additions.

My father also said that Yeshua innocently boasted, while writing everything down in Greek, that he could speak and write most of the languages in the Empire, including Arabic. Tiernan effortlessly dictated, often repeating important stages of the mixture back to him. Yeshua would speak about any fact or feeling that caught his attention when it entered his mind, while he wrote the instructions on how to make the potion as it was dictated by Tiernan.

Yeshua continued his joyful behaviour, humming, whistling, as it caused much frustration to Armaigen who patiently waited for Tiernan to finish. Armaigen was a secretive man, a calm and humble man, with the strength of a permanent apparition. He seemed to have many things on his mind, perhaps not achieved or completed, and a determination to complete some unknown task or journey; he now just wanted to leave and be somewhere else. Both he and Tiernan seemed increasingly restless, uneasy, in the dim room.

Armaigen became agitated and uncomfortable while pacing slightly and glanced at Yeshua. He seemed anxious that he would say too much of truths that did not concern us.

Afterwards, my father said that he thought Armaigen would have preferred that Yeshua kept to the essential actions of the moment, of just recording the ingredients and instructions of the potion.

Tiernan was observed as a man, more straightforward and practical, a paradox of feelings that was insightful, compared to his secretive appearance. He wanted to finish his job quickly and leave us; he appeared troubled.

When my father asked about how they had all met, Tiernan said, "Where do I start? It is not a simple story. The ending is more important than the beginning, even *we* do not know what exactly will happen in the end, but we are hopeful. Armaigen and I have been together for many years. Like he said, we are healers, keepers of the land. It won't mean much to you but we are Druids. Yeshua has been with us for a short time. He is not an apprentice like me, but essentially, Yeshua is simply, Yeshua."

"What is a Drui?"

Armaigen became mad, "Forget that word and never speak of it again. We are an enemy of the Romans. As I said, it could put your own family in danger, if it is spoken outside this room."

Tiernan went back to his work. He studiously emphasized noteworthy facts over and over to Yeshua who was writing every word down.

Armaigen repeated it again to my father, "Only your son can take the plants and herbs we have left you. They are not for you. We are *truly* sorry. They must be locked up in a wooden box, stored in a dark, cool place, especially in this climate. The location is known only to you and remains a family secret forever. Otherwise, not only you and your son will be in danger, but so will the earth we all live in. Every seven days, Galenus must drink the mixture. You must always have plenty made up. Do not forget! Do you understand?"

Alarmed and afraid that he correctly heard every detail, and that he was not missing anything, my father repeated, "Yes. Seven days. But what will it do? It is safe?"

Tiernan, "Of course it is safe. We all take it and we are all well. But only your son can take it – you understand this? You have no need of this." Tiernan gave a cold stare towards my father.

My father, who was quick to please, nodded, "Yes, only my son, every seven days."

Tiernan, "That's right, only your son."

The travellers did not want any money. Any mention of money for payment was abruptly ignored, with one of them saying that they did not need it. But they would be grateful for some food and water from our well before they left.

The thunder and lightning had stopped; the veil downpour of hard, conspicuous rain continued.

My father sent servants outside to make sure there were no Romans about. The sky was still dark. The strangers left, as they had come: unrestrained and sculpting clear of the rain until they were no more. They had gone, slipping into the narrow street, leaving Pergamon forever.

Chapter 3

THE EVIL DEMONS

I awoke the next morning and saw my tired, but grateful father. He had tears in his eyes, so happy that I was now awake and well.

I no longer thought as a normal child; I felt different, yet my body was the same as yesterday. He told me to lay still; the servants had been instructed to take care of me. Soon, I was so bored with being in bed for so long, that I jumped out of bed to look out of the window. I asked whether I could go outside. My father grudgingly relented, so I was instructed to not leave the veranda but to stay in the shade away from the hot sun. I was so hungry that I am sure that I ate most of the food in the house, as the servants went out for more food to be brought in.

I was just a boy who was now well; I quickly forgot what it was like to be sick. Obviously, my father saw more importance in their visit.

As a child, I only thought of them occasionally; obscure faces covered with elegant opaqueness. My memory of the dark, healing room was caressed with the lines of daylight; the faces of the strangers sometimes haunted me, as the shadow of a tree moves during an interesting storm in the night.

I was impressed, looking back, that my wealthy father had the good judgement and discipline to keep writing down as much as he could remember from that night. All the notes from my father about the three strangers, along with my daily journals, were stored in my secret potion room.

The next day, my father told the servants not to bother him for several days. Food was to be delivered to his room. I was allowed into his private room and played quietly, but he was easily distracted due to his frustration. Quickly, he tried to focus on writing everything down that was said by the three strangers. He called them 'strangers' but I felt a connection to them that I could not explain, like relatives that you do not often see.

He would read back his notes to me and would ask what I had noticed or remembered. The questions were very detailed. It also included my father's attempt at sketching the face of each man, with small notations about any unique physical features. I contributed more when he was drawing the shapes of their eyes. Their faces were so close to mine and their breath smelled like the breeze of warm, wilted lilacs in the spring. I even drew my own pictures of their faces, which my father said looked more realistic than his own.

At every spare moment, my father studied his notes from that important night. He did not sleep for nearly one week. He scribbled notes, then revised them, and spoke out loud often, when I was present or not; what did it all mean? As I child, I did not see the complete significance.

As I got older, and entered medical school, it was obvious to those who knew me that I looked younger than most men my age. My father noticed and would review his journal and add extra thoughts regarding why I had been chosen; he told me often that I would save the earth. It was a sobering thought that frightened me, for I was now a physician and did not like violence.

How could *I* change or save the earth?

So, as he aged, and his business slowed down, he spent his spare time reading and researching all the words and phrases that were spoken that night, even paying people to translate the meaning of their names in numerous languages, dialects and accents.

Mostly, he did not make progress, defining the many possible meanings of the words and phrases spoken that night: 'refuge', 'the ending is more important that the beginning', 'Aelius Galenus would save the earth'; all which would be impossible under Roman rule. Still, the potion was working and I was not aging very fast at all. Why was I not aging?

Even the circle drawn on my head by Yeshua made my father think back to that night. Sometimes, he would trace the circle on my forehead and pause, trying to receive some sort of illumination, but it only prompted more theories and questions with no answers. The three strangers did not appear to be gods. But one fact that we both noticed was that I was beginning to look exactly like the man figure carved by Yeshua.

My father studied the wooden statue Yeshua had carved, often feeling it. "Can you make any sense of this? Are they ghosts of the night? I felt no threat. They did not seem like killers, yet they honestly admitted murder. What are we to do? It must be some sort of confusion."

"Are they coming back?"

"No." My father handed me back the small statue. "I know they healed you and I've told you not to mention it to anyone, but I don't want them back. Be grateful that you are alive and that is all that matters."

"What you say makes me afraid."

He hesitated, as he paused, still thinking, "Sometimes, you will meet men who are not like us. I don't know how to put this because they healed you. They certainly meant no harm, but I felt slightly difficult around them, like they knew everything about me; they knew what I was thinking. They were men who lived in a certain way that is not for us. Our place is here. It is a comfortable life." He paused again for his thoughts were a tangled mess of inconsistencies. "I honestly don't know. I only know that they are not like us and never will be."

"Should we stay away from them?"

"No. We will not have to. I don't think they will come back here. It is you who will go to seek them out. Yes, after so many years, this is what I feel will happen."

For years, local stories and myths were told of the travellers throughout the Empire, especially by other strangers passing through our village. When prodded for more information, many said that they, too, had heard of them, some had even seen them. These strangers would call them, 'spirito del male' or evil spirits and demons. Of course, as any interesting story goes, more facts were invented than could be possibly true; many said that they were not mortal men, but evil gods disguised as men.

They were feared by the Romans, who had placed a price on their heads; alive or dead. My father told me that it was likely that many innocent men and women were being accused of being these evil gods and killed in the colosseum.

These stories eventually stopped. After many years, the so-called 'reliable witnesses' of the demons had moved away or died; my father and I became the only survivor of the truth, which we kept secret. Occasionally, unscrupulous men and women still passed through our town, seeking a drachm or two to tell stories to those who would listen about the demons. By now, the story had been relegated to a desperate Greek myth; a story of fiction as the Roman gods now ruled our lives.

The Romans continued to hunt everywhere for them, and there was a rumour that they had even created a special cavalry unit to find them. By then, most citizens were occupied with some other new dilemma or Roman threat that they did not really care; a new generation had replaced the old. The plague that I had survived was a distant terrifying story; a fading memory to most.

Chapter 4

GOOD AND BAD VIRGINS

I was born as Aelius Galenus, in Pergamon, Greece, a half days walk to the beautiful, blue Aegean.

My mother, like many other women died in childbirth. I am getting better at saving lives but even I cannot prevent all deaths, although I possess the surreptitious medical knowledge of physicians living thousands of years from now.

The Romans were a capricious lot to any conquered lands. My name was changed by the Romans to just, *Galen.*

It was not formally altered with any imperial edict; it would have been nice for that to happen to any Greek, in any position. It was not that important, for life is an ephemeral transition. Other personal matters consumed my attention; but one day it was somehow mispronounced carelessly by an outspoken, near deaf soldier during their occupation.

Even the round sign outside, with two white, entwined, winged serpents stated my full Greek name proudly; the Romans seemed to think it was some sort of a joke. Maybe it was not the name, but how I appeared to them; I was a tall, sad, young-looking man with a thin face and a long slim nose. I knew I was not the most attractive man, compared to Roman standards but I more than made up for it living an interesting, covert, hidden life.

Quite by chance, a thoughtless soldier visited me one day and had several abscessed teeth. He saw my sign and came in. It was odd to treat a Roman for they had their own physicians. I just wanted to quickly get rid of him, so I removed his teeth and gave him an antibiotic without thinking. Soon, my skill of treating abscessed teeth was well-known; I was young and it was a nervous, depressing time. Teeth were easy and so wearisome to treat; I craved a higher level of knowledge.

Strangely, my new name did become permanent, even accepted, by my fellow Greeks. However, I heard that numerous Roman physicians had told most soldiers not see me. These same inquisitive Roman physicians, from time to time, would come to me and question how I was curing gum abscesses. Of course, I did not reveal any of my secrets but acted the fool, for that is what they expected.

My father's name never changed: Nicon Galenus. He was older and respected by the Romans as an architect and more outspoken, often bragging when drunk, that his buildings stood like gods. He sometimes picked on me that my physician healing was transient in nature for the sick would eventually die. What did it matter? He would tease me, sometimes in front of other people in our own house when feasting on astakos (lobster); he said that my good nature and knowledge was wasted on patients who were like sardeles (scavenger fish), hunted by the useless seagull vultures.

"You deprive yourself of wealth and privilege. Your deeds are unnoticed by the gods for you do only ordinary acts. What is the matter with you?"

I kept quiet and never reacted to these outbursts and perhaps that is why he felt free to say them so often, because he knew I would not say anything back. He felt life cheated him, for he loved only my mother, but she was dead and he was alone. He was never really angry at me but frustrated that I could not be an architect; the decision had been made for him by strangers.

But with his wealth, my father was a friend of many powerful men. He lived in a large house, almost the size of the Roman Governor, but it was still not enough for him. He knew it was cruel to say such things to me. I knew he was jealous sometimes, for I stayed young as he grew old; I could not age as fast as a normal person. I was cheating death and he could not.

It all began because of an event that happened in my childhood, when three strangers visited and healed me. They told my father that the potion they had made was only for me.

My father was a rich, educated man. However, his instincts told him reluctantly, that his great intellect and talent had created a complicated life without an innate happiness. He once said to me that, "Stupid people were much happier, for they stare and think of nothing."

The three unusual strangers had made it very clear that the potion was made only for me and any attempt for him to take it from me or to stop taking it, would result in the death of me and most people on earth.

Of course, as he grew older, death crawled closer and he became even angrier at the smallest thing and sometimes he was very unpleasant to be with. These sudden outbursts, while embarrassing, were predictable and I began to avoid all contact with him. That is one of the reasons that when I became a man, I moved away into a comfortable, modest house enclosed by a high wall.

My father's life became one of enjoying as much pleasure as his position could dictate. There were dinner parties at his house several times a week and I was always welcome but cautious of how my father would be that night.

Often, he would say, sometimes shouting, "Get married! There are plenty of women looking for someone like you: a man who will inherit his father's wealth one day!"

I know it sounds childish, but I could never accept him seeing other women in what was essentially my mother's house. It was a lack of respect to my dead mother's memory. Yes, the women were beautiful, their bodies designed by the gods, but, at the end of the day, they were only a passing distraction.

I knew they were invited as possible marriage prospects for me. I was flattered and attracted to beauty like anyone else but I knew I could not marry anyone.

I should give my father credit, for he would not give up. Once, with several potential candidates standing close to me, all staring at me and acting happy, my father would quietly tell me, "I know, from a person who knows of such things, that all these women are good virgins. Take one before they are all gone."

It was like shopping in the market; I suppose I was a lucky man but I wondered how you could tell what a bad virgin looked like, for they all looked the same to me as a physician.

He waved his hands, shouting above the sound of music. "I have done all this for you."

"I'm not interested!"

"You do not want children? You live through your children. One day you will see that. Is there something wrong with you?"

One night, I took him outside away from the noise and people. "Look at me. You know I was to wait for a sign when I was healed that night. You even told me that they said I would save the earth, so stop all this. Be happy in knowing I enjoy being a physician; I am good at it. You should come around more to see the work we are doing."

There was a scream and more laughter coming from inside, as my father's name was called. He looked at me, slowly nodding; deep down he understood our fate. Then he would directly change back to that laughing old man as he walked away, desiring to squeeze as much fruit as he could from the young grapes before he closed his eyes for the last time.

I stood outside alone, looking at the full moon and the infinite number of stars. I knew that the universe was not a string puppet operated by the gods, but that there were laws of nature and physics; all things were made of atoms and gravitational singularity theorems. It was increasingly fascinating to me. Still, I was content in knowing that something had been planned for me. It was stimulating but sometimes distracting from more important, practical and immediate matters of my practice, which required my attention.

Something I cannot control, so I wait.

Inside, I could hear my father and looked in the door. I saw him dancing with women young enough to be his daughters. He shouted as he danced, "Omorfos! Omorfos!"

Several women came and pulled me in to dance with them and I followed smiling; for I was a man and the temptation sometimes was too much.

At that time, I had spent many days alone, thinking too much and I was often sad. It was somehow in my nature to feel a despondent anxiety. But with every bowl of wine, women became so beautiful and I knew it was not healthy to be sad at those moments. I had everything to live for.

Unknown even to my father, my intellectual knowledge of the future facts and events was greater than he could imagine. It was beyond the understanding of any person alive, except the three strangers.

Chapter 5

GODLESS OUROBOROS

In some way, we all eat away at ourselves, not seeing it or understanding what is bothering us at each moment.

The Romans were emotional cannibals.

Armaigen had instructed me to drink the bitter potion once a week. The plant mixture delayed aging and when I fell asleep, I had numerous visions.

One fact persisted, one that was constant and true: my visions predictably occurred in a hypnotic trance brought on by drinking my potion. It was my own true '*god particle*' which took place alone in my hidden room, once a week.

Interestingly, through many decades of visions, I observed and recorded the exact date in time, when these visions seemed to occur, in relation to my many other dreams.

I decided to let the Romans play it out, for I have glimpsed into the future and I am shocked and troubled.

I did not fully understand the famous string theory of all things real, which seemed important in some of my visions. I suppose one day I would pull together thousands of the educational talks that I have witnessed.

Over the years, I absorbed a vast, comprehensive, understanding of earth and did marvel at the phenomenal events that I saw in my visions.

This was not always easy, for it continued to be frustrating and wearisome as most of my visions would last for a short moment, and give me only a glimpse. Sometimes, randomly, a longer vision would occur filled with seemingly unrelated visions, until months or years later, I began to put all the knowledge pieces together. It was very confusing sometimes. There was no pattern at first and no reason why I saw what I did every week when I took my potion. I witnessed events that happened at any moment in time, up to well over 2000 years from now. So, there was bound to be an inexplicable oddness, incompatible and strange to the life we lived in Greece. But I still recorded every fact and detail in my journal, thinking it might be useful one day.

On the bright side, documentaries in my visions had shown me new fields of study. I witnessed how other future civilizations lived and died; a disobedient reverse of knowledge I could not change, for I was only an observer of historical events. My visions sometimes proudly announced that the information was for the minds of a scholar. It was really a misconception, for the visions were occasionally assigned stars; the more stars meant the better vision and this was overall called a *rating*. I did not understand or care why this seemed so important. The visions were like pertinacious anomalies of my existence.

I learned so much through the years. So many new fields of study: archaeology, anthropology, even forensic anthropology and psychology including vast medical knowledge of the body and surgery including DNA. Hundreds more fields and related areas of study were crammed into my brain; there was no end to it. The learning of the *cosmos* was especially of interest to me for it supported my theory that there was no god and why. Other areas of interest were wide and varied, from the Vikings, Egyptians, the British Empire and the powerful Mayans with their dark birthmark blotches and human sacrifices; including the belief that they were descendants of people coming down from the sky.

I could discuss and understand most things as a physician up to the end of the 22nd century. There was almost too much information, yet I sought more knowledge because my inquisitive nature dictated it. Stem cell research was fascinating and how one could be cured including the manipulation of the aging gene. As was the information that we all have Neanderthal DNA, it was truly intriguing. I did not like those visions that included the world wars, mass killings by a madman or religious terrorism; it was too much to take, knowing that there was no god. My mind easily jumped from one vision to another, as I reflected of my present life in Greece versus the future when we are all dead; we all live an abortive life.

Events happen, but who remembers the common person after so many years have passed? I often think of Trafalgar and Waterloo; the battle between three or four countries, with only one victor without any significance, after one hundred years or so. Immortality is wished for by losers. What does anything matter but being healthy and happy? Sometimes cynicism seeps through me and the saying from some 20th century slang expression sums it up best, 'we are all legends in our own mind.' I also grew to love colloquialisms; 'ain't life a bitch' or 'shit happens'. I suppose there was too much information and analysis; in the future, quick negative summaries permeated all cultures.

Wait, do not delete me yet. The program is not over and we can create more insight for the viewer if we promote another interpretation or make you imagine a sense of temporary gilded greatness; inferring there is a link between intellectual knowledge and the creation of more wealth, which leads to driving bigger cars, if this is your thing. And just when a vision began to get interesting there were always commercial breaks at critical moments: food, household cleaners and even vacations to Greece! Or, "if you phone the number on your screen in the next thirty minutes, we will give you a set of plastic lunch containers." What is a plastic lunch? What is a phone?

The rich created greed; it is an easy emotion of desire for the poor that spitefully consumes everything they see, for they can only dream it into their lives, like an empty lottery.

Sometimes, the visions became so relative, without meaning; for there were so many of them. The sheer number of pictures dilutes the absolute sum. Perhaps there is no absolute sum because comedy, drama and tragedy waver like several burning oil lamps in a windowless room; that you cannot escape from. Trapped senses; trapped multiple lives without substance or integrity.

After I take my potion every week, I fall asleep and my visions begin. I cannot stop what I see; sometimes, I am very disturbed by horrible events. I did not fear what I saw but found them captivating. My brain sought more knowledge and I was thankful that I would likely live a long life.

The curious insuperable spectacles that I view are randomly presented to me. I'm not sure whether what I have seen is true or not. Is it all a fabrication of facts and theories? However, it would be nice to have one of those MRI machines in my practice.

Chapter 6

THE GREATER GOOD

Life and death is my profession. Nothing will ever change that.

My father always wanted me to be an architect. After the three strangers came, they left me with the wooden figure of a physician. My father decided that it was a sign; I would be a physician one day. Years of taking the potion and then having hundreds of visions made me well prepared to enter medical school. My father was always amazed at the advances in medical science in the future and slightly frustrated that he could not benefit from that knowledge.

My father submitted my name when I was a very young boy (or I appeared as a young boy), though I was the same age as any first-year student, but we kept the ruse going that I was a child genius.

I easily passed my medical examinations. My teachers quizzed me on any medical topic, and while it was not the answer of the established thought of the day, I would always be five steps ahead with any prognosis and possible cures. My answers were theoretically correct but sometimes they remained only a concept to them. I could not prove much without the required technology shown to me in my visions. Having no electricity was a big problem.

I was even asked to become a teacher at the school at graduation, despite the objections of some older, envious teachers who said I was not normal; I might have some sort of possible contagious mental disease. I had to be careful to not know the answers to everything; so periodically, I would show my human miscalculations by giving a ridiculous prognosis, which I knew was not the correct answer. This seemed to appease the more old-fashioned teachers of their superiority.

I politely turned the offer down to teach, for I sought to keep my potion and visions to myself as we do with the personal scents of our body. I was soon known as a very good physician, who could heal an illness easily. I became a trusted member of the community. It really was not that difficult.

In my practice, all surgical instruments were cleaned in boiling water and laid out, covered the night before in our private consultation room. There were many different sized scalpels, crushing forceps, hooks, catheters, vagina speculums and a host of other instruments that would make a healthy person vomit. Lots of freshly cleaned cloths and a host of dried herbs and fresh plants which grew in the courtyard were available for many ailments.

People began coming from all over the country and different points of the Empire. My practice grew. I also became a teacher to other healers and mystics at my villa. We would all share our knowledge freely with each other; it was like a 20th century commune without the free love. I enjoyed this interaction immensely; many of the concepts were not Western but more Asian in their influence. I was surprised at how many visitors knew Asian philosophies.

Despite the added initial commune expense, it was a rewarding time in my life in more ways than one. My wealth increased beyond expectations and people sought me out to help them or their family.

In my early years, I supported a large medical community of non-Greeks, with food and drink. I wondered from time to time, how many people were really serious physicians or just naturopathic healers? I had my doubts. As I became older in years, I decided to stop sharing my knowledge for I felt that the calibre of skills shown by the visitors had declined through the years for some reason.

I enjoyed my educational visions which explained atoms, genes, DNA and fighting germs in cells with other germs. I usually prayed for medical visions before taking my potion; it never really worked but I kept trying. Too bad I couldn't send texts and ask questions.

Funny-looking Darwin would have been proud of me. I had seen a biography vision on him and I personally related to his struggles on whether to release his research to the world. It was an interesting contrast to me; his research on the selection of the species versus me supposedly saving the species.

Most of my Greek colleagues were too proud to ask me in public, but continued to approach me privately on how I was curing so many patients. I would tell them that I was doing exactly what they were doing and had no idea why their medicine or treatment was not helping their patients. They could never understand and I'm sure they became insecure regarding their own medical knowledge.

I had saved many lives throughout the years. I gained knowledge by dissecting human corpses, apes or any animal. It made me feel miserable: examining and slicing into the flesh and organs of dead bodies. It bothered me that death is so final. It was sad that there was not any more to life itself, for all the effort we all put into it. It was not fair.

It disabled my resolve to seek out a relationship and have a family like other people; one day everything and everyone, including the Romans, would become dust and forgotten.

I performed gallbladder operations along with treating blood clots, eye and heart surgery. I emphasized to my patients the importance of eating well and exercising, which was difficult because during the time I was practicing medicine in Greece, a sign of prosperity was being overweight.

Imagine what they would have said, if they knew there was a pig organ inside their body. Or that I had opened their skull, removed tumours, shaved corneas, opened the chest cavity to fix their heart or removed the eye and stitched it back in so that they would see straight.

In those days, most people who came to me for help were not educated. When I performed an operation to save their lives, I would make up something to calm them down, something that they could relate to, which would support their faith in the gods.

This process of faking a diagnosis and cure sometimes bothered me. I learned from Jeremy Bentham that overall it was acceptable.

It was amusing using 21st century medical knowledge and technology while surrounded by primitive wisdom. I would explain the cure to a patient using the weather, plant and animal analogies, even their moral attributes! I knew they trusted me enough to put their life in my hands; they had no idea how lucky they were choosing me over the physician down the street.

My patients connected with me. I began inventing stories of mythical rewards and cures; for that was the only language they understood. It caused me to sometimes burst out laughing as I looked down at a patient in the recovery room. Everyone was glad to be alive and ignored my lack of professionalism. I usually told the patient that it was my tears of joy and happiness, seeing them well again.

Chapter 7

IDLE PLAYFULNESS

I was proud of the knowledge I had acquired through my years as a physician. I had secret visions of a way of life that even I could not truly understand. Sometimes, I did not know what I saw. People seemed to mostly possess an idle playfulness of all things innovative in the future. It did not matter who you were.

I had witnessed thousands of visions. Or were they premonitions? Was I observing the gods at play? Perhaps. Where do all these people that I see, live? I felt this was not what they did for a survival, that they were all actors maybe? I saw tall, godlike, rectangular, shard-flaked temples, as people went in and out of them all day. The buildings were never dark even at night. What did they do in there?

The retold statements in many visions repeated themselves in some ways: 'popular right now', 'trending', 'you can skip in 5 seconds', 'just released music videos', 'anyone can make it in America' – what is America?

In my visons, there was no end. Stories were retold, recapped, recited, resaid, restated and replicated. I began to develop my own vocabulary to include wacky, madcap, weird, silly, zany and pissed off; there was no end to new words and ideas. Too many ideas filled my visions; I suffered many panic attacks after watching my visions, and it would take many days of sleeping peacefully under the shade of a tree to recover.

I had never treated panic attacks as a physician before. I did not know what to do. Wine made me feel better but the affect wore off; then later I thought I was having a heart attack. Despite the chance of another panic attack, I still could not stop the visions as I continued to enjoy, for some depraved reason, more information and entertainment. Slowly, I began to learn how to control the attacks with my other herbal medication.

Still, I felt I had lost my personal freedom. I could not look away for the unpleasant facts were often relieved with a good news story or event. I did not understand the word 'stress' at first, but it was a word I believed that described anything that did not make you happy.

I was observing strange people and worlds. Naturally, I wanted to see more, for I was intrigued and enticed with the diverse newness, the colours, excitement, even the music that enhanced all visions. Everything you needed was in these visions and the 3D printers made food, if you did not have time to make a good meal. We always had time in Greece to make a good, long meal and enjoy it with friends.

I had a specific vision only once; it troubled me. I saw millions of people starving in a thick fog. There were few trees left. It was not an island like the Rapa Nui documentary but the entire earth. I could never understand where all the people came from in the future. It was so overcrowded that there were no countries or empires fighting each other. People did not have homes and migrated to wherever there was space, food and water. There were many small battles with men and women wearing no uniforms and it was difficult to pick the right side; for everyone used the word 'righteous' and it lost all meaning.

I only had this vision once, so I do not a have a lot of detail. Very sad, for I believed it was the end of the earth. It was confusing, because I was told that I would save the earth.

It did seem like a godless moment without hope, which is interesting coming from a person who does not believe in any god. I was a physician, so I believed that when you died, that was it. My advanced medical knowledge could help cure a person and I was happy in my own little ageless body. But I could not control events bigger me – how could I? I did not understand it all. It is only normal for us all to be an addicted observer of all things as breathing is a paradox.

I'm not a depressing person, although I am more often sad than happy, but I blame that on knowing too much. In the 21st century, people are advised not to 'overthink'. My father was predictable in his observations, ahead of his time, but correct when he said life was easier for the simple-minded. My visions showed me that nothing in the future was easy.

In the future, people had mastered nature. They could think and act faster with the help of computers; they were smarter, quicker and often told that they were lucky and happier. But men only seek simplicity in their lives.

Every day my knowledge grew. I felt the visions guide me. I lacked control of what I saw. Yet week after week, there were too many visions to make sense of. Sometimes they dulled my inquisitive mind.

It helped to record the details of my visions for future reference. Every now and then I got desperate and felt uneasy; especially if my practice was busy that week. Sometimes, I prayed to the gods (that I did not believe exist), for the visions to stop; it did not make sense, but I did it anyway. I didn't have close friends to confide in and never will, because my potion had to remain a secret. I begged for mental peace, a respite from the full and concise precision of continual thought. I desired a life of quiet contemplation but knew this was impossible.

I observed that life was a series of a priori statements. You could prove anything you wanted to prove. Was my interpretation in my written journals of the future correct? I had the knowledge of great advances in medicine and used it to cure people every day. But what about the rest of the knowledge I possessed about future historical events; how was this to be used to save the earth?

Chapter 8

FOLLOW YOURSELF

I was taken by surprise and worried when a servant from my father's household burst into my room and said that I must come quickly; my father was dying.

I knew it was coming, but I did not want to think about it. That sunny day I was busy and content; there was a confident peacefulness in being respected in the community. I was recognized as a reliable physician who had compassion and the ability to heal people, usually on the first attempt. Other physicians predictably tried many ongoing treatments often without success. Most of my knowledge was gained through my visions and I was not going to share my secret with anyone.

My father was very old and had lived longer than most in those days, thanks to me. But as he aged, he became quiet and more reflective about his life; what he should have done and would do differently, if he had the chance. He was sad and guilty about the full life he had after my mother's death; he always said that she was the only woman he had ever loved. He was sure he would live with her again after he died. I kept the truth to myself.

Walking as fast as I could over to his house, I passed many of the temples and buildings he had designed and built through the years. I was glad that I had taken him around in a cart during the last year whenever

I could, so he could see what he had accomplished. He would leave the cart and slowly walk around the buildings with my help, looking up to examine any stone decay or movement in those areas of the structure which the columns were holding up; the capital blocks at the top of the columns, the metope, triglyph and the tympanum. The last trip we had made was a month ago, when he was very frail and wanted to see the Altar to Zeus.

"Magnificent! I wish I had built it!"

"But you did complete some work on the reliefs and the altar?"

"Yes, repair work. It's not the same."

I looked at his face as he was looking around, holding his arms outstretched, "Zeus, the king of all gods, the sky, the law, all order, thunder, lightning and most important, the fate of all lives!"

I carried him up to the altar with a bag that was full of food and good wine. He spoke in a weak voice, thanking me for taking him. I could imagine he no longer had enough strength in his lungs to ever shout again; I was losing him slowly and he was receiving his fate well.

So, I picked him up and could feel his thin bony arms and legs. It was not a good sign.

I carried and placed him carefully down, as he leaned against the altar, smiling, touching the stones on each side of him. "You still have the strength of a young man."

I sat on the steps quietly and looked out as I ate some of the fruit. We were high off the ground and I felt the perspective of the situation. "That night changed my life." I am not sure whether he heard me; but I did not pursue my thoughts with him. This was his day.

My father was happy, "Look at everything; the stones elevate our position. You can see everything like a god."

I finally got to my father's house, delayed by the slow-moving market crowds and went right in. It was very quiet. There were servants talking in hush tones, making brief eye contact with me as I passed them and entered my father's room. There was a group of servants and friends around his bed looking at him as he slept. I had known all of them since a child; they greeted me warmly and left us alone.

I sat down beside him and held his hand. He opened his eyes and squeezed my hand. He coughed and I gave him water.

In a low voice, "You are here. You might not think so, but I have always been proud of you." His tainted, dull eyes were covered with lifeless white mucus; I could still see touches of his soft blue eyes from when he was younger.

He gave a quick grip of my hand. "You look healthy. The gods smile on you." Then he closed his eyes again; I knew he was thinking and not asleep.

I urged him, "Don't speak. Rest."

He spoke in short, choppy, slurred sentences with his eyes closed. "I must speak. I dreamed that you will leave Greece. You will fight. Many will die. You will cross waters to a fertile land with many trees. Do not be afraid; you live. I saw you smiling."

"Where?"

He opened his eyes and turned his head towards me, "Not here. You change history. I have seen it." He lifted his hand slightly off the bed, moving it about, "All that we have, all of this, will not matter. It will all be gone one day."

My eyes began to fill with tears. I encouraged him to remain positive, even though I knew the buildings in Greece would all be in ruins one day, "No. Your buildings are strong."

He coughed again and could not stop. I turned him on his side, and gave him more water wiping some blood from his lips. He fell back onto the pillows studying me for some time. I'm sure he was recalling happy moments in our lives.

I held his hand and squeezed it. I did not know what to say. He had been a good father; we lived a fortunate life. Overall, we saw the good in people. But we were not like other families due to the unannounced visit of the three strangers and the prophesy.

To humour him, I said, "Maybe the gods will want you to design and build more temples for them in the clouds." Even though I knew that was impossible; for water vapour settles onto the condensation nuclei, it could not hold any weight.

※

My father became tired in those last days, slowly losing his appetite, as his eyes became a blind, grey inert tissue; without life. I had seen it many times before.

Soon, his memory quickly faded and he began talking slower. The day he died, he said, "You are still but a boy. Be a boy as long as you can." He paused as his head slumped over; I placed a hand on his chest, thinking he was dead, but he awoke suddenly from my touch and spoke softly, "Did you every miss not having brothers or even sisters?"

"I think our lives have been busy enough."

"I suppose. Your mother wanted more children." He looked away through the window over the far-reaching hills and valleys, against the never-ending, plainly decorated blue sky. I helped him drink, holding his hands steady. Then, afterwards, I wiped some tears from his face; he looked at me as he stroked my hand. "Look at your body, your smooth skin. How tall and straight you sit. I am old and hopeless. You will go somewhere soon."

"Yes, perhaps."

"I want you to do me a favour. Listen carefully. When I die, cremate me. Bury me in the Altar of Zeus. Near the back altar there is a loose stone with the letters 'AAG' on it."

"What about my mother?" As I finished the sentence, I understood. My mother's name was Anthousa.

"She is already in there. Many years ago, I moved her to the Altar of Zeus. I did not tell you." He closed his eyes, speaking slowly as he breathed with difficulty. The words were strained with a series of unknown moments between each word; I felt he was going to die at any moment.

"Do it at night, alone. Scrape the filler and the block will slide out. It was never properly done. Mix new cement, so that the stone will never move again."

He took several short, wheezing inhales which filled his lungs. As he exhaled his last sentence, he seemed to think carefully of what to say, "You have your potion; your mother and I will live with Zeus forever. Be brave."

Then, he was gone.

Chapter 9

MATTHEW

One day, I heard three, measured, firm and determined knocks on the door of my house.

I stopped, interested in seeing who was behind the seemingly distinct knocks, expecting someone young and determined. I am a sceptic of life and enjoy listening to the false idealism of youth. It is unfortunate that their creative enthusiasm is wasted; for the thought of making the world a better place is a lie. I stood behind Abrux, my friend since childhood who lived with me and his kind wife, Glenna. Abrux cautiously opened the door.

I quickly glanced. He was a sick beggar; old beyond his years and I turned away to let Abrux handle him. However, despite his first hesitant words as he cleared his throat, the full abundant voice became strong and clear. There was something unusual about him so I returned and stood beside Abrux.

The man looked at both of us; he was unafraid and confident. "Shalom. Hello. I am seeking Galenus. My name is Matthew. Yeshua told me to come here. My Lord said that if I ever needed a refuge, Aelius Galenus would help me."

Abrux looked at me for a response. I wanted to speak. The name Yeshua was spoken. I had so much to say and ask. The old man had a long grey beard. He concentrated his stare at me. His eyes became wide and alive; his beautiful smile acknowledged his search was over for now, as he looked relieved. His donkey made a disturbance, jerking his head as it patiently stood tied to his derelict cart on the street.

"I am Galenus. My name is now Galen. Call me Galen." He shook both of our hands. "You know Yeshua? Come in. My servants will take care of your mule."

Matthew looked up at the physician's sign on the front of the building. "Please forgive me, but you look so young." He turned and attended to his donkey, waving a hand back at me that he would just be a moment; the donkey lurked uneasily wanting attention.

I assured him that I was Galenus and that it was too many decades to count since I had seen Yeshua.

"There is so much I want to ask you."

I had no idea what had happened to Yeshua; I thought that he would still be with Armaigen and Tiernan. "I remember he was travelling through Europa."

Matthew turned and stroked the face of his donkey. His long hair appeared dirty and tangled. I knew he had heard me, as I saw his head nodding a response. "I know nothing of that." He wore a dark cloth, which was a mix of a harsh weave, clearly from across the Mediterranean. He turned and smiled at us. "I am happy to be here Galen. This mule carried my Lord Yeshua."

Where?

Abrux lifted all the bags off the cart that Matthew had identified and brought them into the house.

I told him that the mule would be watered and fed.

"Can he be brushed? It has been such a long trip; he deserves it." He patted the mule on the back and then walked towards me. "I fear his time will be up soon. Poor thing."

"Yes, of course he will be brushed."

Matthew slowly passed me and touched my arm, as I followed him into my house. He suddenly looked relieved and a little tired as I now led him into our large dining area. "I'm afraid to tell you that Yeshua is gone. I'm not sure where he is. That is why I am here."

"Gone?"

I still have the present that was given to me by Matthew when he left. I knew by the shape and size it was the lyre Yeshua had played during his ministry; for it was not just his words that drew people to him. At the beginning, his words were very unassuming, almost too discreet, but his words, music and lyrics began to travel eternally in the air through Judaea and the earth, forever raising the hearts of the poor in spirit. I suppose this includes me. He once told me that sometimes Yeshua would sing before his sermons.

I ordered a full table of food from the servants who were scattering everywhere to make the larger room more comfortable and personal. More pillows, wine and a variety of plain and exotic foods descended upon us.

All the lamps were lit and as the sun set the night became day inside.

Matthew went around the room as I encouraged him along; he was inquisitive, looking at all the antiquities from other countries I had collected. It included some frightening medical instruments that I had found very useful through the years during surgery. He was very interested in learning. I explained how I healed people through medicine and different treatments.

"Yeshua also healed many."

Matthew continued touching and examining the pieces in my collection, even the sharp instruments; carefully holding them, turning them over and remarking how light they felt.

"Many of these I have made myself."

"How?"

I could not help but smile for the potion had given me the knowledge. "Research and practice, I suppose."

"I have never seen or heard of such fine craftsmanship. You are very smart."

I felt relaxed and at ease. This was a person who knew Yeshua and had a direct and real connection to him. But how was Yeshua now gone? Was he lost? I thought perhaps Yeshua had told him about me and would be able to help explain what happened to me as a child when I was cured.

Matthew smiled appreciatively as wine was given to him, as he lowered himself onto the pillows.

"Galen. Thank you. You live like a king. I had no idea of who you were. My Lord never hinted at such a lifestyle. Yet I am sure you have worked hard and he would not have sent me to you unless you were honest."

I still was trying to understand him and where the conversation would lead us.

Abrux came into the room with Glenna. Matthew stood and hugged Glenna; we all sat on the floor. "Matthew, we usually sit at the table. But I thought this would be more comfortable for you after such a long journey."

Matthew took a long inhale and exhale. "I am so glad to be here. It is always dangerous on the road. At least I have Yeshua with me." He drank a full goblet of wine without stopping. "Good. That is good wine! I thank you."

"Did you not say he was gone?"

"He has gone away but is with me always. That is why I am here. I am writing about Yeshua the man, the son of God."

Abrux, "What God?"

Matthew looked certain and absolute. "Why, the only God there is. The God of Gods." He held his glass up as it was refilled. He smiled holding the glass up again as he toasted us and hurriedly drank the complete glass of wine and placing it on the floor. It was quickly made full again as he encouraged my servant to fill it up.

There was so much food he was confused, like a hungry, excited child not knowing where to begin. "Thank you. I seem like a bad guest. I am not. I am so grateful and have not drank or eaten in days. I was lost. It was frightening and it was only by chance that I made it here. Go left or go right, most decisions are so simple but sometimes have severe consequences. I believe that Yeshua guided me. Ask and you shall receive; only sometimes you do not get an answer until you are so desperate. Patience; I am still learning how to be patient."

Matthew apologized as he continued, "Galen, I am so hungry. Sorry. I am not always like this. I will explain everything."

We all helped ourselves to more modest quantities and kept politely quiet until he was finished. I waved the servants away thanking them, wishing for us to be alone with Matthew.

I sat closely across from him. "Galen. Thank you again. May the Lord bless you; and this house. I can see you have been blessed. Yeshua told me to come here if I found a need to quietly finish my work. There is much to tell."

"You are a man who knew Yeshua. You are here and do not have to ask for anything. My house is your house. You are not just a guest but a friend, you may stay as long as you need."

Matthew laughed. "You may regret that offer!" He finished the last of the fruit he had placed on his lap and laid back onto the pillow. "I hope I am a good guest. I will go anytime if I get in the way."

Glenna, "I feel you are a generous man and have lived a good life. I trust you and we welcome you to a good household. Galen has given his life to helping and healing people. I do not know how he does it."

I thanked Glenna, for I never talked of what I did to others; I did what came naturally. I did lead an interesting life, but it frustrated me that I did not know how I was going to save the earth.

"Matthew, tell me where Yeshua is – do you know?"

As he wiped his mouth, "Yeshua changed everything. I don't know where he is. That is why I am here. To finish his story before I forget and to talk to you about what I should do."

"Why me? I don't know how to help you. I thought you would help *me*."

His smile was one of relief. "Maybe we will help each other. Yeshua would not have told me about you unless it meant something. Everything he said meant something! The blessing of Yeshua is with all of you." He made a sign in the air with his hand. It reminded me of the circle Yeshua had drawn on my forehead as a child. I did not know what it was. But Matthew did not motion the shape of a circle.

Matthew explained himself, "Ever since Yeshua disappeared, I make the sign of a cross. It is a blessing and can be felt by Yeshua and his Father as we speak; he is watching and listening to us at this moment. I am sure of it."

"Yeshua?"

"Like this." Matthew did the sign slowly.

I tried to make the sign for the fun of it and got it in the wrong order.

Gently, "All of you try. No, it is like this. Watch and follow the movement of my fingers."

We tried again and after several attempts got it right and I felt a strange, unspoiled feeling when completing it.

We were both quiet for a while and felt no need to say anything to each other. We all sipped our wine including Matthew, and for the first time, he seemed contented and safe with us. I had always felt there was a certain gratification in silence when meeting friends, almost sensuous. We stared at each other knowing we did not have to speak because the wordless conversation was enough.

Matthew nodded, "You understand?"

"What do you mean, disappeared?"

He looked disturbed as he ignored the question. "Of course, I will not be in the way in your own house. But there is much work for me to do. There is much for me to think and write about. That is why I am here: to finish the story of Yeshua. I have decided to write it in Greek but I will use the Aramaic name of our lord Yeshua which he preferred."

"Has something has happened to Yeshua? What about Armaigen and Tiernan?"

Looking confused, "I know nothing of Armaigen and Tiernan. Our Lord spoke nothing of them."

Matthew then explained everything about what had happened to Yeshua. The CNN version. I was shaken and dazed. It could not be true. I hated the word crucified.

I knew that in the weeks to come I would hear the more serious, well-documented, BBC version. Perhaps because of Matthew's visit, I would be able to see visions about Yeshua, which I had never experienced before.

Time went fast as I let him do most of the talking and it lasted well into the next morning, until the slow-moving, soft glow of the new sun burned the night away.

He covered stories about sharing water with Yeshua. He talked about how all the disciples would huddle together as the cold came up from under the earth each night, and how the name of Yeshua was beginning to be spoken in many lands. There were many people, whole families, well or crippled, Roman or Jew, rich or poor who followed Yeshua, trying to get as close as possible so that they could touch him.

"Why would people want to touch him?"

Matthew sadly shook his head, "Healing. He had the power to heal. It was not fair. His Father allows so many poor to exist who become lost souls." There was more silence as I waited for Matthew to continue.

"Even Romans followed him secretly; they were clearly Romans in disguise. The shape of the face, the hair, but they would not dare to wear the Roman uniform around us, even though we all knew they were

Roman. Still, they were accepted because, to Yeshua, all men were just children. I know that many Romans deserted and that was one of the reasons Yeshua was secretly hated by Pontius Pilate.

Before he spoke more, I was tempted to tell him what had been going on in my life, but I did not speak about my visions, for I felt Matthew had a bigger story to share at that moment.

I knew my servants well; they were not slaves, but free men and women, all schooled onsite. I was aware that this visit would cause gossip, yet I trusted them completely, for they were family. Even though he did most of the talking that first night, we got to know each other and understood that we shared a common bond and a need for friendship.

The next day, he followed me about asking many questions. He watched me treat patients and followed me into the town. I felt he wanted to get to know me better but later I understood he was seeking to feel and see how Yeshua had described me to him. I did have a direct connection to Yeshua and soon Matthew became familiar with his new family. His confidence grew and he became more independent, concentrating on what he had come here to do.

I was glad of this change, but I could not afford the time to be with Matthew all day. I was running a business.

Days arrived and departed like planes; every day created a new endless memory. Each day was swallowed by many quick months as Matthew stayed as a welcomed guest, always offering to help whenever there was a need.

Looking back, it was a flawless moment in time. Although he had the villa at his disposal, he spent most of the time alone with his books, writing notes as he gave speeches out loud to himself; sometimes he would go on for whole days and nights, without sleep, wandering around at all hours. Increasingly, he became very troubled.

During dinner, he would speak of Yeshua having to deal with the harsh Roman attitudes, the responses from people and usually finishing off a day of ministry with a song. He would play Yeshua's lyre singing about life as a Jew in Judaea.

"It seemed to all of us that Yeshua did not like performing miracles but somehow he would be at a place where a healing was needed. He did not seek out miracles. We did not see this as a contradiction betraying his beliefs. Near the end, people shouted for more miracles; I think he disliked the word 'miracle' itself, for it was a command directed personally at him. Yeshua knew that his Father believed more in faith than fate. It wasn't that he didn't like being told to do something or take a suggestion, but he knew that wisdom is the greatest miracle of all; one that ties everything together."

As a physician, life would be much easier if I had that kind of wisdom. Matthew said that Yeshua did it reluctantly, "He sometime hesitated and seemed to choose to perform a miracle if it seemed like the crowd interest was waning, or if his Father told him to; the moment when there was no other choice. He never spoke of the details of his decision, either."

I thought of my potion. I must take it later today.

I picked up on Matthew's last words and was confused, "Where was his father?"

"God. The creator of all things; *his true heavenly Father*. His earthly father was Joseph; he looked after their children, but died young. Mary, his mother, travelled with all of us, with his brothers and sister. We would bring them along whenever we were able to, especially if he was preaching close to their own village."

I had never heard of such a story; "I don't understand."

Chapter 10

BONDS THAT BIND

Sometimes, Matthew would talk so fast and then get confused. He would repeat himself and then try to write down his thoughts, but he could not keep up. I eventually offered him some help.

At first, he refused. I explained that we had a school for the children of the families who worked here. Other children from outside in the village also attended. Some were orphans or children of parents who were dying. I did what I could for anyone, for in one of my visions I once heard the expression you "reap what you sow." I thought this was a cool saying even though I did not need any more money. In these days, the Romans were the only troubling influence, and most Greeks avoided them as much as possible going about our own business.

Abrux was the best teacher in the school and he was more than happy to have a break from the classroom routine. He was excited to learn what Matthew was doing. Abrux became his full-time scribe. Matthew was pleased at this offer for he knew his own limitations.

On many mornings, I would lay awake and would listen to Mathew and Abrux speaking.

I would lean out of the window and see them under a tree and shout a happy greeting to them. Mathew would stop and wave, giving a diverted, hesitant smile as he continued to share his thoughts with Abrux. Even as I treated patients, I would sometimes see them through the window sharing a meal as they became close friends.

Abrux was laughing more than he ever did in the classroom. Teachers have too many distractions and only the good ones actually live the life they expect their students to live.

On some days, he and Abrux would leave early in the morning for long walks. We would not see then until the end of the day. Abrux would scurry beside him, taking notes, never complaining of the heat of the day, but calling out to Matthew to slow down as he sometimes could not keep up with the dictation.

Abrux became a close advisor to Matthew; another disciple. I wondered what effect this would have on Abrux after Matthew had gone.

When Matthew was in a groove, he could not get the words out fast enough.

Abrux's patient teaching skills helped. He encouraged Matthew to explain the implied meaning of a sentence and better, more specific descriptions of the people he had encountered during Yeshua's ministry. Matthew said many times that Yeshua was funny and would joke with people to put them at ease. He was good at reading people and knowing their innermost thoughts.

Over the coming months, Matthew's presence began to change our lives. I do not believe anyone saw at first the direct relationship of his arrival and all the changes that occurred. The household seemed happier; it was easier to get along with each other. Life became exciting as we were all concerned and interested in all the people we came in to contact with.

Gossip did not go away, but stories and rumours became anecdotal, almost humorous; stories were not to be taken seriously. We all developed a light heart. Even on the hottest days there was no complaint, for the heat made us thrive with insight and compassion. A woman servant said that every day was like having an easy childbirth.

The human senses in all things were enlarged and all smells became more enjoyable. We began playing with our food: tossing and juggling oranges, singing, providing happy entertainment whenever we felt the urge, even as food was being prepared in the kitchen. Our strict and sour cook became happier and more easy going allowing this behaviour in her clean kitchen. She now seemed to appreciate the presence of people more.

The servants seemed light-headed and almost any minor event became amusing. Somehow plain water and food had more delight and taste in it, everyone seemed happier, as laughter was absorbed easily into our natural being again like children; as nature unanimously inferred that this was a time to appreciate each life, each momentary breeze on our face. Contact with another was a singular moment of pleasure with unforgettable appreciation.

I was not sure whether it was Matthew talking about Yeshua playing songs but one night my potion created a vision that took me to a place called Woodstock. I did not see a town but a large group of people in a field dancing, sitting and sleeping, as some sort of music played.

The vision happened so fast; it was confusing to understand what it was all about. It was a rainy weekend. Many happy but lost people were there. I thought Yeshua was going to be on the stage based upon how Matthew had described him. He said people were drawn to him because of his songs. But I did not see him. I saw many people singing different songs and I was disappointed that people came and stayed only a few days. That was all.

I learned from a song that a certain pill could make you small or big. Then there was 'The Pill' from an earlier vision, which decided creation itself; I often wondered when I saw an innocent child what Yeshua's true father would think about all the implications it would have on mankind. I guess he agreed with it, that is, if he were a god.

I did see many years later, a vision with many with seemingly learned people. They were discussing the social and political implications of Woodstock which I really did not care to understand for it was like discussing with the Romans the rights Greeks should have; nothing would come out of it.

I liked most of the songs. They were different; a frantic, desperate, screaming message of shared love and understanding without jealousy; I thought it was catchy, but naïve.

I had seen many naked bodies in my practice. I had heard so many of my patients talk about the lack of attention from their wives or husbands, that I secretly wished they would visit Woodstock together on a vacation. Perhaps it is the perfect place we will all want to go to when we die; *love the one you're with.* Men and women dream to be monogamous and happy. My vision of Woodstock, I'm sure, was more a temporary fantasy than fact; like animation.

As for myself, I did need *somebody to love* for I could not feel the sound of love in my mind or body. I did have needs myself; secretly leaving the house to have sex with women in dark places, where you pay for it. I had been doing this for years and the women say they love me. I know they don't, but I do feel better afterwards. No harm done.

The last act by Jimi Hendrix was great; he was a ghost on stage. Too bad many people had already left the concert as he played *The Star-Spangled Banner*; it had an interesting sound to it. I thought it would have more meaning with lyrics sung along with it. I briefly thought that perhaps given enough time left at our house, perhaps Matthew could come up with the words for *The Star-Spangled Banner,* but it would be selfish of me to take him away from his work right now.

Jimi Hendrix was angry at something and smiled in his own way, ignoring what was around him. Sadly, too much talent given to one person is not good. I remember he was briefly mentioned in another documentary profiling the life of Janis Joplin. He and Janis had died of a drug overdose, which means to a physician, taking something not necessarily bad, but taking it every day. I thought, at first, she was taking my potion and was worried I would suffer the same fate, but when I saw her aged face, I was assured and relieved that it could not be the same potion. Her body screamed with a beauty that captured the emotion of human pain and the light of the non-existent god praising creation itself. I wish I could have been able to talk to her, but my visions only allowed me to observe and record events.

Jimi and Janis both died in London. I wonder whether they knew each other. I have a suspicion that Roman Londinium becomes London in the future. I have never heard or seen drawings of Londinium and doubt that Londinium has taller buildings than Rome or Greece. But once I had a vision of London thousands of years from now and its streets were filled with people. There were very tall, red narrow carts going somewhere, with many other people heading down into the earth. I wonder what is down there?

Chapter 11

I FEEL HAPPY HERE

When Matthew was present, the servants would gather in small groups, in and around our large house, unnecessarily. They would make up excuses to serve Matthew or talk to him about any simple or uninteresting topic.

At some point in the day, our servants would make themselves present in the kitchen to bring Matthew food, or ask whether his room needed cleaning. Even some of the older women without husbands, would send flirting glances towards Matthew. He was unaware of anyone but Abrux coming and going out of his large room which was now stacked with his writings.

Interestingly, the actual number of sick patients increased with Matthew's presence, or so I thought. In the summer, the number of patients traditionally decreased. However, every day before sunrise, people came from all around Pergamon to lineup. At first, I thought it was some sort of epidemic, but I soon realized that they all wanted to see Matthew. I am sure that someone in our household had told somebody in Pergamon about our new visitor. I do not know what was said, but it was enough to attract attention. I hated attention.

Some even joined the line not knowing what was going on, others because they thought we were giving out free food. On these crowded, hot days, I sent the servants out with water to ask whether they were here to see me or Matthew. Most wanted to see Matthew and then they were told that Matthew was unavailable. Some would lie and eventually see me and make up any symptom. I always left the doors open to the large inner room where Matthew was working for air circulation. It was interesting to watch people slow down, almost stop to see Matthew, his head hunched over writing away with Abrux nearby. Some would whisper a shout, 'Matthew!' but he would not look up for he was oblivious to the attention. I was fascinated why everyone wanted to be near him.

I once asked someone why they wanted to see Matthew. They did not know why, only that the thought of him made them feel good. A child said, "I feel happy here."

I did not need this interruption and distraction. I was around 70-years-old, but looked no older than 25 and I had a beard to disguise my real age. Abrux's wife, Glenna, would dye parts of my hair and beard grey. Sometimes, my lack of patience and frustration was caused by playing this charade when I really didn't have to; I wanted to be left alone. Imagine a wise old man with a young body, possessing more knowledge and facts than anyone on earth. I was a hybrid enigma.

I could think faster and smarter than any tactless, young person. I could run and out-swim almost anyone. It was easy to defend these results, for I would say 'you are what you eat'. I heard this once in one of my visions and while it was true, it was an easy way to remember good eating habits. Also, most people did not live long during my time in Greece compared to the visions; so many people did not have a point of reference when thinking about my age.

But I had to be careful not to be too smart or too quick, as it was important to show occasional infallibility.

Despite my own infrequent miracles of saving and prolonging life, most memories of my accomplishments were short and there were too many to keep track of. I was too preoccupied in surviving day-to-day, then to think and worry about myself too much. I suppose this was my coping mechanism.

Most days, the number of people lining up did not worry or concern me; many times, small numbers of people were always waiting outside my practice, giving what they could afford to be treated. There was no fee, as I provided a volunteer medical service. Contributions were of course accepted, especially any offerings that included food, or the offer of labour which would take care of most of our needs.

Some others, mainly farmers or craftsmen from outside of Pergamon, feared the initial sight of the crowds outside my office. They thought something was wrong. Most patiently waited to see Galen, the 'famous' physician. Many had no knowledge of Matthew until they lined up. Most of these people lived on the outskirts of the town and would only come in to see me when they were seriously ill.

Usually, they would keep to themselves in the country. I'm sure many were nervous that summer, before they had a chance to see me. There were many exaggerated rumors of leprosy. Illness could kill people fast in those days and most physicians could do nothing, except me.

I was more worried about the people in our town, especially those in authority. I heard from the servants that many citizens were talking about me quite often and about the old stranger Matthew; he was a *friend* of Galen. On many instances, Matthew would be seen walking on the paths outside of town or in open fields talking, as Abrux followed him closely, taking notes. My paranoia was justified.

One day, we had a scare. A group of Roman Legionnaires, I guess they didn't have anything better to do, suddenly pushed themselves into my office to see what the problem was. They all crowded into Matthew's room, picking up books, examining scrolls amongst other things. Matthew looked up, very disturbed at being interrupted. He stood and asked what they were doing.

The Romans were surprised at this old man with a deep, gentle voice who stared unafraid into each one of their eyes. There was a disquieting tension as all thought and movement stopped. The Romans seemed to become very uncomfortable sharing the same space with him. I suppose it was almost unnerving to their basic beliefs, like meeting a dead Caesar, who had authority without a sword or guards to protect him. They were afraid. Outside, a restless soldier who chose not to enter, shouted from the door, "There is nothing for us here!" It seemed to be the excuse everyone was waiting for as they all scurried like bewildered rats into the sunlight.

Chapter 12

APERTURE ABERRATIONS

Matthew was obsessed with the need to tell me about final day of Yeshua's life.

"Yeshua is dead?" It was a shock to me when Matthew said it referring to the crucifixion. It was tragic, I always remembered Yeshua being a young, bright boy with a good sense of humour.

"No. He's not dead. I do not think he is dead. But he was supposed to die. I saw him die for a passing moment and then he was alive again!"

I was confused. "I do not understand."

Something was bothering Matthew. It was not logical to me. Even Abrux took me aside and told me that Matthew was troubled and confused. "He carries a heavy weight. You must help him."

"What kind of problem?"

"It is a theological problem."

"What?"

On some nights, our routine occasionally provided an opportunity to talk without the disturbance of servants. All three of us would sit with wine waiting for Matthew to begin. He would read from his notes and tell me of Yeshua's life, and then, he would suddenly stop. He could go no further for he explained that there was one sad, yet beautiful event in the life of Yeshua. It must be written correctly, or all the good work of his ministry would be for nothing.

Yeshua had told Matthew to tell the story of his life for all to hear; the difficult part was that Matthew did not know what version to tell.

Matthew then decided to tell us the complete story of Yeshua describing his death first. I was still not clear whether Yeshua was dead or not. I don't know why it would be told to us backwards but Matthew seemed to infer that he needed to get the story straight before he went any further; because he might forget something.

Matthew exclaimed, "I can't think until you all know the final ending, everything is connected to it: my language, my thoughts, how I will describe things in the beginning, and so on."

Abrux had confided to me that there was a good reason for it.

Matthew, "Do you both understand?"

Not really. But Abrux nodded in agreement, "Of course." I went along with it.

Matthew was clearly troubled. It had been several months since his arrival. He said the decision about the ending must be done now or he would stop writing. We agreed to pick a certain quiet night where we would listen to what was so important.

Chapter 13

CRUCIFIXION

Surprisingly, I don't think I had ever seen a documentary vision on the life of Yeshua.

I could not believe what Matthew told us that night.

I did believe Matthew was telling the truth describing what he had witnessed. I knew that recalled memories can be false. He described Yeshua's life, it was so incredibly real, that it had to be the truth. The story was detailed, including the human nuances which supported the natural thought processes. It described certain incidents in a way that had all the elements of a Shakespearean play. It gave an illumination of good confronting evil, eliminating any possible deception; less staged without any pretense.

I was shocked and disturbed. Matthew told us that the intention was to tell the story and see both of our reactions. He hoped to gain another perspective, so he could make a final decision of how to describe Yeshua's final moments.

Matthew told Abrux to make rough notes, in case new ideas somehow flourished. He wanted to add in any general thoughts, observations of what any of us said during any discussion; so he could remember everything later.

I will never forget that night; it was a pivotal moment. It was like Yeshua on the night he cured me. Matthew cried. Large Abrux cried, I tried, but was just plain suspicious and diffident. I tried to convince myself that there was a god, despite my visions. But it was of no use, I was born this way and despite my cynicism, I promised myself to keep an open mind. Still, I was hampered by my lack of faith and my knowledge as a physician, I knew with certainty, that when you die, you die. Shit happens.

I cringed when Matthew described Yeshua being nailed to the cross and then watching him bleed; the same happy, bright boy who had showed me kindness and had carved me a wooden physician.

Matthew said that Yeshua would change the earth; I was getting confused again about what the message meant for me. Does change and save have the same meaning? If Yeshua was now dead, how would that happen?

Maybe it was wishful thinking on my part; was I more important than Yeshua? Maybe it was a translation problem.

But the potion did exist. Yeshua was physically present in my father's house. My life was saved and I was involved in this story somehow; it was likely more complex perhaps than I had thought.

I thought Matthew had finally arrived at the climax of the story, for I sensed Yeshua's actual death was coming, but remembered again Matthew saying that Yeshua had disappeared.

But at that moment, another thought came to my mind, a quote from a previous vision of a quite short, unremarkable man, walking around buildings in ruins. There were big, wingless birds or spears crashing into the ground, destroying buildings, which resulted in fires; there must have been a war going on. He had an excellent command of language. I had seen several visions of him speaking in a strange tone which made me feel good: 'now this is not the end, it is not even the beginning of the end; it is perhaps the end of the beginning.' The man seemed to cry a lot and there was something honest and good about him. I did not know who he was.

Matthew had finally reached the point in the story where Yeshua seemingly had only a few moments left to live. He had been nailed to the cross for two days; most were surprised he had lived this long. Matthew said that only he and Mary, Yeshua's mother, were present along with a few Roman soldiers. Matthew could only watch and hold Mary close. The storm had eventually driven everyone else away.

Yeshua was in pain. He cried out, "Mother, do not fear, I have lived a life of joy. You are innocent."

Without any disrespect for the moment, I whispered a prayer to a god with my eyes closed.

I could not see or imagine the picture of god in my mind, but I did try. I thought of a few words that I knew were prayers to Zeus, seeking some insight or communication from Yeshua's father; I was sure he would forgive me, even though he apparently knew my own heart which was essentially a muscle. He was mistaken, for the heart was just an organ; it did not retain the essence of any soul.

At that moment, I thought of a recent documentary on Blake, thinking of the word *symmetry* for some reason. I suppose in a sense, Matthew's story, taken holistically was symmetrical. Perhaps all elements of life that keep us alive are related, working in conjunction. A complex muscle like the heart might hold an invisible, secret innocent soul somehow.

Matthew continued, oblivious to my own internal struggle. Yeshua spoke slowly and murmured, 'Tell them I love them. I will not see them today.' Yeshua then fell asleep again."

"Dead?"

"I thought that. No. he was asleep."

Matthew said the Roman soldiers were getting annoyed because it had started to rain hard; they had orders to stay and not leave until Yeshua was dead. "One meek and small soldier, a boy, was present. His armour hung loosely on him. His helmet was too large and awkwardly covered his face, adding to the almost absurdity of the moment."

The son of man was surrounded by other Roman soldiers and this was the real and oblique drama Matthew spoke of.

"The boy was being cheated in a game of chance. He became mad at losing his money, and knew his youthful limitations but wanted to prove himself to his new older friends. He stopped playing and swore as he looked up at Yeshua, shielding his eyes from the rain."

Matthew continued, "The boy moved towards a spear lying on the ground; I knew what he was thinking. I left Mary and tried to pull it from his hands, but was pushed down by one of the other soldiers. The Roman kicked me as I lay on the ground."

The legionnaire motioned the boy, tempting him to use the spear on Yeshua; then he stabbed our Lord in the side. He left the spear hanging from the wound, while he stood back and looked up at Yeshua, seeing what his reaction would be. There was no response as my dear Lord had passed out. The boy shoved the spear deeper into his body, twisting it and smiled as he pulled it out, dropping it to the ground. Mary went to the boy shaking him, cursing him and his family. "What have you done? That is my son!"

A legionnaire got up and withdrew his gladius. He fought the rain and the wind as it held him still for many moments, as he could not move. I went to Mary again, coming between her and the soldier.

Yeshua woke up, as there was a crack of thunder and lightning. He angrily looked down at the boy, and although it strained him, he moved his hands and fingers, unfurling them like a claw with sharp talons, pointing them down towards the frightened boy.

Yeshua screamed a loud, penetrating, hateful scream at the boy who stood still. The soldiers stopped playing. They looked to see what was going on. This was the first time I had ever heard him shout, other than outside of the temple market where he had pushed people out of the way, destroying most of the market goods. This sound was different, something you would hear from a dangerous wounded animal. Not the son of man; not the voice of Yeshua.

Yeshua then shouted again, I did not know at first what he was saying but slowly, as he suffered, I heard him say to the boy, 'I will give you my pain without mercy.' The legionnaire was now closer to Mary and held up the hilt of his sword ready to strike her head. I held up my arms over her, pulling her away, when suddenly the wind picked the Roman soldier up, into the air, tossing him onto the ground, dead.

Yeshua then said to his Father with his eyes open, looking up, saying, "I seek no forgiveness. I am not you. I am only a man."

Yeshua then closed his eyes. There was a long pause as we all waited; I was sure he was dead for his body and head gave out.

It was a miserable moment. All the time I had known him, he had always been physically strong, despite his slight tall frame. It was difficult to believe that he was broken and near death. I was sure he was going to leave us forever.

Yeshua's eyes remained closed. His whole body appeared different; lifeless.

We both looked at him and knew he was dead. There were no signs of life and his chest had stopped moving. Mary stroked his feet. Yeshua was dead! That was it! I looked about and prayed there would be some sort of sign from his Father, an angel or a message but all I saw was a dead body nailed to a cross.

There was an unexpected noise, almost inaudible and incoherent. I knew that slight sound he made as he woke up each morning, always taking a full breath of air. He was alive again! He had come back to life!

I heard exactly what he said and so did Mary. He said with no emotion, "I am here. I will not forsake you." His downcast eyes were half open; Mary looked at me smiling and then back at Yeshua.

She told him to rest and we would take him someplace safe. Yeshua then exhaled another long breath, emptying his lungs as he said, "Help me. Get me down."

He continued to take long gasps of air as if he had been swimming underwater for a long time and now needed as much air as possible. He looked so tired and said very clearly, "I want to feel life and love again. I have seen my Father's house. It is not for me. I am not ready."

Yeshua called out, "Let me go, I want to live as a man. I will go far from here, away from this cursed land!"

The rain and wind seemed to increase, blinding us to the surroundings or any complete understanding of what he was saying.

<hr />

Yeshua pleaded impatiently, "Get me down!"

The boy screamed. He was frightened, as he stumbled trying to escape, but he could not go anywhere; he was alone and weak; on that fearful, dark night. The boy's hands were covered in blood as his side was bleeding. The same side Yeshua had been struck with the spear. He began to cry. Mary left me to comfort him.

She was alarmed as she felt the heaviness of the boy's body in her arms; he dropped to the ground, groaning in pain. Lightning and thunder brought another outburst of rain like I had never seen before. You could not open your eyes. We were all on our knees, crawling about, keeping our heads down for the rain cut into our faces. I was still on the ground as Mary fell beside me again. We tried to get up, but it was impossible. We both had our heads down and were huddled in prayer, but we were not expecting a miracle. Who could hear us with all that noise?

The rain was strong and steady. The wind had momentarily slowed down, allowing us to look at Yeshua. My Lord's bleeding had stopped on his side and the skin was clearly healed with the rain washing it clean. He was awake and his normal skin colour was returning.

I saw Yeshua smiling at the boy. It was a smile of some sort of contorted revenge; it was uncharacteristic of Yeshua. He seemed glad that the boy was hurt and bleeding. I was right there and I saw what Yeshua had just done. I know what I saw and felt, having spent many years with him. I knew that he enjoyed hurting that boy. He wanted to kill him – he wanted him dead. I was so confused.

The boy panicked and squealed as he lay on his back with his arms outstretched towards Yeshua, looking up; he was scared and trapped. The remaining two soldiers were crawling over to the boy. He continued to try and stop the bleeding with his hands, but to no avail; there was too much blood. One soldier tried to pick up the spear again to throw it at Yeshua. The guard was on his knees, as he held up the spear, but it slipped out of his hands and rolled away. The rain continued to drop in a hard downpour, as the crack of thunder and flashes of lightning seemed to rest right above our heads.

The soldiers tripped over each other as they tried to stand up, looking at Yeshua who was still smiling. I am sure they expected Yeshua, who was still nailed to the cross, to hurt them in some way. They were horrified. Mary and I feared for our lives because we were still scared of the Romans.

But the soldiers were more afraid than us. They panicked, running away, and left the boy behind. The boy went to get up slowly, but had lost all strength as he fell dead at the base of Yeshua's cross. I went over to the boy as the rain and the wind now began to ease; blood ran like small streams over his small, distorted body. I tried to wipe his skin clean for some reason.

I closed his eyes. I looked back up at Yeshua and he just stared at me. It was if we had lost our place of who we were, and did not know what would happen next.

Mary ran after the soldiers who were now just moving shadows running away into the darkness. She scratched the ground picking up rocks, throwing them at the soldiers as she sobbed. The rain had stopped to a trickle but the occasional lightning and thunder still rang out as it moved away from us. I led her back to Yeshua.

"We must get him down!"

Chapter 14

THE GRACE OF GOD

There was a silence between us. I knew this was difficult for Matthew. I handed Matthew and Abrux a cup of wine. All of us took a sip and waited. We could not look directly at each other; we were muddled, for it was difficult for me to understand the total life of Yeshua. We all knew that at some part of our lives, events do not go the way we had hoped. Sometimes, we have all done something wrong against someone, occasionally justified, because we felt they had deserved it. Guilt always remains, despite what we should have done or said; no matter how big or small.

Poor Yeshua.

I broke the silence. "But he was not just a boy; he was a soldier, a killer." I wished I had kept silent. I knew the comment was without analysis and weak on facts.

Matthew was not finished and gave me a firm look to be quiet, "Mary touched Yeshua's feet and kissed them.

She stroked his legs and said to me that they were still cold and rubbed them. Yeshua would begin to feel warmer. Mary said, "You are a beautiful boy. Matthew will get you down."

Matthew looked at me, "His words were strange. Yeshua spoke more as he seemed to regain his strength. He told his Father not to forgive men; they know what they do. Do not forgive me, for I have denied you and the forgiveness of all sins. He told me that we must revolt against those in authority. Destroy them all!"

Matthew continued, "It would confuse everyone and destroy the message he had always intended. I know he believed the meaning of his words during his ministry and what his ministry was all about. He even confided to me. Yeshua used parables to tell stories, to make a point; we all enjoyed them for they were easy to remember. But sometimes his stories had many meanings.

Mary did agree with me later, that he could have meant we were to fight back against the Romans, but we could not be completely sure. He could have meant that everyone should fight until there is only one sacred winner on earth. Mary said it was my decision, and that either way it was in God's hands, by the grace of God.

I was the only other sole witness. The Roman soldiers that escaped would never speak of it. If I was not here speaking, who would know of his life? It would be like sand having no purpose; like our lives right now."

I disagreed with Matthew, as I thought it through. I did not feel that my life had no purpose. I had worked hard in my life, saved lives, in a way just like Yeshua, and yet I knew nothing of his life.

I thought again about the three strangers that had saved my life, including Yeshua. Now, here was Matthew, a friend of Yeshua's, living in my house. I still did not know what it meant at all, yet there was a mystery here that needed solving.

Matthew looked at me. He had a sober look on his face like he could read all my thoughts. He said, "Right, Galen? You live, you die. Shit happens."

Since I was cured by the three strangers, I learned early in life that there was always another story, another point of view. I'm sure, that with my knowledge there were times I must have appeared smug to my servants, but inside I knew most events were out of my control; I suppose that is why people believed in a god or wanted to.

How did Matthew know what I thought? I then remembered why this all seemed familiar to me. I had seen Yeshua in a vision about the future. I did not see *him*; people in my visions spoke of him and how history had been changed because of him. These events concerning Yeshua had happened in the past, but the events would affect everything in the future.

I sensed that Matthew was now more interested about my visions after speaking.

Shortly after he had arrived, I had told him of the time Yeshua had been in my father's house and the side effects of the potion. I did not age and I was able to see the future through my visions. I said that the three strangers had told me I would save the earth one day. Matthew did not take this too seriously, for he had always thought that Yeshua had implied in his short ministry, that forgiveness, not retribution would change mankind; everlasting life changed everything.

Essentially, I did not know what to think.

Matthew could have said more to me at that moment, sizing up my comments, questioning me on my thoughts of what happened to Yeshua but he did not. This was not a time for an argument; we both knew it. I knew that this was Matthew's life work. It was not my life, and I would never use my godless intellect to embarrass this thoughtful man.

Matthew stopped and reflected with more determination. "I am sure of it. I am not wrong. No one must ever know about his last words and actions. It would ruin and destroy everything. Mary was right, Yeshua tried and the only ultimate solution is a perhaps an uprising.

However, Yeshua's life was more important than what happened at the end. He stood for love; that was his main message in his life. I knew him, and even if he did give up on that message at the end and decided a revolt was the best course to settle the reign of goodness and godliness over the profane, so be it. It was said and it is over. It does not have to be mentioned in this story of his life; I am but a disciple of Yeshua, and my final insights come from God the Father."

Matthew was still slightly worried and confused; anyone would be. It was easy to say anything, but it was still not over. I knew he would not let it go, for in his heart it would always be hard to accept what he saw and heard. He was not a liar, but he would have to lie to tell the truth.

We were all quiet. We did not wish to disturb what Matthew was thinking. "He praised life and told us not to fear death. He would never kill anyone."

Abrux, "The boy?"

Frustrated, "I know! It does not make sense. It was sudden revenge." Matthew shrugged.

Abrux, "You said Yeshua was also just a man?"

Chapter 15

HUMAN WEAKNESS

I felt sorry for Matthew. I saw the anguish in his face; I got it and wished Abrux would just keep quiet, for this philosophy question would take too long to answer. I wanted to keep the conversation going, so I interrupted. "It's not your fault. Yeshua made a mistake. We all make mistakes. Do not second guess yourself! The sun will rise in the east tomorrow."

"How can you say that? There is more at stake than just the sun and the light of the day.

It was different being there with him. He spoke on behalf of his Father, for Yeshua was a God."

I said, "Which father? You are going to rewrite history? Don't feel guilty it's been done before. It's going to be rewritten many times after you. History is just words replaced in the future by other words at different times by men not even born yet. No one cares. Don't worry about it. So, Yeshua lived."

"No. Yeshua died; I am not finished! How can I *not* worry! I will leave out exactly what happened at the end of his life, for it was human weakness, it was not him. He would agree on my decision, I'm sure of it! He would never kill."

"Die? You confuse me. Well, he did kill the boy; how could anyone ever forgive a god for murder?" Matthew was disturbed at the slight sound of pessimism in my voice.

Abrux, "But maybe the word revolt was a metaphor for action?"

Abrux had caught Matthew's attention again. "But it is too powerful to be a metaphor. It also infers violence and conspiracy. He would be no better than a Roman, yet I can't ignore that he did kill that boy like Galen said."

I was glad that he had agreed with me. "He was dying, fed up with everything. I would have defended myself and I am a physician who has sworn an oath to save people. I really don't see anything wrong with it."

Matthew was slightly frantic and lost his temper, "Of course you don't! You can't even see your own nose on your own face, for your visions blind you, confuse you and distort the truth!"

What did he know about my visions!?

I was annoyed to the point of getting angry at Matthew, but I knew he was suffering and struggling; this was his life's work, "I do not. What truth is there but life?"

Abrux agreed, but not completely with me. "Matthew, do what you must or all is lost. I think you have made up your mind, but you don't like what you must do. The story of Yeshua would mean nothing if the boy was mentioned. It would become simply a story of death not life after death."

Matthew was not listening but did feel the support of Abrux, encouraging him on; whatever Abrux said confirmed his thoughts, "Yes, I must. It is what I saw and heard all the years I was with him. It was all wrong at the end. It was not like the Yeshua I knew."

Abrux, "Should I destroy the notes I have taken and throw them in the fire?"

Matthew took his time, carefully thinking, "Yes. When we write the end of Yeshua's life on earth, he will die on the cross, but speaks to his Father these last words: 'Father, forgive them, for they do not know what they do,' He motioned Abrux. "Then he dies. A spear does pierce his body, but only to make sure he has already died. Don't worry, we will work it out and Yeshua will be pleased that we did not give up on him."

Matthew continued, excited, knowing the revised version would be acceptable. "He dies on the cross and becomes alive again in his Father's house. There must be a resurrection for all men; without that there is no story. Then he travels secretly to Arabia."

I became more interested at the new information, "Arabia? What has this got to do with anything?

"You will soon find out. I have not finished the story yet."

Chapter 16

A GLIMPSE OF HEAVEN

Mary and I were left alone on the crooked rocks. The lightning sparked right in front of us; the crack of thunder again announced his presence as we huddled together beside the dead boy. Yeshua groaned as he struggled trying to break free of the nails, but could not. The lightning continued hitting the earth all around us, until it struck the back of the wooden cross near the base. The wood cracked and split. Mary and I were knocked back onto the ground, stunned, but unafraid. We were in the presence of Yeshua's Father. It was a sign.

The cross began to split apart and slowly fell sideways coming to rest on the cross beside Yeshua. Those men on each side of Yeshua had died at the end of the first day but were not taken down.

I got up and rushed towards Yeshua, trying to stop the fall of his cross as it began to slip. I did slow the fall of the cross to the ground. The crossbeams where his hands were nailed hit the rock hard and the cross fell back, facing up. Yeshua cried out again as the nails tore his wounds. He turned and faced me. I took the crown of thorns off his head and threw it away.

The rain was washing his face, and there was still blood that trickled down from his hair. Mary was now beside him and held his face, stroking it, wiping the blood away from his eyes with her clothes and she kissed him on the lips. Yeshua seemed to enjoy the cool water. He smiled that slight smile that all people loved to see and be near.

Yeshua seemed to be waking up from a dream as he told Mary, "I saw it. I was there. I saw heaven."

Matthew nervously refilled our wine glasses. His hands were trembling. I was beginning not to think clearly. I had drunk too much. Abrux held his hand over his glass and told Matthew he had enough to drink. "I must copy. I must copy your words."

Matthew sounded severe. "No! Stop. Do not write everything that I said tonight! Only that last part where I said he asks for the forgiveness of his Father. I have changed my mind for now; it is not over." His face lightened, "It was a miracle!"

Abrux, "A miracle?"

We all were silent and disturbed. There were so many thoughts and impressions in the air. The unpredictable Matthew was deep in thought. It was a long time before we spoke. Abrux looked at Matthew concerned.

I thought the story was over.

Again, I felt no rush, but wished he would get to the main point. I was interested to hear what Matthew would say next; I like creative fiction.

Excitedly, "You see, Yeshua did die on the cross but came back to life."

Abrux, "But...?"

I could not be silenced, "You said that Yeshua did not want to live in his father's house. He wanted to live and love life. Be like us. From a physician's view, Yeshua was unconscious and simple woke up."

"Everything is so easy for you. Yes? But he did die and went to his Father's house. What is wrong with that?"

"He saw only a glimpse of heaven; a momentary glance! Yeshua sounded like he did not like what he saw! He seemed angry at his father."

Matthew was insistent, "Yeshua refused to die. Is that not a resurrection? He went to his Father's house but I am sure his purpose is not over."

"Don't you think this was not what his father had planned for him?"

"Who are we to say what God has planned or not?"

Abrux, "Oh, so he will be seen afterwards when everyone thinks he has died, but he has not."

"Yes! No one survives a Roman crucifixion! And his tomb will be empty."

Yeshua was on his back facing up to the sky; his body was so thin that the bones were almost twisting out of his flesh. The blood on his body had matted and still streamed from his head where the thorns had scratched open his skin. The cross lay on a slant, propped up on one side by the uneven, sharp rock mound. It looked unnatural like a large anchor hanging against the bow of a ship. He screamed again to be taken off the cross as he struggled, but could not escape; the dull looking nails held his flesh steady.

We did not know what to do. Mary and I were mesmerized. We had to act, but momentarily we felt so alone and empty of immediate solutions. The thunder filled our ears, we were wet and the darkness seemed to play tricks with our eyes, for we were surrounded by empty shadows; images of dark destruction and death.

We went searching about and I found a Roman gladius and the spear that had been driven into my Lord. Yeshua moved his head trying to follow our movements with his eyes.

Mary located the malleus that had been used to beat the nails into the cross. She went to Yeshua's feet as I moved the dead Roman boy away. She lifted slightly the base of the cross as I picked and stabbed at the wood where the nail had penetrated out through the other side as I tried to loosen it. I took the malleus and began striking the nail back out through the wood, through Yeshua's feet. He did not cry out in pain, but urged me on with each blow.

He shouted, "Don't stop!"

Finally, his feet were free! Mary quickly wrapped them in her own shawl as Yeshua looked at his mother satisfied. Then with each hand we did the same. It seemed to take a long time, but as I look back, our fear of the Romans returning made the moment stand still. We knew that until we had taken Yeshua off the cross, only then, would he be safe with us.

When the last nail came out and dropped to the ground, Yeshua rolled into Mary's arms as she cradled him like a child. He was shaking. I covered him with the cloak of a Roman soldier, as his purple robe was drenched. We all stayed there on the ground as Yeshua seemed to regain his awareness. Mary held his head as she continued to kiss her son.

Yeshua did not say anything. He was comforted by Mary's touch. After a while, he tried to move his body, nodding his head with his eyes that it was time to go.

Mary took his feet and legs, as I lifted his shoulders and head up. As we passed the dead boy, Yeshua stared without emotion. Although Yeshua had lost weight, his long body was awkward to hold as we slowly maneuvered down the hill; half-dragging and carrying him. Stopping to rest for only slight moments, when Mary could not carry on.

We went to the closest house outside of the wall. There was no one around as a soft gentle warm rain began to fall. I banged the door once, with a free hand, as we did not want to lay him on the ground again. I dreaded the door opening for I did not know what to expect. We were greeted with a smile and rushed in as the whole family of the house helped carry Yeshua in to a quickly cleared table, placing him on top.

The man and woman of the house welcomed us. They invited us to stay. We would be safe from the Romans in their house. The woman cried as she recognized Yeshua. She told us of seeing Yeshua preach once. She felt guilty when she saw Yeshua carrying the cross through the streets and doing nothing. "The Romans, what could we do!"

Mary and the mother of the house washed and dried Yeshua on the table. They wrapped his wounds as he slept peacefully. The father had lit a fire and went outside with his sons to get some clothes and food for us.

I was concerned how we could get Yeshua out of Jerusalem, but my main concern was keeping close to my Lord watching him breathe. Mary told me not to worry so much. I was tired and did not know what to expect.

Mathew looked at us like a man who had been given back something valuable; something he had lost. A man who was poor but had discovered sudden great wealth and didn't know what to do with it. His face was a flame of excitement.

"He was alive! Don't you feel it? Yeshua, the man who lives!"

He continued, "But what do I do? I am so troubled and uncertain. I can't have Abrux record he died on the cross but escaped. He did kill the boy, and why did he say the word revolt?"

Abrux, "Did you not say once that you could never understand why suppressed people allowed themselves to be unfairly treated?"

Mathew shook his head, looking away, not listening. "I don't know right now."

I was the logic person and it was my turn, "Look, he was bleeding, near death; he did not know what he was saying. He was angry and perplexed. You must be honest and say what happened and let the storytellers interpret the event. They will respect your honesty and truthfulness even though what he said is a shock that distresses you."

Sympathetically, "Matthew, are you sure he did die?"

I still felt the whole story had not been told. The different converging thoughts of Matthew had interrupted the story; I don't think it was possible for him to have a logical thought process. I did not care too much about the boy. "What happened to Yeshua?"

Matthew awoke from his thoughts of recollecting the events. "Yes, he died! We record the original story! You all confuse my thinking. I suppose it is because Yeshua did live and still lives somewhere."

"Is this one of your own parables?"

"Don't be clever. I was thinking of something else right now. You take away my concentration."

"But you left us with Yeshua in a house of strangers. What happened?"

Abrux gently, "Matthew, you must tell us."

"If you must know, I will tell you. I was going to tell you after I figured out how I was going to explain the killing of the boy first, because it bothers me the most."

Matthew, "Galen, is there more wine?"

"Yes."

"May I have some more?"

"Yes, of course."

"Well, for the next few days the Romans searched for the murderer of the boy. I heard that they could not get any sensible information from the soldiers who had run. Consequently, they were punished with a hundred lashes each. The thief and the murderer who were crucified on each side of Yeshua were buried somewhere and the Romans believed that Yeshua was dead and had been taken down and away by his disciples and friends."

Rumours did persist that Yeshua was taken off the cross by his Father. Many of the disciples knew that they had not moved him and the family tomb had never been used. The stone had been rolled away and never closed because Yeshua was never laid to rest in there.

Yeshua healed fast and as his appetite grew; so did his strength. Within a week, Yeshua was on his knees in prayer with everyone in the house at sunrise and sunset. One night, with the help of the family, we escaped out of Jerusalem. I asked several of the family members to find the disciples, if possible, and have Peter organize a meeting. Yeshua would be waiting at the hidden cave which everyone knew. Mary requested that her family must come, including Yeshua's brothers and sister.

Chapter 17

YOU COULD NOT THINK AHEAD OR BEHIND

It was some time before everyone was gathered together. We had enough supplies and food for all of us. It was in a cave, in a secluded valley, away from any path or trade route. We had used this cave many times before, hiding from the Romans. It was barren except for a few tables, chairs and a hot spring pond. The rock walls were covered with colourful pictures showing Yeshua's teachings; during his ministry of three years. The oil lamps glimmered a trembling light as the people on the frescoes moved as if they were alive.

You could only get to the cave by squeezing through a crevice; once there, it opened to a wide cavern, exposed to the sky, high on a mountain, full of grass and lush luminous moss growing on all the rocks within the cave. No one wore their sandals for the grass was soft. There was a feeling of peace and harmony created by the muted, unbroken light.

So there we were, as we all sat nervously in a large circle. There was plenty of bread and wine.

On each side of Yeshua were Mary and Salmone. Most of the disciples were there, including Yeshua's brothers and other close friends; men and women who had formed a close relationship with him. His hands were healed and showed no scars from the nails.

Yeshua was hesitant and troubled as he spoke in the heavenly dialect, he used with his Father. He was speaking directly to his Father, and as we listened, his voice sounded sharp and serious.

This was likely to be the last time we would all be together and hear this spiritual voice. After, he had finished speaking with his Father, he said each one of our names; slowly telling everyone stories about that person and related events. Some of the stories were sad, some were humorous and all were inspirational. He completed a series of ceremonies blessing everyone present. He explained about what his heavenly Father looked like and what it was like to die and come back to life again. He said it was as easy as going through a door struck open by light; into a glorious endless space, where everyone you had seen or spoke to in your life was there.

It would happen as you thought about them, or you had a feeling about a past event, the feeling of laughter or sadness; it was all about feeling the emotions of the Holy Spirit, sinless and forgiving, as an innocent child.

Speaking was not necessary in the afterlife as thinking took on another form; you could not think ahead or behind. It is. Yeshua said it was like a continuous calling of pleasure, a reward for the faith you had showed to his Father. It was an inherent inborn goodness that made you understand that there was no need to pursue destiny or riches, for they were only fleeting desires; a trick to test your true nature. In heaven, there was nothing to seek. Every moment was appreciated, and there was no word for time. For in the afterlife, the *self* was imagined to life and you lived by using your sensory abilities without touch.

I asked, "You said that Yeshua's father spoke through him. His father was not mad at Yeshua being alive on the earth?"

"Yeshua said he had a new purpose. He did not know at first what his Father thought but knew he was angry for his tone was one of indifference."

I thought that Matthew was trying to give me an interpretation to soften my atheism, which was impossible for I could never see or feel god. "No, I don't. I really do not understand and I don't seek to hurt your beliefs and feelings."

Matthew, "I am an honest man and must tell the both of you what Yeshua told me in private when he was alone. What I am about to tell you is unknown to his family and disciples. It is something that troubles me and makes me unsure of his Father. Yeshua did tell everyone in the cave what he saw during that transitory moment in heaven, before he came back to us alive. I think most of it is true, but he had personal reservations about his place with his Father.

Yeshua said to me that he was disappointed with heaven. He saw it and immediately did not like it! The souls of people were happy, but were not emotionally and spiritually evolving. He described it as a placid place. There were no physical bodies but a collection of countless souls immersed in a cloud of water, ever flying and floating; everything repeating itself, over and over. His Father had told him that all of mankind's sins would be forgiven because of his death, but Yeshua believed there were no sins in the world, only simple people, who lived, loved and sought illumination.

He told me that he was tired of his Father telling him what to do. He had mostly always been a listener, but wanted to think for himself more. The Father told him that because he was not in heaven that the forgiveness of sins was in doubt."

A scientific thought came to my mind, "It sounds like a process called osmosis; there is no control over the cells. It is a process that continually happens under the right conditions. Essentially, it is very clinical and predictable."

"What?"

"Never mind."

"You see, Yeshua was a modest speaking man. Seeds need water to grow and in heaven there were no seeds to grow, and without personal enlightenment, there is no growth. The souls were content, but not passionate enough about where they existed. That is what he hated about heaven and why he awoke on the cross, deciding to live on earth again. He did not seek contentment, he sought a feeling of excitement, he wanted to grow and love and experience what life had to offer, enjoying the emotions his Father had given to us all. At one point, I thought he said it would be dull for him to just observe and guide the lives of others on earth, knowing that one day they were all going to heaven anyway."

Abrux, "What did his Father say?"

"His Father was furious! He threatened to not speak to him again or help him perform miracles."

"What happened?"

"Well, I don't know. I don't think they are on good terms. It is something that was not settled. Yeshua did feel bad that he did not join his Father, but suspected some other motive for his displeasure. He felt that his Father was ill and that he needed the human enlightenment that he had only experienced. But the Father did not want to admit it. Yeshua was a fresh and powerful life spirit.

Perhaps Yeshua's presence in heaven would have changed heaven to be more like living on Earth; but without the violence and evil. It had been written that a man like Yeshua would come to Earth; but his Father did not expect Yeshua to go back. I can understand why his Father is mad but I am glad that Yeshua still walks among us."

"When everything was said that needed to be said, Yeshua told everyone in the cave that he was going to Arabia and his new name translated while there, would be Issa. Mary would guide him to a religious order that she was brought up in as a child; he would spend the days in silent prayer. His brother, James, would also go and help Mary back to their home in Nazareth."

Everyone cried, begging him not to leave and to continue preaching. Yeshua told them in his way, for he understood the nature of all things, that the word of God he preached would be known without him. "It is your vocation now; it is the will of God that you still believe in me."

Salome, Yeshua's sister was sad, "We will never see you again."

"Treat me as if I am living but I will not be physically in Judaea again."

Everyone exclaimed, "No! You can't! Stay!"

"You will see me and hear me, you only have to ask. I will live a long life in a new land.

When I was young, I travelled to Europa with friends. One day, I might go back but I cannot stay here with you. My purpose will eventually lead me somewhere else. You may visit me anytime in the monastery. If not, you will only see me when you need me. Just say my name, wherever you are and I will answer your prayers and be there with you."

Chapter 18

STRUGGLING OPTICS

The worst was over. We had all lived Matthew's spiritual journey. I did not want to talk about Yeshua anymore; Jerusalem or Arabia, it did not it matter to me. It was selfish, but I could not listen to a story centred on a belief in god. I was just a man who healed people in my own way. I preferred to enjoy the warmth of the real sun.

Matthew had decided that Yeshua died on the cross, was buried and on the third day he rose from the dead. Abrux was glad he was writing something that would not be revised again. However, Abrux was a changed man and despite the story taking place many years ago, he would speak of Yeshua still being alive somewhere.

I started to live in the present again.

So, there was a very important reason that life goes on for all of us; we will it to happen.

Matthew became a figure larger than life. He remained through the hot summer into the late fall, until his notes were completed by Abrux.

As he made progress, Matthew seemed relieved; his face changed and he allowed one of my servants to trim his beard which made him look younger. His presence was a peaceful radiance, which paraded through his whole demeanor and being. It was a gladness that said all was now well; tomorrow would be full of more delights and pleasing surprises.

I admit Matthew did change us, all in ways that mark us as being different from one another.

There was no fear or lingering doubts in our conflict about Yeshua's death and resurrection; it was a situation that we thought was best not to be discussed. Before he told us the truth of Yeshua's life, Matthew was descending into a deep hole. I would call it more of a black hole that destroys people and complete universes.

Without dreams, we are nothing. Matthew was following his and fortunate that he had met Yeshua on the same road sometime in the past. His current world would now be filled with happiness until some random contemptible shithead came along to destroy it. He was the type of person that would not see it coming; for Matthew believed that all people were essentially good.

I suppose at one time or another, bad situations affect all of us; my mother dying was a tragedy. Who has ever experienced pure happiness or pure love? Not I, for I have hardly left my house for nearly 70 years waiting for the signal or sign that I am to see Armaigen and Tiernan again.

I have died many times, in the Elizabethan sense; but that was never pure love. Yeshua was now gone, and yet I felt more pressure, for I had been told that I was going to save the earth. I hope that did not include a crucifixion.

Where is Yeshua?

The timing was not right to tell Matthew what I knew and suspected: that the story of Yeshua would be told all over the Mediterranean. It would be an unpleasant, brutal, and spiteful journey for him and his disciples. It would be so difficult; I feared many would be killed. I did not have the heart to tell him.

It did not really bother me that the ending was revised, because I had seen visions of what people thought of Yeshua in the future; Yeshua lives. I thought that if I ever met Yeshua again, we could be good friends for different reasons that I could not readily explain. Matthew would be pleased to watch and know how famous Yeshua would become, especially for the economy at Christmas.

At one point, I decided to tell him of my visions of Yeshua and the gospels of Matthew, Mark, Luke and John sometime before he left. It would give him something to think about and hopefully get him by for now; not to mention that I could help him avoid some possible accident or future sudden death.

My intentions were good until I thought it all through. I thought of that humorous movie about the time travel car that stressed the importance of the space-time continuum and even the more technical interpretations in my documentary visions, hosted by physicists, explaining time as a fourth dimension.

I thought I would tell him the overall effect of being a follower of Yeshua in the future, only the good, happy parts. I must let him live his own life and leave out the detailed facts, for I knew the theoretical dangers of fooling around with the super galactic and subatomic levels. Serious shit.

The rest of Mathew's visit was truly enjoyable. I started to believe that Mathew had made the right decision on the ending of Yeshua's life; the real version was too complicated.

I came to terms with his beliefs. It was not really a serious lie, for Yeshua's story needed to be told to our violent and sometimes cruel world. Random, unexplained shit does happen. I would be dead if it were not for Yeshua. Fate is always expecting us.

I believed it was good just to tell a simple story and leave it as that. Who was I to say any different?

I did love Mathew. He was not an ordinary man; he was the main event. There are eternal questions and realities even for atheists. Matthew would never be a follower of YouTube or the inventor gods of the future, like Bill Gates. It took courage and humility to say what he did. I respected that.

My visions continued during Matthew's visit. Some would say it was my subconscious working overtime for my documentary visions began to include the religions of Asia. It was really, just a coincidence.

Yeshua and Matthew had travelled for years. My visions began taking me to different lands to study different philosophies. I even prayed silently to Yeshua for the fun of it; just as he had told everyone to. But I never saw or heard from Yeshua to get his opinion about Asian religions.

I really had no interest in understanding a different point of view, although I did find Taoism and Buddhism to have some appealing, different perspectives about life in general. It also seemed full of riddles that I did not comprehend or care to solve.

However, Asian-thoughts did create a calmness in me, unlike Yeshua's story. His life, through no fault of his own, always seemed to have an inherent sense of impending violence and doom.

I suppose that is why Yeshua always felt so real, and why I always had an uneasiness to have long talks with anyone about Yeshua, including Matthew. I decided to be a student of Yeshua and just listen; without the pressure of marks and attaining a credit.

I would heal bodies, not souls.

One day, I decided to tell Matthew about my potion and what I had seen in my visions. I planned to be very selective and even lie if required, so that Matthew's own vision and future history of Yeshua would not be disturbed. I was sensitive to the fact that Matthew had written a new religion. Damn serious shit.

I explained everything from the beginning: Armaigen, Tiernan and Yeshua. How they had saved my life with the potion that night and that the potion delays my aging process.

Only a few people knew about the potion; Matthew deserved to know everything.

I felt I was a part of some sort of euphoric noble cause; a joint sunrise and storm pulling me into a conflict of excessive joy and danger. It was very exciting. Maybe telling Matthew would give me more insight on when and where I was going.

I told him that the plants kept me young. They were grown outside of the village by a reliable farmer who proudly delivered his plants directly to me on a regular basis. He was told they were important remedies for my patients. I paid him the usual going rate for this type of crop, because I did not want to arise any suspicion.

"Did Yeshua take the potion?"

"Yes. We were told that he did; like everlasting life."

"Stop."

"What?"

"You know."

Matthew was momentarily lost in his thoughts. "That night, did he touch you?"

I knew he meant Yeshua. "Yes. On the head. Here. What of it?"

His face responded with a silent courteous applause. His eyes smiled as he experienced a sudden revelation.

"Have you ever thought that Yeshua's touch keeps you young?"

"No. Why should I? Armaigen and Tiernan were not touched."

Matthew grinned, "Or were they?"

Then Matthew murmured, "Everything is faith."

The only faith I had was in science.

My thoughts quickly cleared, I was surprised. He reached for my head and I felt his rough fingers touch me. He made the sign of a circle several times on my forehead; moving around. He stepped away and scratched his beard grinning. "I can still feel the impression of what he did to you."

"Like Taoism."

"What?"

Chapter 19

MADNESS

After much trepidation, I convinced Matthew to see my secret room. I had the only key. He was going to observe one of my trances for the entire night.

It was a relaxing, quiet and comfortable place below ground level. I locked the door behind us.

As we went down the stairs to the bottom, my feet could feel the cool air with each step. The fading heat departed out of our bodies, the lower we descended.

I lit all wall and table lamps, making sure there was enough oil for the night. There were many blankets to keep us warm. After many years, the servants knew I was not to be disturbed.

I showed Matthew how I made my potion. I told him the ingredients and amounts, plus some useful steps I had learned along the way to make it perfect. Plants hung down from the ceiling drying and were placed in picked order. Every time I was to take my potion, I always made another batch, which was stored in my floor chest. I opened it to show him. He was taken back by the number of potions I had already prepared with dates on them.

I did not realize his knowledge of plants as he told me he lived off leaves and roots for years as he travelled. He had learned to survive. He felt the coarseness of the hanging plants and easily identified each one, which was not easy for they had all dried out: borage, comfrey, puffball and burdock. It sounded like he had gained knowledge of these plants by eating them at separate times. But he did question the choice of one plant, "Why burdock? It is sharp and sticks to you."

"Would you like me to make you a good supply of the potion?"

Abruptly, "No. Never. Yeshua believed that dreams could be a warning."

I took a knife and cut each of the plants open. I explained that some plants were scraped and leaves and stalks were crushed, and then boiled in water.

Maybe it was the steady, low tone of my voice, my helpfulness or my detailed sharing of knowledge with a physician's confidence that helped Matthew accept my fortune.

When I was finished, Matthew looked at me and said, "I want to see these visions. I want to take the potion with you."

"Are you sure?"

"Yes. I must. But a small amount only; less than what you take. Have you ever seen Yeshua in your visions?"

"No. Not in person. Once I saw different pictures of him and listened to people discussing his life. I thought nothing of it. The pictures did not look like Yeshua at all. It is called a documentary. I have never seen him in person, other than when I met him as a child. But that does not mean you will see what I have seen and heard. The visions are never the same."

I thought the chances are slim to none he will see Yeshua; but you never know.

I had awakened before Matthew and sat up. I was still not fully awake. I was used to the hazy feeling and the routine of drinking water right afterwards, for the potion always made me thirsty.

I looked at Matthew and was surprised that he was still asleep. I could tell he was not at peace because as he slept, his legs and arms shook. He moved his face from side-to-side and then unexpectedly, he shook and fell out of bed, suddenly standing up. He stumbled about blindly, dripping with sweat and edging his way around the small room holding onto whatever he could find, until he held onto a wall and looked back at me.

I went to him and guided him back to a chair, giving him some cold water.

"Madness! How can such dreams be allowed to exist? I do not understand. I still feel the fear inside. If Yeshua saw it he would cry." He looked miserable. "Get me out of this place. I need to go outside for some air."

I tried to explain, walking with him as he hurried to the stairs. "You will not see what I have seen. I have had only one vision of him; the one I told you about. I'm sure that I have never seen what you just saw. I did not mean any harm to you."

"Galen, is having a longer life worth all this?"

"Yes. This is my life. Yeshua knew; they all knew the truth!"

"What truth?"

Matthew rushed up the stairs and opened the door; the coolness of the room rammed into the heat of the morning which had filled the ground level of the house.

The servants were surprised to see Matthew, as I followed him closely behind, talking to him as I hurriedly closed and locked the door to the cellar.

Matthew was outside our garden wall, still walking fast. I was catching up to him, but he walked faster wanting space between us. I saw him turn and follow one of the paths, which led outside of the town away from people and nearby farm houses.

He continued to walk fast, waving his arms, "I need open fields!"

I shouted, "Stop! Matthew, please stop!" He turned and knew he could not gain anymore distance on me. He was exhausted and drenched with sweat. He stopped and sat down on some supple green grass, under the shade of large trees.

He did not look up at me as I sat down, "I'm sorry. Sometimes my visions are terrifying."

Matthew, "Why didn't you tell me?"

"I never thought about it. I am sorry. When I was a young boy I was afraid to take the potion each week. Sometimes it made me scared and I know now, it has made me quiet by nature. But as I grew older, I tried to learn something from the visions. Bad visions linger on for days, but I try not to think about them too much after I record them."

Confused, "What did I see?"

"I don't know." We had one of those silent moments. We both stared at each without speaking.

"Where was I when I saw it?"

"The future."

"It can't be."

"But it is. What I have seen has made me a cynic most of my life; a cynical physician with amazing knowledge. Sometimes, I feel that no matter what I do, there is so much more life and events to come, that nothing really matters here in Greece."

"I've noticed. Sometimes, I feel sad to be with you." He hesitated again and was thinking. "Tell me the truth; does the story of Yeshua live on?"

"Yes, to some. But the world changes in the future."

Silence.

We saw a lone figure coming our way, carrying something. It was Abrux. He called out from a distance, "The cook said that you might be gone awhile. She told me to bring this out to you."

I waved him forward.

My mouth began to water as he got closer. My cook always exceeded expectations. "Well, let's see what you have. Open it up."

Abrux was careful and slowly laid out the food on the ground. It looked delicious. It was a grouping of every colourful, tasty food possible, including red wine; almost enough food to feed an army. The cook knew our tastes very well.

Matthew asked Abrux not to go; to sit and listen. He said that he had a story to tell about the vision he had last night that disturbed him. We all reached for our favorite fruit, cheese, meat and warm bread. We made sure our bowls were full of wine, as we waited for Matthew to begin.

Chapter 20

PICASSO

Matthew began telling us about his vision.

I was an observer and free to walk around. People came and went without noticing me. It took me many moments to see the complete long room for it was large, plain and imposing; the high ceiling and long windows made it look like a room made for a king. I heard lots of noise coming from outside, like geese honking when they are mad but did not look out of any window, for I was afraid and thought it best just to stay where I was.

Everywhere, in every possible space, cloth paintings in no certain order or pattern filled the room: on the walls, against chairs and other paintings. Only small spaces were available on the floor to walk and explore. There were no tiles on the floor; it looked as if it was made from wood. When people walked, it creaked. There were no Greek or Roman murals on the walls.

Then I saw him. I did not move, for now I was facing him, but he could not see me. I saw a short man sitting by himself. He was thin, with a bare chest, a large, old head and great, deep brown eyes. He was sketching a picture of something as he sat in a round, wooden-framed chair.

I could understand in some way what was said and the thoughts of all people.

A woman shouted from one of the corners of the room, "Pablo. Pablo. Come back to bed."

I looked over and I saw at least three women in bed, waiting for him. Then close by, another two naked women waited patiently on the floor, blowing smoke out of their mouth. I did not understand what was going on. Then there was a knock at the door, and several other people came in, all talking and very relaxed, like they lived there. The room was now full of people chatting and laughing. Other men and women were smoking through their mouths. Everyone seemed to be drinking or drunk, except for the old man called Pablo.

One man appeared to be the leader of this group; he was tall and took off his hat, waving everyone about. He went up to the old man, turning to the people following him, then pointing down, "This is the great Picasso! See him work. Walk around and see the paintings that only a god could create!"

Picasso looked up and sneered, "Yes. Come look at the monkey."

Pablo continued to concentrate on his drawing on the papyrus and said, "I hate you! You are my agent, but you do not come in here uninvited. I have told you before!"

"I was just around the corner and thought I would drop in."

He stopped and got up, rubbing his hands on a dirty cloth to clean them. His face looked angry but slowly it changed into a soft, gentle smile, as he greeted everyone. I felt and saw a cruelty or selfishness in him. I did not clearly understand what language he or anyone was speaking, but I did pick up some slight Roman accents. Through time, I understood what everyone was saying.

The group had wandered off by themselves, looking at all the paintings.

Pablo shouted, "Don't touch the paintings! Just look!"

The man called the agent pulled Pablo aside and quietly said, "They are rich and are here to buy something. See that beautiful woman in red with the floppy hat? She is Catholic. Look at her legs and breasts. Her father owns an automobile factory in America."

"You know I don't like to sell my paintings. I have no need of it!"

Picasso looked at the women who sensed someone was looking at her, and he raised his voice, "Does she know that anyone who purchases a Picasso must be painted by me naked?"

She heard what he had just said, looking back at him smiling, like she didn't care.

The five other naked women grinned, acknowledging the spell of Pablo. One said, "Can we stay?"

"You're not here to watch, for I am Picasso who paints what you cannot see in yourself; I pay you, for I am to watch you and do anything I want you to do! I pay you good money. In this room, I am god."

The agent sensed his interest in her by his concentrated long stares in her direction. He saw that Picasso had not taken his eyes off the women, who kept looking back at him, walking slowly as she studied each painting; clearly flirting with him.

"Why don't I introduce you to her, and you can show her your work?"

"Picasso can introduce himself. I can speak. What do you think I am? How old is she?"

"She just graduated from college. Making the tour, you know."

"What is her name?"

"Francoise. If you did, you would have to change her face. Her father is very powerful."

"Every face I have painted I have changed."

Matthew paused and took a deep breath. "You may wonder why I am crying. Well, it is what happened afterwards and what Picasso paints."

I do not know where everyone went. They vanished. But I only noticed this man called Picasso and Francoise. He kissed Francoise's hand warmly.

I knew what was on his mind. The girl did have adventure in her eyes, which only encouraged him even more. If I may say, property was being bought and sold right in front of my eyes.

Francoise, "Would you like to paint me?"

"Why?"

"Because you are the great Picasso and I want to be immortal."

"No one will recognize you. Is that what you want?"

"I will still live forever."

"I will paint a disturbing vision of you. I already see it. You remind me of the *'Weeping Woman'*."

"But I am not sad."

"My job is to distort reality. Your menacing soul is trapped by your own amoebic beauty; it is so simple." Picasso did not move and watched her turn away as he smiled; many women were afraid of him at the beginning.

Francoise looked from side to side at the hundreds of images he had painted through the years and was feeling less inclined to be immortal in these types of paintings. It was so easy to get caught up in the moment. She was now not too sure that she should be here at all. One hour ago, she was outside in a café, sun shining with her friends, laughing. Now everything seemed so dark, despite the bright colours almost jumping off the white walls, like water, enveloping her eyes.

The more she saw of Picasso's creased face, the more flaws she saw on his old skin. Men she had known in America were flawless; they had to be like her. 'I can be immortal right now,' she thought.

She asked, "What is this painting called?"

"That Francoise, is called *'Les Demoisells d' Avignon'*. Do you recognize it?"

"No."

"Look at their beautiful eyes, they follow you. Look at their bodies. Do you ever see your body like that?"

She giggled, "I guess sometimes". She stared at the faces, "I like their faces and eyes. It looks like masks. Would you paint me like that?"

"No. You are different. Every painting is different. This one here I called, *'The Kiss'*."

"Looks like they are biting each other, eating each other?"

He traced a line from the top to the bottom with his finger, "See the continuous line joining the couple?"

"The couple seems in some strange way to love each other very much."

"More than that, they are fused together, already making love right before your eyes."

Francoise looked, following the lines, finally seeing through the eyes of Picasso; acknowledging what he had intended. They both smiled at each other; his yellow teeth, hers a small white grin. She said, "Yes, I see that."

"Have you ever been fused by anyone?" It felt good to play with words.

Silence. She wanted to say yes for no reason at all. Then she felt a slight embarrassment to admit the truth to a stranger. "No."

"Let me show you a painting I keep at the back. It is the only painting for sale. It is called the crucifixion. All painters paint a crucifixion scene. This one is very different." He pulled back a large covering. "Here it is!"

Francoise gasped. It was a mockery of those things which brought her peace and safety. It frightened her.

"Beautiful, is it not?"

Matthew loudly shouted and we nearly dropped our wine glasses!

"Instantly, without warning, I was standing watching them, everything went black then light again. I heard only words at first, Pablo describing how beautiful the painting was."

He paused, assessing what to say next, "I think I heard something like, 'we are proud to present today…' and I did not hear the rest, for I vomited all the colourful paint onto the painting. I was now not just a part of the painting, but the painter himself, as I saw his work through his eyes; unbroken, flowing fluently, colours of disbelief and sarcasm."

My body was now lying on the papyrus; it had lost its human shape, as I look to you both now. I was surging tunnels of paint, curving through every shape and figure on the cloth, running like watery paint without control, not knowing where I would go next, unbroken, absorbed into the painting by some sort of spirit or trick unknown. I was trapped and all I could see was Francoise and Picasso looking at me, but they could not see me. I felt nothing but pain and anguish. My whole being was floating in and through the faces, arms, legs, strange shapes and objects that Picasso had painted; even my terrified Lord. I could feel every thought and purpose of each color and shape. I felt naked. It made no sense to me.

It was a nightmare, for I now could see and feel how Picasso viewed life and people. There was no soul or promise of any joy in life now or in heaven. To him, there was no God or heaven or salvation or hope in the painting at all, only distorted evil and damnation.

Then, unexpectedly, I found myself standing beside Picasso and Francoise.

I was so close to Pablo's face that I poked his cheek and felt his skin recede. He swatted away my hand, like I was a fly. He still did not see me.

Pablo, "You like?"

Francoise stood there, not wishing to speak, as her eyes tore at each shape trying to understand what was going on.

"You are confused?"

There was still silence and she began to feel older, more in control of her feelings and thoughts. Now, she did not need to impress anyone; she did not want to betray herself to him any longer. Inside, the need to suppress the good around Picasso was gone and she became a child again in her heart, just playful memories of fun. She wiped a tear away, which was swelling in her eye.

"No. I am not."

"That surprises me because everyone usually has questions...You are crying? Why are you sad?"

Francoise turned to him to say something, but she knew it would not matter. She stood looking at his dark eyes for a moment. She raised her hand in a quick burst and gave him a hard slap to his face. As she walked out of the room, she did not look back.

Francoise opened the door as another woman entered, nodding a blissful appreciation.

What I was seeing was slowing fading away. I suppose I was waking up.

Picasso swore and shouted something at Francoise in that loose Roman accent I had earlier recognized. I took one last look at him. I did not understand what he said; the words were now a slur, as he suffered a sudden mental paralysis, losing his temper. Furiously, he picked up a jar of blue paint and threw it at the wall shattering the colour into some other form. Roughly, without control, he cleared the table of his paints and brushes with several sweeps of his arm until he was covered in his own paint.

Mathew stared reflectively, at nothing, "I suppose he has servants to clean the room."

There was an immediate moment of quiet for all of us. We were trying to understand what Matthew had said and whether there was any significance.

A few birds came out of nowhere; darting towards some other trees close by. Our concentration was relieved as we watched the farmers work in a distant field. We finished our breakfast in silence, as there was nothing else to be said.

Chapter 21

A NEW CONTENTED STILLNESS

Matthew seemed to enjoy living in my house more each day after he had come to terms with the crucifixion. His disposition became more carefree; he seemed to act younger. He was less serious, with everyday personal observations and conversation with staff, enjoying the differences of opinion. He easily loved all people. He was very courteous and pleasant with most of my patients, as many seemed drawn to him. On many occasions, he would help out with my practice, greeting patients, cleaning instruments or any job that needed to be done around the villa. The servants were happy he was there.

Despite all the activity we all felt a new contented stillness in the household.

At certain times of the day, usually early morning, he would settle down to work on Yeshua's final story; he became focused and careful with every word. Still, I know he was enjoying the process with his trusted friend, Abrux. The servants knew enough of their habits to avoid his presence while he was working. Matthew's room was never to be cleaned.

We continued to enjoy each other's company despite the odd communication conflicts and implicit boundaries of silence. Sometimes he would enter my examination room when I had a patient. Despite these petty and minor encounters there was an invisible spiritual bond between us. He continued to write short notes every spare moment, stuffing them in bags and pockets. Eventually, there were scraps of papyrus everywhere throughout the house.

It was important to him to record all thoughts and impressions, including the songs Yeshua had sung. I gave him as much papyrus the town could supply. Stacks of it were delivered, sometimes many times a week.

The papyrus supplier did become suspicious. But in those days, it was easy to make up almost any story; I told him that chewing papyrus helped make teeth white and clean, while reducing tooth decay.

Matthew's bizarre OCD habits became a source of humour in the household. It was all innocent fun and compounded by his daily routines, unmindful of the people around him.

The servants were all sworn to secrecy. They began to accept the existence of a historical Yeshua, including the many miracles. Matthew and Abrux's friendship continued to flourish with Abrux enjoying the intellectual challenges that Matthew presented.

At meals, Matthew was self-absorbed with his own glossy-eyed thoughts; we did not take offence to his behaviour. He would write and eat at the same time, as I spoke about the patients I had seen that day. Abrux and Glenna ate with us every night. Sometimes, a guest would be invited. I would warn Matthew in advance not to talk about Yeshua or my visions.

Matthew was a part of the family, a fully-grown child who would politely nod and agree with almost anything anyone said during social occasions.

As a physician, I learned to avoid using certain words or phrases like: saving people, returning people back from the dead, and discussing the heart muscle in detail. I told Matthew once that I knew how to make a heartbeat after the heart had clearly stopped.

It only irritated and broke him from his concentration of his studies and notes. He begged me to stop tell him of such things that could not be true. Maybe he thought that I had taken too much wine. "Only Yeshua can do that. No offence, Galen, but it is a sin."

Out of respect and friendship, I stopped discussing advanced medical matters and observations given to me in my visions. I tried to keep it simple supporting the times we lived. I would discuss the simple leech medication and setting broken arms. I made sure whatever I said did not relate to the cataclysmic future I had witnessed.

For now, I tried to be a humble physician, full of superstitions. It was interesting being an actor, for you had to be careful not to fully forget who you really were; when treating a patient the next day. I always sought a cure and to extend the life of all my patients.

Sometimes, Matthew would ask me about Yeshua when he was young. This would usually happen when he was tired or stuck on his story, frustrated by not be able to describe a specific situation using the exact words spoken by Yeshua.

I even let him read my father's notes made right after the visit by the three strangers. He read my own journals, written when I was a boy. It contained vivid descriptions and thoughts about my visions. But Matthew quickly skipped over any description of visions and only wanted the early journals of my father and myself as a child that contained observations of Yeshua, remarking once, "I have never heard of people called druids."

I told him that it was cool with me, as bad is the new good.

I let him keep the wooden carving of the physician almost from the very beginning of his visit. He carried it wherever he went during the entire stay with us. Matthew would smell it and say, "It smells like Yeshua." He would then respectfully hand it back to me, like the Japanese do with their business cards, asking me to smell it.

"Yeshua is in there." I did not really know what he meant. Looking back, I should take people more literally. I did not give it too much thought at the time, for I was trained to think like a physician.

Chapter 22

THE NEED FOR SOFTNESS

Matthew told us that Yeshua would fill the air with so much love and joy. It was a stark contrast against Roman cruelty and seeing people die of starvation in the streets. The young and the old would follow him anywhere, like hundreds of ships pushed by a calm, warm breeze with no opposition.

Matthew said that people could feel the kindness in him compared to the unkind world.

They would touch him and he would caress them; when he was alone. He fed their need for softness; for the hard, sharp rocks on the ground everywhere had pierced not just the feet of people most days, it had hardened hearts.

Glenna, "Yeshua dated women?"

"Yeshua was attracted to women and they loved him back."

Food was in short supply, as it is now. The Romans hoarded food behind high walls for their own people. They did not care about us.

Poverty was deeply entrenched. The people were searching for something. Most were poor and they were especially vulnerable. This helplessness was felt by Yeshua and it troubled him. Yeshua gave them hope that all things were possible and not eternally dormant.

Matthew continued, "Weathered fathers did not always breathe the same air as we did around Yeshua. He would sometimes get into trouble, for some fathers demanded marriage if they suspected anything was going on. Some would confront him, most were hesitant, for he could read them before they had even spoken a word; he knew what they would say. No one is without sin." Mathew shrugged, "Who is? He understood what real life was like and that the fathers had a responsibility to their daughters."

Those fathers, who objected to Yeshua's flirtatious advances to their daughters soon felt his goodness. They knew they were not without sin and it became difficult to confront him. The fathers seemed more embarrassed about responding to rumours or sneers of disgrace from village elders about their daughters. Daughters needed good and stable husbands, not a man who questioned the Rabbi's teaching, as he wandered about the Roman Empire with his disciples.

Yeshua would greet a father with an embrace. Usually this was rejected, as the father would shove him away or even push him down to the ground. Other family members would be present, like the mother and her children, but never the daughter in question.

He would not fight back, but stand up with that slight smile of forgiveness. It was as if all wrongs in the world were just a temporary, luminous mist. In his innocence, he truly did not believe he had done anything wrong. He did not like blind traditions, for he had a new message to the world. Yeshua said that one must live in the world we are given. The feelings of desire he had sometimes, was no different.

He would try to lead the father away, slowly in silence and deep in thought, asking them to sing a song above love. Most times, the father's fear of family disgrace left, for the love he spoke of was pure. Most trusted Yeshua; they knew of his reputation. He was known to be a man of God.

Sometimes they would eventually sing with him as he walked or even gather in a small village with his disciples to learn more; everyone knew he was more than just a man.

At other such times, Matthew told me that Yeshua would recite complete poems he had created. Many were about the beauty of women and love. His memory was excellent as he would point to the heavens and dance as he sang encouraging us to follow a simple, tranquil melody.

Fathers seemed to be soothed by the tone of his words. His voice was different than most men. The sincerity of Yeshua was real. He convinced the fathers of his integrity and that love was an offering from heaven.

Yeshua had a genuine beauty about his face. He understood what it was like being human. All gladness had been stolen by the Romans. Everyone who had contact with him, discovered that happiness and eternal life did exist.

I asked him whether the part about fathers and daughters would be included in his story.

"No. These are not important details; Yeshua was a man. It would be a distraction. Some say the body is weak. Yeshua said the body had a soul that needed love. We were all mostly good men and women. The poems and songs will be recorded and placed in the story where God tells me to, whether it is real or imagined."

Chapter 23

IMMEASURABLE

My resilient scientific knowledge regarding the eternal question began to waver a little.

I developed, more often, an open mind; a new mild general approach. I was sure there was no god. I became less angry discussing the topic and was less cynical when I spoke about Yeshua. The strength of the human spirit always surprised me, even when you were not telling the truth, for change is possible.

Matthew told us all about the miracles he had witnessed. I could say they were made up or I could say it was the grace of god. Matthew was not a liar and I did believe his stories. Unfortunately, I also knew of the law of physics and the creation of the universe.

My visions had always provided too much information for me. My father was right about the value of a simple mind, because you never second-guessed yourself. I knew about behavioural modifications and much of the knowledge I had acquired, while important, took the fun away from living a full life.

I enjoyed visions from the 1960's that endorsed impulsive behaviour telling everyone to turn on, tune in and drop out. Life then seemed so natural and organic.

Mathew was excited to let me read, what he now called, 'The Gospel of Matthew'. I was not allowed to take it out of his room as he sat watching me go through it, slowly.

Squinting by the light of oil lamps, I read late into the next morning. It was a long story. I found myself asking questions to Mathew after I had finished it. He was euphoric at my sudden interest as he embellished the written words I had just read, even more than I thought possible, with details that I had not known before.

I was not sure whether I was now an atheist or an agnostic. Yeshua meant no harm.

I lacked the faith but I patiently sat listening to Matthew. I knew Yeshua's message would survive for thousands of years. I did not have anything to contribute. It did somehow provide great comfort, like loving a woman. Life is more than what we just see. But unlike loving a woman, there seemed to be no end to his story.

How could there ever be order in a world of human disorder?

What Matthew witnessed and wrote is immeasurable. It is without context or comparison. It is not science fiction. Like it or not, Yeshua was telling all of us that Earth is it. There was no E.T.

I had to give Matthew some practical advice, "Have you made copies of this?"

"Yes. Abrux has made two copies and this is the third copy."

"What will you do with it?"

"I will hide a copy known only to me and the disciples still living. I will have many copies made and use them to spread the word of our Lord."

I stared at him in those final few moments. I knew I would not get a chance to read the Gospel again. Matthew had such a kind face. I could see and understand why Yeshua loved him.

He finished by adding, "You know, this story is not just a routine event. It is connected to all the blinking stars. It is a human drama on the largest scale possible and that's what makes it so real and true."

I continued to sit, thinking as Matthew spoke, that it was like an astronomy vision I had seen about the cosmos. It showed how a star is really a sun that sometimes folded in on itself and exploded. It remained full and true; this star was Yeshua.

Chapter 24

STARING INTO YOUR SOUL

Matthew finished his gospel.

Yeshua, the perfect infant man with all the answers, came out of nowhere.

The story was complete, except for the *how* and *why*.

Matthew was here for a limited engagement. I never saw a vision of Yeshua or a 'trending right now' notice. But I never witnessed random quantum mechanics as a trend, either.

Without Matthew's presence, Yeshua would have been like an interesting-shaped cloud. Memorable for a brief moment, but not to be confused with cloud computing. Yeshua was all real sky and clouds: beautiful and ominous.

I understood clouds, for it was another curiosity for me, called a 'hobby' in the future. My favorite is the circulating altocumulus lenticularis duplicatus cloud; very rare, like Yeshua and Matthew.

Matthew told us that Yeshua liked to sing short songs. He told me that Yeshua did not speak for long moments. He preferred to speak in short sentences, his songs tended to be simple and memorable.

I told him that my father said that Yeshua whistled a lot. The night I was cured, he whistled and sang softly the same song over and over again.

Armaigen told him not to sing *'Blackbird'* anymore and to be quiet. He said he was tired of the same songs.

"What about Tiernan?"

"He was smart and kind. Determined. He had a strong, inner strength for an apprentice."

"Tell me again about the night the three strangers came, especially Yeshua."

"Sort of like sparkles, flares of magnesium coming together, more important than the highest-grossing movie of the year; like the genre 'mystical realism', real life but a miracle happens that you cannot explain. I always wanted to solve the equation of why I was cured as a young boy. It troubled my father more than me back then, perhaps because he was an adult with important responsibilities. Many boys and girls died in Pergamon that year; I should have died, but I lived."

Matthew looked at me strangely. "Why do you think you were saved, while others died?"

"I don't know. The potion makes me live longer and I know what the future holds. I have no idea of how I will save the earth; I am only one person. I was just a boy, reckless about most things; there was nothing special about me. But the three travelling men did appear, healed me and left. Yeshua was one of them and gave me a small painted wooden carving of a Greek physician. I played with it for countless days when I was a child. It never left my keeping, even to this day, except when you borrow it. I usually keep it stuffed into my inside pocket."

Matthew left as he came, with no notice. He mentioned one morning that the sunrise was brighter than usual which seemed like a good sign. He also said it was going to rain later which didn't make sense for it was a sunny and hot day. He said the rain would be "Good for the vegetables. Good for *my* special vegetables."

I had told several servants that Matthew was leaving and to prepare supplies for his journey. He asked Abrux to come with him to Judaea. Glenna encouraged him to go. "You need rest. You should see new lands and keep Matthew company. You are his friend. We will be fine here."

Abrux asked me what he should do. I told him not to worry even though I thought it would be a dangerous journey. He asked what I knew about the future, following Yeshua and his teachings. I told him what I knew: it would be a violent, but exciting start to a new religion.

Abrux wanted to go, but he had lived a quiet, comfortable life making a real difference in the lives of his students. Glenna and he were so close that I suppose he felt that he was already in heaven. Abrux decided to stay.

It was not an ordinary day. When the morning meal was over, the servants took all of Matthew's personal effects, including his notes and additional supplies that I had purchased. Food and water were also secured on his cart.

Matthew stood in our large meeting room and looked at all the servants. There was a nervous, happy anticipation; almost all of us were waiting for something important to happen. The servants had left their usual morning duties and were now waiting around and watching everything Matthew said or did in these last moments. It puzzled me what was happening, for I found myself acting and feeling the same way, as if the day had slowed down and every breath was important.

There was a variety of mixed feelings as we anticipated his departure. The amount of increased activity was pleasing; there is nothing more enjoyable when you see people happy and excited, running about with a good purpose. That is what it was like the morning Matthew left.

The entire household knew; school was postponed to the delight of all the children as everyone huddled inside the great room, waiting. We quietly watched what he looked like, how he moved his hands when he spoke, his soft eyes as he stared into your soul taking time to thank each person. He slowly moved, selecting an anecdote for each person, ending with a kiss and touching each face before moving down the line. Many kissed his clothes, and when some bowed before him, he became embarrassed, and quickly pulled them up straight.

At the end, everyone was quietly crying, for this was a *man* in the simple definition of the word. He gave hope to everyone that there was life after death, but not me.

Matthew stood silently in front of everyone and said he would sing, as best he could, some of Yeshua's favorite songs. The songs he sang that year had lively lyrics; many reminded me of the 'Beach Boys.' He sang many more songs and said that all of Yeshua's songs were already written by God and the melodies were just floating in the abiding air; waiting to be heard.

Matthew smiled and sang as he lifted his arms up at different times of each song for emphasis, enchanting our senses. Everyone sang along, singing the chorus over and over until it had played itself out. Afterwards, we all clapped and shouted with appreciation and delight.

Matthew crossed the room and hugged Abrux again who was now sobbing.

Matthew, "Don't cry. Without you, I would not have been able to complete the story."

"It is true. All true?" Now every servant was crying, including myself.

"Yes. The same story his Father wanted to be told." Abrux cried even more and it was several moments before he let go of him.

Matthew took his own sleeve and wiped Abrux's eyes. "These are the tears of God. Do not cry."

"Yeshua lives?"

Matthew, "He does. The story is not over"

Matthew then came closer to me. I allowed him again to draw a circle on my forehead. Before he gave me the physician carving back, he smelled it. Both of us smiled.

I nodded, yes. "How could I forget?" After all these years, the carving was but a smooth round piece of wood, almost colourless, worn down by human touch and sweat.

"You will remember this." Matthew picked up a package that was leaning against the wall and gave it to me. "It is from Yeshua; it is his lyre. He wanted you to have it."

"No. I cannot." I felt guilty of not being a believer; it was not logical. How could he still believe in *me*?

"Yeshua told me not to tell you this until I was returning back to my land. He said that when you are on an island, you will begin to save the earth."

"An island? But when? Has it begun but I cannot see it?"

"You are not listening. I know nothing more."

I was suddenly disturbed and sad. I suppose it was because every moment since I had awakened this morning, my house had been full of anxious people. Matthew was leaving and we were all happily downcast.

I said to Matthew, "It has been so long since I have seen Yeshua."

Matthew walked out of the house and everyone followed; talking and wishing him well on his travels. We all wanted to touch him before he climbed up onto the bench of his cart. I offered him the reins, as I stroked the head of the donkey, the beast licked my hand. Matthew pulled an apple out of his clothing and gave it to him.

Matthew adjusted some straps and stroked his back, "This is a very famous donkey, aren't you?"

I thought the donkey must be much older than I was. "How long do donkeys live?"

"This one still has some life left, but this I fear is his last journey. We will go slowly. When he gets tired, he lets me know and we stop for a rest. He can be stubborn. Mostly, we walk and we talk about anything. At night, when I am alone, he is good company. I sleep up against him like I did with Yeshua. When I get home, he will spend the rest of his days where he was born in a cool, dry stable. He has done his job."

"Where will you go?"

"Home. My disciple family is there. First, I will visit Yeshua's family. Joseph died many years ago. The children are now married, and have many children of their own. They all help with the talents God has given them. Mary is old; she speaks quietly with Joseph and her Father. Her will to live is strong. Mostly, she sits under the shade of the fig trees. She is visited often by close friends and her grandchildren. When I see her, I will read the story to her. She knew I was coming here to finish it."

We studied each other's faces.

Matthew, "Galen, my friend, waiting for an answer involves patience. Patience and persistence go together. Be glad it is you. Patience is everything. It is written that you will have a chance to save the earth."

"I don't understand."

I went to speak again. He held up his hand and moved a finger on his lips, speaking quietly to me, "In your own time, it will come to you. It will mean more to you when you discover it yourself. You've seen it in your visions. Think about what matters the most in your visions and it will come to you. Don't you think I have an idea of what you have seen?"

The face of Yoda flashed in front of me. It was like saying some important one-liner before a big fight, or the moment before someone solves a mystery; it was of no real consequence, for I usually forgot riddles because they were often too abstract or too dry. That is how my mind worked.

He turned and looked around as he sat on the cart. He made the sign of the cross to everyone several times around the group. "May the blessing of Yeshua always be with you. It shall be given to you. Seek, and ye shall find. Knock and the door shall be opened unto you."

He looked about again and then glanced toward the direction where he was heading. The donkey knew what to do and moved away. Once on his way, we all stood waving, then he suddenly stopped and twisted looking back, smiling a little as he waved his one free arm. Slowly, Matthew began singing loudly in the street for us all to hear.

Matthew disappeared down the steep path made of small tight stones. The old donkey carried a heavy load and slipped. Matthew steadied him and motioned upright with the reins; helping the beast regain his balance.

We all waved to Matthew until he was out of sight, not like the 1960's saying, but the Greek saying. We did not notice that some dark clouds had appeared behind us with the sun still shining in front of us. A small, brief shower poured down on us. We all stood there looking up to the sky, not moving, knowing the deliberate rain would stop soon; it was a new day for all of us.

Matthew moved away, as his song turned into a faraway sound; a faded, empty ricochet of clanking cart wheels and rounded worn hoofs on stone. He disappeared around the edge of the last building. None of us would ever forget Matthew's visit.

Chapter 25

SORANUS AND EOLUS

It was the end of another hot day; it was going to be a fortuitous, warm night.

Everyone was in bed and I was about to lock the main door. There was a weak knock on the door; at first, I thought it was the wind unsettling the door in the frame.

I pulled the door open. Two boys, dressed like beggars, stood looking up at me. They appeared tired, dirty and hungry. It seemed to me that they had waited until all of my sick patients had left. I was looking forward to being free and alone.

I was tired and routinely said, "We are closed. Come back...." I stopped in mid-sentence.

The taller, alert-looking boy with long, blond hair introduced himself quickly, "My name is Soranus. This is my brother Eolus." I felt he would continue to do all the talking.

Eolus had curly, short brown hair; he was of thin stature. He stood slightly behind his brother, warily sizing me up. They were the most prime example of fraternal twins I had ever seen.

I watched Soranus speak and knew by his use of words and complete, convincing sentences, that this boy was educated.

Soranus, "Sir, we are tired. We have come to see Galen."

"Why? It is late."

Eolus stuttered, "We have been lost."

Soranus spoke evenly to his brother, "No, we haven't. It just took us longer. We have been waiting."

I looked at Eolus as he had difficulty saying words and sentences. Clearly, simple-minded compared to Soranus, but likeable for he lightly hovered over the importance of their visit. There was no malice in his voice, just the sound of fatigue and frustration.

I stood and listened with a detached stillness; thinking.

"I am Galen."

Eolus, "You? You are very tall."

Soranus ignored Eolus, "Our mother died in a fire and the Romans took our house. She told us many times of a famous physician called Galen of Pergamon. We had no father to speak of and she was worried we might be left alone one day. She said she knew you and had met once when she was much younger. She said you were kind to her."

"What was her name?"

"Adonia."

The name sounded familiar, but I could not picture her. My father had introduced me to many women; I was sure I did not know her personally. "Did you ever know the name of your father?"

"Nicon Galenus."

It was mispronounced, but I knew it was him. I was shocked and speechless. I tried to understand the involvement of my father, although I knew there were many times in his life when he had younger women live in his house.

I was aware and ashamed he was capable of such things. Somehow, I was partly to blame of his reckless behaviour for I could have made more of an effort to stop it. My father missed my mother, despite his talent of creating grand buildings, he had a lonely heart. He did feel cheated and knew the gods were likely not pleased with his actions, but his wealth and lust for women made it too easy for him. The temptation was too great and he was just a man.

I studied the eyes and the shape of the faces. Yes, it was true: I felt that these two boys were my brothers!"

"My own mother died when I was born." Soranus was carefully listening to me. "It seems none of us have a mother."

Eolus, "Bastard!" The pronunciation was incoherent. I could tell that the boy was not used to swearing.

I asked, "What do you know of him?"

Soranus, "Only that he was fat and a liar."

"Rich. Tell him Soranus, he was rich and raped her. Threw her away like garbage."

"Yes. My mother was with child. He sent her away!"

"Two childs." I sympathetically smiled, not at the facts, but that Eolus held up two fingers to make his point.

Soranus seemed annoyed at me and his brother's interruptions, "He gave her money and told her to leave. She chose Athens. We had relatives there."

"But they are all dead now."

"He sent enough money every year for us to live."

"My mother said she was ashamed of what she did."

Soranus sharply stopped his brother, "It was not her fault!"

I then remembered my father saying before he died, 'Did you ever miss not having brothers or even sisters?'

Sorrowfully, I said, "No. It was not your mother's fault. Never, ever, think that."

<hr>

They agreed to come in and stay the night.

Later, after Soranus and Eolus had been washed and fed by my servants, we all sat comfortably in front of the fire staring at the flames. Eolus said he could see different shapes in the fire.

I saw them more clearly now. They were on the cusp of being men. It would take many months and years of care, feeding them, continuing their education, so that they would grow into healthy, good men. Despite everything they had suffered in life and in their search for answers they were both quiet, seemingly generous boys, and at ease with themselves.

There was this strange feeling that we all seemed to know each other from some past life. We were completing the sentences of each other, before they were finished; it was another suspicious coincidence. Nevertheless, they were comfortable enough to speak of their long walk from Athens to here; then it was followed by a pleasant pause when nothing would be said. They trusted me; I liked them and was glad they felt safe in my house.

I estimated Soranus and Eolus to be around twelve years old. I realized that Eolus relied on his brother and could not survive on his own. Soranus was more mature, quick witted and had a good eye for detail.

I could feel the stare of Soranus, "Why are you helping us like this?"

I could not hold back; it was not in my nature. I told them outright that we both shared the same father; his name was Nicon Galenus.

Eolus, "That's the same name as you, sort of."

"Eolus, don't be stupid, it is the same name."

"I don't understand."

I explained, "My father, your father, lived sometimes an unstable, selfish life. I'm not saying what he did was not true; it could have happened. There were many parties with men and women. I did not like what was going on."

They sat quietly and said nothing; they had the right to be angry. I told them they would likely feel anger for the rest of their lives.

Soranus did not seem mad at me but was more solemn at his response, "At least you knew him."

"I am sorry. You are both here now."

Eolus broke the silence, tapping the arm of Soranus, breaking him out of his pensive thoughts.

"Soranus, so we have a big brother?"

Soranus sat up on the pillows. He spoke but chose his words carefully, not taking his eyes off me, "Yes, I suppose we do." He continued to think.

Eolus, "This is good, right?"

"But if all of this is true and our father is who you say he is, that he died an old man and you lived all these years with him, then why do you look so young?"

I could not reply to Soranus's question. The truth was even too much for me, so much time had passed and the unknown complications and possible outcomes were vast and unknown. There was nothing to tell, at least, not now.

I was surprised at his insight. I did not really look too much older than them. I had planned only to tell them the main facts for now. I did not leave out any relevant detail except the visit by three strangers, generations ago and the potion. I talked about my life with my father and the type of man he was. I told them I exercised every day and ate healthy foods. That affected everything and nothing at the same time. I was as truthful as possible.

It was one of the few times in my life that I could not express the right words. So, I gave an abandoned look of sympathy when I was finished and looked back at the fire. I felt Soranus's stare for a moment as he eventually gave up any further questions for now.

They were my brothers; my new family. I was wondering what I would do with them and whether I should just let life take its course. I did need help in my practice. I could place Eolus in the school here. I looked over at Soranus. Oddly, I felt he knew what I was thinking, for he was a confident boy and I always needed good, reliable and intelligent help.

"You both are welcome to stay with me. It is busy and I can train you to be a physician, like me."

Eolus, "We can stay here, forever? It is so big."

"Yes. We are brothers and need to be together." A momentary thought crossed my mind; when I leave Pergamon one day, the boys will have to come with me. I could never leave them.

It never occurred to Eolus that I was speaking mainly to Soranus; he knew of his own limitations but was proud for his brother. "Soranus, you are going to be a physician. I can help you!"

Soranus was a quick study and eager to learn as much as he could. There was no need for him to go to medical school. His progression and knowledge of medicine grew at a fast rate, participating in operations, giving suggestions, and asking questions. I trusted his capability and as time went on, I observed he knew more than I did at his age. Of course, most of his advanced knowledge came from my own visions, unknown to him.

He never pursued the question of why I appeared so young and in return I never brought the topic up. I was unclear of my precise age unless I sat down and figured it out. If you did not age at the normal pace, years were of no consequence. Once, I did calculate my estimated real age and I was surprised I was that old; afterwards I burned the papyrus.

Soranus grew in his medical ability as he became a man. Eolus was happy in the role of being the main assistant. He had the unique ability of making patients feel relaxed as they came in, checking off a list of possible ailments and symptoms of each patient before we saw them.

We were a good team and it was a happy time. As another year passed, their company made it easier for me to minimize my obsession with the prophesy. I accepted my life knowing my father had something to do with it. It connected my past to my present.

I continued to keep my dark sealed room a secret. I kept the key to my potion room around my neck. As each new plant shipment arrived, I would disappear into my secret room, hanging up plants to dry. I would spend my time cutting, mixing and preparing what I referred to as 'my brew'. No one in the household would ever interrupt me for they knew my routine and my reputation as a great healer; I was working and not to be disturbed. In the corner, I had additional chests for the storage of extra plants and herbs.

Chapter 26

PARANOIA

I felt like a Greek renaissance man as my intelligence and practical knowledge grew. There were only a few people in my life that understood what I was saying about the human body. I naturally felt self-assured, although there were still many days that I felt insecure.

I woke up feeling nervous. I did not have a good night of sleep due to a reoccurring panic attack; I likely had the only panic attacks recorded before modern times. I felt I was developing a mental illness, what Hippocrates called paranoia; too many unresolved issues, I suppose. There was going to be a change of some sort or was there going to be a death of someone close to me. The paranoia continued, as I lay in bed wording the song something about only good die young. Absurdly, I was not young.

For weeks, this strange concept was building into fear. I was getting distrustful and reading too much into the motives of people. I had gone through this before. But people outside my house truly began to stare at me for long moments. I would over hear people speak of me when eating in town or become quiet when I walked into a building or a small crowd.

Even patients would hold onto my arm or not let go after an embrace. Once, I noticed some legionnaires point at me as I pretended to ignore them, looking straight ahead, walking right past them. But I clearly heard one of them "Charon, Charon!" followed by laughter. The Charon was the person or spirit who transported the Roman dead across the river Styx.

Was my great hoax exposed? Was this the end of my deception?

I felt that my trusted brothers Soranus and Eolus had noticed something different or they were becoming familiar enough with me now to discuss my situation: why was I not aging?

I noticed on several occasions, when we were not busy, that Soranus would prompt Eolus to have a good look at me, until I diffused the action by a good, friendly smile back at him. They knew I meant them no harm. They had both grown so tall since living here. Soranus became more articulate and was the same height as me. Their faces had changed and they were healthy; their mother would be glad and it made me feel good.

Soranus was also suspicious of one specific medical protocol in which he was not allowed to assist me. I never got sick; everyone else would get sick once and awhile. We were always surrounded by sick people. So, my rule was that when a patient arrived with open sores or bleeding not from an injury, I told them it could be a contagious disease. If that was the case, then the patient would only be seen by me. They were to keep their distance.

Why is he never sick? What does he do in his secret room?

Soranus kept his thoughts mostly to himself. I knew he was smart enough to know, like me, there were no coincidences, just medical facts and logic. He knew I never got sick, and Abrux confided in me that Soranus once asked him why I slept in my secret room once a week.

I had to try and ignore what I thought I heard, and stop trying to read the minds of everyone. It was difficult, for I would sometimes forget about my problems and joke with Soranus during surgery about how clever I was during a certain type of surgical technique. He must have thought that I had mysterious, god-like powers. Perhaps I was the evil Diabaulus or the attentive Ascelpius.

I knew that the distinction of good and evil was very different, but to most people they were somehow related and both feared.

Soranus continued to indulge me, not saying anything as he admired my insights. I knew his placated thoughts and silence were a mirage. He knew I was not a normal human being, but he remained patient because he was my brother. I was not a god, but acted like one.

Chapter 27

THE GIFT

The sun rose. Our simple, quiet routine was retold in a comforting, undeclared way. The early warm air was bleeding into the house. The cool morning air withdrew, as the newly created light flooded the darkness.

We had our separate rooms. The servants laid out our clothes for the day every morning, keeping their distance as we all preferred to wash and dress ourselves. Then all three of us, along with Abrux and Glenna, would meet in the main room to eat an enduring breakfast on the long table, littered with books and papyrus. Our morning meal was enjoyed not only for reasons of taste and hunger, but after several years we all felt in command of our upcoming duties for the day.

We were at ease with one another, as were the servants who were free men and women.

Our house in Pergamon, was a respected place; an honourable house. Almost every week, someone would come and ask me or Abrux, who did the hiring, and if we had any open positions. We rarely did hire, as most of our help were families who had been with us for many generations.

We had to be especially careful not to take the slaves of other households without the permission of their owners, so any new prospective person required a delicate, tender investigation of their background and experience. My reputation was important to maintain and I did not want to attract any undue attention.

It was a very busy practice, chaotic at times, especially if a patient was in pain and feared our suggested treatment or surgery. The falling sickness was the worst situation, for the patient could choke or bleed profusely after sometimes hitting their head on the stone floor. That is why we tried to persuade families to stay out on the street and wait until we had a prognosis or treatment, except mothers and fathers with sick children who were allowed in. Eolus was very good at organizing this, and keeping the door shut if the room was already full.

During our morning meal, we would sometimes share observations of a new malady, symptoms and possible treatments. At those moments, we would get out medical books and read them out loud for all to hear. Sometimes, people would fake an injury or symptom and ask whether we had any coins or food in the examination room. We all would laugh at humorous situations.

For example, people repeatedly came in when nothing was wrong with them, because they were lonely, a toothache requiring the three of us to extract it, diarrhea and flirtatious men and women. It was all innocent talk, which relieved the tension of the upcoming day. If patients were dying, we had a separate building and rooms where more senior servants attended to their final needs.

It was a conventional morning. Our modus operandi was guiding us forward.

A noise caught my attention; it was an unexpected, unknown sound from outside of the building.

I was with a patient and trying to concentrate on pulling a needle through the skin, closing a deep knife wound. Soranus held the skin tightly together as I sewed.

Doros was a large powerful man. He had been given an unusual name which meant *'gift'*, he was the first born of a large family. The family likely did not know any better at the time, for he was a bully who lived off the weakness of others. He was always in trouble fighting and drinking and I was surprised to see him alive that day, for I had heard he was dead. I mentioned this to him.

"Dead? Do I look dead?" I wanted to punch him in the mouth and knock out the last few teeth he had. He was very annoying.

Soranus was beside me and was not intimidated, clinging to the loose skin with the tips of his fingers, as I worked away stitching. With each push of the needle, Doros squirmed in pain. "Hold still, don't move and it won't hurt as much!"

Doros caught Soranus looking at him, "Who the fuck are you?"

I pricked him deeply into the wound and he shouted. "Ah, shit!"

"He is a physician just like me, and only the gods know why even *I* want to help you. So just shut up for now."

On the table, Doros slightly moved his leg again, "Stay still!"

He stopped and did not move, but you could see the pain in his face, as he forcefully squeezed his eyes shut. I stopped sewing.

Doros looked up, "What?"

It sounded like horses far away, many horses. The noise was coming closer, faster with the uniform thumping of feet and the sound of shouting, people screaming, deep voices, more men shouting, horse screams, scraping of wood or metal on stones. I thought, "The Romans! They have come to arrest me!"

I looked up at Soranus, "You finish up!" I waited until his hands replaced mine.

I left quickly, pointing at Doros, warning him to be quiet. He stopped whatever he was going to say, laid his head back and closed his eyes again as Soranus carefully continued.

I ran down the long corridor and as I rounded the corner to the front room, the chaotic noise became louder. I dreaded the Romans for a variety of reasons. I did not fully understand the seemingly excessive ferocity of the outside panic and uproar; maybe they were passing by my house and not stopping. I was afraid, not for me but for my brothers and servants who were a part of my family. I had no fighting skills, yet I was not planning on resisting.

The Romans had stopped outside; my worst fear was confirmed. The patients waiting to be seen outside were herded quickly out of the way, like animals. Inside, there were people standing still, not knowing what to do. They were scared and breathless.

The door was violently kicked and it exploded inwards, as a group of soldiers charged inside. Each waved a gladius around like a sharp cloud of pungent smoke, knocking Eolus on the ground. The large shields pushed everyone out of the way, others hastily escaped squeezing past the loose hanging remains of the door out to the street.

Many people screamed and fell over, then recovered, crawling away until they stood again, moving faster to avoid the sharp swords, as the soldiers slapped their backs with the long shields. People too sick to get up were dragged out of the building and thrown onto the street.

Tables and chairs were knocked over, searching for anyone missed and the large breakfast table was cleared of all books, papers and numerous organ jars were smashed into pieces. I moved towards the table holding my hands up, "No! Stop!" But I was shoved back until a shield knocked me on the head from behind. I looked around at the soldier and he hit me again. My nose was bleeding.

Ignorant people; he spoke Latin, a language I knew, but mostly refused to speak, for I was a proud Greek. I faced forward and thought of the quiet, peaceful breakfast we had earlier that morning.

Eolus had somehow rolled away, crawling into the corner of the room and eventually found his way to me. I did not know what to say, I feared my life would soon be over. Eolus held my arm, shivering, as soldiers rushed past us. Suddenly, there was a hoarse scream, some swearing in the back room and I thought of Soranus; at that moment four legionnaires dragged Doros past us as he struggled to get away. I looked at his leg and could see the needle still in the skin and deep red blood dripping down his leg as he was then thrown out the door, stumbling off-balance. Soranus stepped up beside me and stood on my other side. I was glad he was safe.

The imposing soldiers stood all around the outside of the room and behind us. It was stifling hot and smelled like sweat, dirt and dust. It became dark and closed in. There was no one to talk to; no one in authority. It was frustrating and I just wanted to tell anyone of my secret so that Soranus and Eolus would be released and safe.

The legionnaires looked very serious at attention, waiting for someone. Outside, Romans continued to be moving, seemingly spinning about, until all my patients had left. It became quiet as the street was now secure.

Chapter 28

PAX ROMANA

"Out! Everyone out!"
A large, tall high ranking Roman officer shouted as he took off his plumed helmet entering the room. This was no ordinary officer, but a battle-hardened Legion Legate, a man who had command of an entire Legion. He pointed at me, "Not you!"

A few legionnaires and a Centurion were told to stay and directed to continue guarding us. It seemed like so many bodies were now being pushed along, feet shuffling, all wanting to leave at once as they took up all available space, but only one soldier could leave at a time through the door. It was still not fast enough. The Centurion repeatedly hit their backs and helmets from behind with his stick, "Move! Move faster! What's the matter with you? Faster!" He walked about behind the tangled group leaving, continuing to smack the last legionnaires out of the room.

He shouted at the Commander who nodded, "All clear. Bring the Consul in!"

A man wearing simple nightclothes was carried in on a stretcher by some attendants as others carefully lifted him onto the table. "There!" The Centurion pointed, as he tapped our eating table.

The thin man was clearly sick; his head was dripping with sweat and rolling about, delirious, in and out of consciousness. The Legion Legate went closer and made sure the sick man was made comfortable and talked to him, then shouted to the others, "Stand back, give him air, and bring a pillow. Water, we need water!" I went to help the man who was clearly very sick; near death, I thought. The soldiers behind me held me back, as another one blocked my way.

The Legate looked over, almost imploring to me, "Galen! Are you Galen, the Greek physician?" Just his tone of his voice made me feel more at ease. The tone was not of Roman anger against a Greek, but it was a genuine search for help and assistance. I thought this sick man must be someone who means a lot to him, as he stood holding his hand on the sick man's shoulder.

"I am." There was relief in the officer's face. I tried to move, but could not.

"Let him go. All of you move back! Come!" The legionnaires guarding me, stepped aside.

All the attendants were still crowding around the table. Some were fixing the sick man's clothing for appearance sake, some adjusting the pillow, dripping water into his mouth; they were all meaningless tasks that re-focused my attention to curing the sick man.

All the multiple of hands and people was frustrating and I shouted as I looked at the Legate, "I need room, so everyone needs to move!" I waved my arms, "All of you! Just leave, go away!" I looked at the officer's face. "Please."

Soranus appeared on the other side of the sick man, with Eolus keeping his space behind his brother.

"You heard him, everyone move away. Now!"

I motioned for Soranus and Eolus to come closer. "Don't be afraid. Come." I felt I had established some sort of trust with the Legate, who likely made logical decisions based upon facts and not superstitions. I thought this was going to be a curious encounter, at least I felt I had one Roman on my side.

A sole Roman physician came beside me, looking annoyed. I suppose it was because I was now taking his place beside the sick Consul. "I will be watching you, Greek. He is an important man. If he dies, you will die."

The Legate spoke up, "Shut up! You have had your chance. Let him do his job!"

I asked, "What is your name?"

"Barrius. Legion Legate of the IX Legio Hispana. This is Proconsul Gaius Suetonius Paulinus. We have travelled from Egypt."

I did not continue the formalities. I spoke directly to Barrius, ignoring the Roman physician. "Colour of his urine?"

"Like dark water."

"Shit?"

"No shit. Yellow bile, some brown water. Not solid."

Strangely, I suddenly remembered that my initial fear of being arrested had disappeared. I felt relief. A hidden freedom was reaffirmed and my mind was untroubled. The Romans had not come to arrest me, but needed my skills as a physician. It seemed that my reputation as a healer was known, even to the Romans.

I stood there and became concerned. I examined the face of the Consul. I had been given a dead patient and was frustrated for I knew that the Roman physician had waited too long to bring him to me. It would detract him from any blame, for his death was imminent.

"This man is near death! He is dehydrated. Look at him! Look at the colour of him! How long has he been like this?"

"Some days he is better." The Roman physician looked at Barrius for reassurance. He continued, "The Consul is strong. I'm sure he will be better in a day or two with proper Roman medicine."

Confidently, I turned and stared at the Roman physician, "If he dies, I'm sure you will not be practicing medicine again. You have done nothing for this man." A grim, forbidding look came over his face.

I hated this minor bickering and petty jealousy. Barrius seemed to acknowledge my medical knowledge by offering his hand to mine. It was a sign of trust. I was now going to be the physician to look after this man. He also acknowledged Soranus and Eolus. He picked up the hand of the Consul and looked at him. "This is a very important friend and man. Please, do anything to save him."

"What is his name and rank again?"

"His name is Gaius Suetonius Paulinus, Imperial Legate and a Proconsul of Rome."

I bent over Paulinus and held his eyes open. I looked inside the pupil. He was almost unconscious. I felt his skull and looked at his neck and shoulders. "How long has he been like this?"

The old Roman physician became angry, "Be careful, Greek."

I stopped and scowled at the Roman physician, then at Barrius. "There can only be one physician in this room and it is me."

"No. This is not possible. I have been treating the Consul!"

Barrius glared at the Roman physician. He turned back as he looked at me; I nodded, confirming the other physician must leave. "Leave, now!"

"But..."

"Go." Barrius cut him off as he waved his hand; he did not look at him anymore. "Do not say another word until I tell you to. Go back to the Consul's villa and wait. Do not speak to anyone." He shouted after him as he moved slowly away. "If I find out you have spoken and spread lies, I will kill you myself!"

Barrius looked at me, "For the last month; the fever comes and goes. Many have died in the legion. He is getting worse and falls in and out of sleep. And now he does not eat."

"Where was he before this started?"

"Africa."

"Where in Africa?"

"Alexandria."

"Damp and marshy?"

"Yes."

I bent down and smelled his putrid breath as he coughed. Hot sweat drizzled down his face, soaking the pillow and clothes he was laying on. This was not a good sign. The sweat was slowly draining all water out of him. I instructed Soranus to take all the clothes off the Consul for a complete examination; he took a knife and cut down the front of the Consul's clothing.

Eolus had seen many cases that were similar; he went without my instruction to get cold, clean water and extra cloths. Upon his return, he began gently washing his body and applying some herbal plasters over the rashes.

"Eolus, Soranus will finish up. You prepare an intravenous with sugarcane juice, fill his body with pure clean water and have the servants fill a bath full of cold water. When you are ready we will move him there"

Barrius, "Intravenous? What is this?"

"A last resort. The Consul is near death. We will try to put water back into his body through his arm, but not through his mouth."

Barrius looked perplexed, and then sent everyone out of the room, including all the legionnaires. "Do not let anyone in. Guard the door. No one enters without my orders."

It was one of the few times I had an opportunity to talk to a Roman with some authority; he was in my house, yet I was still wary of him, for he was a killer of men. His friendship with the Consul was sincere and I am sure he was thinking on behalf of the Consul, dismissing the legionnaires so that they would not see him so ill.

Barrius, "They say you perform miracles?"

"It is science, cause and effect, simple as that. No different, I'm sure, then you planning a strategy for battle."

"I suppose."

The Consul felt the cold wash of water stream down his body to his toes; his body reacted by suddenly moving. Soranus lightly stroked his whole body, avoiding the rashes and inflamed areas. The Consul woke up and said something unremarkable that we could not understand.

Soranus, "Galen, there seems to be bite marks all over his body."

I looked closely with my magnifier moving all over his body, "Insect bites all over his neck, shoulders and legs. Move him to his side. Up." Soranus and Barrius lifted him. I pulled his wet outerwear off his body and tossed it on the floor.

"Not good. It is now infected; malaria." I stood up and looked at Barrius with sadness as they laid him flat again.

"Malaria? Can it be cured?"

"A week ago, maybe. Now I'm not too sure. If I had only known…it never really goes away and comes back if the insects bite him again and even then, it gets worse than before. If he lives, he would have to be very careful of where he travels from now on."

"He must live. The Emperor…" Barrius stopped and thought. "Galen, do whatever you can do."

Barrius was a thinking man like myself and had chosen his words well. I also realized the importance of the situation; we were both realists. At this stage of the disease, the Consul's chances were slim, even with the medicine and treatments I had at hand.

A servant came back into the room and told us the cold bath was ready. Soranus and Eolus both stopped and looked at me knowing no treatment would cure malaria at this stage. The bath might help his fever. It was up to the gods, who I'm sure were deaf and blind.

Precipitously, I thought of something that was objectionable to me, but could provide a cure.

It was a quick decision. I would do it. I stood there in silence, staring back at my brothers, planning how it would happen. There was one way I might be able to prevent the death of the Consul; I would have to move fast, but I knew Soranus and Eolus would now know my secret and what I had been doing all those years in the cellar.

My father had been told to keep quiet and to share it with no one. I justified my change of opinion knowing I must try to save the Consul. Only my brothers would know of my potion. I trusted them. Now was the time for action and I could not see any other way out of it; the Consul would be dead sometime today without my potion. I knew I was breaking an oath made many years ago, but I saw no choice in the matter.

Barrius stood back to give us more room. I shouted for the servants and instructed them to carefully lift the Consul into the bath. Soranus and Eolus looked at me and I could tell that they knew this action was hopeless and not logical, but they followed my instructions.

"Eolus, you start the intravenous in the bath, Glenna will help you."

I looked at Glenna and she nodded in agreement. "Make sure the Consul is sitting upright and his arm is resting on a table beside the bath. Wrap a cold cloth around his head."

Chapter 29

IN DUE TIME

"Soranus, you come with me. Barrius, you stay with the Consul. We will be right back with some other medicine."

I left in a hurry and Soranus caught up with me as we walked to the back of the house, "Galen, what are you doing? You know we don't have any medicine for malaria. He is going to die."

"If we don't at least try to do something who knows what will become of us? This could be our last day if we don't try something. These are Romans, not Greek philosophers."

"But it's not our fault."

"I know what I'm doing. Trust me." I walked fast and felt with my hand, holding the wooden carving through my clothing and thought of Yeshua.

I got closer to my locked door which held my plants and herbs. I pulled off the leather cord around my neck with the key, and opened the door. I turned to Soranus and said to him, "What you see must be kept to yourself, do not tell any Roman, even Eolus for now. I will explain everything later. Come."

Slowly we made our way down into the darkness, feeling the damp walls beside us; the cool air churned the deeper we went into the ground. I kept lighting the oil lamps until I reached the bottom of the stairs. I lit the last one sitting on a table, which I handed to Soranus. "Hold this."

He followed me other to the other side of the room, our heads brushing against the drying plants hanging upside down from a wooden beam.

Soranus, "What is all of this?"

"You will know in due time, but for now we have to try to save the Consul. Our lives might depend on it. I think I have something for him. Stand here and don't move."

For many years, I had taken thousands of my weekly doses. I always had prepared potions; we just had to add water. It was like one of those instant noodle soups I had seen in the future. I opened the chest and felt the watchful eyes of Soranus over my shoulder, as I smiled to myself. I enjoyed the inquisitive nature of Soranus; it humoured me at this critical time that he was so confused at what was happening. I wondered what he would say when I told him of my secret.

But then again, I always smiled when I opened one of my chests. It was like a treasure full of eternal life and unlimited knowledge.

"Remember you were asking several years ago, about my age?" I picked around the contents, sorting things out. I looked back at his face and he said nothing, but was clearly thinking about it.

I groped around in the shadows, feeling many dried plants "Here!" I pulled out a small bag, "We have no time to waste! Close the door behind me and blow out the lamps. Follow me! Lock up. Put the key around your neck." I ran up the stairs and left Soranus behind. I quickly walked towards the Consul, and entered the outer room.

Eolus, "I did what you said. I think the intravenous is working, because his temperature has dropped. He is now sleeping."

Soranus arrived, "That is just the cool water."

"Wake him up!"

Eolus seemed confused; he was not used to helping us out by himself. There were so many details to think about. He was confused, and panicked slightly, not knowing what order to do things. "Eolus, pull the intravenous slowly out of the arm of the Consul. Soranus, you give him a hand."

"But I just put it in?"

Barrius, "What is going on?"

"And now you will take it back out."

Barrius looked uncertain and stood back as many people were moving in all directions following Galen's instructions. "This does not seem right." No one paid any attention to him.

I said, "Someone get me a clean bowl with a pestle and bring it to the table here. Bring a jug of clean water. Hold him up more in the bath. Straight up and don't let go of him." The servants held him up from behind under his arms. The weak body of the Consul sagged as his head drooped forward.

"Hold his head up! Right up, so he can breathe clearly. I have something for him to drink."

Barrius was perplexed and on edge. I could understand any soldier being tense without holding a sword for protection, or for that matter, waiting for the enemy to attack. It must have been difficult for him to just watch.

I knew what I was doing. I felt I had the upper hand. The image of Armaigen, Tiernan and Yeshua flashed in my mind. I felt confident. Barrius grabbed my arm as I rushed past him to mix my potion. I stopped. "Barrius, let me try to heal your friend. I don't know what will happen but you must have faith in me." He released my arm and stood closer to Paulinus.

"Will he live?"

"We will know soon."

"When?!"

I ignored his question, knowing he wanted more details, but I did not have the time.

I gave Barrius a blank look; I had said enough. He understood and knew he should stop bothering me.

Eolus, "What about his temperature? He is burning hot again."

"You said he cooled down before. Replace the head cloth with another cold cloth. Place another cold cloth on his chest."

The Consul was barely alive, but made comfortable

Everything became eerily quiet. Many were gathered around Paulinus in the bath. The occasional person glanced over at me, but didn't dare tell me to hurry. They watched me crush the contents of the dried plants into the bowl. It became a green, leafy, powdered mixture.

I felt the same urgency Tiernan must have felt looking down, pounding away as fast as he could before I died a certain death. I felt the same pressure, but then thought it was strange that I was doing the same act and wondered whether these two acts were connected.

I decided to double the potion I would normally take; I had never given it to any dying patient before.

I finished and dipped my fingers into the potion and then sucked the water off my fingers. Good. I went over to Paulinus.

Everyone made room so that I could slip in beside the Consul and pour the potion into his mouth.

"What is that?" Barrius did not really care what it was; he cared more about knowing whether it would help Paulinus.

I lied. "It is an old Greek remedy, used many times on cases like this." Soranus and Eolus looked at each other having never seen it before.

"Will it work?"

"Only the gods will tell us if we are too late." I was trying to divert attention and blame away from us, for I had never used this medicine on anyone but myself. I really had no idea whether it would work.

"Soranus, he has to swallow all of this. Come. Hold his nose. Eolus, hold his mouth open. Watch your fingers! It is bitter, so he will choke and try to spit it out. Shut his mouth after I pour it in for he must swallow."

I carefully dripped a small stream of the solution into his mouth, Paulinus reacted just like I had done as a small boy; he came alive trying to spit it out, shouting commands to stop. His head turned from side to side avoiding the drink, "I can't breathe." He spit up, some of the contents.

"Hold his mouth open! Keep his head still. He must swallow all of this! Hold his body. Do not allow him to move!"

I shouted at Soranus, Eolus and the servants; it was unusual for me. I was quiet, smart and the logical one, who never loses his temper. "Soranus pinch his nose and don't let go! Don't worry who he is, he must swallow everything I give him, hold his nose tight, and bring his head up!"

Again, with more determination, we all did what we had to do and once more the Consul resisted, trying to twist his shoulders to get away, but he could not. His strength had vanished and we all felt his body relax until the entire potion was emptied into his mouth.

"Give him some cold water to wash his mouth out. Turn his head over, force him to spit the water out, it will take some of the taste away and make him more comfortable."

We all stood there as Barrius came close watching for any change or sign. The Consul was alive, but asleep.

Eolus felt his face, "He does not feel as hot."

I felt it. "He is still too warm. Keep replacing the head cloths with new, cold cloths again." I looked at Barrius. "There is nothing else we can do but let him sleep."

"Everyone, lift the Consul to the bed. Cover him with light sheets. Plaster his bites. Make sure the sheets are clean and cover him up to his shoulders."

The air was stale in the room. Hot from the passing noon sun. We were tired and it was difficult to wait about, for we were restless from the morning. Food was prepared and brought to all of us; we were all hungry from the excitement of the morning.

It was quiet at first, while everyone grabbed food and rushed about, pushing in and piling their plates up, as they ate as much as possible. Some talked, telling stories of the Romans kicking the door down, as other stories began to overlap until every experience was retold. We all felt sorry for the patients who had been knocked down.

Barrius, "Sorry if any harm was down. Some of our legionnaires can be bullies."

Then many talked of my plant mixture, for they had never seen me use it before. I was not going to tell anyone. I was pleased that it would remain a secret, but Soranus still had that serious look in his eyes. I noticed his broken, half-smile as he held up the key around his neck and showed me that he still had it. He told Eolus that he was proud of him and of the good job he did with Glenna. He had not done that procedure before.

We talked in hush tones for some reason, as Glenna sat by the side of Paulinus, occasionally taking his blood pressure. It had stabilized and she recorded all the results.

I thanked everyone. "Eat and drink as much as you need. Take food back to your wives, husbands and children. Tell the cooks to give you more bread, cheese and wine if you need it. You all deserve it!"

The servants busied themselves before they left, lifting all the chairs that had been toppled over that morning. They put everything back in its place. I told them to stack all the books and papers in the corners and to throw out the broken jars and the decaying organs that were lying all over the floor.

Barrius, "Galen, we will replace whatever is broken or damaged."

Paulinus was asleep and I had no idea whether he would ever wake up. His body temperature was normal, which was a good sign. I remembered that as a boy I had slept all through the night during the first time. As mid-day moved to late afternoon, our bodies became impatient. I dismissed all my physician assistants, who sometimes doubled as servants.

The room became cooler as the sun went west. The temperature became bearable as the moving of our bodies produced wafts of cool air.

Barrius was still standing, looking down at the sleeping Consul; he held his hand. He looked lost and beaten. "Is there anything else we can do?"

I touched Barrius reassuringly on the shoulder. "We wait. We have done what we can. He is a strong man. Many would have not lasted this long. There is nothing more we can do. Come and sit with us; eat, drink. He is not in pain and should sleep through the night. We will stay here for him if he wakes up."

"What happens if he does not wake up?"

"Well, that is something I have learned never to talk about. As a physician, I like to deal with the present moment. We wait. You need rest, too. Let us refresh our bodies and minds. Eat before all the food is gone."

I watched Barrius slowly undress away from us, down to his sweaty tunic and bare feet. His body was in excellent shape, even with no armour. I thought that even in that state, he could easily defend himself. Some gave him a quick glance, as he stretched out beside me as food was served to him.

"Thank you, Galen." He looked about. "Thank you all for what you have done." He raised his goblet as a toast, "To Paulinus." In a single gulp, he swallowed it, wiping his mouth afterwards.

We all toasted, looking at each other disconcertingly, for I am sure it was the first time any of us had toasted a Roman to get well.

There was no use for all of us to stay up with the Consul. I felt it was a good sign that he was still alive. I covered the Consul with a light blanket to keep him warm from the cool, night air. The lamps were all lit around the room. I would stay beside him; I told most of the others that if I needed any help or if something changed, I would call them.

I arranged with Barrius that food and drink would be brought outside for his men as they patrolled the street; some slept along the outside stone walls.

Barrius, "They have their supplies and rations. They will stay there until I tell them any different. The Greek night air is acceptable to them.

Much cooler then compared to what they have been used to for the last couple of years. The air was so damp that you could hardly breathe in Egypt."

There was silence between us. I wanted to talk to him about Roman law and the cruelty I had witnessed; I thought it would be wasting my time for he would likely justify everything for the glory of Rome. There was no point; it had been a long day and it was time to sleep.

I am Galen. I had no need to spend my time on small talk. I'm sure he had many questions about me as a physician. I did not want to present an opportunity for him to question what was in the water I had given to the Consul. It was time to stop talking.

Barrius spoke as he stared at the fire, "I suppose you are wondering how we knew to bring the Consul to you."

This comment surprised me because I naively believed that my work with the Consul was finished and I would be left alone by the Romans. I had forgotten my initial thoughts that they were here to arrest me. I was selfish in my own self-importance, probably because I had no medical competition.

"No. Not really. I am a physician. I am known to the people of Pergamon. There are not too many physicians around."

"And a damn good one from what I hear. You take anyone, even those with no money. You are respected by many people."

"Thank you."

"To be honest with you, we didn't care too much about that. Working for free is for fools. What is the purpose of work to start with?" He stopped. I was too tired and wanted to avoid an argument. I thought of Karl Marx and his beliefs of a society where everyone is equal.

He continued, "What we heard were the rumours of your closeness to the Gods, and that you never get sick. Clearly, you are very well-educated, for you speak like you have lived and seen many people. The Gods must bless you, for some reason."

"I am just a quiet man who likes to read about everything. My father left me money. It is true, I have seen many ailments."

I felt Barrius stare at the side of my face; I was not going to make eye contact. I felt he looked at me with a patronising smile. "Perhaps. Another drink?"

He got up and poured two more goblets of wine. He handed me one and sat back on the pillows. We both said nothing, staring at the colours of the dancing fire.

The silence of time flowed out like the night tide. We both fell asleep in a perfect peaceful balance, until the next morning.

Chapter 30

GAIUS SUETONIUS PAULINUS

Several plates crashed onto the floor! Followed by bouncing breaking plates and clanking lead goblets! Barrius jumped to his feet like a cat. In one persuasive movement, he pulled out his gladius from the sheath that had lain beside him all night.

I quickly stood up and noticed the eager sunlight pouring into most corners of the room. The night shadows were sliding away. Within moments, we both looked over to the Consul's bed and he was not there! Over at the table, we saw the Consul steadying himself, as he dropped down into a chair with a heavy sigh. With his booming voice, he shouted, "Barrius, I thought you were supposed to take care of me?"

Some servants had come in and bowed as they looked at the Consul. He had wrapped the sheets around himself. His strong presence dominated the room. This man controlled life and death. Most servants went quickly back to their quarters where it was safe. Some did not show themselves fully but took turns peering at him around the corner of the room.

I approached with Barrius. Paulinus had made a remarkable recovery. Other than his body looking thin from not eating, his face had colour in it.

Paulinus banged the table, "Whatever you did, Greek, you made me very hungry. Food! I need food and lots to drink. My mouth tastes like a horse's arse." He smacked his lips together.

I nodded to the servants and they quickly went away to tell our cook.

I came closer, "How do you feel? May I feel your temperature?"

"His name is Galen, Consul." Barrius interjected.

The Consul was speaking and was almost giddy. "Yes of course. Feel anything you want," he laughed. "I was ill for a long time. This is the first time I have been able to sit up in a whole month. Praise the gods! I feel good and strong." He felt his chest and stretched slightly, twisting his shoulders.

"Barrius, make an offering to the gods, make it a Greek god." As he waved his hands towards me, "What say you, physician? Do you have a god of healing?"

"His name is Asclepius."

"Barrius. Make a gift to…what did you say?"

"Asclepius."

"Yes, Consul."

"Galen, call me Paulinus. Gods, they're all the same anyway. Greek, Roman; gods are gods. Do you believe in the power of the gods?" He looked around the room. "Where is *my* stupid physician?"

Barrius, "I sent him away."

"Good!"

I was not sure whether Paulinus ruled his life by the gods or was superstitious in any way; most people feared something or ruled their life by things they could not see. The tone of his voice led me to tell the truth of my own feelings, "No, Paulinus. I believe in facts, logic and men using proven treatments to heal."

"Like a soldier following orders. Finally, an honest physician who speaks his mind and is not afraid of the consequences. You *are* just as clever as they said you were! But, I would have thought you to be an older man?"

"No." I felt his stare and he broke into a grin.

"I feel like there is some mystery about you, some cryptic obscurity, maybe there is nothing, but as you get to know me perhaps you will teach me some of your healing secrets to keep me well. I would say I am a good man to have about, right, Barrius?"

Barrius, "Yes Consul, you were near death and Galen deserves all the praise."

"I live and that's all that matters to me for now, and to Rome, of course. You shall be rewarded."

"Thank you, but other people helped."

"A humble and shrewd physician who sounds like a politician. Do you always give credit to others?" He was very pleased as he studied my face again. "We must not lose this one, Barrius! He will be my new personal physician!"

He stared thoughtfully at my face and our eyes locked; I was not going to be the first to look away. He nodded, "Yes. I must take you to Rome with me. You are a loyal man." He turned, quickly looking at Barrius, flicking a backward motion of his fingers in the air, "Barrius, make the arrangements!"

Paulinus stopped talking and looked at me again. "There is something about you. Yet, we have never met. Is there something you want to tell me?" I knew this was an insightful man and at that moment, I was concerned.

Paulinus wiped his mouth and hands. "Give me your hands. Let me look and hold them." He examined both sides of my hands rubbing slowly his fingers into my palms, thinking. He became serious and would not let go. "How did you save me?"

I hesitated. My silence was broken by the noise of servants in the room. "Paulinus, it is Greek medicine passed down from my mother." I wished I had said something else; it was too late and all I could think about.

"Where is your mother now?"

"Dead."

He looked at me again, squeezing my hands tightly and seeing my reaction as he shed them from his own skin. "Well. Your mother was a good woman to have a son like you."

"Yes, I suppose."

"Galen, you deserve more recognition than you give yourself. Get out of this dusty, hot town. Yes." There was a pause as he studied me again. "There you have it! I like the looks of you. I am a good judge of character. When I was sick, I swore that if I lived, I would give something to the person and the gods who saved me; this person is you. The gods ruled it, but I know it was really you. In the years to come, we shall have many interesting conversations, I'm sure. Don't take my offer lightly; I know many important people in Rome, including our Emperor."

Rome? Huh! Rome would be an elaborate maze to me, a prison not an escape to follow my quest, where I could wander free. There were many laws for a Greek. I would never be treated equal to a Roman.

I was shocked, but I was safe. Everyone was safe. Perhaps there was a god after all these years. Maybe waiting and worrying without faith was my punishment. Doubting the prophesy all these years had made me insecure. I had to have faith, this was the opportunity I had been waiting for.

Was it that simple? For a moment, I felt slightly guilty. I had lived my life by using logic, my cognitive abilities and the knowledge gained by drinking the potion. I felt good, sick and nervous. I was being released to follow my fate to another part of the world. I was grateful and did not care who or how this was arranged.

I was leaving Roman Greece and would seek out Armaigen and Tiernan, and if possible, Yeshua, wherever he was.

It was difficult to restrain my elation in front of Paulinus; this was my moment. It had finally arrived! Perhaps I should be more open and have faith in that invisible force, whatever it was. These were sudden sentimental thoughts and I tried to clear my head as fast as I could, knowing there were no gods.

I would go to Rome, but I would not become a Roman.

A long line of many servants came in and out of the room, filling the table with more food and drink.

Paulinus continued, "Barrius, Galen, sit and eat. Galen, come close to me. Rome needs physicians like you. The Empire is large and still expanding. I even hear that we will make another attempt to conquer Britannia one day."

Barrius, "Britons. They remind me of the Germanic hoards. They are a very stubborn people."

"Galen, I cannot leave right now, even though I am overdue for a wedding. That's how it works Galen; you give service and you get a reward. I was to marry a cousin of the Emperor; I suppose they think I am dead by now. Barrius, send word to the Emperor that I am very much alive! They will be surprised of my miraculous healing! Nero has been our new Emperor for the last four years, while I have been in Egypt, who would have believed it? I have heard of him, but never met him. I'm sure he has heard of me. I have never lost a battle did you know that?"

"Paulinus, you must rest for a few weeks before you go to Rome."

"He's giving advice, already! We must set out before then. Galen, the Emperor will want to know how you brought me back from the dead after the same illness killed almost one entire legion."

I had heard about Nero; Rome was going into a dark age.

"Hopefully my fiancé has not been married off. I hear that she is a desired commodity with men. You wait until she sees me for the first time, eh, Barrius? Yes?" He laughed. "Look at me, short and stocky. Not a Mark Anthony, that's for sure!" He gulped some more wine as he was still chewing. "She is said to be beautiful and she has no choice but to marry me!"

I had not eaten or drank anything that morning. It was all too much to take all in. I had preparations to make. All I could think about was the potion; I would have to keep it a secret. Everything depends on it; I dare not imagine if all the Romans took my potion. They would never die!

"I need time to pack all of my supplies and medicine. I need much time. I wish to bring many of my assistants with me. I need horses, carts and food. "

"Yes. Yes. Of, course. You know, moving my army or what I have left of it is not an easy task either Galen. You are not the only one that will be moving."

While I was glad I would be leaving Greece; I was not sure what to take and how my potion would be stored and hidden. "Yes, but…"

"Is money what you want?"

I spoke with a more conciliatory tone, to avoid any suspicions or lack of appreciation. "No, I don't need money. Just time to think what I need to bring."

"Take your time. But when we leave, you leave, so be ready."

"I must be able to bring my two other physicians, Soranus and Eolus."

"Yes. Very well. Good. Then it is settled. Barrius, whatever Galen needs, give it to him, and help him prepare."

"Yes, Consul."

Chapter 31

SHALOM, AELIUS GALENUS

The practice was closed indefinitely. I did not want to take such extreme measures, but I had no choice. A notice was posted, referring my patients to other physicians. The priority was preparing for our trip. All the rooms in the villa were in the process of being cleaned. An inventory of all medical supplies was taken and we purchased whatever else we needed to build up our stockpile. I was not sure whether I was just the personal physician of Paulinus or whether I would help with other legion illnesses or even battle injuries.

I sat down with all the men and woman in my employ. I told them what had happened and that the villa was to be used by them and to keep it in good condition. It was not to be a physician's office any longer, depending on when and if I returned. There were many rooms and the most senior servant, Hypatos and his family would oversee the running of the villa. A small token of money was given to everyone, depending on their station and length of service.

Separately, I spoke with Abrux and his wife Glenna asking them to come with me. Glenna said she would be glad to come and get out of Greece. They had never travelled before and both seemed to be looking forward to it. Abrux said he was sure that Matthew would not mind if he talked about the life of Yeshua outside of Greece.

I told him to be careful of whom he spoke to.

Soranus and Eolus also received the news well. They were very excited. Eolus was pleased as he would now be called a 'physician in permanent training'. Soranus rolled his eyes upon the announcement.

I noticed the key on the leather cord around Soranus's neck. He asked me, without Eolus present, when he could find out about the secret room and the plant mixture I had given to the Consul.

I was not ready to go through the whole story. I felt Soranus and Eolus should be told together. If they were told, then they should be given the potion also. It would make no sense for me to be selfish. It was a complicated issue and I hesitated, because of their age. However, we were a family and I felt families should share whatever they had with one another, even the potion.

I asked Soranus to give me back the key for my room. He handed me the key.

"Are you going to the room?"

"Yes."

"Can I come?"

I gave him a short blunt answer. "No. Not right now."

"Why? You said you would tell me."

"I will. I just can't get into it right now." He followed me to the room as I ignored him. I imagined his horrible gaze behind me, as I unlocked the door.

I turned and looked at him. "I love you and Eolus. I promise you, that I will tell you one day. But I am busy getting ready, for all of us to go."

Soranus looked sad but I knew he understood. "I feel the importance of your secret; I respect your decision."

I entered and locked the door quickly behind me. Darkness. I was not thinking clearly, following the routine of lighting the first lamp inside the door before I locked it. I fumbled my key and my feet slipped hard on the jagged, wet rocks. I could not stop myself from falling, slipping down the stairs on my back, until I landed on the ground, at the bottom. "Shit!"

I felt the bloody torn skin on my back; the pain was intense. I did not move for a few moments as my mind charted my complete body for any broken bones, as I moved my limbs, slowly.

Besides some other bruises on my hip and legs, I did not feel anything broken. I saw the small, clay lamp flicker on the table. I was so sore and got up carefully, bending slowly upright. Using the table lamp, I went around the room and lit the other lamps. My mind was alive with incongruities.

I felt Yeshua's wooden statue dig into my skin. I reached into my inside pocket and pulled out the old statue. I took the cloth off but it did not feel right; I looked at it and did not know what to do. It was cracked and split into several pieces. It must have hit the coarse rocks when I fell.

What could I say or think? Frustrated and angry, my eyes swelled with tears, as they ran down my face. I felt like a distressed desparate child. Life would never be the same again because I had lost something important. My only direct link to the three strangers.

I noticed some rough papyrus rolled up on the ground by my sandals, as I picked up some other pieces of the statue. I unrolled it and sat down at the table, reading the tiny print. It must have been hidden within the small statue all these years. I felt like some glad, foolish boy decoding a message; evidence of some kind. I nervously pressed it flat on the table.

C.H. BYART

I knew it was written by Yeshua for me:

Shalom! Aelius Galenus
Imagine dreams achieved,
Hope endless joy believed.

You are there in the sun's glare,
The brave physician, our heir.

The wait is over; bird voices sing a new song,
Rome is only one stop to where you belong.

Despair not, for all air shows your answered prayers,
Rome is drowned sound, full of self, so beware.

Only two of the three you knew is living,
Yet the old and the young one is still giving.

Joy to simple earth,
Tiernan's ways give new birth.

Where legions are Britannia bound,
There, Tiernan will be found.

Follow the drums and screaming omens,
You will help Britons defend off the Romans.

Across the water will sail the remains of earth,
Hope bathes, cleans well, a new rebirth.

Accept all, for it is a moment in passing,
It-is. It-is. It-is not lasting.

I silently reflected, thinking about everything I knew about Britannia. It was a mysterious, unconquered, wild Roman province on the edge of the known world. Why did Paulinus just speak of it?

Julius Caesar had tried to conquer the land in 55BCE and failed. A century later, Claudius invaded in 43CE and had difficulty controlling the tribes. Many tribal clans occupied Britannia. The philosopher, Agricola, said the Britons were fierce, dangerous fighters who lived in swamps. They wore no clothes, and tattooed their bodies with strange patterns and animals. It is now 58CE, well after Yeshua's factual recorded death and resurrection.

I remember in my visions that the Britons were victorious against a dictator called Hitler in World War II, but that was in the 20th century. That is not important right now, for it is too far ahead in the future to think about.

There are not three strangers anymore; only two are left. Yeshua said they would be in Britannia.

I was captivated by the poem. It had been written so long ago when I was a child. Yeshua had the power of prophesy. He was a special man, just like Matthew described.

Yeshua mentioned that the old and young ones were still giving. The young one must mean Yeshua is still alive. Yeshua is not in Arabia but waits in Britannia.

Yeshua also mentions that Tiernan's ways give new birth. My first thought was that Armaigen was still alive, but he is not mentioned in the poem. He also said that Tiernan will be found in Britannia, so the two still giving must be Tiernan and Yeshua!

I was nearly 90 years old, but did not age beyond the look of a 25-year-old. I had remained a young man because of the potion. I was in excellent shape both physically and mentally.

I was heading in the right direction following Consul Paulinus. I would have to refresh my memory by reading my journals of the future and see who commanded the next Roman invasion of Britannia.

PART II

Chapter 32

THE LIGHT IS FREE

**Ynys Mon
(Isle of Anglesey)
61CE**

My name is Tiernan; I have been alive for over six hundred and forty equinoxes.

I am a Drui and husband to my beautiful Orin, who is pregnant with a little, strong oak. I am father to our Drui warrior son, Egan. Our dear, youngest son, Caeoimhin, has Orin's cunning mind; he is a new, budding pine tree, still bursting through the ground, sometimes tripping over his roots when he is not looking. He is always running in the open, free from the moving shadows of the forest, with no shade to stunt his growth; where the light is free for all to enjoy.

Alana, who barely flowed her first white flower, was found by us one day in the forest. She did not have a family as we know it. We adopted her and treated her as one of our own children. She was a female forest spirit, who had lived with her unborn child in the trunk of an old oak tree. She told us in the language of the spirits, that there was no father to her child. She was frightened of us for quite a while, and still has problems speaking our tongue. With Orin's tender encouragement, we are hopeful that she will soon give birth to a healthy, baby forest fern.

Our life is blessed, for every thought that we have, and every action we take is guided by the earth spirits; there is no hurry to do anything. The signs are everywhere and we are told what to do and how to live by what we feel. Truthfulness and integrity are treasured as the earth is praised every day, for we are surrounded by pure honesty.

Everything we see, speak to, breathe in and eat is the unspoiled truth; we are one with that same veracity. The very earth we stand on is sacred, as are the eggs we produce and the seeds we grow, the air we breathe, the red fire, and the water we drink. The animals, the plants, the sun and the moon possess the spirits of all of us and our ancestors; made for all of *us*. We have our sacred oak groves, which are mainly used for equinox celebrations, but we can channel the richness of the earth at any place we occupy. It is all ours. A shared earth. An eternal gift. We must protect this sacred earth, at whatever cost, for we are the curators of that revered trust.

Chapter 33

THE WELL

Before I came to Ynys Mon, my family lived in Aquitania. The Romans burned my family alive, as I was made to watch. Afterwards, they laughed as they threw me down a poisoned well onto a dead stag with large antlers.

I awoke cold, scared and hungry. I could not stop weeping. The smell of the stag was foul and disgusting. The eye of the stag was open staring at me. Soon, I became accustomed to the smell and the warmth of it's body thinking that it was still alive.

Earlier that day, before the attack, I had tied some sheep guts around my arms, as my father had shown me, to make a lyre. I cut long, thin strands tying them tightly to the antler tines at different lengths. I made up silly songs about anything I could think of: the forest, wild animals, the sky, the stars, the wind and the moon. I thought of rhymes describing my family which seemed to bring them alive providing some solace. I played and prayed each day and night, calling for the spirits of my mother, father and sister. I could not see them, but I heard their voices, reassuring me not to worry.

All I could see above were the things I could never touch: the birds, the sky, swift-painted clouds and the sun. My singing voice was clear and loud as I practised singing long, high, supple notes, like prayers without words as I felt the presence of something. My mother said that the spirit world controlled all life. I cried out 'help me.'

The spirit voices responded and began to speak to me. They told me to scrape the bones of the antler and bite into the soft core. Every day, new small roots grew out of the earth, hastened by the power of the underworld. These roots wrapped themselves around me, as a small blanket of leaves rested on my body. White flowers and black berries of the elder appeared, as well as several protruding trees and plants that blossomed quickly before my eyes. There were the red berries of the yew and the white berries from the mistletoe tree. As I ate each berry and the soft, sweet leaves, I could feel the spirits fill my body, as they told me not to worry; I was safe. Someone was coming to rescue me.

I spoke in the dominion of spirit speech and understood even the fast hummingbirds that came to visit every day, dripping sweet nectar into my mouth. The animals of the above world heard my words and would peer down at me, into the deep, dark hole. Some of the animals would bring apples and drop them into the well.

The spirit of all divinity spoke to me. I began to see that the air was not empty space, but full of spirits wanting to be with me. All types of rocks, dirt, ants, bugs and minute specks of dirt would speak with me. They were interested in what the world was like. They asked many questions about people they had known in a variety of villages. I was able, to answer their questions. All of nature was nothing more than the actual living spirits of people who had lived previous lives as humans; including the stag that I used as a bed. Everything was alive in the upper and underworld.

I prayed every moment, giving thanks for all that I had; which was life itself. I asked and it was given. I swore that if I survived, I would protect all earth spirits.

As the days turned into weeks and months, the roots continued to wrap around my body. Water was directed from the sides of the old well, trickling down the curled roots, as the water seeped into my mouth. I never stopped praying and singing to the earth spirits.

Then it started. One raindrop hit a happy stone that sat on my shoulder. I heard it squeak and it caused a slight panic as everything moved around me, twisting, rolling to take cover. The day sky darkened as if it were night. Up and far away, we watched from below the lightning flashes. I heard repeated thunder. We could see the rain sweep across the land as the water began to fill the well.

The water from the storm ran like a river down upon us. I was choking for air as the water reached my neck. I begged for the rain to stop but it continued. The roots released me and my stag as we floated upwards together towards the sky.

As I got closer to the surface I heard what I thought was a donkey, followed by a man's voice shouting so loud that it was deafening. It did not make sense. I feared that the Romans had come back. All the living earth that had helped me survive for many months, squealed like hungry baby birds.

A thin, tall man, with a long, grey beard leaned over the edge of the well and asked me something. I did not understand his language at first and hesitated; I had heard those words before. That was the language I had used with my mother, father and sister, but they were dead and I could not get the words out clearly.

I called out in a stag's voice, wanting to be free and live on the ground again ruled by the sun.

We were now at the top of the well. The rain had stopped as the man pulled me off the stag. He left me standing me near the stone wall of the well.

"Help me drag the stag out of the well!" He grabbed the thick fur of the animal. I did not know what he was going to do. "Just don't stand there. Pull!" I pulled as hard as I could, as we dragged it along the ground, away from the well.

The noise of the spirits continued. I looked over at the cottage in ruins that was once my happy home. I felt sad. The tall man brought me a blanket. He looked at me, "You must try to put that behind you." The man seemed annoyed and distracted at the spirit singing that had interrupted his thoughts. I knew that the spirits were only saying goodbye.

He looked down into the well and shouted a series of garbled sounds. He turned to me. "Sometimes you can't hear yourself think! They make such a noise."

The spirits in the well became silent again. His shouting had broken the spell.

I went over to the stag and stroked its head. The man knelt beside me. "A beautiful beast."

"It helped save my life."

He looked at me and smiled. "Let's see what we can do." He placed his hands on the head of the stag. He had his eyes closed as he whispered some words. Then he leaned back on his legs and clapped his hands!

Suddenly, the stag moved. I jumped back afraid. The animal layed there on the ground as it began to slowly breathe. "Go on, feel it breathe." I was hesitant but placed a hand on it as the body moved, breathing stronger. Then it struggled, pushing itself along the ground, grunting and wheezing until it was up on all four legs! The stag stared at me for some moments and within an instant it was gone, running back into the forest.

"Who are you?"

He said in a deep, friendly voice, "My name is Armaigen. I am a Drui. I was called by the underworld to come here. I am sorry I am late. I have travelled far."

I asked the stranger, "What is a Drui?"

"I am a Drui; there is only one of me. You will become the second Drui and we will be known as Druids."

Chapter 34

TRAVELS WITH A DRUI

I travelled back in my mind, picturing a time when Armaigen, Yeshua and I used to wander from village to village through the Roman Empire; making due and being fed by simple strangers.

On most nights, we were usually very talkative, full of energy, excited to rest and enjoy a good full meal, under the stars, beside the warmth of a fire. We would reminisce about our travels, as we spread the knowledge we had of the spirit world. Yeshua would speak of his father; which usually confused me.

Sometimes, the days were long, as we would visit several small villages. We would perform charmed tricks, sing ballads and help heal those who were sick. We always tried to stay close to the Roman roads for fear of outlaws; though outlaws were not always the problem.

Occasionally, a small Roman patrol would try to steal from us but they would learn with their lives that we would defend and kill anyone who was planning to kill or steal from us.

On most days, our travels were peaceful; full of merriment, new friendships, as the children were always glad to see our colourful cart arrive; like a festive occasion.

Armaigen, always did some magic tricks or slight of hand. Many liked to talk to us about the outside world, in exchange for food and comfort. We freely offered the seeds of new crops we had come across from lands far away, and tell them of the magic of the secret oak groves and mistletoe.

When it was dark and most of the village food and drink was gone, Armaigen would ask if anyone would like to hear the spirits of the ancients that were watching over them. I did not ever remember anyone ever refusing; except respected village elders who felt a loss of prestige and control.

I would play my part and ask for complete silence as everyone was sitting on the ground in a circle, as many fires and torches were lit.

Armaigen would say, "You must all slowly breathe in the spirits of your ancestors for only they have the power of prophesy through me. Slowly, picture their face or hear the laughter of their voices."

He would sit upright, in the middle of the circle. His eyes were closed, hands stretched out upwards, as some villagers squinted to see what he was doing; all excited but not wanting to break the spell, as he named the ancestors of each villager along with a specific feature or saying what the person was known for. He could describe their favorite clothes, their eye color, teeth appearance and speaking habits, like stuttering to those who were vain. Sometimes he would speak of the bravery of those ancestors who had saved someone from drowning or known for giving food to the poor; it would last four stretched hands of the moving moon, depending on the size of the village or until the sunrise of the next day.

Armaigen would call out the name of each villager, telling them what they were like as a child. He would prophesize about the health of a villager and tell them what they must do to stay healthy when the winter comes. Then he would speak about everyone's future; who would get married, who was with child. This sometimes was embarrassing to those unwed women resulting in laughter and anger, with many shouts; and hand pointing. Many vocal sounds from 'ahh' to 'ohh', to mutterings of fear and terror. Many repeated what Armaigen had just said, to make sure everyone heard it around them; some got frustrated because they could not hear properly.

There was only one rule to carefully follow. He warned me that the spirit world does not understand hatred and violence; in a spirit's airy world, greed and anger does not exist. Only a good and faithful Drui can redirect the spirit goodness to confront evil.

Humans exist in different earthly forms and there were times one must be practical; for you must survive in the non-spirit world. Therefore, make the life of a Chieftain, anyone who is important in the village; make their present life sound positive for they want to hear good acts of their ancestors and families. "Say something like, 'your ancestors are powerful spirits', which is impossible, for in the spirit world, all spirits are equal; their strength only increases acting as a collective through you or me. Say to them, always being careful at your choice of words, 'many rely on you to live, keep the villagers safe for they love and respect you', make it up as you go depending on the Chieftain or village elder and the situation."

"If you do meet a villager who has committed evil, cruel acts; then place a spell on them before you leave the village. Eventually, they will be taken care of; the circle takes care of the good and the evil."

In such spirit trances, Armaigen would fall asleep right where he sat for days. There was no waking him, even during the daytime. Many villagers would gather around him, looking up under his cloak to see whether he was really sleeping; which he was.

In many villages, there would be interest in becoming a Drui. Our advice was to live in the forest alone for one year and see whether the forest spirits talk to you; even feed you. For the act of a spirit feeding a human was the ultimate gift a spirit could give.

After many years, we began to hear of other people who called themselves Druids or followers of Armaigen and Tiernan; two powerful hooded Druids. Armaigen was dressed in his blue hooded cloak and me in my green cloak. We did not meet any other Druids in Europa until we returned to Roman Britannia.

Chapter 35

ORIN

Orin came from the air one day and planted herself on the island of Ynys Mon; we knew nothing of her.

Being a stranger and not a Briton, she was not welcomed immediately. Her skin was an olive colour, and she had the facial features of someone from southern Europa. She had an enticing warm smile that only a few at that time appreciated, for her eyes were mostly sad and weak.

I knew that she had been broken at some time in her life. But none of us bothered her as we sensed she was here to help, while seeking safety.

Brithomar was a Silures Chieftain and warrior. On the outside of his large, round house he had hung Roman heads; it was a reminder that he was still alive and would seek revenge against any Roman for nearly destroying his tribe. He had taken in Orin as a wet nurse for his own wife Morgana, had given birth to a child whom she could not feed. She was weak in the mind and sickly after she had been bludgeoned on the head during an attack; she was very frail.

Brithomar hunted down the Roman who hurt Morgana, and after following the cohort for days, he killed the man responsible, along with a few of his friends. The head of the Roman who had injured Morgana, now proudly hung outside his home along with the other prizes from many years of battles.

Morgana was known as a happy, loving wife who was now a gentle woman. She would have occasional outbursts, sometimes cloistered in the corner of her room for days with unstoppable nodding, not speaking to anyone and afraid of any contact. But she seemed happy when Orin was about and trusted her, keeping close to her as she completed her household daily tasks.

Orin did not develop any deep friendships when she arrived on the island. She was very independent and did not seek the shelter of any man for protection, as most women did. She was a plain-looking woman back then, with tangled, black hair, streaked with grey, which hid her face. She was quiet and walked with her head bowed, living in her own thoughts. I knew of her through Brithomar and saw her working hard in the fields without complaint. I had never spoken to her or gone out of my way to meet her, for some reason.

Interestingly, I was attracted to her from a distance, yet she seemed to appear to me the more often I thought of her.

I was Tiernan, the powerful Drui. I was sure she knew of me but did not have the same feelings I had for her.

Orin was different. I did notice on many days her sitting on the earth speaking to the plants as she touched the ground. Even when the grain had been planted and was still small in the earth, I watched her on her knees talking to the furrowed earth. Some called her mad; she did not seem to care or notice. When it rained, she was outside picking up handfuls of earth, smelling and stroking it. Then she gladly spread the earth about her face, arms and legs; as if she was cleaning her body. People thought her strange. Orin developed a reputation and I began to know her routine, watching her from afar.

She had a gift: loving the earth as though she was a child.

Orin lived in the same house as Brithomar. There were never rumours about Brithomar and Orin living together. I was not jealous, but wanted to spend more time with her. Brithomar loved Morgana and followed the spirit order of loyalty and truthfulness.

This code of honour gave Brithomar the strength to be the feared warrior he was. We all knew that any tainted conduct would likely result in death in battle. I had witnessed him fighting like a madman, unafraid; his sturdy shoulders were as wide as a horse's chest and he stood like a tall pine tree, as if the light of the sun kept him sturdy.

Orin had now been with us for a year in our community. I continued to secretly follow her ways. Sometimes when I was alone in the forest, I covered my body like her with the damp earth, feeling the strength of the spirits fill me. I imagined what it would be like to share our love of the earth.

One night, after an equinox blessing in the large grove, it was not quite dark yet. Most of the torches had burned themselves out. Everyone had gone home blessed by the spirits, happy and drunk.

That night, for some reason, I noticed Orin more than ever. Almost the entire night, everywhere I looked she was there, lingering about, glancing at me while she took her time cleaning up. I was sure she was making her presence known to me.

We were the last ones left in the grove and I had never been alone with her; her closeness to my body allowed me to breathe in the sweet air coming from her mouth as we cleared the tables. Her hair had been tied back in two braids; she looked beautiful in the torch light. I noticed her wide blue eyes staring deeply into mine. I saw the spirits in her eyes moving from the lively music played that night.

We stood by the altar, cupped by the shaded branches, hidden in the darkness. Her face glowed, as did mine. We could not move as we were inseparable. Our hands touched as we both leaned forward and lightly smelled the skin on our faces without kissing. We spent the night telling stories of joy and pain in our past lives, living in each other's completeness. We both felt a growing excitement as we began to understand each other, completely devoted to our shared existence.

Orin told me that her family had been killed in Tarraconensis. Her husband and her four children had been slaughtered by the Romans. I felt the pain. "The Romans were everywhere, shouting and killing, as my children called out for me!" She had panicked and hid from the Romans to save her own life. She looked away from me, tears in her eyes, guilty and ashamed that she did not defend her family. "I will never forgive myself. I should have died with them."

I recollected a time in Aquitania, when my family was also killed and that I had escaped. Although I was older than her, I was familiar with the land and the location of where she had lived.

Afterwards, we continued to talk and explore our past lives. Slowly, our hidden despair was shattered, overcome by the desperate happiness we both sought. It was selfish but pleasing. We were finally together. We both knew that this love for each other would never die.

Orin led me away deep into the forest as my spirits guided us to the dry pond. We slowly undressed each other and we blessed the event by silently covering every part of our bodies with earth and warm moss in the moonlight. When we were finished, we kissed and walked into the pond, washing each other off. As we floated on the warm water, we fell asleep, holding hands until the morning. We were protected by all the spirits; which I am sure sanctified our union many years ago.

As the years passed, our love for each other grew. It was good and right for us to have children together.

We enjoyed our own company and naturally created different routines of affection.

Orin and I would often walk naked through the perfect forest together. Our intimacy with each other was accompanied by a soft chorus of humming from all the forest trees and plants. The melody of the sounds we heard depended on the age of the plants and the type of growth.

Our physical and spiritual feeling for one another always felt new and fresh; for we had great expectations of how long we would likely live. Our love was intense but gentle as the air made our skin prickly free; as the filtered sun warmed our moving bodies through the forest, filled with the sightings of past and present spirits.

As we danced, we would stare and touch each other, ending with our fingertips. Our desire would grow during those moments. Our bodies would separate, moving away, then move in again as we softly caressed our hands and fingers, parting and joining, so satisfied at just touching, fulfilling our senses.

We enjoyed sunning ourselves in our secret meadow; Orin with her arms and legs open to the sky as I enjoyed the heat on my back. The sun on Orin's face would slowly flow through her body, as I slid my single root inside

I was proud that Orin told me that I had the stamina of a young man, which was a nice compliment to a man 160 years old.

Chapter 36

THE UNDERWINGS

I had spoken of Armaigen to Orin often. I was careful to be selective of my stories of him, for I did not want them to become tiresome for her. But Orin was different, for she seemed to enjoy listening to what I did in past. She called my travels endless adventures. I was quite a contrast to her past life. The death of her children was very disturbing. I have seen the cruelty and death of others, but when you love someone, you can't help but feel their tragedy.

It is now time to tell the story of an extraordinary life of a man who was reborn. Like me, he was given another chance to show everyone the enchanted reality of earth spirits, that surround us all.

Orin and I had enjoyed each other early that day. We now lay on our backs relaxing, talking about whatever came to our minds. We felt the comforting grass slip out from behind our bodies, reaching towards the sunlight, as the blades rested on the ticklish nape of our sides. The moss purred as it grew in the crescent of our feet, settling in between our toes.

"Tell me about Armaigen. He is still a mystery to me. It seems his powers were great."

"Armaigen taught me that any word is such a fleeting sound. It gives no homage to the man or woman when they are gone. Words are full when a man is alive; almost speaking for themselves. I will tell you of him and hope that my words do not come out as hollow, single letters and sounds."

"As you know, I was his apprentice. He died years ago, in Europa, after the ill-attempted crucifixion of Yeshua in Judaea."

"Our Yeshua? Why is he not dead?"

"Yes, our Yeshua. The crucifixion did not kill him. I have a problem with it."

"He is still a young man."

"No. He is not what he appears to be. He travelled with us, as a boy, before the crucifixion."

"I don't understand."

"You will; I will tell you everything. There is much to tell you. Armaigen, Yeshua and I, long before coming to Ynys Mon, travelled through Europa, Asia and most areas on earth. We visited many small villages. We learned many things; spoke many languages, healed many and entertained anyone. In return, people gave us food and shelter. The three of us did this for over 30 years."

"Thirty years?"

"The thiry years only includes when Yeshua joined us. Just before I met you. Armaigen and I travelled for well over 100 years before Yeshua. I know, somehow it doesn't make sense." I paused thinking of some of the faces I had seen in my travels. I thought about where I had just finished telling the story. "Armaigen was much older than us. I never asked him, but I believe he was nearly 2000 years old when he died. I know it sounds inconceivable and farfetched, but it is true. He wandered the earth by himself for almost a timeless eternity."

"Near the end of his life, he would tell us, when resting at night around a fire, that his moment on earth would soon be over. I did not realize that he had secretly stopped taking the potion."

"The same potion you and I take?"

"Yes. And Yeshua."

"Yeshua?"

"That is why Yeshua looks young."

"Oh."

"Armaigen would not say it every day. It seemed to come at the end of a day when we were all tired from walking too much or our food supply was low; sometimes, we were just lost and frustrated. He was a private person and I have always had a natural-trusting naivety and respect for him. He did save my life and was like a father to me. Armaigen had mastered control of all earth spirits. I saw him sometimes shift his own spirit into a plant or animal, as he continued to physically sit and talk to us."

It was night. Yeshua had scouted the area for Romans and returned safely. The sun had dropped fast from the sky. As usual, we huddled together as the flames from the fire became tossed glowing embers. Sometimes, at night we were too cold to move. Yeshua and I would take turns to adding wood to the fire. Near the end of Armaigen's life, he seemed withdrawn and tired, almost anticipating his oncoming death.

During that last night, we had all agreed to head south the next day and enjoy the heat of the sun. Winter was coming early that year. Armaigen joked that cremation would be a relief. I did not think it was funny.

Yeshua looked at him then up at the sky saying a prayer to his father. I always waited for a response from his father, but his father never talked to me. Yeshua cannot speak to my earth spirits.

I suppose, it is what the Greek scribes call satire.

"His father?"

"Another story. On the night of Armaigen's death, he seemed livelier and happier than usual. He said that he would tell us how he became a Drui; it was time for us to know the beginning."

"Armaigen told us not to worry so much about life; the spirits only hear the lightness in a man's heart and voice. Even in the darkest moments, men should stay calm and be lighthearted about their circumstance. He recollected his childhood and his home with the UnderWings."

"UnderWings?"

"Yes. Interestingly, the last story he told us was similar, to what had happened to me, but without the UnderWings. You know that I was thrown into a well as a boy." I became more serious, "Orin, I am going to tell you something. An incredible story. This is a secret you must take to your grave, that is, if you ever have one."

"What?"

"Long before we knew him, Armaigen was told about a clandestine plant mix that allows all of us to live a very long life. It keeps you young and prevents aging. That is the same potion we take."

"We are immortal?"

"No. We can be killed. We both can die, but we cheat aging and death."

"You told me it would keep me well?"

"It's much more than that."

"That explains a lot." She smiled at me, still perplexed.

"Armaigen was born on an island called Eire. It is a distant and ancient land across the sea from the Britons. He lived in the County of Kerry, in a large house on a cliff, with a square tower."

One day, as a child, Armaigen went on a walk. The field appeared as a normal meadow, covered with grass, shrubs and some rocks. There was a hidden sinkhole filled with water deep under the surface; it was a danger unknown to anyone. Armaigen fell into the sinkhole. After a long search that lasted for weeks, his family and local villagers assumed he was dead. However, he was not, and when he awoke, he was surrounded by hundreds of small, odd creatures who looked after him.

He was terribly upset and missed his family; it was impossible to leave for he was now so far underground. He did not understand where he was or how to leave, as there was no escape. He was made comfortable in a large cave with vegetables growing and enough other food for him to survive.

The light throughout the UnderWing world came from a thick, luminescent light from plants. It grew everywhere: on the ground, rock walls, trees and bushes. The light never ceased, as there was no day or night. The UnderWings never went to sleep. Armaigen said this was difficult to get used to. He made a bed in a smaller cave where there was less light and the UnderWings were less noisy. They respected him and were careful never to wake him up until he was ready. His new friends were very accommodating and genuinely concerned for his welfare.

Armaigen called them initially *the underling people*, but eventually shortened it to *UnderWings*. He remembered taking a bird nest, with eggs in it, home to his mother. They placed it back on the branch as he watched the mother bird return and keep the eggs warm under her wings. He thought it was the perfect name for them. He could not speak to them, for any normal sound from him was too loud. The UnderWings had very sensitive hearing. So Armaigen had to whisper or mouth his words, ensuring the UnderWings were looking at him, as he silently tried to communicate.

Only a few of the UnderWings had ever heard of English, and that was not very often for the UnderWings had only heard the muffled echoes of people in the above world; as they walked and spoke, innocently passing the hidden sinkhole. Sometimes, sheep were heard 'baa-ing', which only confused them more. The UnderWings could not distinguish between the words of men or animals. They stopped trying to decipher any language long before Armaigen arrived, for it seemed too complicated.

They did try to guess at the words Armaigen was pronouncing but had no idea what he was saying. It soon occurred to him that no two UnderWing translations were the same. So their interest of ever learning a language stopped.

Armaigen did not give up. He thought of nothing else after he arrived. There were no equinoxes so there was no time. Remember there was no day or night. He was initially successful with a small group of his learned small friends, as he patiently made each UnderWing pronounce each syllable of the word 'UnderWing' slowly.

It was difficult at first, pronouncing every letter, but the word *UnderWing* became a proud description of their civilization. He told them through a bright interpreter that 'UnderWing' meant *goodness or the ones that give goodness*. This word had many forms of communication; drawings on cave walls, making letters, symbols and pictures on hands, arms and faces of all UnderWings.

It was interesting, for any touching of an UnderWing's hand was like a permanent record or impression, as if made in a book; it was a permanent mark or record like old library in Alexandria. But the skin of an UnderWing had layers and you could retrieve information and past discussions through simply brushing the skin, on any part of the body which allowed another word or past conversation to appear.

Armaigen said the word UnderWing came to mean more than just a hello or a greeting, but became a word of affection, like saying you loved someone. The UnderWing vocabulary was only one word, but they could say the word in thousands of different tones, pronunciations; which could even include all the letters of the word jumbled. It created a vast complex vocabulary.

Armaigen said it was difficult at first pronouncing every letter and syllable, emphasizing and elongating a combination of letters and sounds, but the word evolved to become a proud, honourable description of their civilization.

That single word, *UnderWing* began to have many interpretations and came to describe the purpose and personal identification of each UnderWing in their society, as well as a friendly greeting. Armaigen noticed it was all in the way it was said; the tone of any sounds was important and how long you held the sound before saying another letter, creating a different tone. It was not unlike the different accents Armaigen had already heard as a boy, traveling from one town to another in the upper world; no two voices of the UnderWings were the same or the interpretation.

The UnderWings appeared human, but were only as tall as a human finger. Personal wealth was not evident. Each had two small eyes which sparkled with light, two arms and two legs. There was no hair on the creatures, but they had the same soft wet skin as a salamander. They never stopped working; their sole purpose was to dig tunnels and holes into rock.

The UnderWings never complained, never slept, never got sick, never gave birth and never argued or died. Armaigen said at the time, he did not know the exact UnderWing word, but he said they were immortal. When they were hungry, they were all hungry at once and would all stop at the same time to eat. They ate almost anything that was growing in the underground caves. Numerous farms grew additional food for variety and special occasions.

Armaigen said he studied them at first, following them around and thought it was gold or some precious metal they were digging for. However, it was not gold but something much more meaningful.

He questioned them, asking them what they were doing, as he used a blade of grass on the palm of their hands to communicate as he squeaked and grunted the variations of the word *UnderWing*. It was received with a blank face, as if he should inherently know what they were thinking. Then, he watched a small, bright light appear, as the tiny finger of one of the UnderWings slowly coached a small flicker of light from the rock. It drifted out onto the palm of Armaigen's hand. He looked at his hand, wanting to touch the light and the UnderWings nodded in agreement.

As Armaigen touched the blueish-green light, thousands of unified voices clearly told him he was in the presence of the creator of all things seen and unseen. He knew that one small speck of the light spirit would protect him. In return, he must use all the powers he would be given to protect the earth. Then the light floated up to his face, split into two and was absorbed into each of his eyes.

Armaigen said he did not know what to say or do. It was overwhelming, as he did not understand the knowledge that was flowing through his body. With time and as he became older, he understood what the UnderWings felt and thought.

At that moment, the UnderWings gathered around Armaigen, some jumping up onto his legs and shoulders, all wanting to be closer. Armaigen understood and accepted their affection. He gathered them up and placed them all over his body as they scrambled about on his head, until they all squeaked at him, calling out, over and over, 'Drui! Drui! Drui! Drui…'

Armaigen was surprised, for he thought they could not speak any other word but *UnderWing*. He said he had never heard this sound before and accepted it, shouting back without knowing what he was saying, 'Drui, Drui, Drui, Drui'!

At that moment, Armaigen came of age in the UnderWing world. He worked alongside the UnderWings, in the mines, helping them release the infinite spirits into all the air we breathe. He followed their own unique journey through all the crevices up and down the rock face, while they tunneled into the earth under the seas.

When Armaigen was sixteen, he decided to leave the UnderWings. A meeting was held in the largest cave and millions of UnderWings attended. He found his voice cracking, using the one word to discuss his appreciation and love of the UnderWings. It had become very difficult to move around the caves since he was now so tall; that was the main reason he had to leave.

On the last day, he was sitting down cross-legged, covered with UnderWings, they all wanted his attention. He touched the soft heads of as many UnderWings as possible without hurting them.

He was presented with a blue robe that had been made with a concoction of plant spirits and the wool of sheep that had fallen into the sinkhole, from the field in the upper world.

"*Your* robe?"

"The exact robe."

Armaigen said he could not stop crying. He wanted to get his emotions under control; a new lake had been created from his tears. He spoke in the UnderWing language, touching thousands of hands lightly, as many UnderWings licked his tears as their eyes glowed with light. They repeated together what he mouthed slowly, in the language word 'UnderWing' with the following meaning:

> *'My imagined dreams have been achieved,*
> *Spirits hope endless joy believed!'*

Armaigen mouthed the rhyme several times before all the UnderWings understood what he had just said. There was silence afterwards, followed by the UnderWings encouraging him to participate in a mass, spirit coupling. They had never shown him such an event before; he was too young and the UnderWings had kept it well-hidden. He was now of age, and as the spirits filled his body, he became excited and they helped him spread his own spirits far and wide. He was surprised that his simple body could make him feel so good and relaxed.

Orin was confused, "What a strange way of describing the act. I thought spirit coupling was a myth."

"No. It is real."

"How is it possible with other people around and watching?"

"That is what Armaigen told me. I know it happens but I have never been involved."

"What about you?"

"You are the first woman I have ever been with. I enjoy you so much."

"I was afraid to ask you. You have not been with a woman for nearly 160 years?"

"No. Yes. I never really thought about it."

"What about Armaigen?"

"That was his first and his last time with the UnderWings or anyone, as far as I know. He said that the love of the earth spirits on that occasion was so powerful, that he could have the same feeling anytime he wished for it, just by thinking."

"What about you?"

I shook my head, genuine in my sole attraction to Orin. "Until I saw you, I felt numb inside. But I can arouse that feeling, just as Armaigen could."

"My dear Tiernan, you are certainly different." Orin kissed me. "We will try to make up for all those lost years."

I paused grinning, "Are you ready now?"

Orin took a deep breath and looked more serious. "Go on. I want to know what happened."

I continued. "Afterwards, the UnderWings said one final message in *UnderWing*."

'I Am—It Is'

"What does that mean?"

"Unequivocal acceptance of who you are and others. Only then, can you truly love yourself and the earth."

Although that is the literal Briton translation from *UnderWing*, they continued in unison, all making millions of different sounds meaning the same. They were trying to tell Armaigen that they wanted to give him another gift before he left. They said that eternal life lives in the light and dark.

The people of the upper world needed a *Drui* and Armaigen had been chosen from birth. The UnderWings told him that they were sorry that he was not able to live a normal life with his real mother and father, as other children do. Men of the upper world have not seen the spirits of the earth, although they do feel them, but do not know what they are.

Armaigen was advised to live a long life to save the earth. He was given a plant mixture which would keep him young and live long. He would be able to perform what humans call *miracles*, but it was nothing more than speaking to the earth for help. He was told to use it sensibly and to share it with only a close circle of friends, whom he trusted; only those who would also defend the earth.

The spirits would be ever present with him, would comfort and protect him. He was to seek their counsel and they would appear in some form to him. Armaigen was told that he would never be alone again. The UnderWings called out, '*I Am-It Is*'.

At that moment, the light from the spirits drifted out from all the eyes of the UnderWings. The spirits encircled his body; the light lifting him off the ground. He floated into the air, slowly back through the openings of the sacred rocks, ever upwards to the surface of the upper world he had not seen since he was a child.

Chapter 37

MISSING EARTH

It was not difficult to speak with Orin about Armaigen and the UnderWings. We knew he was not dead but alive in spirit. Telling her about Armaigen's death reminded me of the finality of each moment. I found it curious that most of us avoid ever thinking about the end of our lives and the need to leave a small legacy behind.

I was fortunate that I did not have to dwell on getting older, for my life was a collection of lifetimes. Although I have lived through many generations, I only had glimpses of the past for I cannot remember everything unless prompted. The life of the present always seems to consume my attention in a self-sustaining way. Not unlike most people living

---

Orin, I will tell you of Armaigen's death but also the torment Yeshua lives with every day.

My master died a discreet death. We had stopped for the night. It was cold, despite the fire we lit. He simply did not wake up the next morning; yet he had the face of a child.

We had seen him aging quickly, every day for the previous two weeks on the road. He had refused to take the potion any longer. He said that he had seen enough of the earth and it was time for both of us to carry on.

Yeshua said he expected it. I was not sure whether Armaigen would ever die, for he had been with me always. I felt a responsibility to declare his death to the world, as the Romans would with the death of an Emperor. But there was nothing to do, for we were all alone in a quiet and tranquil forest. I felt anxious but glad afterwards that he had crossed over.

Yeshua told me many things about himself as we prepared Armaigen for his journey to the spirit world. Yeshua was a quiet and strong man. Whenever I am around him, he always makes you feel good about yourself. He does not have to speak, or do anything; for his company alone makes you smile at the human condition. However, he would get serious when matters of the eternal soul came up, or he had to defend himself against the Romans.

We were all warriors and defended ourselves when necessary. We never went looking for trouble and avoided it when possible. Yeshua was naturally very skilled with a sword from the moment he travelled with us before his ministry.

Orin, "How young was he?"

"I will explain that to you later."

I witnessed on many occasions, fights in which he was outnumbered and would move with the speed of the wind. Afterwards, he would smile at what he had just done, saying the person would now be in heaven; judged by his father. He also had another side to him. He is so kind to the less fortunate, the poor, the crippled and children. Yet, he can strike fear in men and he has no trouble with women, unlike me.

Armaigen said to us one day that I was the earth and Yeshua was the sky. It was an easy way to explain our purpose. He said not to worry about all the facts and details that were created by man, for they did not exist. He told us to accept the water that falls from above. Likewise, take pleasure in the water that comes up from the ground.

I learned from Armaigen's death to think for myself. As I developed my earth spirit powers, my confidence grew, but they never were as great as my master. Armaigen will always be with me; he is everywhere and you need only to call his name.

Orin defended me, "It is all a matter of perspective, for you were a follower of Armaigen, which is why you are uncertain of your powers. Armaigen is someone who will always be hard to live up to."

I told Orin I was grateful for her words. "Thank you."

Yeshua and I washed and wrapped his body in the largest fern leaves and the softest, damp moss we could find. We tied his body with fresh ivy, as if he were a newborn.

I was upset that my master was dead. I asked Yeshua whether he remembered all the times Armaigen would separately take our hands and raise our arms to the sky, guiding our fingers with his long, thin, tired hands. I would look up into the sky, as my fingers followed the constellations, tracing out where the stars would be in the next equinox, and the alignment of the moon, in relation to the planets.

We quietly lifted him over to a tree and leaned him against the trunk, so that the sun would shine on his face. We made sure that he could see what we were doing, as he listened to us prepare the way for him.

Yeshua told me that Armaigen muttered something to him the night before he died. He talked of the other battles we would fight. He said the final fight against the Romans was not the main battle. There was a new place somewhere and that we must seek it.

Orin, "The final fight? I don't understand."

"Yeshua became captivated by the thought of it. At the time, he thought it was one of Armaigen's riddles, which he enjoyed telling. He told me that Armaigen had said, a few days earlier, that Yeshua and I would stop wandering the earth one day. He told Yeshua to 'sail away.' I said to Yeshua, sail where? I can't even swim!"

"Then Yeshua divulged, that his father once told him that he knows of a new land. It is called the *old* earth."

Yeshua said that we must think and act on this. Armaigen and his father were essentially saying the same prophesy. He told me that we must all go there one day. Circumstances will present themselves to us.

Yeshua also told me, that before Armaigen closed his eyes for the last time, he whispered, "The new land will save you. Save the UnderWings and the spirits.

A late, midday meal was prepared. Armaigen's favorite foods were laid out on the ground, in front of him. All of us sat in a small circle.

We reminisced about all the moments that had made an impression on us. We laughed and cried tears of happiness, interrupted by private images and silent thoughts of meeting many people in a variety of lands. We had all lived many different lives as men in this world, so we were appreciative, compared to those who only live once.

The day had exhausted itself. The dark tree shadows began to appear in the east; night was coming. Armaigen would soon not be with us as a man or a child. He did not eat any of his favorite food, so we decided to put it in his cherished leather bag and place it on the funeral pyre. We were sure he would be thankful, eating and sharing it with others on his eternal journey.

We worked, not speaking, as Armaigen watched. The sound of broken branches cracking, dried twigs and the crunching of dead leaves broke the silence, as we built the funeral pyre for our friend. We stacked all the wood, working in unison, without speech, knowing where each of us was at any moment. The simple work distracted our minds far away from our grief. The pyre was soon completed; we could not reach any higher. It was a glorious monument, fit for a king.

We were quiet and both of us carefully kissed him on the lips and covered his face for the last time with a cloth. His blue robe hung off a branch; he had told me many years before that I would inherit it after his death.

We cried as we lifted Armaigen closer to the pyre, placing him gently on the ground as we tied some rope under his arms. I climbed the pile of wood and slowly pulled Armaigen to the top. Yeshua pushed as much as he could and climbed up higher to the peak, helping me arrange his sword on his chest, with his hands on the hilt.

I covered his body with mistletoe and oak leaves, as was the Drui way. I took one last look as we both jumped to the ground. We stood silently, saying a prayer to each of our spirit worlds. We heard some birds chirping and saw many trees filled with different types of birds and squirrels, also saying good night before they slept on the branches around us.

It was dark.

The cool night air was coming, a slow childbirth, sinking leisurely down from the sky. It would form a damp, banished layer of frost on the ground; as it allowed the forest to sleep.

Yeshua spoke:

> *"He that believeth in me, though he were now dead, shall live: and whosoever liveth and believeth in me, shall never die."*

I said it was a comforting poem. "You speak like a god although you are but a man."

"The last time I said this was in Judaea, during my other life. My Father told it to me and I spoke of it often. It brought comfort to many."

I asked, "Did it work?"

Yeshua did not answer right away, as he thought. "Why would I say it, if it were not true?"

I asked him whether people were praying to him or his father.

Yeshua said that people prayed to them both. "My Father did not talk to me about the earth spirits, like you and Armaigen have described."

I said that Armaigen had told us both that the earth spirits gave birth to Yeshua's father, not the other way around. The earth spirits came first.

He looked at me and said it would all be revealed one day.

I was ready to defend my master, but thought that Armaigen would not approve. I knew Armaigen believed that the spirits were everywhere. The earth spirits listen, watch us and take care of us. They provide a home for us when our bodies decide not to breathe any longer.

I asked him whether he prayed to his father.

"I pray to Him and seek His guidance. Sometimes I just want to share my feelings with Him. My disciples were very loving and understanding, but in many ways, they were like sheep and children. Just like I am with my Father, I suppose."

As I spoke to you before, Yeshua could not remember many events in his past life. He believed that his father was controlling his memory for some reason; he told me his father was angry with him. Armaigen said to me that Yeshua had created a new way of life in Judaea. It was spreading to all mankind, beyond even what a Drui was capable of.

Armaigen said it did not matter, for in the end, the same result would be provided to all.

I once tried to remind Yeshua of different events in our lives together, trying to revive a past memory when he had his ministry in Judaea. He calmly reflected, saying it was not possible.

I think he had given up, for his father was not speaking with him at the time. Yeshua did try to talk with him. His father was selective about when and what he would talk about. He told Yeshua, that if he wanted to live as a man, then he would not have all of his prayers answered, all of the time.

Orin, "Oh, dear. I could never imagine."

Yeshua told me that he had been crucified on the cross, and, for just an abrupt moment, he died. He said it was like an arrow catching up to a shooting star, it had all been foretold. He ascended, but he never really left his earthly body. He believed that he had to finish something that he had started on earth.

He lived in heaven, as fast as it takes to snap your fingers! Yeshua did not like what he saw. He felt empty and that his purpose had been extinguished. He is related to his father but his feelings of being a man were gone. In heaven, he was the same as all the other souls for his father still ruled. He wanted to live as a man again.

Orin, "Why? I don't get it. His father is acting like a child! Look at Yeshua; there is nothing wrong with him. Yeshua is trying to reconcile, but his father continues to be difficult with him. His father seems to be an angry selfish god."

"Life is what we share together. I live. You live. The Romans will upset the balance of life on earth. Therefore, we must seek this *old* earth Yeshua speaks of, where the spirit world flourishes. I have travelled everywhere and have no idea where that land is."

Yeshua did say something else to me, which I will never forget.

We were ready to light the funeral pyre. He paused and looked at me, as if he could read my mind, "I am here where I belong, where I want to be. I do not want to leave; I cannot leave for I would be *missing earth*. My Father said I can stay for a little longer but one day I would have to go back."

"My Father needs me now to complete this new journey. He did not like my decision to leave heaven and come back to earth. He thinks the flesh is weak but that is all too simple of an explanation for me to accept. He looks upon my refusal as an act of rebellion, not unlike the angel, Lucifer. He will never understand that *I just want to live*."

I did not know who Lucifer was.

Yeshua continued speaking, telling me that it was a complicated story and that he would tell me about it at another time. He made it clear that he was in no way like Lucifer. He finished explaining his situation, saying, "The heavens declare the glory of God; the firmament will showeth his handy work. One day telleth another and one night certifieth the next."

I had no idea what he was talking about.

It was likely well overdue to have this conversation between us. We now had to live our new lives without Armaigen. We waited for our words to disappear into the air. Each of our spirits from the different realms would remind us what to do next.

Yeshua then told me it was my turn to say a Drui prayer to Armaigen.

"The earth is alive,
Armaigen will never die.

All the air is for you,
You spirit wondering Drui.

Flowers will grow wild on your face,
Joy to everyone, to smell, kiss and embrace.

Spirits from the earth flow up through your feet,
Guide and give you an eternal spirit sleep.

Look how quick you will now run,
Live with the UnderWings; your new journey has begun."

It was a pleasant night. We did not have to speak, the wood crackled and the fire danced as it took Armaigen's soul away. We continued to drink to ease our pain. The heat from the flames filled the forest. All creatures, trees and plants did not sleep as they sang praises to Armaigen; we joined in singing, as best we could.

The excited, colourful spirits of light came from all over the earth, flitting about until the sky and the earth had reversed its positions; up was down and down was up. The spirits carried us, up and away to other worlds, as we soothingly walked together on the moon and the boundless path of hot stars. I held up my hand and the blue earth disappeared behind it. It was so small.

We drank too much that night, as we wished Armaigen well on his journey. I told Yeshua that Armaigen had told me what to do with his ashes. His ashes were to be placed into two separate bags. One bag of ashes was to be taken to Ynys Mon, and brought deep into a forest surrounded by pine trees. Pine seeds were to be gathered, and combined with his ashes and planted into the ground where there is a patch of lilacs nearby.

In the future, we were to take people to Ynys Mon and make it a place for all Druids. There, we would watch Armaigen grow into a tall, strong tree; the tallest tree in the forest. The tree grew to maturity in 10 years! It grew so tall that you could see Europa from the top. The other ashes were to be brought back to his childhood home in Eire and given to his sister Muriell.

Later, Yeshua fell asleep. I stared up at the sky. It was still dark, but the sun would appear soon.

I awoke to Armaigen's gentle voice. He told me that he was happy in the spirit world. It was a place where you did not have a physical body or a thinking mind. You dreamed as a child and all good thoughts came true. You could wish for anything, for there was no earth or sky but spirit and pure emotion. You could switch spirit bodies into any form; anytime you wanted. Imagine becoming a deer running free in the fields! All the people that had made you happy in your life were there, along with new friends that you had never met before. All wishes and desires came true.

There was no place for evil men in the spirit world. They would never ascend as a spirit but live as they were born in a place of never-ending darkness, touching other wicked angry people, with no appetite to live or die. Forever lost.

I looked at the pile of white ashes containing Armaigen, still smoldering. Two small lights burst out of the fire; dashing right at me. Armaigen said he was giving me his eyes so that I could see as well as he did. The lights flew quickly into my eyes, without hesitation and were absorbed like drops of water. It was an ignitable obvious moment, everything looked different. My knowledge of the spirit world had increased and I now knew how to harness all my powers over nature.

Orin apologized for crying. "It is a gloomy but happy story. You can't help but love and admire Yeshua. He carries a heavy burden. He does not have a father. A real father would not torture him like that." She paused and thought. "Did he have no family as a child?"

"Yes, he did. Armaigen and I met them. His father Joseph was a kind man and gave him a good life. He had two brothers and a sister. They were very protective of him."

"How can anyone have two fathers? Why would he leave his father, Joseph, if he was so happy?"

"He left them and came with me and Armaigen. It was in the same year we met Galen."

"How could you take a child away from his family?"

Chapter 38

FINDING YESHUA

In the early days, when I was still very young, Armaigen and I traveled through Europa to beyond the very edges of the Roman Empire; countless times for many years.

We saw beautiful lands and came to understand that the world is a dangerous place. You must always be on your guard, whether you were in open fields or darks forests; you learned to expect unforeseen events. This was especially true with strangers, even the people you had travelled with for many weeks would sometimes steal from you. A few would try to kill you if you tried to prevent them from stealing valuables or food.

Once out in the country, one had to be careful of the Roman patrols. Most of the army was made up of peasants who, for most of their lives, had nothing before becoming a soldier. Away from their forts, beyond the reach of Roman law, many patrols indiscriminately raided villages, raping and killing innocent people. They would kill you and get away with it, or imprison you for some trivial reason. You learned to kill first, when you had to.

Armaigen and I did not plan to go to the great Roman port of Ostia. We had killed many Romans in self-defence that spring; more killings than usual, and we sought a place to hide out for a year or two. We were now wanted men and conspicuous because of how we dressed and looked. It did not help that we did not cut our hair and beards. We were described as 'the demons' who had a lone donkey to pull our heavy cart.

Our original plan was to cross the land using the roads above Rome and not go near the capital. We would go to Greece, then onwards to Asia. It was also rumoured that the people in Asia, also believed in reincarnation.

We really had no idea where we were going to end up. We sought new ideas about the spirit world, for we had heard much about Asian earth spirits; they seemed more Drui-like in their philosophy. We were not seeking out Asia for trade, but we always purchased cloth and spices if an opportunity arose.

Strangely, meeting Yeshua happened because our cart was broken. Armaigen and I had been sitting on a hill, meditating. We felt the wind carry our thoughts and prayers to the foreign spirits somewhere in Asia, very far away; we told them we were coming to learn.

At some point, later that morning, when were finished with our prayers, we met an old merchant selling his goods on the side of the road; he had travelled from the far east. He told us about the thousands of colourful prayer flags that were called 'Dar Cho' – the 'Dar' meant one's future and wealth, the 'Cho' meant a person's feelings, hearing, smell and taste that would travel within the wind spirits. We were sure that the prayer flags had received our thoughts.

We were on a rough, dirt road, more a path than a Roman road. We stayed away from the Romans as often as we could, but it meant we had to push our cart over the uneven, rocky ground. It is interesting how nothing can go wrong, then the worst possible thing happens; our axle was broken. We repaired it as best we could, but knew it would have to be replaced. The closest large city was Ostia and we would have to change our route.

We had been to Rome many times before. We went there to pray in their unholy, empty temples. We had left many earth and sky spirits behind to grow and multiply with the desire to destroy the Roman Empire.

Our prayers never worked in their temples as the Romans became even wealthier through the years. We were usually ignored in the city, for we appeared poor. Most thought we were harmless beggars; but now we were criminals.

Armaigen said that we must avoid entering Rome.

We had a guarded optimism on this trip to Ostia, despite the fact we were wanted men. We hoped that we would be able to enter and leave unnoticed; come in one day and leave the next day, after the axle was fixed.

Armaigen never liked any Roman city or village. From his view, the Empire was covering up the ground with roads, aqueducts and buildings; the earth spirits were being suffocated. He said Rome was a perilous place, for it lacked any earth spirits. People were strange there; happy for all the wrong reasons. He had taught me that a spiritless earth makes people weak. It makes men and women hollow, empty and barren, in the sense that you cannot see or feel a virtuous life.

We were just two holy men; our small presence would likely be unnoticed.

However, it only took one serious argument, or the way you momentarily stared at a Roman, to arouse some sort of arbitrary suspicion, leading to our arrest and death.

Obviously, we did not fit in easily in a crowd. For the most part, we used our abilities to protect ourselves. Romans would cross a street to hurt us for no reason at all. We tried to avoid conflict by following uninhabited quiet streets, away from the large buildings and crowds. But drunken men would somehow find us, for we appeared weak to them. During those instances, we would use physical force, especially when there were no witnesses or soldiers around. The young attackers were always surprised when the two old beggars showed such quick sword skills, killing without remorse.

We were familiar with Ostia and knew of a small Roman gate in the city wall, that the poor mostly used.

The soldiers, who guarded it in the past, wore tired looking uniforms that had not been washed; the metal they wore was dull and scratched, like the consigned legionnaires assigned to this post. These soldiers were old and suffering from some injury or affliction caused by serving the Empire for so long. They were now relegated to guard and check people coming into the city. But because this gate catered to the unimportant and poor; questions were rarely asked. It was an easy job, boring with some imaginary prestige to it. By the end of the day, the guards would be tired and thirsty and want nothing more than a woman on the way home while getting drunk.

But this time, it was different.

Armaigen always protected the back of the cart as we walked, knife ready, as I led the donkey. It was very crowded that day, too many people going through a small gate, like water being poured out of a narrow bottle. As I got closer, I could see it was not necessarily the crowds that were slow, but some new polished recruits had been mixed in with the old warriors; they were keen to make a name for themselves, while enjoying their new authority.

I shouted back to Armaigen that we might have some trouble ahead.

Armaigen came up front for a moment to look. As he spoke, he removed his notable, blue robe and threw it in the back of wagon. He came back to me telling me to say nothing unless asked. If they asked, we were merchants and he would take care of getting the coins.

We were close to the gate. The road was not in good shape. It was uneven and needed repair. I suppose the more important, high-profile entrances got all the attention. I could feel the axle give way as the cart tilted; I slowed my pace down over each stone, at one point stopping to look at the wheel, which was now on an angle, slanted inwards. It would not last much longer.

The two, inquisitive new guards had seen our tall cart ramble its way slowly forward; pots clanking and the stubborn donkey braying as it resisted all the stops and starts. But we were not moving fast enough. Some of the people behind us were calling out to move faster and hurry up. The two soldiers walked down each side looking at the wagon. One young soldier walked up to me and I pointed to the wheel, telling him about the axle.

I kept moving as fast as the cart would allow. The soldiers continued to move towards Armaigen.

One guard pulled open the back flaps, to have a look inside. He asked what was in the cart.

Armaigen said that we were merchants. He asked whether they were interested in buying, saying there were many good deals.

I looked back at Armaigen and knew that the bright legionnaire would not give up, as I continued slowly guiding the cart forward. I saw the old lazy guards sitting on a bench, on the side of the road, not worrying about anyone passing by. I stopped the cart just inside the gate, leaving only enough room for rows of single bodies to get past the cart.

More people begun to shout and complain that they could not enter because of the wagon blocking the gate.

The old soldiers awoke and reluctantly moved their disheveled bodies. They were clearly annoyed at me, until they saw the wheel.

They sighed as they got up and yelled while waving at me, "Go! Go!"

I told them that I could not move. The axle was broken, and I needed help to push it through.

They ordered some Roman citizens who were standing about; that were waiting to leave the city. They grabbed their arms and told them to help. A number of men, on both sides of the cart began to rock the cart as the guards shouted instructions, as our donkey became irritated.

Armaigen was concerned at the young soldier who had jumped into the wagon; he went to the back, looking at everything. Throughout, there were casks of water, basic food, grain for the mule, dried fish, jars filled with herbs, much clothing, wine, oil lamps, terracotta figurines, ceramic jugs and bowls. There were also numerous artifacts picked up along the way: walking sticks, sea shells and colourful crystal rocks. At the back of the cart, well-hidden, were swords and many other weapons, including a massive, locked, iron chest that held our potion.

Armaigen warned the soldier to be careful, for there were many breakable objects.

The ambitious soldier had pulled back all the cloths covering the chest, asking what was inside.

At that moment, the cart suddenly jolted and the soldier was pitched forward. He regained his balance for a moment, but the cart immediately jerked back and he fell out of the cart. He was caught by Armaigen before he touched the ground; he was not hurt. The cart was moving forward again.

The friend of the fallen soldier sniggered as he dusted himself off.

Armaigen was a good actor and extended his humble apologies, explaining that the old wagon needed repair. He explained that there was nothing of value in the cart. He offered a present for the legionnaire's trouble.

Armaigen was now walking with the cart as he talked. The soldiers on each side of him were fascinated by Armaigen's coin purse and the solid sound of the coins which were enhanced by the thin, vacant clatter of the tin pots, hanging on the side of our wagon. He took his time trying to find a coin.

The soldier that had fallen looked at the purse seemingly more avaricious than the other legionnaire. The other soldier looked ahead at the old sweaty soldiers who had helped move the wagon along, not wanting to share the coins he expected to receive.

The ambitious soldier told Armaigen to hurry. He even called him an "old man" and told him to hurry before the other guards saw us.

Armaigen conveniently found the coins. He told him that he thought it would be enough to pay for the delay. They released his arm, and he placed a gold aureus in each hand of the two young soldiers. They were shocked and smiled at each other.

Armaigen told them, "I am sure you will use this, and make sure to give thanks to the Goddess Venus tonight."

The soldier that had fallen out of the cart grabbed the purse from Armaigen. He pulled out another coin not looking in the small bag, as he stared defiantly at him. It was a silver denarius. He dropped the purse back into Armaigen's hand. He later told me that if he had known that this was his last day on earth, he would have killed those men. 'Roman greed knows no limits!'

Armaigen put his shoulder against the back of the wagon and helped move it forward. He said to the young soldiers, "Boys, can you give me a hand? I am out of breath." The two young soldiers looked resentful at being asked, but then they quickly stuffed their coins away as Armaigen stood back and watched the soldiers continue to move the wagon until it was safely inside the gates of Rome.

As we left the gates behind, the streets became less busy and we had time to talk. We both walked together on the same side of the wagon, with Armaigen more at the back, watching for thieves.

I asked, "What happened back there?"

"Gold. Gold will do it every time."

I looked back. "Tell me later."

"Just follow this street. It will lead us to the harbour."

A series of dense buildings were still blocking our complete view down the shaded, narrow streets. The coolness of the air was good this early in the morning. The sun was cutting through the streets on either side of us. The light slowly moved with us, as the earth turned over, changing its position in the sky. We both felt it was going to be a hot day.

I could smell the open water. The odd scavenger seagull flew overhead, making its annoying, screeching sound. One mast appeared between a building, followed by the tops of many other masts, sticking up even higher above the buildings as we got closer. Now, hundreds of masts filled the low sky and the whirring noise of thousands of people jammed the air. I had not yet seen any groups of people, but knew that they were close, possibly around the next corner. My heart raced, excited to see the ships.

As we came closer, we heard the noise and the shouting of men, as many wagons passed us, coming up from the harbour. There were full fish baskets, as well as many different sizes of clay jugs and wooden boxes. Everything was going back to Rome to be sold in the city markets. Then more noise, as men and woman shouted for attention from anyone in the thick-moving crowds. All the sounds combined and plugging our ears, as the variety of smells topped our senses; it made us hungry.

We did not want to be there but knew we would not go to sleep hungry that night.

The wide dock was overwhelming but impressive. Hundreds of ships and masts were now fully visible.

There were ships of all sizes that had moored already. There were still more at rest, in the harbour, anticipating their turn to dock while waiting for the other ships to unload. Food and articles were stacked everywhere along the docks beside their respective ship, as still other crates were being lifted out of ships by pulleys, manned by many hard-looking, dark-bearded, bare-chested men.

We walked more into the square and found an empty wall to place the wagon against. The wheel had a definite tilt to it and we could not go any further. We were fortunate to find an unoccupied place; it was under some gnarled trees, clutching to a wall. Some branches reached away from the wall seeking the light, as the numerous, green-clustered leaves fell over like grapes; creating some shade for us. Our dependable, but annoying donkey told us he could not take another step. We would now search for a carpenter. We did not know where to look, or who to ask.

Orin interrupted me. She put one finger on my lips for me to stop talking. I took her finger and kissed it. She leaned over and took her time kissing me. We held each other for a long moment; her skin was so soft and I was aware of every subtle curve of her body. The lofty afternoon sun had moved directly above us. I felt our sweat almost glue us together. It was too hot for us to lie in the grass any longer.

"Tiernan, my love, let's cool ourselves in the water. I have the feeling this story will take some time. I want to hear it all, especially Yeshua's life and what he thinks about."

"I need to finish the story. I need to talk to you or someone about him. It bothers me. I appreciate his beliefs but I do not really understand him. I don't think he understands himself either. But I love him as a friend. He is on our side but is alone. He needs as many friends as possible, but he will never be a Briton, or a Drui, for that matter. He is a man without a country."

After we played in the water, Orin suggested that she prepare some food for us. The cottage by the dry pond had plenty of supplies that were replenished by the forest spirits. I enjoyed preparing food and helped her bring everything we needed outside, under the pleasant shade of some trees. We were dressed again and felt dry and clean. I poured some wine for Orin and we toasted our health and that of our children.

I was now very excited. "I enjoy this next part of the story the most!"

We gave the donkey grain and water. We stood looking about for someone to fix our cart.

The ships were all joined along the dock, bow to stern, and all the sails had been furled, hanging down at odd angles, resting.

There was too much to look at and we knew that one of us would have to go searching for someone. At that moment, someone shouted and waved at us. We heard it, but did not know where it was coming from. Then, suddenly, we both saw him; it was a boy waving at us!

I felt he had been staring at us all the while. Armaigen and I both had to cup our hands above our eyes to block the sun in our eyes; we could see his thin outline.

Yeshua was a skinny, tall boy. He was dressed loosely in cool, blue stripes. He smiled easily, showing that boyish smile that never went away, even in manhood. He was standing on top of a group of scattered wooden crates. Loose wood planks were strewn all about on the ground below him. He always liked to be higher whenever he could. He had the same instincts as a bird.

Yeshua stood alone, but had a presence about him. He seemed to infer that he was the overseer of the entire harbour. He waved at us, sweeping both arms around, as many who were close to him stopped to see what he was looking at.

Men started shouting at him from the small ship docked beside him.

"Look up! Look up! Yeshua! The chairs are loose! They are coming down on you!"

Yeshua was too preoccupied, maybe it was his age, or maybe it was seeing our unusual bright blue and yellow wagon covered with pots. The harbour was a unique confusion of life itself. It was so loud. There were so many languages being spoken, bright-coloured clothing from many lands, disreputable men and woman settling arguments, other people making deals and the smell of food from many countries being sold in the numerous and abundant market stalls.

Armaigen and I saw the ropes coming apart that held the chairs, curling and thrashing upwards, flying free and away. The chairs were slipping; some were only dangling above him and ready to drop. I ran over to help. I did not have any plan, only that a young boy might get crushed without my help.

As I gathered speed, it seemed that everyone was stepping in front of me. I started shouting, but nobody understood what I was saying. I began pushing people away.

I was getting closer to the boy, Yeshua still stood oblivious to the danger above. He did notice I was coming towards him and stopped waving. I leaped up and over the wood crates, taking one last look up and noticed the complete load was giving way and about to fall on him. I reached up as far as I could and pulled him back on top of me, rolling over some crates with hard sharp corners. We came to rest on a small mountain of thick rope.

Yeshua was on top of me when I opened my eyes and said with a smile, "May the Lord bless you!" He rolled off me and got up quickly, "I must go!" He ran to the chairs which had fallen to the ground. Other men, a little older than him had left the ship and were now shouting at him on the dock. An older man went between the men and Yeshua; until the shouting and tempers settled down. It was quiet again, but the men were still mad by the looks on their faces.

A woman came up to me and helped me to my feet. "We are so sorry. Thank you for what you did."

I looked at her. She was beautiful with a dark complexion, large round brown eyes and black thick hair. She also had a strong presence about her, a woman who could take care of herself. I did not know what to say and glanced over at Yeshua again. I suppose my confused and bewildered look made her want to put me at ease.

"My name is Salome. Those are my brothers. Sorry to say I am stuck with them."

I held out my hand, "My name is Tiernan, and that is my friend over there. His name is Armaigen." Armaigen looked serious as usual and raised one hand, waving me back to him. He was acknowledging that I should not waste any more time.

Salome started pointing, "The older man with the beard is my father, Joseph. That one over there is James; he thinks he is the boss. The one beside him is Simon. He is a good worker, but is quiet most of the time. You have already met my younger brother, Yeshua."

"Yes. I have met Yeshua. He was staring at us when we came into the square. He caught my attention."

"That's Yeshua. Never misses anything; head in the clouds. James calls him lazy. But I think he's more of a dreamer. No one likes a dreamer – do they?" She glanced at me, sizing me up. We watched everyone get back onto the ship as Yeshua stacked the chairs on the dock and set aside the ones that were broken. "Yes, he is a dreamer."

"There is nothing wrong with being a dreamer. At heart, we are all dreamers."

"Exactly. But who listens?" She looked at me for a moment. "I like you, Tiernan. I'm sure we will get along."

"What about the broken chairs?"

"Yeshua will fix them. He might be a dreamer, but he is a very good skilled carpenter."

"We need a carpenter. Our axle is broken."

Armaigen and I waited under the shade of the tree, drinking water, nibbling on some fruit that Salome had given me. She took us to the ship and we quickly met the brothers who were still working, unloading the shipment of tables, other chairs, benches and long pieces of flat stacked wood.

Joseph thanked me for saving Yeshua from getting hurt, or worse.

Several merchants with their slaves verified and counted the shipment under the watchful eye of James who had left the ship and stood beside them. He counted the actual shipment again. The merchants counted and recounted until an agreement was made. Money was exchanged and still James counted the money, until he was satisfied, followed by a handshake.

Joseph kept Yeshua separate from his brothers, for now. I did see him talk to him quietly with a hand on his shoulder. Yeshua was looking down, but listening. I did hear him say at the end, "Yes, father."

Then Salome, Joseph and Yeshua stood with Armaigen and I. Yeshua said he was sorry, as he embraced me. I formally introduced Armaigen, who greeted everyone graciously. Joseph suggested he and his family would provide a dinner for us, as a way of saying thank you.

Joseph, "We have been on that ship so long that it will be good for us to sit on the ground again. And Yeshua has something to say to you both as an additional favour."

Yeshua, "I will fix your axle and wheel."

Armaigen, "We will pay you for it, of course."

"No. We have some extra wood on the ship. It will not take long."

Joseph said proudly, "Yeshua is very good working with his hands. He also knows many languages, don't you my son?"

Yeshua gave that infectious, boyish grin. "It's easy."

Salome, "The market is a good place to pick up many languages. You must remember to count your fingers before you leave! It is also a good place to learn the ways of men and negotiate. It is a great place to learn business!"

Yeshua, "I'm not too interested in business, or making money."

Joseph broke the brief silence, "Yeshua is young."

James and Simon arrived and we greeted them. They were strong, healthy-looking men.

James, "Yeshua is foolish for nearly getting killed and wasting all of our hard work."

Yeshua looked sad and timid. James and Simon gave him a warm, friendly embrace, kissing him. "Be more careful, my brother. We forgive you."

Yeshua looked suddenly relieved.

The brothers and Joseph stood in the shade with us. James quietly told his father and Simon about the profit they had made today.

Armaigen, "We have plenty of wine. This will be our contribution. I will bring it out."

He motioned me to the back of the wagon to help him.

"Look at Yeshua's eyes."

"What?"

"There are flecks of gold in each eye, in the pupil. It reminds me of the spirits growing in the rocks in the UnderWing caves."

It was agreed that Salome and Yeshua would take me to the large market.

We stayed together mostly, but Yeshua kept wondering off, like a child adrift. He was easily-distracted and always saw something that caught his eye. It could be a colour, a smell, unusual-looking people or strange-looking fish. This happened often until Salome told Yeshua to explore the market by himself, but warned him to come back soon.

"Since he was small he would walk off by himself. He never gets lost and always seems to know where we are."

"Doesn't mean that I don't worry. He enjoys his own company but he loves speaking with people. He will return. He likes seeing all the foods from different countries and practising different dialects. He's very good at it. I don't know where he gets it from, for our family has difficulty just speaking to each other in one language, let alone all the languages from around the Empire." She laughed a little, not embarrassed at all.

I took the initiative to buy some blessed meat and other foods under the careful eye of Salome. She knew this market and the owners of the stalls. We were jostled and pushed, as others interrupted our presence since many were bargaining for the same items.

One seller did not recognize me and immediately paid more attention to my voice; he was thinking where I was from. I had done this many times before, and knew when I was being taken advantage of. I felt that I was not making any progress negotiating.

The price seemed high. I felt the elbows of Salome dig into my side, pushing me out of the way, "I hope you don't mind." She took over, telling me to stop speaking. "We can get him lower, I will get him lower. They are all thieves here because you are new. They would take your sandals off your feet, if they could."

We came back with a treasure of good food, bread, blessed meat, more wine, a variety of cheeses, fruits, figs and olives; fresh off the ships. My arms were full. Salome walked ahead of me and for the first time I noticed she had a slight limp. I felt sorry for her. I thought I must talk to Armaigen about her. Then we both stopped, for we heard Yeshua shouting for us to wait. He also had an armful of food and was running to catch up to us.

Salome said to me before he got much closer, "That's Yeshua for you! He has no money, yet he comes back with food, which is given to him freely. All of us don't understand it, except his father for some reason and he won't tell us how he does it. No wonder he avoids work."

We had more than enough food when we returned from the market.

Armaigen had made a canvas cover to shade us as the sun came around. We laid carpets and many pillows on the ground. The whole family joined us on the flat stones close to the wagon.

Many beggars came asking for food. They stopped and seemed to notice Yeshua. After he gave them some food, he would hold their hands and bless them. I thought this was very strange for a young boy.

It was the late afternoon; the area was still crowded. Many ships had left the dock and others had replaced them, but the unloading continued.

The tall, red legionnaires stood at attention, carefully watching people and protecting the tax collectors, ensuring the proper merchant and shipping tax was paid.

It was one of the most pleasing dinners I have ever had outside of our marriage. It was almost equal to the meals villagers had given us in our travels. Of course, I have also failed to mention the equinox celebrations in the sacred groves.

It was like we had known this family for years and that we were all related or connected for some unknown reason. I asked how often they came to Ostia and they said as much as possible, as well as other Mediterranean ports in Greece; they had even gone to Alexandria once, but mostly Roman ports and some surrounding islands.

Joseph said, "As we sit here many of our relatives in Judaea continue to build wooden tables and chairs for the family. Business has been good, but our old ship is starting to leak and we have to be careful how far we go."

"What is the name of your ship?"

Yeshua, "Mary. Named after our mother."

"Your mother?"

Joseph, "Mary is my beautiful wife."

Armaigen was mostly quiet during the meal, thinking. I could see he was enjoying himself in his own way, as others soaked up his warm company. I thought that he would have talked more, for he was not quite 2000 years old and had the most stories to share.

It was as if Armaigen had just read my mind, for he began asking questions about the Roman conquest of Judaea and what that was like for everyone.

Joseph said quietly, as he looked around, "Bad. The Romans and leaders are cruel people."

James, "What is it like in Europa?"

"It is the same for us. We are all a conquered people to some degree, my friend, no matter who rules. I know this first-hand for I have lived through it, and seen it with my own eyes: Romulus and Remus creating Rome, the conquest of Greece, the conquest of Egypt then Judaea, Germania, Gaullia, Alexander the Great and Hannibal of Carthage. I don't need to go on, for we have all heard stories. It is a story of life and death and not much in between for most people. It saddens me that there seems to be so much death lately."

Simon and James both spoke at the same time, "You said you have seen it with you own eyes – this is not possible!"

"James, Simon, stop! Watch how you say your words. Honour Armaigen's words and what he speaks of. I'm sure it is a slip of the tongue."

Yeshua, "Armaigen, how have you seen such actions? Those events took place hundreds of years ago before you were born."

James, "Father, listen to Yeshua."

Yeshua leaned back, grinning. "Five hundred years would be 2000 equinoxes. That is many seasons but only one season breathes for my Father." His family looked at him, for they were surprised at his quick logic, for once.

Joseph looked at Yeshua surprised, not shocked, but speechless. James, Simon and Salome did not know what to make of it.

Joseph resumed his attention back to the group, "Armaigen is a scholar. Look at him. He would not spread such lies. Surely, you have read about these events?"

We had all drank too much wine. We were not drunk, but our thoughts took time to express themselves clearly. We were very relaxed and happy and enjoyed the fellowship we shared. Our hearts felt warm towards each other.

Armaigen did not speak and I did not know how he would answer, for I had never heard him lie. I had heard him talk about his life outside, like the things that he has done and seen.

I wondered why he would even bring these events up. My mind was working as fast as a waterfall. I thought it would be impossible to tell these people how old he really was.

There was an uneasy silence and I knew that Joseph and his family were beginning to think Armaigen was not a liar, but confused, for he appeared old and a little unkempt.

Then Salome reached for the last grapes in the bowl. She took them before Yeshua had a chance. "You're getting too slow, my little brother." She then threw several grapes at Yeshua, some of them hitting his face.

Yeshua just grinned and picked up the last grape, and ate it. "Perhaps, sister, you should be busy finding the face of a husband to throw grapes at?" We all laughed.

Salome then spurted out, "Father, see how I am picked on? You should have had more daughters!"

Armaigen filled up all the glasses with wine. I dreaded what he was going to say. I was nervous, but it was too late.

"I know not all of you, but I wish to tell you a story about myself and Tiernan."

I thought why would he do this now? He told everyone that we were healers of men, who have wandered the earth for so many years that we had lost count.

"Of course, young Yeshua is just starting off in life, learning about the ways of men and you will all find it interesting, I'm sure. My story will take time to tell, but it must now be told."

Armaigen looked at Yeshua. "It will be of importance to Yeshua, I'm sure."

I took a big mouthful of wine feeling the wonderful warmth of the drink seep slowly down my throat. I thought this could be a big mistake. We had already been together for nearly 70 years. Armaigen began and as he spoke in a low, clear voice, I felt more composed and tranquil. He was going to release the secret life that we had led for so many years amongst the pagan Romans. It was *now* the time for it to be told, and I was not going to stop it.

Armaigen swore them to secrecy. Then, skillfully, over many hours, told them of the UnderWing world, what it meant to be a Drui, the potion which prevents aging, his travels through most of the villages in Europa, his powers and communication with the earth spirits, rescuing me and everything that had occurred to us, including killing Romans in self-defence. He described countless deaths, including killing thieves. He did not go as far as his prophesies, for even Armaigen understood that the future was never completely certain.

When Armaigen had finished, he gulped an entire glass of wine without stopping. He burped and wiped his beard with his sleeve. As he sat waiting for a reaction, he poured himself another glass of wine.

It was too much for everyone to take in at once. The silence was broken by the laughter of disbelief as many began to speak all at once.

James, "Surely, this is some mystical story; an exaggerated story passed down through your family, through generations that are just rumours and not true."

Both Armaigen and I sat silent looking around at the faces. It was difficult, for no oil lamps had been lit and it was dark except for the small fire that had almost burned itself out from dinner.

Armaigen asked Salome to get some oil lamps from the back of the wagon.

It was a peaceful quiet that allowed everyone to review again in their minds what had been said in relation to whether the story of Armaigen and Tiernan were to be believed or not.

Joseph did not look up at us, "Why Yeshua?"

There was no answer as we both looked at Yeshua, then back to Joseph. "Why Yeshua? You said the story is important to Yeshua, but you did not mention Yeshua in your story."

Joseph looked worried. Armaigen and I knew that he had a bad feeling in his stomach. He loved Yeshua so much. He remembered the birth of Yeshua and hiding Mary and the baby. He had hoped that the many prophesies were not true. Many years had passed and most people had forgotten. James, Simon, Salome and the rest of the family did not know anything, just Mary and Joseph.

Armaigen, "Yeshua has the same gold fleck in his eyes that the spirits of the earth carry. Even now he has great powers. He does not think about it because he is young and the world is already in his carefree command. He senses something, but is not sure what it is. He is not the same as others his same age."

James, sounded indignant, replied, "This is our brother. We were all the same at his age. He does not care to know the business right at this moment, but I am sure he will when he gets older."

He smiled at Yeshua, as he pushed his brothers' shoulder away, knocking him off balance; both were laughing. "You know what I mean!"

Yeshua, "In a dream before we sailed, someone told me to look for both of you, so I climbed on top of the boxes today, waiting. Then I saw you. I knew you were important, but I did not know why."

The family looked at Yeshua and listened. They had always called him a dreamer. Maybe he was different, but he was still a son and a brother with a family in Judaea.

Armaigen, "I know this is very difficult and unusual. We are strangers to you. We have not been here even a day. Tiernan and I are the only Druids on this earth. No one has ever been told the story I have just described. Now you all know. Yeshua, I believe, is somehow connected to me and Tiernan."

Armaigen sat more upright. He pushed his hair back, so that you could see his face properly. "I have a question, Joseph. It involves a personal sacrifice on your behalf and your whole family. This is my question and I know it comes as a surprise even to me, for I came to Ostia just to fix my axle, nothing else."

Armaigen waited, so the question would be taken seriously.

"Is it possible for Yeshua to be our apprentice for one year? Don't say anything. I do not know why I ask you. After one year, we will return here and place him safely on a ship. He can return to Judaea. During the time with us, we would send you messages and keep you informed on how he is doing and let you know he is safe."

James, "No Father, it is too dangerous. We do not know these men. He is only a boy!"

Salome was looking at Armaigen. "How could you guarantee his safety? No one could do that. Anything could happen."

"We both can't guarantee anything, except what we control. There are the earth spirits, which control everything; they work through us. To answer your question, I would protect Yeshua every day, even if my life depended on it."

Simon, "I agree with James. This is foolish. Why one year?"

Yeshua, "No one has asked me how I feel? I want to go. I need to see the world. My Father calls me. These are the men I want to go with."

James, "Nonsense! What do you know? What do you mean, 'my father calls me'? Your father does no such thing!"

Joseph held his hand up to James, to stop talking, "I have seen firsthand only one other story like this. Armaigen, it was not like your story at all. There are slight facts to your story that make me pause." He looked at his children. "There are prophesies that are known only to your mother and me."

Joseph shook his head, "God knows, what I would tell your mother! She is a good woman; a woman of God. God speaks every day to her. People come from all around to speak and pray with her. God speaks through her, not unlike your earth spirits."

Joseph studied Salome and his sons. "We all know this to be true about your mother."

The children were all quiet.

Joseph stroked his beard several times, distraught and confused. "It is so late and I am tired. I think we are all tired. I will pray for guidance. You will have your answer in the morning."

━━━

That night we helped Yeshua fix the axle and the wheel. We said nothing to each other as we worked together. Yeshua said good night and returned to his ship.

Armaigen and I lay under the wagon. We wrapped the blankets around us, keeping us warm from the sea winds. We said good night to each other and prayed to the spirits as we fell asleep. We did not know whether Yeshua was going to come with us; I think we both believed that he would stay with his family in Judaea. If that was the case, we felt confident that our story would remain a secret.

Judaea was so far away. As our eyes closed for the last time on that day, we heard Joseph's family trying to keep their emotions in control; it was late and their voices carried to our ears. There was shouting. The tempers seemed to be rising as the tone had a sharpness to it, one of mistrust and anger. Suddenly, I heard one voice that had a fatal firm finality to it. It was Joseph commanding everyone to be quiet; it was a lasting peace and we finally fell asleep.

My body shook. "Wake up! Wake up! I am coming with you!" We both looked up and saw Yeshua's excited face.

"I am ready, let's get going!"

Armaigen and I looked at each other, but it was too early. We felt damp and our skin sticky with sweat. I was hungry. I knew we were not going anywhere until we ate something.

We kicked off our blankets, rolled over slowly, and pushed ourselves up, rubbing our eyes and faces, trying to see clearly. Yeshua was eager to go, but after so many years, we had a routine that worked for us, and it was deep in our nature to follow it.

Besides, we needed to speak with Joseph.

Armaigen cleared his voice, "We must get out of Ostia before Ostia wakes up. We're wanted men and this city will kill us if they find out who we are. We must keep Yeshua out of it."

"I agree."

I noticed Yeshua's possessions had been piled up near the wagon. I said to him, "You feed and water the donkey. Place your belongings in the back of the wagon. Try to keep them together on one side."

We made our way to wash at the public fountain. Mothers were already washing clothes as their children played, some chasing each other, some playing games as they jumped in the cold water.

When we got back, Joseph and the family were sitting on the ground. Salome was stirring the morning meal of boiled fish in a cauldron over a fire.

Armaigen, "Where is the cloaca maxima?"

Yeshua, "If you mean the latrine, it is quick walk from here but in the other direction from the fountain." He pointed at the water behind Armaigen.

Joseph said, "We may be poor but we have the largest latrine right there and our ship floats on it."

Armaigen, the first Drui who had been chosen to be the protector and leader of all earth spirits, needed directions to release himself; he looked disgruntled and embarrassed. I didn't care; I just wanted to go, too.

"Go to the stern, under the deck and behind the curtain, there is wood with a hole in it."

It was humorous to Joseph, that such men, who had complete authority over nature, could not find a place to piss.

When we returned, we were greeted as friends and sat down as we did the night before.

"Sit. Sit. I went to the market early and bought bread, fish, and milk. I was even able to get fresh eggs - can you imagine? There is wine, milk and oil to dip your bread, some more honey over there and these fishes should be cooked soon." Salome turned the fish over. "I hope you are not offended, but James and Simon got more food supplies for your trip, since you will have an extra mouth to feed."

I said we would pay for the supplies and Joseph said it was not necessary.

We sat down in the morning sun, much like yesterday, feeling good at all the caring attention that we were not used to. There seemed to be an indiscriminate undercurrent of emotions. I suppose if one of our sons were going away with strangers who you had only met the day before, we all would feel that something was not right.

Salome continued, "Yeshua will eat anything, but make sure he eats plenty of fruit."

Joseph, "And pull his weight. Give him jobs to do. He works best with a daily routine."

Armaigen and I noticed that James and Simon were quiet and polite, passing the food around while receiving food from us, but both said nothing.

The obvious anger from the night before had disappeared. They were still carefully appraising us, still wondering whether they could trust us with their brother. I am not sure whether they thought the story was too incredible to believe or they were thinking what it was like to be nearly 2000 years old.

I went to say something to reassure everyone, but Joseph interrupted the silence before me.

"Now I am going to tell you Druids why Yeshua is being allowed to go with you. What I am going to say, you must also keep it to yourselves until the day you die – and in your case, only God Almighty knows when that will happen!"

I wondered who god almighty was that they kept talking about.

He looked at his children. "We feel Yeshua needs to grow up. It's not his fault, for he is supposed to be this way. Salome says he is a dreamer. The world has its place for dreamers, but the Romans crush dreamers. There must be a balance. He is a good and honest boy that any father would be proud of. I am so proud of him and all my children. But for him, he must fulfill the ordained prophesy. He needs to see more of the world and become wise on judging human nature and tactics of men who control the world."

Armaigen went to say something. Joseph held up one finger, for he was not finished.

"Last night you told us a story that some would say was a lie. Many would say you are cheats and thieves, preying on people like us. Last night, I was forced to explain to my children a story from our one Lord, our Father Almighty that was written when our earth was born, perhaps even before your earth spirits had everlasting life.

The prophesy is about Yeshua. It is not like your story at all, but there is a strange connection between us, like Armaigen said. It is more than strange that we would meet here."

Joseph went on to tell us some background information about their family lineage and brief details about Yeshua and how he was to spread the word of God.

Yeshua did not seem to be listening or really understand what his father was saying; he just wanted to leave as soon as possible.

Joseph continued, "Yeshua is young, and you are both old and wise. It is written that Yeshua's time will come when he is older. It is the voice of our Lord that speaks through all good men. You both are what we would call righteous men, seeking what we all seek, binding all life together, so that there is an eternal value to our lives on earth.

We are no different than you, the spirits of angels are upon us, protecting us and helping us to see, speak, and feel the spirit of our Lord."

Joseph stopped. He took his time going around to each of his children and us, kissing our faces.

He was quiet and bowed his head in prayer, offering his hand to either side of him, as we all held hands. We were in a circle. "This is our eternal bond. There is no need to speak anymore of this. We feel the protection of God Almighty. It will be shown to all of us."

We finished our morning meal in a beautiful silence. Then we helped each other organize and pack the wagon, for it was heavy. We all would have to help the donkey on the initial uphill climb from the harbour. James told us that he meant no harm towards us. He was less outspoken than last night, and told us that much had been revealed by his father. He stared at Yeshua with disbelief and wonder.

We all embraced each other again and we cried, as we stood about, going over last instructions.

Salome made sure Yeshua was listening to her. He kissed her and told her he would be careful.

She told Yeshua to follow and obey us; she said we were very wise men.

Yeshua placed his hand on Salome's face, blessing her. She was in shock. "Where did that come from? Growing up, already!"

Yeshua smiled, "You will always be my little sister."

"But I'm older than you."

"But I am taller than you, like our mother."

She looked at her shorter leg. "I will never be tall."

Simon came running from the direction of the ship with a large, leather bag and shoved it into Yeshua stomach. He said, "Brother, some fine carpenter you will make without your tools!"

Yeshua was grateful and placed them in the wagon.

I turned to Joseph, explaining that in the winter we would likely be staying in many villages. I was sure Yeshua would be busy repairing roofs and making furniture.

Armaigen was restless and insisted that we should go. He would lead the donkey today. I knew he was still worried about the Romans arresting us.

Yeshua and I started pushing the wagon from the back. The brothers helped, until we gained enough momentum. We waved goodbye, and I concentrated on pushing forward, as my toes squeezed into the small rock holes between the stones.

I looked back at Yeshua's family and felt I would never see them again.

There seemed to be something wrong with Salome. Yeshua's family tried to keep us visible, moving around, trying to keep a clear view of us through all the people. Salome followed our slow progression away from them.

There was something going on between the members of the family as they stopped and looked at Salome again. She was leaning on James' shoulder. Joseph had bent down to look at her feet.

Our cart was nearly out of sight, engulfed by the crowded streets. We had to stop. There were more people going down to the harbour than leaving it. Our path was difficult, for we did not have much room.

Salome turned away and wiped a tear from her eye. She seemed to stumble and her brothers caught her, as she eased them away from her. She was trying to walk by herself in a straight line.

She laughed holding out her arms for balance, "Goodness. What is the matter with me?"

Joseph, "What is it?"

"My leg. Something is wrong with my leg. It feels strange. It does not feel right."

Both brothers assisted her, holding her up again under both arms. "I'm fine. Let me go! I want to walk by myself!"

Salome held her hands up, moving them away so that she had enough room. Her legs felt different; they were both strong and she stood tall for the first time. Both legs were now the same length.

She stepped forward, then again, bending her knees as she carefully moved. I smiled, watching, as she shouted, "I can walk! My legs are strong! I'm not limping. Look at me! Let me go. I want to do it myself!"

She stretched out her arms for balance, as she shuffled along slowly. She moved faster, as she walked normally without her arms outstretched; walking through the busy crowd without limping!

I shouted ahead to Armaigen, "Did you see that?" He was not really looking.

"Yes. We must keep going."

Yeshua turned his head towards me, "See what?"

"Keep pushing. Put some muscle in it."

Simon, "It was them. Armaigen and Tiernan did it!"

James, "He's right, it was them. They said they were healers. Oh, Salome!"

Salome was overcome with joy; she turned and ran to her father; holding him close crying.

Joseph stood there, as his eyes flooded with emotion. He was happy for Salome but distressed; it had begun, God Almighty had given him a sign.

Chapter 39

SPIRIT OF MAN

I watched Orin's face as she absorbed what I had just said. She spoke quietly and straight forward, "You and Armaigen did not heal Salome, did you?"

"No, we did not."

"Yeshua healed Salome and did not even know he was doing it."

"Yes."

"Yeshua seems happy enough on the outside but he is tormented. His tie to his father is permanent and he cannot release himself from it."

"His father will never liberate him, even though his father tells him to follow us on our journey, wherever that may lead."

"Perhaps Yeshua's father has the power of prophesy, like Armaigen."

"Yes, he does. Sometimes I get tired of any prophesy, unless it is to prevent deaths, for there is no real meaning to a prophesy, when we all know of the outcome. Is it really a

journey for men, when it is already pre-ordained? Where is the spiritual growth?"

"Tiernan, we are all following you. I don't get it. His father puts limits on him and he is a grown man who seeks only goodness and peace; like you."

I was unsure what Orin meant. "But Yeshua is not just following me."

"Yes, he is. Right now, we all are. You two have something going on but you both are too close to see it. I don't know what it is, but there is something there. I do not know how to describe it. You are a *Drui* but what is *he*?"

"I will tell you what I know. I have considered the same thought. Yeshua decided to live like a man. Armaigen avoided the same question from me. Even Yeshua is not sure. Oh, he feels a personal connection with his father but it is never clear to him. When I asked him about it, he hesitated and had to think before he gave me an answer. It is sad to see him suffer. I wished I had never asked him."

"What makes him suffer?"

"Yeshua's father has selectively taken key memories away from his time in Judaea. His healing powers, have been indiscriminately diminished by his father."

I do not know where it came from, but one night as the sun was setting, I asked him about his past life in Judaea. There was an inspiring sunset that had captured our attention; we were both distracted, so the conversation was open and easy.

Yeshua, "I was meant to be crucified and die. It had been foretold; I expected it. It should have taken place. I stopped it. Sometimes my Father is annoyed with me about that; it comes up now and again. But I was not just a man and the decision was mine to make."

"Why is he angry that you lived? What good would have come of it if you were dead?"

"He understands you. He believes you are good for me. What you think and do also affects my Father's view and sometimes His care for all living things."

"What do *you* want to do?"

"There is no question; I want to live with you. Continue our travels. Take the potion." Yeshua stopped and drank some water as he gave the sack to me. "Maybe we should find that new place Armaigen spoke of. I told you that even my Father speaks of such a place."

"What will your father do?"

"It is what He will *not* do. I feel that He is trying to teach me another lesson."

"Has he said something? Is he listening to us right now?"

"Yes. He knows the words and thoughts of all creatures. He loves you and me."

"It a strange love. Are there are no statues or drawings of him? Describe him. How does he see?"

"He is like everyone and everything and not like anyone or anything."

"You sound like Armaigen. So, he could be tree? A horse? An ant? A rock in a river?"

"We see him in those things but he does not live there. The answer is a yes and a no. There are things even I question and don't understand after meeting you and Armaigen. How did you and Armaigen come upon me and my family in Rome? My Father must have wished it."

"We only spoke to Joseph."

"I travelled through Europa, as a young child with you, before I went back to Judaea one year later. I see my Father's hand in all of this. It is all those things and none of those things. Sometimes, I live through Him, sometimes He lives through me."

"Then the crucifixion was inevitable? I don't understand your father. You were young. Why would he want to harm you? My spirit world keeps it simple. I do not feel or see your father, but I should be able to, like you do."

"I was supposed to die for the forgiveness of sins."

"I don't understand your father. What is a sin? It is an absurd incongruity."

"Well, your spirit world is very complicated to me. Armaigen is more like me; he ascended as a child and lived as a man. I can't see or feel your spirits, yet there is really no difference between us. Sometimes, I feel childish and don't understand everything."

I looked at Yeshua. I don't know what came over me, the thought just came into my head. I had to ask him. I did not want to make him feel confronted or trapped, "Are you the son of god?"

"Do you feel that when you look at me?" He had spoken plainly as he continued to stare at the sun.

"I really don't know. I don't know what it means."

"I prefer to be called the spirit of man."

I asked Yeshua, "Are you a spirit or a man?"

Yeshua replied, "People have given me many names, but I am just a man who is a messenger of God. Are we not both messengers?"

I shook my head, confused, "I am a man, but I do not call myself a spirit of the earth. The earth spirits flow through me from all living things; sometimes it comes from Armaigen. But Armaigen would never call himself a god. I know you are a man, but I don't think your father knows what it is like to be a man."

Yeshua, "He knows very well what it is like to be a man. The problem is that man is sometimes treated unfairly by Him. He does not disguish between the young, the old, man or woman. He wants man to freely interpret one's action, hoping there will be some illumination of praise towards Him and the heavens. My struggle is that heaven is waiting for everyone, so why inflict pain into the hearts of man? I agree my Father has made it complicated and the earth spirits you speak of seem simple enough but I don't feel them like you. I want to live life, like any other man. I am afraid that my Father will never release me."

"Then you are not really living as a *man*, are you?"

"Just as much as you are a *drui* but will never be a Briton."

I will tell you one other story. Once, we met a well-travelled old man on the road. He was hungry and Yeshua fed him. He asked Yeshua whether he had ever been to Judaea or Galilea. Yeshua preferred not to speak too much of his past, but this man kept staring at him, wanting to touch his arm as he passed food around, trying to get his attention. He asked whether he could sit beside him as he ate. He told Yeshua that he looked exactly like someone he had met as a young boy, with his *own* father. That this man he had met played a lyre, sang songs, preached about love and forgiveness, but was crucified by the Romans. "There is a large following of this man. Many have been saved by him; he is a *God*. There was a rumour that he did not die."

Yeshua stared into the man's eyes not speaking; he had beautiful eyes that spoke for themselves.

Armaigen looked at Yeshua and told the man, "Yeshua is a warrior; see his sword? He is not a Drui like us, but here to protect us."

I was self-conscious and could not look at the old merchant. Armaigen quickly changed the subject, as he asked whether anyone desired more wine, ending the old man's interest.

Orin said that overall, she felt sorry for Yeshua, "I can understand why you say he is not happy. But he is happy in his own way; he is trying to be *happy*. His father is holding him back. Yeshua is not free like you and me. He is not even as free as the men his father rules over. It is a terrible dilemma. Why doesn't he just go away and start his own family? Find a new purpose and not be so alone."

"Well, he did go away once, for many years, but the life he sought was thwarted and destroyed. I will tell you the story from his point of view as it was told to Armaigen and I. It raises more questions than answers."

Chapter 40

BECAN

Armaigen was still alive and the three of us had been travelling for some time. We decided to stay longer in the forest, so that we could increase our food supplies. We built shelters and made sure our camp was placed in an area hidden from view.

We followed the same routine. Once we had settled on a location, Armaigen would drag his staff in a circular pattern around our camp, far beyond our immediate view. He would plant hemlock and primrose seeds in the furrow and talk to the plant spirits, encouraging the hemlock and the pretty primrose seeds to grow into full plants, overnight.

This was to prevent intruders and thieves from harming us. The beauty of the primrose was hard to resist and when combined with the hemlock, the scent would make one sleep for days.

It was early morning and we had finished our meal. Armaigen had gone off hunting for dinner. I was enjoying the warmth of the sun on my face as my clothes dried from the damp night. I had a hot drink, which was a welcome relief, for the previous days were wet and bleak.

Yeshua got up and kissed me tenderly on my lips; his affection washed over me. He had never kissed me before, not even on the cheeks. I was surprised and grateful at his show of affection, even though it would never be reciprocated.

I watched him in silence putting on his armour and his weapons. I did not say anything at first, for I felt good that day and was enjoying the moment. When he was finished, he turned and faced me, I said, "What are you doing?"

"I must go for a walk."

"But where? In all that armour? We are safe here." I knew he liked to walk in the forest alone for days at a time.

"I don't know."

"Is it your father?"

"No. This is for me."

Yeshua left that day and never came back. Armaigen was angry; I think it was the Irish in him.

We waited and searched for him, but eventually gave up. With the loss of Yeshua, we felt empty. He had been with us for many years after the crucifixion. Afterwards, as the years went by without him, we gave up hope of meeting him again and thought he was likely dead. It was dangerous to travel alone.

Nearly five years later, Yeshua returned to us and said he would never leave again; without telling us where he was going. One night, when all three of us were alone, he told us what had happened to him.

One day I needed to walk far away, very deep into the generous forest. I did not know why, but something was pulling me forward, drawing me away. I had brought no food. I could not stop walking, even when I slept or stopped for short moments, my legs would ache. Walking seemed to relieve the pain and kept me going. For one full moon, I walked without much food or water, living off the land.

I finally entered a small, poor, farming village. They had not seen anyone for some time. They were afraid of me at first, for the village had been raided so many times; family members had been killed for no reason at all. The villagers had nothing, but the worn clothes on their backs. But they still found a few scraps of food somewhere, which they offered me.

I have always wondered why innocent people are killed. That is not what I would allow if I were with my Father. That is likely why my Father allows me to stay on earth with you, for perhaps he hopes I will better understand what he does and thinks. I cannot ever see myself allowing indiscriminate suffering, pain and death.

I told the villagers that had gathered close to me that I meant them no harm. I was a tired traveller, coming a long distance and would pay for food. I went into the small inn.

A small boy would not leave me alone, and was holding onto my sleeve. I asked him whether he would take care of my armour and weapons.

Many villagers shouted, all agreeing, "You don't want *him*! He does not understand!"

Someone said, "I have a boy who can do it for you!"

The shouting annoyed me. I knew they wanted my money. I felt drawn to this small, simple boy who now stood closer to me. He was afraid. "What is your name?"

"BeBeBeeekan. My name is Bessan."

"I thought you said, Becan."

"Yeeas. Beeekan." He rubbed his tired eyes with his curled, warped fingers. "Taaaak mee hummm. Sissturr."

"Home?"

He held my hand with both hands, kissing my sleeve. He said, "Hummm. Hummm."

"I will." My eyes looked about the room. "Where does this boy live?"

Another man said, "He lives far away, they keep to themselves; their family is a strange lot. His father is a demon, and is not allowed in the village. We see his mother sometimes; the boy's hopeless, lost mostly. He will get himself killed one day!"

I had stopped listening from the moment the man began to speak. I looked at the boy. "Do you want something to eat?"

A woman shouted, "He doesn't want anything to eat, always scrounging; that mother of his should tie him up!"

I said calmly, "Let the boy answer for himself."

"He doesn't understand anything! You're wasting your time."

"Muummee."

Many said that I should not feed him with the food I was about to be served. They all agreed that the boy did not deserve to eat. He should go without. "Make him go away!"

Several went to pull him away, thinking he was annoying me, but he was not.

"No! He stays." I looked everyone in the eyes and they stopped talking.

The Innkeeper served me many types of warm food and drink. I was in full armour. As I took it off, the villagers became more relaxed and trusting in my presence.

The whole village crowded into the inn. A blazing fire lit up the room. It felt good, for I had not been with anyone for some time. I always enjoyed having people around me. I sat and ate in silence as everyone watched me chew and swallow; I washed it down with wine.

Many asked questions about where I had come from, and whether I had seen the Romans or thieves on the road.

I assured them that I had not seen anyone. I told them that for now, they were all safe and was sure that if anyone came to the village, it would not be for another moon.

Becan was sitting down on the floor beside me, with my armour on top of his outstretched legs. He was holding as much as he could with his short chubby arms, plump hands and stout fingers.

I gave him some meat and milk. He was hungry and ate holding the food with both hands, for his fingers were not long enough to use one hand only.

Soon, I stood up, ready to go and thanked everyone for their kind hospitality. The owner told me that I did not have to pay for some reason. This did not surprise me, for it had been happening most of my life. I still left a generous tip.

As Becan stood up, he dropped the sword and maille. Some of the knives clattered and spun across the floor. I told Becan that I would get carry anything heavy. I asked him to pick up the knives and slide them into his belt. He was confused, so I helped him.

The villagers laughed. "I told you. He is no good to anyone."

I bent down and whispered. "Don't listen. You are perfect just the way you are. Show me where you live. I will take you home."

"Fooorist. Ththiiiiisssweehhh."

We left the village together.

Behind, I heard several people shout, "His father is Balor! You will be sorry. People die because of him."

Tiernan stopped retelling the story and said to Orin, "I asked Yeshua who Balor was and he said he would tell me later as he continued telling us the story."

Yeshua explained, "I did not listen to the villagers, for their words were full of anger. I looked at Becan's eyes. I saw what I wanted to see. I knew I had made the right choice.

Most of our walk was in a forest, far away from the village, along a narrow path with Becan limping in the lead; I enjoyed listening to him talk to all the plants and trees by name. I asked often whether we were going in the right direction and all he would say is, "Muummee heeer."

It was getting late and we had walked a great distance. The sun was falling below the horizon; a sleepy darkness fell and the leaves began to close their eyes. I asked my Father to keep the light of the sun shining on the forest and it became day again.

Up ahead, I saw lights through the trees and, surprisingly, I left the forest and entered a huge, open meadow, with full, soft, flowing wheat that appeared ready for harvest. It was an unearthly paradise, for I smelled warm bread in the summer air. I noticed off to the side a fresh grave.

Becan pointed and said, "Daaddeee. Daaddeee."

Becan ran further into the field. I knew he had recognized something or someone.

I saw a woman in the middle of the field, holding a lamp up high, and I caught a glimpse of her golden face. There was a small girl shouting out Becan's name.

Becan ran and all you could see was the top of his head moving about the stalks of wheat, as he plowed through the grain. His mother hugged him as she spun him around into the air with his sister jumping up and down, by her side. He pointed back at me as I came closer, still carrying my breastplate and armour in front of my chest with both hands.

Becan slithered down to the ground and pulled his mother's hands towards where I was standing.

As I stood close to Becan's mother, we did not move but stared into each of our eyes. Her eyes had flecks of silver. There was nothing to be said. We both seemed to silently drift away, our eyes drained, the heat running through our souls to a secret and private place, where only the essence of each of us lived.

Elestrem, Becan's mother, quickly turned away as I began to smile. She looked back at me as she hugged Becan, not sure of me, and sneaked another peek as she giggled. Her giggling made me laugh. She smiled and inhaled a deep satisfying breath as Becan's sister, Rozenwyn hugged my legs.

I couldn't help myself, as Elestrem offered her hand to me, and I felt the warmth of her skin. In this place, there were no social or cultural rules. I told her that she was beautiful and that I would never leave her. She told me right then that she would always love me. I could not believe it. I have never known the freedom of such honest, true emotions. We both knew that our feelings had been cut in stone, during some ancient time before we were born.

My head felt light and throughout my soul I felt an exhilarating happiness. I told her that I fall in love fast, but I would always make her happy. I knew nothing about her, but I knew it was right. She told me that we would have a lifetime to learn about each other. I thought how she would react when she knew who I really was. Becan took his mother's hand; Rozenwyn took mine as I held onto Elestrem's hand and we walked together as a new family to the cottage. My Father allowed the sun to sleep and it became dark."

Yeshua, "I lived a wonderful life, for four harvests; Elestrem grew more radiant every day. She was an innocent, free-spirit flying about and through all living things. I did not want to be anywhere else but there. There was no point, for our family was so happy. I had buried my weapons and my previous life."

I asked Yeshua, "Did you have children with her?"

"No. We both wanted children. I think my Father had something to do with it, for we were both very healthy. I asked my Father to let us have children, but there was no response. We made beautiful love whenever we could. We were so perfect together and despite not having children, I still thanked my Father for the gift of Elestrem.

I had made up my mind never to follow my Father into heaven; the responsibility was too much for me. I had nothing now to contribute. I had seen what heaven was like. My present life could not be any better. I was living a kind and loving life, free of tragedy. It was so natural and so good. We were all Becan's.

Many days we would all be working the fields, subdued by the yellow, golden wheat and blue skies. Every day, I desired the salty sweat of Elestrem on my lips, sometimes it was all too much to take, but it was real, and I was blessed.

It did not matter that there were so many jobs to be done, for at night all of us would sit outside during the warm summer and talk about anything and nothing. The simplest things would make us laugh.

Every day, both of our bodies seemed to be drenched in a sensual scent; Elestrem and I could smell each other across the fields. Distance never separated us, as our powerful hearts were beating as one; we both felt our lungs swallow the shared air.

When the children were safe and asleep, we would walk naked in the fields or the forest, sometimes down by the warm stream. We would lie looking up at the stars through the unmoving branches; I'm sure my Father knew where we were, for our sinless love likely reminded him of the beginning of the earth itself.

Sometimes, I would sing many songs. Her favorite was a song I wrote called '*Greensleeves*.' Elestrem would question me about my life in Judaea and I would tell her as many details and parables that my Father has allowed me to remember. I would speak of Armaigen and Tiernan and tell her of the earth spirits.

Elestrem would tell me of her young, simple and modest life growing up on the farm before her parents had died. Nuada showed up one day. He was lost and the villagers had told him he was not welcome and he left. She was not afraid and never judged anyone."

Orin, "Who was Nuada?"

"Nuada was Balor. But there was no Balor; the real Balor is a death demon. Balor only existed in the minds of the villagers. Nuada was a kind, wounded warrior who had fought the Romans somewhere. His face was disfigured. He had one leg and could see out of only one eye. Elestrem took him in, gave him unconditional love and they had two children, Rozenwyn and Becan. Nuada died of a fever just before I had met her."

Yeshua, "One day, after the fourth harvest, Becan and I went into the village to sell some grain, barter goods and pick up some supplies. It was going to be a short trip. The villagers had accepted me through time. I think they felt safe knowing a warrior lived near them; I was still a mystery to them and many distanced themselves from me. My relationship with the village was mainly business. They were a suspicious people but there was a rumour that since my arrival, prosperity had returned to the village; due to great harvests. Many gave me credit for it.

Looking back, I remembered that strange, cloudy day. Some villagers had guilty, blank stares on their faces; no one could look me in the eye. They all avoided my presence. It was as if something bad had happened, which they had no control over. It was unusual and I felt a need to get back to the farm as soon as possible.

One known trouble maker in the village, called Borvo, made me feel odd and uncomfortable, as he sat drinking inside the inn. He gave me a smirk and quickly looked away shaking a bag of coins. He shouted for more service.

I was just finishing a cold cup of mead and Becan was patiently waiting to sip a little that I always left for him at the bottom of the cup.

Borvo's eyes were small slanted orbs; it was the wistful smile of a cynic. I knew his present position was connected to me somehow; he knew something that I did not know. It alarmed me for some reason. There was some sort of a power he held over me.

It was strange, for this man was not a member of the village or loyal to it. I did not know him but knew of him. He only seemed to appear when he wanted something and he would usually do a poor job at anything he attempted.

We returned home at sunset. There was no one at the farm. The cottage lamps had not been lit. I searched everywhere; my natural instincts as a man took over and my heart was pounding. I ran about in a panic.

Becan told me to stop and look at all the bees on the flowers in the garden, near the front door.

The cottage had been ransacked by someone looking for something, but we had nothing.

I did find blood on some stone near the fireplace; I thought the worst. I did not tell Becan, but knew I must go and find our family.

I searched for my weapons and dug them up under the earth in a barn stall. I thanked my Father that everything was still there. I unfolded the cloths. I did not realize that I had so many weapons.

At that moment, I had a feeling that I would never see them again; life would never be the same. I feared that I was going to return to my old life before Elestrem. I was fuming, like a trapped thoroughbred. I could not think straight, as I knew that I was faster and stronger than any other animal, but my very soul was consumed and seething with anger.

Then my Father spoke to me. I was surprised, for I had not heard from him since I lived on the farm. He told me a group of cold-blooded men had visited the farm. I saw the images of their faces. I thought of Borvo back at the inn.

I walked out of the barn in my armour. Becan was impressed; he told me I looked taller. His presence reminded me that I could not leave him here alone. I would have to take him with me.

I knew that whoever had taken Elestrem and Rozenwyn did not head back to the village, for I had just come from there. There was only one path in the other direction and I was going to take that path and bring them home.

This next part is important. For the journey with Becan made me understand inadvertently that my Father should have made all men the same as Becan.

So early the next morning, before the sun, we started our journey.

I took Becan's hand and told him not to worry.

"Whaare r weee goeeen"

"We are going to find your mother and sister."

"Whaare r thaaa"

"I don't know."
"Wiii haaav thaaa gooon awaaay"
"They have been taken."
"Thaaa wi beee laaat fooo soupper. It waaas hott biscuttts steeew toonigh."
"Yes."
"Nooo stooree toonigh"
"No."
"Woo tooc theeem"
"Men. Strangers."
"Wiii?"
"Because that's what they do."
"Thaaa wi miiis mee. Rozenwyn doos noot liiik thaa daarc."
"I will find them."
"Whaaa yoo doo"
"Not sure. It depends."
"Will yoo huur theem"
"Why do you ask such things?"
"Yoo haav kiivves swoor."
"Those are to protect us."
"Tee boos iin tee vaage hiit mee. Poossh mee doon. Sii oon mee tiil I crrii."
"When?"
"Ween u arrr noo arooon."

I felt so sorry for Becan for he was becoming tired from speaking so much and trying to get the words out. He did, however, live in the moment, forgetting the importance of anything I said.

That was his way, as he would sometimes change his thoughts to a completely different subject.

I slowed down and picked him up in my arms; he needed a rest as he could not walk as fast as me. He was pleased and played with my beard and long hair. We walked more without anything being said, as he fell asleep on my shoulder. He was an innocent, harmless boy, much like the person my Father wanted us all to be without His help.

I wondered why we could not all just be Becan's, for it would be so easy giving praise freely to the heavens and the beauty of the earth.

I kissed him and he woke up. I told him he was perfect, to not worry. We would find his mom and Rozenwyn.

"Yoo sahhd ammm puurfecc."

"You are."

"Noou yoo r puurfecc."

"No."

"Maaak mee ike yoo."

I lifted Becan down. I stood there looking at his face and body. I stroked his face and he looked up and said nothing. I knew I *could* do it, but *should* I do it? My Father knew what I was thinking and told me not to change him. I just had to do it, and I placed both hands on Becan's head. "Close your eyes, my son. Think of my face. Do not open your eyes until I say."

"Isssss itt ah sirprhiisss?"

"Yes, A big surprise." I waited for a few moments and felt many changes occur. I felt weary and hoped that my anger would not affect the outcome; I told Becan to open his eyes.

Becan opened his eyes and staggered slightly. He touched his face and smiled as he looked at his hands, turning them about.

"What have you done?"

"Given you what you wanted."

"The air tastes different. I can stand up straight. I am almost as tall as you. The plants and flowers are not as bright."

"Take deep breaths. Now sit. Here. Have some water." I got out some food.

I kneeled beside him, for I could not sit with all my armour and weapons.

"I have so much to ask you. I suddenly feel alone, very lonely. It is not the same as before."

"I'm here. Have some bread. Slowly, eat slowly and we will be on our way when you are ready. Take these two knives; I have many."

"What are they for?"

"If a man or men comes towards you, pull them out and hold them like this." I stood up and showed him the solid stance and the different directions he could be attacked. "These are bad men. They will hurt you, but be not afraid, for I am beside you."

"I don't know what to do. I have this feeling of loneliness that I have never had before. I am afraid."

"They won't know it. They can't read your mind. Just delay them until I can help you. Attack only if someone attacks you. Protect yourself. I will go to your mother or sister if they are in trouble."

"Like what?"

"If you see that they are being hurt, or are going to be hurt, come up from behind them. You should only scare them, and then run away; I will take care of the men."

Becan touched the sharp points of the knives. "You stab people with these? What does it feel like?"

"It's like poking a stick into a wet, rotten log. Push hard, and do not pull it out. Keep stabbing, don't stop and imagine you are killing a poisonous adder. Close your eyes and God will guide your hands."

We remained there resting in silence but I knew Becan was thinking of many questions, as he pulled leaves off plants, rubbing them between his fingers. He dragged a worm out of the ground, brushing the dirt off, stretching it and watching it go back into the ground.

I told him that from this point on, I would lead. We would follow the path, but he should be ready to hide and run. With each step, he was to be careful of anything he saw or heard. If he felt, or saw anything unusual, he was to let me know right away, without hesitation. I told him we should see these dangerous men by nightfall or sooner.

We walked and talked softly through the quiet forest.

"What is death?"

"You are too young to ask such things."

"You have knives, a sword and a shield."

"I don't mean to kill."

"But you kill deer and rabbits."

"That is different."
"Have you killed men before?"
"Yes. Many."
"Why?"
"To protect myself and innocent people."
"Is killing the same as a person dying?"
"Yes."
"How?"
"To kill is the act, dying is the result."
"Can you die first, and then be killed?"
"You can die, but then there is no need to kill."
"But if *you* die, do we all die?"
"Yes. In a way, but we continue to live."
"I don't understand."
"My Father is in heaven. When you die, you go to His house."
"Why can't I stay in my own house? Your father can stay with us."
"He can't."
"Why?"
"He is God. When you die, you go to heaven to be with my Father."
"Nuada was my father. Why do I have to live with your father?"
"You just do."
"Why can't I live with my mother, my sister and you?"
"They will be there. You ask too many questions."
"Most of it does not make sense."
"When you are dead, you are rewarded."
"I was sick before and now I am well; I don't feel I will ever die. Will the bad men we meet be rewarded?"
"Everyone is rewarded."
"That is wrong. Bad men should just go away like they never existed; erased from all memory."
"The sick become well again. The bad and evil men will sit in judgement in front of my Father."
"Is your father dead?"

"No."

"Why? How did he get to heaven?"

"He is the beginning and the end. He can never die."

"Are you a god?"

"No. I am the spirit of all men and my Father sometimes thinks and acts through me. Most times he leaves me alone to live and think for myself."

"It is not right. The good should never die; it has no meaning. Your father should live on our farm. It would be so much easier."

"Heaven is a place, just like our farm."

"I still don't understand."

"Heaven is the reward."

"It troubles me if all this is true. Before you changed me, I was happy and good. Today, I might kill someone. Why do we have all these rules?"

"My Father is trying to teach us all a lesson, to grow and become good by our own efforts, in the image of him."

"But he does not kill like you?"

"I am not exactly sure what my Father does or has planned. He does not kill in the meaning of how we use the word. He allows killing and death. He is full of surprises. I don't accept everything."

"Wouldn't it be easier and right to keep all the good people living? And if your father is as powerful as you say he is, why does he not just reject all evil, abolish it for good? People by nature, I am sure, appreciate everything life can offer. Evil and greed gets in the way. It all seems very complicated, made up with a series of rules."

"I understand what He believes. That does not mean I agree with Him. I pray to my Father about it, but He always has the same answer."

"I'm sorry, Yeshua, you are a kind, loving father, and even in you there is this vengeance side that quickly comes over you. I feel you are looking forward to meeting these bad men and killing them."

"You are very perceptive. In your new body and mind, remember not all is bad but sometimes we must punish those who for no reason, hurt other people. Revenge does consume me sometimes. We all have a lot of things we must deal with, some very troublesome as we get older."

"How does your father feel about that?"

"He does not agree."

"I still don't see the point. If there was no evil, there would be no trouble. You and mom have always fed us and kept us warm. I am happy with my family. I don't want to go anywhere. It would never be the same."

"God made the world and the heavens above, the seen and the unseen."

"Am I a god?"

"You are the image of God. But you must never act like a God for that is a sin."

"What is a sin?"

"Anything that goes against the divine law of God."

"Why can't god take away free will? Then we will not need any laws."

"Humans by nature are born with free will."

"My mom, sister and you had free will at the farm and everything was good. Before you changed me, I had free will and I was happy."

I wanted to change the topic. "Think of something else you would like to be."

"Can be a King one day?"

"Yes. But be a humble King."

"It all seems like the rules of god have been given to men or maybe powerful men on earth, have given them to god to keep us weak and uncertain."

"All we can do is pray and hope."

"But that is not the point."

I heard the snarling and supressed breathing of many men over the next ridge. It was late and the sun was beginning to submerge. We stopped and listened; it was the animal laughter of men. I knew they were the men I was hunting for.

I led Becan quickly off the path in a direction far away from the men. We walked up a slight hill. It had thick dense bushes, many old trees, distorted branches and large thick unreasonable trunks.

Becan climbed the tallest tree to see whether his mother and sister were there. I told him to count how many men were there. Becan came down after he had studied and assessed the location of his mother and sister. He drew a map on the ground. Both his mother and sister were tied up to posts; they appeared to be sleeping. There was a fire lit and he had counted five men. Many appeared drunk; all were sitting.

I moved slowly towards the camp, with Becan close behind. I checked the placement of the knives in the straps of my belt. I had unsheathed my sword and I tightly gripped my shield. I told Becan not to run; he was to walk behind me. We would walk towards his mother and sister, calmly. I would tell him what to do; he was to keep close by my side.

I knew once the men saw me they would attack but I did not see a reason to tell Becan. I walked into the camp like a tribal Chieftain. I took a quick glance at Elestrem and Rozenwyn; dirty and unmoving. With each killing step, men became startled and afraid, seeing an armed man appear from nowhere. There was no escape. They knew they would have to fight me. My piercing eyes, from under my helmet, selected the order I would kill, as my hot rage grew thirsty for death.

The men shouted and ran looking for their weapons or anything to defend themselves. I stepped forward and went after the closest man. I knew they would eventually come at me from all directions.

Becan was caught up in the moment and did not obey my instructions; he became a temporary distraction for me. He could not resist, as he ran to his mother and sister. I now saw that Elestrem and Rozenwyn had been stripped half-naked. Becan was draping the clothes on the ground back around their shoulders as he nervously wept, trying to cover them up, as he spoke to them. I was worried about his safety.

I don't think I have ever been as mad and furious as I was at that moment. There was no God. I felt my life and all my dreams had been destroyed. It felt worse than the crucifixion. I would not only kill the men responsible, but kill them without pity; break them. I was pleased and knew that it was going to feel good. They did not deserve to live any longer.

I was startled and jumped, as I heard a scream coming from an unknown direction; I turned my head and saw a big, brawny man running at me, holding his sword over his head. My sword moved cleverly by itself. I sliced his chest open. He dropped to the ground. I was overcome with a furious revenge. Who was next?

One by one, each man fell, bloodied onto the earth. I could not stop, as I went on the attack. I felt I was a God and did not have to breathe. Arms, chests, shoulders, eyes – it did not matter for they were now all dead; deformed flesh and bones. I walked around to each man again, stabbing and chopping away, until they were unrecognizable; like butchered meat. I enjoyed being covered in blood.

I had forgotten momentarily about my family!

I did not care that these men were all children once; at that moment, forgiveness would have been a sin. Becan was right, it did not make sense that evil men exist on earth.

I went to Elestrem and Rozenwyn. Becan was crying, shaking them to awake but could not; I knew they were both dead.

Unexpectedly, a tall heavy man, face and chest tattooed, appeared out of the forest charging at me, screaming. My back was to him as I was on my knees. The grief had over taken me. He had been hiding, waiting for the right moment.

I had already dropped my sword and I had just kissed Elestrem, stroking her hair, thinking, why would my Father let this happen?

Becan saw him first, coming towards us, at a full run. He stood up and held his arms out, shaking as he held the knives, like I had taught him; protecting my back.

It was so quick. The warrior slashed his sword across Becan's hands, knocking the knives away. He cried out. I was reaching over to grab my sword, but by the time I stood up to face him, the murderer had thrust his sword through Becan's chest.

I stepped towards the sickening coward and felt the power of my strong arms. I parried, pushing him back, again and again, playing with him, wanting to delay the moment of death, for I was enjoying it. His eyes were full of fear; he knew he did not have the skill to defeat me. I asked him, over and over – 'why, why did you do this?' His fat, sweaty face was disgusting. He stumbled back and away, off balance. His sword was down and he had given up. I could not take his presence any longer. Then, with one powerful stroke, I took his head off like a sickle through a soft stalk of wheat.

I ran back to Becan, wiping the blood coming out of his mouth and cradled his head in my arms.

Within an arm's length, Elestrem and Rozenwyn were dead, folded over, half-coiled and misshapen.

I knew I would never meet anyone like Elestrem or Rozenwyn again. I would bring them back to life, just as I had done before with Lazarus. I leaned over and touched their heads, charging it to be done. My Father then interrupted my command and told me that He would not allow it! I cursed Him as I looked over to Becan's small bloodied face. I cursed my Father again! I told Him that this was *my* family; Elestrem was *my* wife.

What kind of a Father takes a loving life away? I pleaded with Him for the return of my power, yet He still refused. It seemed that my Father desired me to walk on two legs, like everyone else on earth. My mind and body was all I had; all anyone has.

He asked me to understand that miracles were sacred and would show more meaning to a man who has faith. My father was punishing me, I could not believe it!

My Father told me He was angry that I had cursed Him. He said that He would let one person live and that I must make the decision of who that would be.

How could He say this to me? My Father was truly uncaring! Why should one life be saved, when it was so easy to save all three? It was not their fault; they were all so innocent.

Becan gasped, as more blood streamed down his small chin. I went to him, holding him in my arms as I cried.

Becan whispered, "If there was no evil, I would not be dying."

I leaned over and kissed him. "I know. My son, you saved my life. I can heal you and you can live with me forever at the farm."

"There is no forever. I love you. I feel lonely here since you changed me. Everything is pale, dark and without colour. Say goodbye to my mom and Rozenwyn; I love them. Tell them not to be sad." He turned his head to one side, seemingly confused as he looked for them. "Where are they? Tell them to come."

Becan was fading away. He asked me, "Change me back to the way I was. I want to die like that. I was never lonely there. I saw and could feel so many beautiful flowers. I was safe there with my mom and sister."

"I will give you your wish and change you back. I love you, Becan. Close your eyes and imagine my face." I held my hand on his head and he became the old Becan. His eyes slowly opened and he smiled, touching my face with his stubby fingers.

I could have saved Becan. But I knew in my heart that none of my family could live without each other. I could not either.

"Aaaamm hoomm nooow; haappii."

"My Father is wrong, like you said, my dear, dear son." I kissed him on the cheek.

"Loouve yoou miiii plaaass izzz baahahterr." He took a breath, sighing out as he smiled, taking his secret with him as he died.

I untied Elestrem and Rozenwyn. I got them all dressed, making sure their hair was nice and flat, just as they liked it. I washed their faces with warm water. I was sobbing so much I could not see what I was doing. We all huddled together for one last night in the forest, away from the evil men. All the bodies of my family remained with me until the sun rose the next day.

My Father was silent. He knew I was still angry with Him; my connection with Him changed that day. Our closeness became a hesitant greeting, not one out of respect. I called my angels to come down from heaven and take the souls of my family to heaven.

I thought of Becan wanting to stay in his own house.

That night, the angels stood around us in a circle, facing out with their swords pointed down into the earth; all in mourning."

Orin interrupted, "What are angels?"

"Spirit messengers from the sky. I'll explain later."

"The angels emitted a soft, comforting, blue light. It reassured Yeshua that his family was safe now, filled with the Holy Spirit. He joked that he was sure that Becan would question his father on why evil existed at all, that is, if he had father."

Yeshua continued, "In the morning, I left the dead men where they were; sunken, airless bodies. I saw ravens sitting in the trees, waiting for me to go; I knew the birds would take their eyes out. They would suffer a sightless despair. I was told from my Father during my early ministry in Judaea that when evil men die they enter this first house to account for their sins. Even though I did not preach or speak of it. He said that when evil men die, they suffer a perpetual fear of the dark. It is a crowded place, full of people like themselves, crawling all over each other naked, feeling sick with the desire to consume anything, even all physical temptations. They suffer a mental madness tormented by their past evil deeds. It is a soulless desolation; you cannot breathe properly, always gasping for air. I found out that these people do eventually get to heaven, but I have no idea how or when."

I thought of Becan saying that everything was too complicated.

I placed my dear and loving Elestrem, Rozenwyn and Becan in the wagon belonging to the men I had killed. I called my angels to walk with me. I did not want to be alone. I could not think of anything or anyone but the three innocent bodies behind me as I led the horse. My Father wanted to speak with me but I told Him to stop.

As I approached the farm, I imagined my family walking the same earth that I was standing on. All they had ever wanted was to be loved. I found a nice place in the wheat field, where there was plenty of sun. I buried them in one grave so that they would always be together.

That night, I slept peacefully on their graves looking up at the stars and wondered what they were doing. I felt they were looking down at me.

I stayed living on the farm for three days. On the last day, I washed in our river and dressed for battle, again. I said my goodbyes as the sun dropped from the sky as I left slowly on my horse. I thought about burning the house and the barn but felt there had been enough destruction. Let the farm live, for Becan had said that he wanted all of us to live together, as a family. Before I took one last look, I said a prayer and saw Elestrem, Rozenwyn and Becan waving to me, as they stood in front of the cottage.

My Father said nothing, but my family told me not to be angry. We would all be together one day. Elestrem and Rozenwyn were still confused at where they were; Becan only smiled and told me he would explain everything to them.

I arrived in the sleepy village at full gallop. I pulled up on the reins and led the horse around all the old buildings, letting my presence known; saying nothing. Many villagers appeared in small pockets and were alarmed that I was there. Some ran away, while others huddled for comfort, for they knew who I was looking for.

They were all guilty, to some degree, of the attack on our farm. They had done nothing to warn Elestrem or me. I tried to calm myself, but could not. I dismounted and went into the inn. I knew Borvo was there. As I pushed the door open, I saw the worthless shit.

"Borvo!" I walked to him without stopping.

It was early and he was eating a morning meal. Many dirty bowls and plates were spread out in front of him. There was a foul woman close by who quickly left him alone. He cut his tongue on the knife he was feeding himself with and stood up cursing. He could not see me clearly at first. He spat out the food in his mouth as he touched his lips, soaked with blood. He looked at me like he had seen a ghost; terror and panic riddled his face.

I was surprised he was still in the village, since he was not well-liked. I suppose it was the money he was spending that made the poor villagers do nothing.

He knew why I was there, "I can explain." He shrugged his large, round shoulders, holding his arms out, "Men came here looking for a woman. I said nothing, I swear!"

I looked at the bag of coins on the table as I pulled out my sword. He moved back and away, as I took the purse and scattered the coins across the floor.

"Did you not think that I would not come back?"

It was nearly dark and the sun pierced the odd-shaped openings through the wooden walls.

There was no place to run as he looked behind and around me, wanting to make a move. I easily blocked his way as he moved about. He panicked and was alone. His knife was no match for my sword. Long, thin slivers of light filtered through to the dark room.

Borvo told me it would be murder if I killed him! He said there were witnesses.

I stopped. I was distracted by all the dust and dirt that was hanging in the air between Borvo and me. The light of the morning sun was holding it up. I played with the floating dust with the point of my sword. It reminded me of the lives of people trying to survive and how we are all so small.

Borvo looked at me strangely, not knowing what I was doing.

"Did you hear me? The villagers know you!"

I spoke casually, not looking at him as I continued to play with the air and the dust, "I do not see anyone. You killed my family. I *will* kill you."

I stopped moving the particles about, wondering why I was there, why I was living at all; I could not come up with a good answer.

Borvo moved back and away from me. "No. No. I beg you. You will be hanged."

I stared at him, giving a slight smile. "That will not happen."

He gave me a curious look. He knew death was moments away.

I looked him in the eye. I thought of my beautiful Elestrem, precious Rozenwyn and simple Becan. I said to him, "Becan was right; you should have never been born."

"Becan? I know of no such man!"

"He is not a man, but a beautiful boy."

My sword easily pierced his flabby, weak chest. He could not move as he shook; his hands touched my blade, and then his arms dropped by his sides. I watched life abandon his eyes. I quickly withdrew the sword, releasing him, as his worthless body collapsed to the floor.

I walked away without regret and left the building. More villagers had gathered outside. I told all present that the coins were to be shared evenly in the village with the poor; for food, not drink. There was a rush past me, for many went inside at that moment and searched for the coins on the floor. I warned them that I would return and make sure it was done.

As I rode away, I cried as I thought of my family. I heard someone shout out, "Balor!" I wanted to go back and see who had said it, perhaps even kill them, but I did not. It was just a word, for Balor does not exist.

Without my family, I was nothing. I cried throughout the first year. Everything seemed to remind me of my family. Whenever I saw a child like Becan, or woman who looked like Elestrem or Rozenwyn I would feel sick. I miss the days we spent together, working in the fields under the sun and swimming in the river.

My Father tells me that Becan is happy; I am not sure what to believe anymore. I will never forgive Him for what he took away from me; it was a perfect love and life. Why would He deny me this?

I never returned to the village again.

PART III

Chapter 41

DOLPHINS

I wondered whether my journey was over or just beginning.

Three years ago, in Pergamon, Greece, I cured Consul Gaius Suetonius Paulinus from certain death. As a reward, I was appointed as his personal physician. My brothers, Sorranus and Eolus, came with me, as well as my best friend Abrux and his wife Glenna.

I quickly gained a reputation of being the greatest physician Rome had ever witnessed. But it was not hard, for Sorranus continued to increase his medical skills under my guidance as Eolus enjoyed his position as a permanent physician-in-training. Abrux and Glenna opened a school and many children from notable Roman families sent their children there to be educated. We had established a new life for all of us. It was a good life in terms of physical comforts but we continued to feel like foreign temporary residents.

Romans would never introduce or speak of us as being a *Roman* but always included the word 'Greek' or 'Greece' in our names. I would be called, 'Galen from Greece' or this is 'Galen, the Greek'. My family and I were treated well but we never felt Rome was our home. Refusing to speak Latin did not help. Paulinus assigned an interpreter, who followed me about all day, except when I was in surgery.

I held myself responsible for our lack of stability, I told Sorranus, Abrux and Glenna my story of the three strangers and the potion. Of course, they were all shocked, except Sorranus who knew something was going on with my young physical appearance. They all agreed to take the potion and knew that they likely were going to Britannia one day.

We did not feel Eolus was ready for the truth but that he should be allowed to take the potion. So each of us, on different days, each week, we would secretly take the potion. Except Eolus, who I personally gave it to, telling him it was to supplement his vitamin intake. He told me it made him feel stronger.

I met with the glib Emperor Nero, when he was in Rome, almost every day. Paulinus did not mind me spending so much time with him, for he was an ambitious man. Besides, I used my new-found influence to design advanced medical equipment using the local Roman craftsmen.

Nero was an average-sized man, with a chubby face and a large belly. He was very young and overweight. I enjoyed his company, even though I knew he was corrupt and prone to compulsive behaviour. He treated me well and was always interested in watching me dissect pigs, sheep, and monkeys. Once, he had me dissect a cat and laughed afterwards. Later, I found out it was one of his own cats that roamed the palace. However, much to the frustration of the existing Roman medical establishment, he continued to give me the support to speak and publish my anatomical reports regarding the circulatory system, the heart as a pumping muscle and how the brain controlled bodily movement.

I never talked to him about his physical condition being a liability, increasing his chance of an early death. His bodily sweating was a concern, for his 'corpus ordour' was a common hidden complaint for those who worked closely with him. He never bathed regularly. Sometimes it was difficult to inhale a breath around him. I did my best in suggesting perfume-scented baths, but he took this to the extreme by having his clothes washed in aromatic oils and issuing an edit that everyone around him must be scented, including his guards and pets. It was extreme, but a temporary situation. According to my journals, I knew he would commit suicide in 68CE. In fact, he was too scared to kill himself, so he had his secretary do it for him.

Paulinus told me I was one of his best friends. I was not, but played along with him; he was just an obscure acquaintance. I was grateful that he was helping me fulfill the prophesy, but I knew our relationship, one day, would be over. Besides he was a *Roman*.

We all did not have to wait too long for there was another tribal revolt in Britannia!

Paulinus was promoted by Nero to be the new Governor of Britannia and assigned to conquer the barbaric tribes, once and for all. Barrius remained a Legion Legate and was to accompany Paulinus to Britannia. When I received word of this I acted fast, meeting with Paulinus, urging him to take me and my physicians with him. He was not a superstitious man but knew that I could help save the lives of his men with my medical knowledge.

I was finally in Britannia. I stood on the shore watching across the straits, studying the Britons and Druids, in between the middle of two Roman legions. I was searching for Tiernan and Yeshua. I still did not know how I was going to save the earth.

The Roman army and the distant island of Ynys Mon were smothered in flash lightning; no wind, sound or rain. Jagged red and yellow brush strokes, heavily repeated, dragging long bright quick flicks of passion in the sky, as if marked by the gods. It was a sign of something strange to most, but not yet defined to me.

Paulinus had fought throughout Britannia. His reputation of slaughtering entire tribes was well-known. The tribal rebellion had seemingly been stopped but not destroyed. There was still much anger and hatred towards the Romans. Britannia was still not a safe province for the Romans.

Before I had even stepped on this wet island, Rome had previously tried to invade this barbaric and pagan land. I was not thoroughly aware of earth spirits but very curious on how this would play out. What a queer and odd race; it was like stepping on Mars for the first time. So many battles had been fought, won and lost against the Britons through the years. There would be no more Druids. Simple circles would be replaced by golden eagles, black and red squares; everything real and imagined would be drawn at unimaginative right angles.

Paulinus had taken two of his three legions and placed them opposite the island of Ynys Mon. The remaining legion was stationed near Londinium. It was to await orders from Governor Paulinus.

I was sure of one detail. The Romans would have their final victory soon. Logic and analysis were everything to me. I had recently witnessed vast resources of men and equipment brought to this island that I had never seen before, even against the people of Gallia Lugdunensis before we crossed the water from Europa.

General Seutonius Paulinus, Governor of Britannia, seemed surprised as he hurried out of his tent and was the last to join his officers and aides. He was assisted to his saddle and nudged his giant warhorse forward. He was surrounded by his commanders and officers. It was the same routine as always.

Paulinus's personal guard of elite, blacked-robed legionnaires provided an ominous wall of protection around him.

With his new, elevated status as Governor, Paulinus became progressively prone to irrational outbursts, as his increased authority amplified his pride. His reputation had been established upon prior events in his career; he quickly became a warrior to be feared. He was famous for his butchery, fast victories in Egypt and being the first Roman to cross the Atlas Mountains.

As the Governor of Britannia, he wiped out any tribe who did not accept or conform to Roman values. He believed that he could not be killed for he was undefeated in battle. He was favored by some unknown god.

I stood apart from the Roman officers, as was my way. It was healthy to keep your distance, for you could think more clearly. Like a tortoise without a shell, I stretched my neck viewing the land and people on the other side. I knew that the Romans would go no further than Britannia, for this province would be the permanent western boundary of the known world, for hundreds of years until their tragic collapse.

Where were Tiernan and Yeshua?

I could have ignored the call from the three strangers. I suppose I could had been a follower of Buddha, and lived a happy, penniless life. But the potion was working. I could have selected, with my vast knowledge of the future, many multiple, strange and comfortable lives. However, I was being pulled here by some natural force that I could not explain. It was an interesting feeling, my overflowing emotions filled me with anticipation to finally have all this drama acted out, like the climax in the final act of most Shakespearean plays.

And, although I knew the history of the Romans, I was unaware of my life being recorded in any history book or being important at all. It certainly made me excited to see how all these events were going to develop. Where was I in all this? What was I going to do that was so special and important?

Up until this moment, I would have thought everything to be logical and predictable. Joy and pain exist to varying degrees; that is all. Somehow, I felt a part of a certain mystery. The thunder and lightning without rain was strange, as I watched the primitive Druids run around half-naked on the other side, shouting hollow insults at the Romans as they shook their shields and spears.

My mind was now like a full sack of wheat, ready to split open. Every one of my seeds had an important story to tell. In my heart, I knew it was time to harvest the knowledge that had grown. I should be happy, but I felt sick; nauseated with a selfish excitement.

I heard Paulinus and the officers' snigger as they made crude comments about fucking all the women they could find. God, I was so tired of them.

⁂

The active murmur of 10,000 crowded men preparing for battle surrounded me; they were scared as their nervous anger mocked their mental insecurity. Everyone feared death in battle but pretended otherwise. I heard around me Centurion's shouting commands, the movement of soldiers, horses, carts, and the banging of wood somewhere in the distance. You could smell food cooking on the hundreds of small fires all around, as the army was scattered in lines and squares, giving the image of strength, real or imagined.

I stared, uncontrollably, in a silent gaze at the moving water, swirling on top. I knew there was a strong, hidden current which prevented an immediate attack from the Romans. Thousands of small boats were still being built at the rear of the legions which would carry the army across. The water seemed to flow towards our position, then out and away to the middle of the straits rolling to the vast, unexplored, anonymous dark sea beyond Eire.

⁂

My eyes were charmed and very still; tears blurred my sight into a trance. I had never had a daytime vision while I was awake, not so much a vision, but a silent apparition. The water reflected Armaigen's face up into the clouds; I saw him looking down at me with that elusive smile I remembered. His face was elongated and puffed out because of the clouds; it was him.

With his whet clusters of bubbling clouds, he announced his presence to my ears without speaking.

Armaigen's face appeared as ancient pictographs on the clouds. There was a story to be told beginning with the three strangers, my life and up to this moment. I glanced about and noticed that the Romans could not see my vision as they were immersed in themselves and the Britons on Ynys Mon.

Armaigen moved his head looking over the Roman legions, as if he were observing their position and weaponry. He noticed me again and smiled.

Most of the Romans were in full battle dress, artillery ready, every position manned. I remained uneasy as I could not understand why the Romans could not see him also. You see what you want to see, for the most part. When I was a child, I often saw different animals in different shapes of clouds.

Armaigen spoke with a gentle quiet voice, "You have come. Good. Not a boy, but a man. I am not dead nor am I alive. Be careful of them." Another lightning flash sprayed over the Roman legions.

I was anxious and had so many questions; I still did not know what I was supposed to do. I waved my arms about, pointing back at the legions, pleading, "What am I to do?"

"Be ready. Tiernan is coming for you when the sky is on fire. Prepare. Gather all supplies, your brothers and people. Watch for them. Escape in the darkness; you must move quickly or all will be lost. You are leaving. The moment has come. Tiernan is coming for you! Look!"

The clouds moved and his face vanished.

I turned to look at Paulinus and several officers had noticed my movements and that I was speaking to someone unseen. Paulinus stared at me; concerned. I knew he would speak to me about it later. I would make up some story.

I deliberately looked at every unusual feature on the island: the rolling hills, the rocks, the vast forests broken by strips of open pastures; there were so many trees. Many Britons were moving about on the hills and some were sitting in groups around fires. I now concentrated on the shoreline looking at a group of people making way for a man with a blue robe.

There was a distraction as women, men and children were swimming in the water, shouting and laughing. Children's voices screamed with happiness, as they were all immersed in a secure moment, unafraid of the Romans so close to them.

The man in the blue robe stopped and held up his staff waving it, as if he were trying to get my attention. It was Tiernan. He was looking right at me!

Immediately, without notice, I was there, walking with Tiernan, following him alone into the cool forest. He turned to me and smiled. We could see each other, but no one around us knew I was there.

I was alarmed to see a large warrior suddenly beside me. He looked angry and many weapons covered his body. I stopped. I was afraid but he did not see me.

Tiernan, "Cathal, go to the water and prepare my raft; I will be there shortly. You cannot come with me; the women are preparing themselves. I will see you on the shore."

The man called Cathal looked bothered and disappointed. I watched him leave to be sure and then walked faster, trying to catch up to Tiernan.

I had travelled further into the forest which opened to a small clearing. There was much talk as I saw many women. They had stripped naked, except for their tight belt; several knives were slipped into their belts. I looked away embarrassed, not wanting to see them. For the first few moments, I did not realize they could not see me. I was an invisible bystander as I moved within their ranks.

They were helping each other apply blue woad all over their bodies, face, hair and every crevice; they smiled at each other. Some made jokes about their husbands or of men in general, especially when they rubbed each other breasts. One even pinched a nipple for fun, giggling and looking for the surprised reaction. The woman jumped and let out a squeal as she crossed her arms.

One woman was clearly the leader; I heard someone call her Orin, as she gave last instructions to the small group of women, handing out hollow flutes, made of wood. She showed how they were to breathe underwater with them.

"We can all swim like dolphins. The dolphins swim with us all the time in the water; they are attracted to us, as we are to them. Stay under the water. Hold onto the raft and don't let go of it. Keep it in the middle of the straits; hold the raft against the current. I will let you know as we move."

I felt a warm rush as my legs nearly gave out; Tiernan had walked right through me and he looked back at me with a grin. He had not changed and looked exactly as I had remembered him.

He went to Orin and gave her a kiss. I knew they were husband and wife.

"What are you looking at?"

Orin seemed distracted, "I thought I saw something. Is someone there?"

I did not know what to do; they were staring right at me.

Tiernan, "Yes."

"How could you?"

"It is Galen. He is a physician."

"It's not right; tell me the next time. Look at how I am." Orin continued to stare and walked in front of me, then stopped, trying to see me. "You have told me much about Galen; it is time you sent him back, he has seen enough."

Within an instant, I was back on the Roman shore; my physical body had not moved.

Paulinus shouted, "Galen, why do you talk to yourself?" All the officers were now looking, waiting for an answer.

"Governor, I was praying for victory." His stare lasted a few more moments; he then looked back at the people in the water swimming.

The killing of Britons would not stop until blood had replaced air, flooded with Roman songs of joy and victory. It made perfect logic. It would be a most fortunate, predictable Roman conquest.

Dreary death and banal euphoric victory; blah, blah, blah. I had heard many slang expressions during my visions of the twentieth century. Be succinct, as less is more.

I sensed this was not like Caesar's invasion in 55BCE and 54BCE or even Claudius' in 43CE. There was a persuasive sense of permanence to it, like a relentless, angry crow attacking a smaller bird. I had reluctantly agreed in my heart, with much sickening resentment, that the Britons would eventually lose everything. Die frantically; fighting back against the inevitable piercing momentum of the gladius. All of them would vanish from this mysterious and peculiar green island.

I should call them the people of United Kingdom of Great Britain, for they would also have their own empire one day, and then it would also die. I prefer not to get ahead of myself and I should deal with the more immediate matters at hand, so I will call them just Britons.

I understood humiliation and worshiping all things Rome, for the Britons were to be enlightened as my fellow Greeks were. It was so easy after a conquest to give in and go about your daily routine and mundane duties. Dulling choices of fight or flight? Why bother? You live and die. There is always some sort of authority ruling us.

I'm sure the Britons knew in their heart what was coming: a new privileged, superior class would enslave them. All the earth, as far as you could dig down, to as high as your eyes could gaze, the stars would now be Roman stars; or so the victors imagined.

I stood looking at the large raft with the tall mast across the strait; the one sail was loosely furled in the light wind and was being opened and pulled tight. The raft was held in the water by Cathal and other warriors.

The turquoise dolphin women slowly entered the water, swimming quickly away from the shore. I suppose they were trying to stay warm, testing the water, as they all disappeared from the surface. Without turning, I heard many Romans close to me make comments. What were they? Where had they gone?

Chapter 42

FROZEN CURRENTS

As I held up my arms, Cathal made sure that my weapons were in place. He looked angry and disturbed. "Fine looking armour." He was admiring the white stag and gave my green breastplate a hard slap, which pushed me back off balance. "At least you will die looking good!"

"Take my helmet off. It is too hot. I want them to see me." I moved my robe back behind the hilt of my sword. My hands pushed my long, brown hair, marbled with some grey, off my face and shoulders. I felt the weight of the long sword on my hip and knew I would not need it. "Remove my sword. Take the belt away."

"You can't go without your sword!"

"My sword will not be of any service on a raft, especially if I land on the other side."

"Ah, you are now plan on invading all by yourself? You tempt the spirits!"

"They know what I am doing."

"You, of all people, know anything can happen in battle."

I went over to my horse and withdrew a long staff from between the leather straps. The staff had a yellow-painted carved warbler, with a black cap and black wings sitting at the tip of the pole.

I looked at the face of the bird, stroking its head and kissed it. "Now, do what I wish. Be not afraid." I held the staff up to give it some room to fly, for I was surrounded by warriors. The bird came to life and squirted away into the air. There were yells and shrieks of laughter as my people were astonished at my powers. I knew they would be reassured at their chances of surviving on Ynys Mon after seeing me visit the Romans.

Cathal was agitated, "I still say this is insanity. You do realize that there are two Roman Legions waiting to kill you?"

"Do not worry."

"How can I not worry? Are you blind?" Cathal pointed at the massed Roman legions and the crowds along both sides of the straits.

"This will not take long."

"I agree; they will not hesitate killing you. But what is the point? You *will* have your chance. Why die now?" Cathal brought his arms up, exasperated, as if he had given up. "Yeshua, tell him this is foolish."

Yeshua had been sitting silently on his horse for a while. He was dressed in his every day, white, casual garments. "Cathal, I agree, but he has made up his mind. I don't think Tiernan will die today."

I looked at Cathal, like I had won, "See?"

"You cannot be completely sure. You know, we all need him here."

"Yes, we do. But it is up to him." Yeshua pulled his horse away and slowly made his way along the shore.

Cathal pointed his hand at Tiernan and Yeshua, looking puzzled, "Both of you are going to get us killed, with all your fucking secrets and knowledge. We are just fucking *men*!"

I started walking down to the water. "I'm not planning to die. Look at the red sky. There is no noise. See how quiet it is. How can anything bad happen today?"

Cathal sniffed the air as the sky flashed an ominous warning, "Looks like a storm."

"It's not a storm to harm us; it is warning to the Romans."

Orin had entered the water with the dolphin women. The water was up to her waist and she cried out saying the water was cold before they all submerged. Soon, they came up for air as several women came out of the water to hold the raft even and still; waiting for me.

Many more warriors had moved closer to me and had gathered from our main camp. Most stood in silence thinking that either I was brave or foolish, perhaps both. There were single, odd calls, deep within the crowd of Britons, cheering me on. The warriors closer to me knew the danger and muffled inaudible, deep-voiced responses between themselves. I heard someone say it was just plain stupid.

It made me feel poorly for a moment, but I recovered, for myself and the men; I was Tiernan, the apprentice of Armaigen.

I looked at Cathal, "Let me surprise you today. I have some earth spirits to protect me, as well as some illusions planned. Armaigen always said simple tricks were the best."

Cathal grabbed my arm just before I stepped up onto the raft, whispering, "Don't be a fool, my friend. Be careful. I know I can't stop you, but for the spirits sake, use good judgement if you get in trouble out there."

"I will be fine. I'll be back before you know it."

Orin raised her voice, "Tiernan, be careful." The other dolphins looked at me with dread. I began to feel nervous for no one wanted me to go and I began to have doubts of why I was doing this at all. I knew that I had to show the Romans what they were up against, yet I felt that the spirits were repulsed by evil and danger. The spirits preferred a subtle mysterious approach, to the ways of man. While the spirits loved clever good people, I knew my actions were not always subtle.

Cathal confessed, "I have hidden our archers; the wind is picking up in our favour. If they make a move I will use the archers to force them back. The dolphins must not allow the raft to cross the halfway point of the straits, you will be in range and they will fire at you!"

"I don't need any protecting."

I told Orin, half-smiling, "Enjoy the swim."

Cathal sputtered, "Don't be reckless. It's not just a swim! There is no need for you to do this. You infuriate me sometimes!"

I looked forward, standing. I held onto the mast with my free hand as I gripped my staff. The dolphins had pushed me out and disappeared under the water. I was more out in the open now and was sure the Romans would notice me at any moment. I was moving in the right direction, with seemingly no assistance.

The raft stammered, uncertain, and then began to glide into the open vastness of the water, floating to confront the entire Roman army, who were masking our sacred, dear earth.

∽⁀⁀∽

My bird returned for instructions, lingering in front of my face as it landed on my arm.

I touched its small face. "Fly. Fly away and tell me what you see and hear. Go to Paulinus, wake him up!" I threw my arm up as it nipped away, chirping a sweet song.

The dolphin women began slowly kicking like frogs, the water was churning around me as the raft moved further from our home shore. Orin's head appeared so she could see where they were going. "Orin, that is good. Closer, they need to see me."

Orin, "The current is beginning to feel stronger here." She shouted back. "Hold on, girls, we are dolphins now. Protect Tiernan." The speed of the raft increased as I gripped the mast tightly, leaning against it, feeling more secure and balanced. There was still a good distance to go.

Orin's dark head was half-submerged; she faced forward as she spat water out of her mouth. She was very serious, focusing ahead at what had to be done; I watched her in the lead as every muscle in her beautiful body moved, stretching the rope taut as she directed the raft forward. She was now pulling hard, moving faster as she gained momentum, in and out of the water, then drifting, easily floating without movement like a real dolphin.

She shouted back, "Girls! The full current is moving us along, I can feel it, swim against the current. Slow the raft down in front of the

Roman red tent, in the middle. Bring it to a stop. Hold it there! Work together!"

I urged Orin, "Closer. Get me closer!" I pointed to the Romans, "There. Move me over there. I must be in that exact spot!"

I looked at the Roman shore, taking a quick glance at Galen's vacant look. I cast my eyes at the Roman centre and there was such a commotion going on, with men and horses being directed in many directions. Colourful Roman flags flapped routinely around, as all the Roman soldiers were hurriedly moving about to get a good view of me.

I looked back at our island, eyeing the massive stone wall at the top of the largest hill. The Britons and Druids were bulked together. A small ribbon of wind came in from the salty sea as our flags blew open – Yeshua's flag was Armaigen's pine tree, my white stag, Orin's dolphin and the flags of the other tribes, including the adder, fish, wild boar, the fire and the deer.

Orin stopped the raft and turned to face me as she wiped some water from her eyes. "Cathal said not to get close."

"Don't worry about Cathal; we still have lots of water between us."

Orin looked up at me; I knew that look. I was not listening to her. I could not control myself. My mind was now apart of the spirit world. I would employ all those abilities the spirits had bestowed upon me. The spirits were my shepherds as my energy grew over all of nature as foretold to Armaigen by the UnderWings. My gifted bird allowed me to see and hear everything it saw and heard.

My beautiful warbler flew to Galen, fluttering about in front of his face. I could still see that boy in him from many years ago, as he smiled like a child. I felt he was cynical to everyday life, suspicious of most things. It had been a long wait. Not all was bad, for it seemed he had taken the potion, just as Armaigen had told him and his father.

Galen reached out for the bird knowing that I had sent it. The bird sang to Galen and then flew away.

I saw and knew every thought of Paulinus. I had instructed my bird to fly back into time before I attempted to float across the straits on my raft. The audacious bold bird flew into his tent coming to rest on his helmet.

I continued to see the recent past as my raft moved closer. Paulinus had started the day alone, with a generous morning meal, going over the last details in his head, deciding when his army would be ready to attack. He wished that Emperor Nero was there. All Romans deserved to see this polished spectacle, this eternal, mirrored birth of perfection, designed and created by himself. He had told his scribes to take down every detail since arriving, not missing any brave acts the Romans were expected to achieve.

There was a shout from outside as a guard issued an alarm. Paulinus was angry, for he had not finished his breakfast, and ran outside to see what all the uproar was about. He smiled when he saw me on a raft coming towards him.

It did not take long for the Romans to mobilize themselves into a fighting force. This is what they were good at.

My yellow bird continued to fly about amongst the Romans.

On each respective side of Paulinus were the Legion Legate Slavious of the Valeri XX, Legion Legate Barrius of the experienced IX Geminia and General Kiefer of the Batavian Amphibious unit. Behind the Generals was the primus Pilus for each legion, camp Prefects, the Aquilifers, numerous priests and a few physicians.

Paulinus waited patiently, watching Tiernan come closer. "See how their forces are scattered about. No match for our legions. Have they not learned anything from us?"

Barrius, "They are easy targets for our artillery!"

"Look at our Legions; forever remembered by the gods, the Emperor and all Romans. We will kill the last of these Britons who refuse to accept us and secure Britannia, for the glory of Rome!"

Slavious, "I know that is Tiernan, but who is that across the water, dressed in white and sitting on a horse for all to see, with their warriors?"

Barrius, "I believe that his name is Yeshua."

Paulinus, "Is he a Drui or a Briton?"

"Neither. I hear he is from Judaea."

Paulinus was surprised, "Judaea? Nothing ever good came out of Judaea."

"He is a friend of Tiernan. I am not sure of his place. Our spies tell me he is a warrior and has fought many battles in Europa and Britannia with Tiernan."

"Well, we will put an end to him."

"Some say he cannot be killed, like Tiernan."

"Nonsense."

Slavious, "That Yeshua is leaving. Riding away, going to hide somewhere, I suppose."

Paulinus sat up in his saddle for all to see, shouting as he pointed, "Men of Rome, there is the great Tiernan! There he is! The famous Drui warrior. I want his head!"

Kiefer, "He is just a man. I thought they were called a Druid?"

Paulinus, "Pliny, the elder, used the word 'drus' meaning 'oak', so the singular is the word 'Drui'. We do it to humour them; soon they will all be gone. The plural is the extended form; I think it means something about seeing knowledge. It is some sort of barbarian sorcery."

Slavius, "He doesn't look like much."

Kiefer, "He looks young, but seems old."

Barrius, "Don't underestimate him, or any of them, for that matter."

The Romans along the shoreline began shouting taunts, screams and insults at me. They were not mobilizing any cohorts to attack. I heard my fellow Britons and the dear Druids call out behind me, supporting me as they yelped and screamed back at the Romans with all the hatred the spirits could endure.

I felt agitated for some reason, as I moved back and forth on the raft talking to Armaigen and my spirit friends. Below the surface, I saw the dolphin women holding the raft.

Instinctively, I corrected my own movements, as I shifted my weight from one end to the other, until the raft slowed down and stopped in front of Paulinus. The sky was dark, although it was day and I noticed my yellow bird fly about unhampered, as I heard every word the Romans spoke while they waited for me.

Paulinus, "Let's see what he is up to. Barrius, awake the sagittariorum! Choose five of your best archers."

"General, only five archers?"

"That is all. Any more would be a waste of arrows. Wait until he gets closer. I want to see his face more clearly. Watch for my signal. The men must see this."

Barrius saluted and galloped down the hill. Legionnaires jumped out of the way, cheering.

The army were waving him on, as the horse pressed through the seemingly crushed sea of men, who scattered about, excited to watch what would happen next.

More Romans ran freely to the water, elated and surprisingly, breaking rank and position.

Salvius, "General, should I stop the men and maintain our formations and order?"

"No, let them go. It is but one man. Some of our men will die soon enough for Rome. Let them be men and laugh. When Tiernan dies, our job will be much easier. Perhaps there will be no battle at all and all of our hard work and preparations will have been for nothing."

The booming Briton drums were opposed by the short, occasional squeal of Roman horns. Everyone on Ynys Mons began to project a continuous, pulsating, humming noise, which sounded like bees around a nest. Their bodies moved with the sound. The trumpets from our island let loose, screeching out long, droning blasts of piercing air, which made my sail flicker as the clouds above churned into the shapes of our tribal flag emblems.

The Romans just stared and talked amongst themselves, many having never seen a spectacle from the earth itself; most became fearful. They knew based upon previous battles, that this was not just a battle; this would be different in some unknown way. They were thinking of death, many deaths, including perhaps their own, especially if they made a mistake fighting our brutal warriors.

I held my staff up to Paulinus not as a salute but as a warning; he did not understand and did not seem intimidated.

In a clear, but defiant voice, I shouted, "I am Tiernan! I am Tiernan!" I stood with my legs apart; solid on the raft. I dared them to attack. I knew it was all too tempting for them. I could see some preparations being made with some men along the shore with crossbows.

My sparrow heard Paulinus say to his officers, "What is he doing? Insania! He stands like this in front of me and expects me to do nothing?"

Paulinus snickered, it was a wafer titter of a sound that all around him found very amusing.

Paulinus, "Let's give him what he wants, shall we?" He held his hand up and brought it down, giving the signal to Barrius to use his archers. Centurions pushed everyone back, shouting to 'make way,' as the legionnaires moved, giving room to the assembled archers.

Barrius shouted commands and directed his nervous horse about, finally bringing it under control. I knew that horses became uneasy hearing the constant humming noise of bees, which was now buoyantly a part of the wave within the spirit winds.

Barrius shouted, "One month's pay to the first man that kills him." The offer only increased the eagerness of the archers and the interest of everyone around. Many knew the men and skill of the sagittariorum.

The entire Roman army was silenced, as many Centurions and legionnaires shouted for quiet so that the men could concentrate their aim, waiting for the expected and predicted outcome.

Behind me, across the straits, my fellow Britons were still shouting commands from all over, as the noise of the Roman trumpets subsided to our humming and drums, which continued; it was a peculiar, unnatural, halcyon tone, as everyone anticipated that the Romans were going to launch arrows at me.

The sheer elation of clean, pure euphoria clouded Galen's eyes as he wept carelessly; he moved even further way from the Romans so they could not see his tears. He was finally reunited with me but dreaded the thought of losing me so easily, after his long quest to locate me.

I knew it was difficult for him to be here. I knew he was thinking about Armaigen, since he had just been told, to be ready and that I would be coming to him when the sky was on fire.

My head jaggedly turned to survey the placement of the Romans along the shore. I searched with interest the mass clusters of men, weapons and artillery.

The dolphin women kept looking up at me through the blurry water, which became a frozen current as they breathed through their hollow reeds.

The Romans could not understand how the raft was not moving with the current.

The water spirits had accepted me, as the surface water flowed around each side of the raft, as the current remained frozen and still. It was as if the raft was an unmovable rock, sticking out of the water, interrupting the natural flow of water.

A group of smiling dolphins were seen in the straits making their way to the raft, repeatedly jumping up out of the water while making quick, loud crying sounds until they had formed a circle, swimming around me. Several dolphins jumped over the raft, nearly knocking me into the water.

Everyone on Ynys Mon cheered when this happened; the Romans could not believe what they were seeing and it only reinforced all the bad omens they had heard.

With my arms outstretched, I yelled another Drui scream to the earth spirits. I told my bird to fly to the Roman archers.

Barrius saw the annoying, yellow bird. It flew around and near the faces of his archers, bothering them more as it sang a light agreeable song, while blocking their line of sight to me. They did not have a clear view of my position. "Kill that bird!"

The bird flew high up, moving quickly out of their range. The men of the sagittariorum tried and used many arrows trying to kill my warbler, but the small, fast bird could not be hit. I laughed as the wasted arrows fell into the water, and my bird turned inland away from the Romans.

Paulinus, "What is Barrius doing? Shooting at nothing? See what he is doing!" Some men rode off furiously, down the hill.

Barrius was annoyed and confused. He saw men riding towards him. Why was Paulinus questioning his decisions? He looked back at Paulinus, standing up in his stirrups, with his arm up in the air, pointing to something in the now empty sky.

Barrius was frustrated by the bird diversion and knew that he should not have delayed the orders of Paulinus. He shouted as he motioned at Tiernan, "Loose! Fire at will! Kill him!"

While the arrows streamed towards me, even more arrows were loaded and released; there was no stop to it. The sky was thick with death. I stood out in the open, not worried of the outcome. Each arrow landed away from me, falling harmlessly into the water. The Romans continued wasting arrows until Barrius shouted a command to stop.

A seemingly unknown force was at work. It was not Armaigen, but I knew a trick that Armaigen had taught me. It was an illusion where I could be in two places at the same time. Fortunately for me, they would see only a vision of me.

Barrius shouted at the archers to fire again and again, "Loose! Loose!" I just stood and watched the arrows fall helplessly into the water. It was such a waste of arrows.

Paulinus could not understand what was going on. "What is happening? The old man is so close? Why can't they kill him? What is wrong with them? Their fucking aim is off!"

The Romans became carefully guarded with their thoughts; some laughing nervously, not believing what they saw. Yet hundreds of arrows were shot into an empty space.

I laughed at the Romans. They could not understand; it made them feel discouraged for everything they had done in support of Rome was now undermined; they were lost and growing insecure.

Cathal saw the opportunity. He called out, "Now!"

Our archers, with the superior long bows stood up and began to fire across the straits into the legions. More archers appeared, coming out of hiding from under bushes along the shore. Hundreds of our men began sending their arrows, as they pulled each tight string back to their eye, the other eye mostly closed, aiming, arching the bow to the sky as they released each arrow with tremendous force and speed. They fired so many arrows that the sky darkened, casting a shadow over the Legions. Cathal shouted again for them to stop so he could view the damage they had inflicted on the other side.

The Romans scattered after the first legionnaires were hit: chests, legs, shoulders, split heads and unruly death. There was chaos and panic as the soldiers huddled, hiding behind anything. Many died standing with a momentarily lapse in judgement as an arrow found them, pricking deep into warm flesh.

Paulinus could not believe that the arrows could fly across the strait that far with accuracy; as he watched his army die. Unknowingly, the air spirits were carrying the arrows across the straits. It lacked any form of justice and logic; there was nothing he could do. The Romans trumpet sounded retreat, for the first time in Britannia under his rule. It happened so fast, and with so much savagery and intensity. He felt a sudden change in direction of the wind as the arrows began hitting the ground around him. He pulled his horse around, as did the others near him, moving swiftly out of range.

<hr />

I saw my small bird flying back in my direction. At first, I thought it was another arrow or just a dark spot. Then I noticed the flapping wings, sprinting about, fluttering like a hummingbird. As it looked at me, I smiled and stroked the head of my bird. "You were a good bird. Thank you." It jumped onto my staff and became wood again.

I was pleased that the Romans were confused and in disarray. The drums of Ynys Mon and the humming of all Britons continued, never stopping. My little show was not over yet; I shrieked a never-ending call up unto the sky. The storm clouds returned to their normal form and the bright yellow and red flashes appeared unbroken. We continued to have flash lightning with no rain.

The dolphin women were getting tired; the frozen current was melting. The sea dolphins gathered together, all speaking to us, wishing us well as they slipped under the water and went back to where they had come from.

Orin shouted, "We can't hold the raft!"

I looked down at their exhausted faces as they had all come up for air and held onto the raft. I stopped calling for the spirits.

"Let it go! I am done here." I looked up and around, turning my body as I looked at the Romans; thanking the spirits from all four corners of the earth. There was much damage and confusion in the Roman army.

I thought that I would show them more of what I can do. I knew it was vanity, but it would be the last sign for the Romans to worry about. I summoned the animal spirits.

Orin and all the dolphin women pushed the raft back and away with their feet; their bodies curved backwards as they disappeared under the water heading back to Ynys Mon.

The current took over and the raft began to move away from the Roman shore; I was glad to be going home. My spell had been given to the animal spirits and from this moment on, my work was over for today.

Without warning, all birds that had lived above and in trees on this sacred Briton land appeared, circling above the Roman army. They had been in hiding, scattered high in the sky; waiting. They had flown beyond human sight but heard my cry.

The black mass lowered themselves, down and down, still coming down towards the Romans, now so dangerously close to the ground. The birds began to drop on them as if they had all died for none of their wings were flapping. I glanced over at Ynys Mon and it seemed that my people had escaped the blitz of the birds, my spell was not for them; the birds were only falling on the Romans.

Thousands of wheezing birds made deep, hollow sounds as they plopped on the land and even the water around me; one even landing on the raft. They bounced with pain and confusion, shaking and rolling about, for they were used to the free open sky.

Some legionnaires ran, shouting and screaming, as they panicked and looked for shelter under anything, pushing anyone close to them out of the way. The Roman soldiers found cover under carts, shields and most stayed where they were, huddled together in groups on the ground, forming a ball, as they covered their heads with their arms. Paulinus held his cloak above his head as he shouted a curse at me. All animals collapsed in the Roman camp, falling to the ground, as well as all cattle, sheep, caged ducks, chickens and rabbits.

I heard the squeal of many horses, twisting in panic, and their legs gave way as they thumped to the ground. The horses fell, as the riders, including Paulinus, rolled away from the body of the horse to avoid getting crushed. Other men were not as lucky, as some horses even fell on unsuspecting soldiers nearby and were killed. It was like all animals were dead but they had only momentarily fainted.

As the animals hit the ground, within an instant, they all became awake again. The birds, once awake, tried to fly off into the limitless sky.

Some were thwarted by hitting legionnaires and other birds and objects on the ground, until they were aware of their sense of direction to fly up. There was so much noise, as all animals awoke; unmindful that they were asleep but terrified, not knowing what had happened.

The Roman priests were in shock as the camp was in general disarray. They did not know what to do, for this was all unexpected and abnormal. The Roman gods had perhaps abandoned them. Many screamed, which did not help things, as others ran away to hide in their tents.

I saw Galen standing calmly amidst all the havoc and confusion; he did not run, but was deep in thought and analysis. Near Galen, on the shoreline, I saw Barrius and the movement of artillery towards me.

I moved the sail canvas to catch the wind. The current was moving me along. I needed to increase the speed of the raft, away from the Romans. I pulled my hood up covering my head; it was to conceal my presence and comfort me, as if I was no longer there. I then experienced a precipitous, dark premonition about my own safety. I felt that I was going to die.

I made a slow course to Ynys Mon. I laid my staff down on the raft as I held onto the mast.

I heard shouting from behind; I knew it was the Romans and prayed that I would make it back alive. I looked back over my shoulder and saw Barrius ordering the preparation of numerous scorpions. I knew he did not want me to escape. I looked forward again and felt the strain on my forehead, concentrating on the people waiting for me on my home shore.

Barrius had seen my raft gently caught in the current, moving away. He dismounted from his horse and had moved along the shore behind the weapons.

Barrius was organizing the artillery and legionnaires to regroup, screaming at them.

Instinctively, he knew this was a momentary opportunity to kill me; they would only have a few shots. Men ran, some tripped, as they toddled, holding large scorpion arrows with two hands. All around there was confusion: pushing, bumping and anger, as the long arrows were placed into the slots. The winches were cranked, the rope tightened and the arrows were pulled back. Everyone was shouting, as men took their positions with each machine they were assigned to.

Orin and the dolphin women surfaced off shore near Ynys Mon, their heads poking out of the water. One-by-one, the loud thoughtful Briton drums, cheering and humming stopped.

Orin nervously looked around and saw the Roman activity on the other shore. The Romans were preparing to shoot and she frantically looked back at me. She shouted something but I did not clearly hear her. The sound of Orin's voice was a warning cry and I felt sick of what might happen. She shouted feverishly again and again; panicking. I saw she was treading water, moving her arms upwards, frustrated at not being able to help me.

As the Roman soldiers lined me up in their sights, Barrius shouted to fire and the scorpions launched the arrows; the wide, sharp, metal heads were spinning towards me. As these were released, other scorpion arrows were fired with a low direct arc into the sky; alive like twirling snakes.

I was still facing forward and continued to see visions of what was happening around me. I did not want to face the immediate danger; I could not summon the spirits when I was afraid. That was a secret only Orin knew. It was a horrific feeling that my survival depended on the skilfulness of the Romans without being able to defend myself.

I had my opportunity and now it was the Romans' turn. I knew that the arrows were coming towards me with a velocity that would tear my limbs off. I did not close my eyes but remained steadfast in my growing determination and fearlessness; I refused to look back anymore.

I readied myself for the pain if I was struck.

I thought of Orin, thinking she was right; I was sometimes selfish. The face of Armaigen appeared; he said nothing. I did not feel this was a good sign because usually, in battle, he would appear and tell me I would live or to watch out for that person behind me. I could hear all the arrows coming, as the wind cried out to me. The first arrow fell short, hitting the back of the raft, rocking it about wildly. I stumbled to one knee but got back up, still holding onto the mast.

Two more arrows overshot the raft cutting into the water ahead, and then several more plopped into the water, on each side of me.

Arrows continued to splash down all around, missing me. Ynys Mons was getting closer. The arrows continued to whoosh and zip by. Each arrow burnt out quickly in the cold water, slapped down and snuffed out without fanfare, drifting aimlessly down into the water; uselessly lying on the sea bottom.

Barrius continued to shout, not understanding why I had not been hit yet; he pushed some legionnaires away from a scorpion. He vigilantly selected an arrow, loading the scorpion himself, turning the winch and then ever so slowly taking aim; screaming as he released the large arrow. I thought that this had to be the last arrow, before I was out of range. In my mind, I had seen him loading it. I heard it coming, alone, closer and closer, splitting the air.

I said a small Drui prayer, repeating it over and over.

'Listen.
Briton drums, Druid screaming omens,
Will defeat, the oncoming Romans.'

I let go of the mast but held on with one hand. I went to pick up my staff but it fumbled out of my hand, back onto the raft. I bent over again to pick it up and as I did, the raft jolted to one side, reacting to my movement. Finally, I lifted my staff upright, as I regained my balance.

The arrow was on a direct course downward as it followed the raft, but the raft tilted slightly as I grabbed my staff. The heavy, sharp arrow nicked the side of my body, cutting through several ribs. The arrow pierced into the bow of the raft, wobbling to a stop.

I dropped onto the rough bark surface of the raft; I curled up in incredible pain. It became quiet as the noises of men on both sides subsided.

I looked up and saw the blue sky for the first time that day, as the clean clumps of white clouds were dispersed; the sky spirits had completed their job. I touched my wound and looked at my shaking hand. It was covered with blood.

I thought there was a terrible nothingness to life as I laid back and accepted my fate. I had harnessed the spirits of earth. I felt the thrumming again of the spirits in my heart that I had always known. A fulfilling breeze touched the skin of my face, waking me up momentarily.

The natural, caring spirits promised me that I would be taken off the raft by the people who loved me. I fell back asleep, enjoying the peace of darkness.

I didn't care if I was going to die, for I would become a spirit somewhere.

I was told afterwards what had happened.

The Romans had swarmed over a stunned, but hesitant Barrius; all praised him on killing me.

Barrius carefully continued to stare in my direction, as I lay motionless on the raft. He half-smiled to his fellow soldiers, but did not feel completely satisfied, for I was only one man. I had caused widespread havoc and death.

The Roman arrows shot by his archers had all fallen into the water. All the animal kingdom had fallen asleep. It bothered him, for everything he had been told about the Druids was likely true. Sorcery was at work and this same sorcery could be spent during the invasion of Ynys Mon. He looked worried and it was too soon to celebrate. legionnaires continued to shout and cheer; the elation was heartwarming, but he knew it signalled their short-sightedness.

Paulinus sent word for Barrius to return; he wanted to honour his skill. Barrius took a few moments drinking water, still concentrating on what he had just seen.

My fellow Britons and Druids had entered the water, pulling the raft ashore.

Barrius climbed back up onto his horse, trotting slowly through the thickly packed crowd, back to Paulinus. He took one last look back at me being attended to, as I disappeared inside the many warriors who had encompassed the raft.

Chapter 43

I WILL NEVER FLY

The raft came to rest in the shallow water near the shore.

I was half-awake and confused. On the side of my chest, there was a throbbing sharp pain. I touched my wound again and looked at all the blood on my hand. I did not move as I heard shouts of men and women coming closer to me. In all my years of fighting, I had never been wounded like this.

I rolled over, pushing up on my good side, propped upright on my elbow. The sun was too bright and I could not see clearly. If Armaigen was here, he would heal me. I knew that only Yeshua could help me now.

I heard Orin shout and visualized her crushing through the water with her body, knowing she was the fastest swimmer on the island. I watched all the dolphin women feverishly kick as they moved their arms, all splashing towards me.

Some Britons and Druids had run into the water, taking the edge of the raft and moved it closer to the shore. Their faces were gripped by fear as they saw me, helpless. The raft was wrenched over the small rocks, scraping its way to the smooth sand. As the front was lifted, my arm slipped and I collapsed on my spine, lying flat on my back again. I groaned, but could not move.

Orin shouted as she jumped up onto the raft; I knew it was her. Some cool water dripped on my face. I felt her loose breasts on my shoulder; I did not care that she was naked. She frowned as she wiped the blood away several times from my chest, examining the open wound on my side. She told me that several ribs were sticking out through my skin.

"You are bleeding, very badly." Her eyes were wide as she continued to examine me.

"Sorry."

"There it is. You are cut wide open, right here."

I cried out and flinched, arching my body away from her hands.

"Don't move; you will only make it worse." Orin held her hand against the cut; the seeping blood oozed out between her fingers, "You silly man!" She shouted loudly, "Someone, give me a cloth! Many cloths, right now!"

"I love you."

"I love you too. Don't talk."

My eyes quivered and it was difficult to see clearly.

"Don't you die, old man!"

"Do I look old?" My eyes closed as I tried to smile, but could not.

Orin touched my face and rolled it gently in the palms of her hands. "You wake up. Stay awake! You hear me?"

I woke up. I felt weak. I thought it was not so bad to die; it was easy. I wanted to cross over, just have a quick peek, like Yeshua and come back.

"Yes…spirits…"

"You're delirious. I told you not to do it."

I came to life again. "Did you see it? I made the animals sleep! The Romans did not know what to do."

"You have lost a lot of blood. The arrow clipped your ribs, maybe your lungs." She looked up and saw some people running towards her with cloths.

"Clipped my wings. I will never fly again."

"Not your wings, your ribs! Can you breathe?"

"It's hard."

"Stop closing your eyes or I will get mad at you."

She pointed at the scorpion arrow, "Someone get that fucking thing off of here! Fuck! We must get him to Yeshua, now!"

There was a great crowd waiting; I'm sure they all felt useless just watching. I know that by now, my injury had spread alarm throughout Ynys Mon. There was complete shade around me; like a sudden eclipse. The strongest and the most robust warriors blocked the sun, as they gathered about me. I could not speak, but felt comforted by their voices, announcing that they were carrying a log stretcher. I caught the odd glimpse of their faces as they looked at me, some grimacing at my wound.

I was worried but could do nothing.

Brithomar, Taryn and Ronat, the strongest and most robust Silures warriors came forward. I felt thankful.

Orin and some other dolphin women worked fast and tightly bound my chest with cloth.

I sensed much activity from many people, numerous voices calling out.

I could feel Brithomar's big hands grip both shoulders from behind. They were taking me somewhere quickly. The pain was too great and I screamed out.

"Tiernan you brought this on yourself. You are a fool, a brave fool, but a fool nonetheless."

"That's what Cathal said."

Taryn looked at Ronat who was already out of breath. "You think you can carry him that far into the forest?"

"It's not far."

"Honestly? Yeshua's house? I know it is. Once we begin, we will be going as fast as we can."

Ronat, "Are you referring to my weight? You are a stupid, selfish pig!"

Brithomar angrily cut Ronat off, "Not another word out of you!"

Orin, "Shut up, all of you!"

I tried to lift my head up as I watched Brithomar pull his great axe from his back. He went into the water and took one great swipe cutting the scorpion arrow in half. It flew up into the air and was taken away by the current. He chopped at the raft, and then removed the sharp arrow head with his hands, throwing it into the water.

Brithomar became very serious as his friend approached, "Ronat, please. You follow us at the rear, just in case there are Romans about. We have enough men."

"There are no Romans around."

"I said, follow us!"

Ronat stared at Brithomar, thinking how far it was to Yeshua. "I will follow you and keep my sword ready."

"Good. Alright, boys, on my word. That's it! Good. I will lead. We will follow the path until it ends. Yeshua's home is deep in the forest. If you feel you are going to drop him, shout, and we will all stop!"

I called out, "My staff! Orin, bring my warbler staff."

Orin, "I'm going with you. I will run ahead. We will stop now and again and check on you. Are you ready?"

"Yes. I pray to the earth that Yeshua is there."

Brithomar turned, looking at Orin as she came closer. The other dolphin women stood about, unashamed. "For the sake of the men and the all the spirits, put something on, woman!"

I don't remember too many details, as I was carried back through the forest to Yeshua's farm.

I was asleep for most of my trip, dreaming of the past and thinking of the punitive realities of the future. My body was pulled and lurched for the entire journey. I was in a lot of pain, but I did not complain or shout out. I kept my jaw clenched, as I strained my face, watching the branches rush by.

I thought of Orin and all the memorable moments we had spent as friends and lovers. Then I relived the birth of my children, cursing that I had involved my family into this mess with the Romans.

The voices of many men surrounded me, mostly grunting and groaning, with the occasional shout 'watch it now', 'steady' or 'slow down.' Orin kept telling Brithomar to go faster but he was careful.

My back ached from the branches of the rough knots on the stretcher. It was sticking into my skin, scraping my back bone, as my body rubbed against the logs that had been tied together.

Brithomar pulled a bag from his belt, rapidly drinking water, pouring it on his face as he passed it around, still moving. All I saw were tired and rough hands blocking my vision. I felt the water splash over my face; I was thirsty.

Brithomar looked back, "Where is that fucking Ronat? He is supposed to be behind us!"

Taryn was gasping, "He didn't last long…saw him stop, a way back."

Everyone slowed down and we rested; Orin came over to me. Someone handed her the remaining water and she poured some into my mouth. She checked my bandage; I was still bleeding and the cloth was soaked with blood. I could hear a wet, patting sound from her fingers on my side, as she checked my wound.

The pain was great and I felt suddenly weaker, like I wanted to fall asleep again.

Orin looked puzzled and irritated, but there were more important things to think about. "Pick him up. Let's keep going!" She began running again, beside me, "It's not far now!" She left me as she ran ahead shouting, "Faster!"

I imagined Yeshua was in his nest at the top of Armaigen. I knew that he had seen everything that had happened in the straits. I was sure he was waiting for me. I hoped it would not be too late.

Everything could be lost, or maybe it is best that that I die now. I could not think clearly.

Does my story end here? We could make a truce with the Romans, and agree to live under Roman law. Disband and promise not to be a Drui. I had been fighting the Romans for a long time. They were selfish animals. I knew it would be impossible to become a Roman citizen.

There was no turning back. The Romans would kill us all regardless; I was sure of it.

I was responsible for the lives of everyone; it was my duty. I remembered Orin saying that Yeshua carried a burden too. All the Britons who had escaped back to Ynys Mon relied on me; they all believed in the earth spirits and that I would protect them.

Ynys Mon had very good arable land. But I knew what the Romans were up to: they really wanted the copper mines.

I thought, if we were all dead, the stories of Druids and earth spirits would never be remembered. It would be a story that was never real, like a Greek myth. No one would ever be told of my exploits through Europa and Asia. Such was the cruelty of the Romans and many before them. Armaigen and I were sure it would lead to the destruction of *our* earth.

I felt weaker, my face was wet with sweat; I was tired again and felt like sleeping. Was death silently approaching? My mind was overwhelmed with stupid facts, but I was not fearful of death. I thought of the Romans again; we would put up a great fight! I needed more help from the spirits, who were sometimes fickle, like Yeshua's father.

Everyone was busy carrying me through the forest to Yeshua. I knew the men were at their limit, as they took short breaths, spitting, with their mouths opened wide, sucking as much air as possible.

They shouted and swore to keep moving! I'm sure it felt a relief to them that we were close.

I felt bad, almost guilty, of teasing the Romans as I floated past their legions. I had a problem caring too much about myself. Still, the spirits had graced me with their presence. In a selfish way, I really wanted to see how this battle was going to turn out, even though people on both sides would die.

I thought of Boudicca. Though I had never met her, I had heard that she was the tallest, female warrior in Briton. She was an Iceni warrior who was raising a great army against the Romans. It was not just me with a grudge who was being threatened with death. Her husband had been killed by the Romans and her daughters were raped by the Romans, right in front of her.

I did not care too much about it right now, for I would likely die before I got to Yeshua.

I was slipping under the dark water. I would not have to live an infinite eternity with the disgrace of seeing everyone die on Ynys Mon. I was going to pass out. I heard Orin shout again to stop running, just before the blackness.

Orin slapped my face. I'm sure there was a previous slap that I did not feel, but the second and third slap was hard; it stung my skin. I woke up as we were moving again. I felt my body tip in many directions as the men slowed down, stepping carefully over fallen logs, raising the stretcher higher as they pushed through the thick bushes, as the branches and leaves scraped my face.

We were leaving the dense forest and moving into a vast, open, sunny field. It was Yeshua's farm and I could smell the fresh crops and spirits abound.

We stopped. The stretcher was lowered slowly to the ground. "Get me off this thing!" I struggled to move, but could not.

Orin, "What did he say?"

Taryn, "I don't know. He was speaking nonsense."

"Thank the spirits!" Brithomar was shouting and acknowledged the warriors for their
hard work.

I could hear the faint cries of the farmers coming to see me. The shouting increased, as the word of my arrival had been relayed to everyone.

More farm workers rushed forward to see what was happening; they saw me and their excitement turned into fear and despair. I could not speak but weakly gazed about. There were so many faces to look at, so many I did not recognize. The stimulation was too much to take. Many of the farmers turned away crying. What had I done!

Was I going to die?

Many more had gathered around me as I was taken off the stretcher and placed on the earth. I felt the warm earth spirits cover my back. I could not see the sun for the crowd was shading my view of anything. My throat was dry and I still could not shout out my thoughts.

Orin pushed everyone back, "Give him room! Back! All of you. Let him breathe!"

Chapter 44

YESHUA'S NEST

Yeshua was known to everyone, but few knew him.

The tall, dark stranger from another land was different. His voice was even and the slight accent made you savour every word; the aroma of sound from his perfect mouth was intoxicating.

Yeshua walked so fluently that his feet seemed to skim the earth. He was known as a quiet and friendly man, who enjoyed telling stories and known to sing in his nest at the top of Armaigen. Children loved him and would follow him everywhere.

Often, he would hide out somewhere, praying. He was not an introvert or known to have fits of temper, but his skills of a warrior were legendary. Once, I heard a humble farmer remark, after meeting him for the first time, "This is a *man!*" He radiated a metamorphic glow.

There had been stories, but no Briton had ever witnessed Yeshua heal anyone. I knew that he had the power to heal, for I had witnessed it after many decades travelling with him in Europa. He took his healing powers seriously and feared that people would think he was a sorcerer, or worst still, a magician. He was graced since birth to spread goodness; that is all.

On Ynys Mon, he was more an observer of the ways of the Drui, respecting me and our beliefs.

<hr>

I did not see him descend Armaigen. The looks on the faces of those who blocked my view said it all. Not a word was spoken; they were hypnotised. I had seen him climb that tree many times and pictured him coming down swiftly, with a dramatic last swing off the lower branch onto the earth.

The crowd around me moved back and opened a path for Yeshua to see me.

Orin broke the silence as Yeshua approached her. "Hurry! Hurry! Tiernan is dying!"

Yeshua reassured her with a peaceful silence, as she followed him to my side. He kneeled beside me and touched my face.

Excitedly, I blurted out, "Did you see it?"

"Yes. It was one of your more foolish moments."

I felt weak and lost, "I'm bleeding."

He touched the skin around the cut trying to see the wound, "I can see that."

The group of warriors and farmers closed in around me, trying to see and hear what was going on. Orin turned, looking at everyone, knowing they also cared for Tiernan. She seemed to become calmer, speaking in a kind reliable voice, "Let Yeshua have some room."

Yeshua smiled at her. "They are fine."

<hr>

Yeshua told me to relax and close my eyes. He wiped his hands clean of my blood on his clothes. He took each hand in turn, as he moved his fingers, slowly tracing the lines in the palms of my hands. He followed the outline of my fingers, finishing with a grip of his hands entwined between the fingers of my hand. He stayed in that position, holding each hand, one at a time. I wished I could have seen his face.

Yeshua stopped and took my arms, placing them down at my side on the ground. I opened my eyes and saw the small, gold flecks in his eyes. He was looking down at me and smiled. "You are an old spirit, my friend." I thought of Armaigen. He then rubbed his hands together, as if he was warming them up to touch me again. He held his hands in prayer with his eyes closed. I heard him say, "My Father." I closed my eyes and waited.

He gently covered my face with his open hands and then he raised his hands away from my face, slowly moving them down my body. The movement was in a circular motion. His hands stopped over my chest, then my heart, down to my stomach, following my legs to my feet and toes. His hands returned to my stomach, making the same circular pattern that the sun followed every day, rising in the east and resting in the west. My breathing became easier and my lungs felt clear.

Suddenly, I forgot where I was and saw Armaigen in a vision. It was a forgiving place and I heard children laughing in the background, as he spoke to me:

'You will be a flat, shale rock,
Skipping across the endless water,
To a free land, full of spirits.

Be not afraid of the storms to come,
Fly all sails, for if there is no wind,
There is no earth.'

This was not a prophesy of my death. The revelation had been given to me before, by Yeshua, predicting our life in a new land; what Yeshua's father called the *old* earth.

The pain raged through my body. I woke up surprised as Yeshua was pushing down on my wound. I cried out, wondering what he was doing or why I was there. I had been far away listening to Armaigen and now I was back, worried what would happen to me. Yeshua's eyes were closed. The hot sensation was almost too much for me to take; I smelled burning skin. I did not want to look anymore, so I closed my eyes.

Yeshua called out for all to hear. "Everyone, hear my words: as Tiernan breathes, you must breathe. Watch his chest move. See him breathe, hear him breathe. I will say my words for everyone to hear, and we will all repeat it together after me. Now let us begin and breathe."

"Oh, good earth spirits from above and below,
Grant this man Tiernan the strength of the oak and mistletoe.

We give thanks and offer our prayers to you,
For he has been a faithful, loving Drui.

Grant that he be restored back to perfection,
And we will be true with everlasting affection."

Yeshua raised his voice as he continued to place his hands over my wound. "Now together, all of us." The prayer was repeated, with some mistakes by the onlookers, as Yeshua had to start over, saying some of the phrases three times to all that had gathered.

There was silence. It was over and no one made a sound.

Yeshua stood up, holding out both of his hands pulling me up. "Rise, Tiernan." I was in shock and offered my hands. That was that. He embraced me, kissing both of my cheeks. "I think you still have a few fights left in you."

I was giddy with excitement. "Was that you or your father?"

"Just me. I did not feel my Father, but I did say a prayer to Him before your Drui prayer. I thought you should have a Drui prayer. My father does not speak much to me anymore but I know he hears me when I speak to him."

"Why would you say a Drui prayer when you don't believe?"

"It's not so much what you say, but what you believe and think."

We looked at each other and knew that it would lead to another discussion regarding Yeshua, his father and my communion and control over the earth spirits.

Orin kissed me. Everyone clapped and cheered; I nodded with a guarded appreciation.

I was afraid to look but lifted my arms up as far as I could. I felt dizzy and could not stand straight. Orin carefully unwrapped my bandages. I only saw dried blood. I touched my side. I was weak and felt like sleeping. It felt like a sore bruise; I was stiff, but the skin was smooth and unbroken. I smiled at Yeshua.

"Thank you. How are *you*?"

"Tired."

I felt uncertain of what to do next. There was still a slight pain and I did not want to move until my head cleared.

I held onto Yeshua's shoulder with one hand. The warriors and farmers took their turn examining the side of my body. I did not mind. They were excited, speaking fast, sharing what they had seen.

Yeshua looked at me, "You will be fine. You need to rest. Orin, take him to the dry pond. There is some food in the cottage there. Take what you need. Rest. You need to rest."

Someone shouted, "Yeshua the healer! Yeshua the healer!" Many people began to be drawn to Yeshua, wanting to be near him and touch the cloth of his robe.

There was a sudden rustling in the forest. It sounded like someone was frustrated and angry. We all heard swearing and snorting. Taryn said it sounded like a wild boar.

Brithomar and Taryn took a few steps towards the sound and stopped, ready to withdrawal their swords.

Ronat shouted, "It's only me!" He was tangled in the bushes before the meadow and stumbled out into the open, collapsing on his back, trying to get his breath back. "Told you…told you I could make it!"

Taryn gave a look of frustration. "You are a pitiful excuse for a man!"

Brithomar walked away, back to his men, as he slurred his annoyance, "Idiot!"

Taryn, "Let's put him out of his misery before the Romans do."

Brithomar, "But we don't want to do the Romans any favours now, do we boys?"

Most of the warriors and farmers laughed, for we were well-aware of Ronat and his physical failings. We knew he made a fool of himself sometimes. He seemed to like the attention, for much of it seemed staged.

He was a brave and trusted warrior. Despite his appearance of being slow and lazy, he was known to fight with two swords, one in each hand, surprising all opponents with his agility and skill.

During these times, it was good to laugh for it was a positive distraction. Ronat was known for his mimicry of Paulinus, around a campfire, acting out how he was a "spoilt child" who women found offensive, because of his small size.

Yeshua did not like all the attention. He held up his hands for everyone to stop. "Please. I must go. Let me go. Tiernan, good health to you." He quickly made that sign of the cross in the air to me and all the others present. Many tried to do it themselves afterwards, but found it difficult to do as they experimented the hand motion as they looked at each other.

Young Caeimhin appeared out of nowhere. He squirted out from between my legs, nearly knocking me over as he hugged me. "Caeimhin!"

Brithomar brought my staff back to me. "You might need this." I nodded.

Orin held Caeimhin still, "Careful with your father. He has been hurt."

My boy's hair and clothes were wet. "Where have you been?"

"In the river, swimming."

Caeimhin saw Yeshua and ran to him, jumping up into his arms. He seemed please to hold him, giving him a protective distance between him and the crowds. Yeshua held him close, nestling into his neck, making him laugh. "Can you swim?"

"Of course, I can; it's easy!"

Orin, "Speak nicely to Yeshua."

Yeshua, "If you don't mind I need to rest. I need to meditate at the top of Armaigen, lay in my nest for a while."

Caeimhin, "Momma, can I go with Yeshua?"

Orin did not like Caeimhin climbing trees at his age. She had caught him once climbing Armaigen and had told him to stay away from the big tree. "Yeshua needs to be alone."

Yeshua, "He can come. I will take care of him."

I looked at Caeimhin and felt guilty that I had not been spending any time with him in the last week. I wanted him to be happy. "Orin, he will be safe."

Orin stared at Yeshua; I know she did not like it. "Alright. Yeshua, watch him. You can bring him, but don't fall or drop him, for spirits sake! He can go. I'm sure he will be asleep soon."

She stepped forward and kissed Yeshua, "And, thank you for saving Tiernan."

"Am I sleeping in the nest all night?"

Orin was hesitant, looking at Yeshua, but reluctantly agreed. "Promise me you will watch him."

"Yes. He will be safe with me."

Yeshua waved back as he walked away with Caeimhin. He took Caeimhin's hand and walked back away from the gathering, into the open field.

We were all watching him; it was not quiet. Many were talking about what they had just seen; I even heard several talking about Yeshua being a powerful healer. We continued to follow his progress, perhaps expecting some other type of spirit support; a few said that they thought Yeshua was going to fly to the top of Armaigen.

Once he had reached this massive tree, he lifted Caeimhin onto a branch. Most could not hear them speak too clearly for they were far away; but secretly I could.

Yeshua, "Don't move. We will climb Armaigen together, branch by branch."

"Do you have the lyre up there?"

"Yes. I do."

"Can you sing to me? Teach me how to play?"

"I will try. There is water and food up there. Jump on my back and don't let go. Your mother would never forgive me if I dropped you."

"Is that a joke?"

"Yes. I will not drop you, but you must hold on tight."

Yeshua reached for the first low bough and pulled himself up. He held his position as he reached up his arms again, crisscrossing each of the sturdy pine branches with careful steps. He steadied his feet before the next move, as if he was climbing a crooked ladder. Step by step, they made their way up the tree, as we all continued to watch until they were both safe in the nest.

The sun was setting. The clouds were stained with yellow and pink flat bands of light. Splashes of angel clouds drifted, changing shape, as they leisurely blew away into nothing.

I thanked everyone for their help, stopping to talk many times, even though I was not completely well.

I moved closer to Orin as she helped support me, allowing me to touch everyone who was present. I hobbled along, still in pain, and could not stand up straight for my muscles were stiff. I announced that the earth spirits would take care of us. "Armaigen is here. He is watching you and protecting all of us against the Romans."

I told one of the overseers to open the grain storage and distribute enough grain for all families. "Open the barrels! Mead and wine for everyone! Food! Bring lots of bread for everyone!"

Numerous cottages and outbuildings stood at Yeshua's farm, storing all the harvested crops for the winter.

I knew that the plants that made the potion were kept in separate, locked, cool cellars, beneath the earth; only Yeshua and I held the keys for the cellar. The potion would be safe.

That night, many fires were lit, as the Britons and Drui families ate and drank until the morning.

There were many songs, and some new ballads that included a story about Yeshua. Even Ronat got into the act with his famous Paulinus imitations. I always believed that it was good to drink and rejoice; it dissolved everyday questions that could not be answered until you were sober again. Even then, serious questions were best forgotten, for all that mattered was to live and to love. I am – It is.

I could have gone into my dream trance and tried to see a prophesy about the upcoming battle, but it had been many moons since I had a drink with everyone. It was a harmless expression of letting go, while I sought to momentarily dull my senses.

Caeimhim was on all fours, moving about slowly in the bottom of the nest. Yeshua had placed a blanket around his shoulders. He tore the bread into pieces and shared the bread with him. "Did you want to see out, over the edge?"

"Can I?"

Caeimhin then moved quickly, in case Yeshua changed his mind. "Hold my arm as we lay."

They lay on their stomachs as Yeshua pointed and named the Briton tribal camps. "Where is your house?"

"There. In the clearing: on a hill, near the water."

"Good. See the Roman tents and men? There must be thousands of fires. All over the land, as far as you can see. The water runs between us and them."

"The Romans are bad."

"Yes, they are."

"I am scared that they will hurt my mother and father."

"I will be there. Many people love them and will protect them and you. Don't worry."

Caeimhin looked worried, "If the Romans win, the spirits will die and the sun and the moon will go away."

"Then we would all in trouble, including the Romans. I promise you that the sun will always be there for you. The earth needs to breathe, just like the plants."

Caeimhim still looked afraid.

Yeshua, "Let's not think of such things. Keep the sacred life spirits close to you. Be like all the animals; they always know what to do. Birds keep spreading seeds to make other flowers. They even fly far away to the other side of the island planting seeds. We can hide and run away. There are lots of people that will take care of you and keep you safe."

"Like Brithomar?"

"Yes. Brithomar, Cathal, your father, me and so many more than I can count; we will all keep you safe."

"Really?"

"Yes. So, why don't we take our sandals off? Birds don't wear sandals in a nest. Have some bread and milk. I'll sing a song, and you can help me with it. I will even let you play my lyre."

Later that night, Brithomar had a serious talk with me.

We both had been drinking and found it necessary to shout at each other to be heard above all the singing and dancing.

There was a sense of urgency and confusion on the part of Brithomar. I was sitting on a log and despite the wine, I was still in pain. "The raid is tomorrow night. You cannot come in that state. Look at you. You cannot even lift a sword and defend yourself."

Orin, "He is right."

My side was sore and my arm was weak. I thought of Galen and the planned raid into the Roman camp across the straits. It was late and I did not know how fast I would heal. I knew he was right, but did not want to admit it.

"We cannot leave Galen there."

"What is so important about this Greek?"

"Everything; he knows things."

"Like what?"

Frustrated, "I don't know. No one knows. Not even Armaigen knew exactly. He once told me that Galen's knowledge would save us."

He shook his head, "Save what? I don't understand. Regardless, we will take Yeshua with us in place of you."

I looked at Orin. "I need to go with them. I must go. Galen is expecting me."

Brithomar, "You'll get us all killed. Then where will we all be?"

Orin looked at Brithomar. It was a look that said 'he would likely not be coming, so let's not argue over it right now.' She touched my arm, "Let's go to the hot springs at the dry pond. The water has healing powers."

"I will rest tonight and see how I feel by the morning." I lied. I had made up my mind to go. If I had to get on a horse right now to rescue Galen, I would have done it. There was too much at risk. I urged Brithomar, "Please, don't go without me."

Brithomar looked at me like the decision had already been made. He did not want me to come with him. "We might not have a choice. We will cross the straits at midnight tomorrow."

"But you don't know what Galen looks like?"

"Yeshua does."

Chapter 45

THE DRY POND

We said our goodbyes, as the celebrations continued. I was sure it would last well into the night. Our horses had been readied for us and our weapons secured, along with my staff.

We left the light of the fires behind and entered the welcoming forest, where the tall trees never slept. We were familiar with the path. I was eager to leave all the noise and return to the cottage on that hot night, looking forward to the warm water.

Despite feeling better, there was a consideration of caution on my part, for I knew the welcoming pleasures that the dry pond offered us would be short-lived. The Romans would attack and we would defend. I imagined how the battle would begin, the ferocious fighting on Ynys Mon, but I refused to think of how it would end.

Orin was in the lead, as we both decided it would be best if we walked, guiding the horses along by their reins. I drank my potion as I walked. We took our time, walking in silence and easily followed the path deep into the forest. The air was clear and fresh, but as we roamed up and down the hills, we felt pockets of warm air that had refused to leave the cool of the night. It was not a full moon, but the sky was clear and it cast enough light for us to see where the path was heading. Besides, millions of dust-like earth spirits had left their homes within the forest, safely directing us to our destination.

The dry pond was a sacred spot where the spirits controlled everything. We were only visitors and anything we wanted, wished for or desired was provided to us, or to anyone who was present. Few knew of the location or had ever seen it. The spirits knew when anyone was approaching and would discern whether your presence was acceptable or not. If you were accepted, you would follow your senses and locate the pond. If you were not accepted, your instincts would lead you far off in another direction and you would never be able to find the pond.

Just married couples and some lovers would know their way to the pond if they had received a blessing from me. The sacred forest spirits around the pond seemed to be able to live within the souls of those in love and endure forever. After living at the dry pond, those respective loving couples would never argue again with their mate and always find a way to handle a family tragedy or that of their friends. It made their bond between them even stronger, as their love for each other made all who were near them feel their pleasure and contentment.

However, unknown to anyone who had visited the dry pond, when you left the forest path and returned home, the memory of the dry pond and the location would forever be removed from your memory.

Orin was the first to see the cottage burrowed into the thick, lavish tree trunks. The cottage had grown out of the ground. The windows were lit with oil lamps as the fragrant smoke from the fire eased out of the chimney. This was one of the many realms of the spirit world, and the cottage was always well-stocked with provisions for those who followed the ways of a Drui.

Orin was beaming with light and smiled, "I can smell the smoke. I am so glad to be here."

We stopped and left the horses. We were lured by our eyes, as we touched our faces. Our bodies came together lovingly. We both felt the warmth of our backs with our hands. We finished with a long kiss as Orin gave a soft bite to my bottom lip.

"I thought I lost you today."

"I was worried. I should have listened to you and Cathal."

"I'm worried for you and the children. We must find a way to get away, for all of us and the families on the island."

"Our backs are to the sea."

"There's always a way Tiernan, that's what you have always told me. There is always a way out of every problem."

"The Romans have us trapped. They know it."

"Why is this Galen so important?"

"You heard me. I don't know why."

"Are you not telling me something?"

"Honestly, I don't know what will happen. But we must get him on Ynys Mon."

"It must be important; otherwise, you would not feel you have to do it."

※

We took all supplies and weapons off the horses, including the reins and saddles. The horses were now free to roam the forest; we knew they would stay close. We decided that it was best if we went to sleep and save the dry pond for tomorrow morning. Orin promised me that she would make a good morning meal and we would see how my wound was at sunrise.

We slept inside the cottage that night, in front of the fire. Much had happened that day and we were thankful to just go to sleep. Orin and I took our clothes off and wrapped many blankets around ourselves, lying so close that our faces nearly touched. We kissed many times. Orin said she was happy to just lay close with me. I felt the same. Women were often just content to be held.

My mind was absent from any sensual moment, wondering how everyone on the island would be able to escape. It was an impossible task. My thoughts of loving her that night melted away. The spirits coaxed us to fall asleep as they blew out the oil lamps, dowsing the light in the room.

In the morning, I woke up slowly and felt rested, as I stretched. Orin was not there!

It was warm in the sunlit cottage. I was in a panic, wondering where she was; I went outside, naked.

"There you are!"

Orin was not dressed and was picking some flowers. She stood up and showed her body to me. She knew what I was thinking. "What's the matter? I'm here, waiting for you. It's such a beautiful day."

I walked towards her as she dropped the flowers. I held her face with both hands as we pressed our lips together, teasing each other, pressing slightly, and then releasing several times until the sensation of our lips were insatiable. We stared into our eyes, until our very souls exchanged bodies and for a moment we became one person.

Without speaking, we turned and held hands, going down to the dry pond, sparkling with light. We stopped again and greeted each other like nervous, secret lovers, as we both trembled slightly with relief.

As the sun warmed our flesh, our hands massaged the heat further into our bodies.

Orin led me into the pond and as we never took our eyes off each other. I stopped and stood admiring her body again. I saw the baby bulge and ran my hands over the small curve.

"What do you think it is?"

"I am hoping for a girl. It would be a nice change."

"You are the most beautiful woman I have ever seen."

Orin modestly ran her hands over her body looking down at herself, "And how many women have you seen?"

"One. Just you."
"What were you up to, for goodness sake?"
"I've been busy. Stop teasing me."
Orin laughed, "You must have been very busy!"
"Armaigen was busy too."
"Just two lonely men on the road! Poor, poor Tiernan."

Orin laughed louder, as she almost tripped over some rocks in the water. I splashed her as she splashed me back, until we were all wet. She turned away to wash her face, pulling her hair back. Her breasts hung down and all I wanted to do was to kiss and touch them.

She timidly looked up at me. "I know what you want. Come and get it!" She dove into the water and surfaced close to the middle of the pond.

My side ached, but it was better than yesterday. I entered the water, slowly.

"What's the matter? The brave warrior, Tiernan, the great Drui, is afraid of water?"

"You know I cannot swim."

"If you want me, come and get me!" Orin then went under the water again and came up right beside me.

She kissed me. "Come on. Take my hand. We won't go out far."

I took her hand and she led me up to my chest, easing my body onto my back.

"She how easy it is? It is so safe here. Everyone can float on this water."

"I know."

We floated with our eyes closed, as we held hands; like on the first night we had made love. The sun dots covered my eyelids in a bright, yellow glow. Our bodies absorbed the water sprits and I thought of my wound. I felt my side. There was no wound or pain. I was healed!

Orin said that she wanted to float a little longer in the open, before the high trees blocked the sun on the water. "The sun is good for us."

I felt half-asleep, but so happy. Orin pulled me to the shore. I could smell her. We stood exploring each other with our hands. I ran my finger slowly around her lips. Then we came close, holding each other. My hands pressed hard onto the base of her back and I heard a sigh of relief. I softly ran my hands around her breasts, and then I sucked her slowly. We then kissed frenetically, as though we could not get enough of each other, tasting the salt on our wet necks. We found some thick, soft grass. There was more kissing, as we explored the curves and the folds of our bodies, while we lightly touched our skin.

We then glided into each other, forever kissing; there was no end to the passion in our eyes, as the heat of the sun healed our bodies and mind from any worry. We went away somewhere, as the earth spirits continued to torment our senses, until we floated off the ground; both coming at once, then falling into a deep sleep, drifting to a safe place far away.

***

We did not get dressed, preferring instead to stay naked and free.

We decided to walk through the forest as the sunlight burned life into all things. The spirits said they liked us not wearing clothes, as we could feel them occasionally slide over our skin.

Orin filled the basket with berries, all sorts of roots, plants and leaves for a stew. I concentrated on finding burdock, borae, comfrey and puffball; the plants that prevented us from aging.

The plants moved with our presence and touch. The branches creaked, as leaves and flowers turned to get our attention, for I was the keeper of the forest. The spirits told us to touch the moist dew, as the leaves patiently waited for our tongues, while we felt the sweet, watery drops in our mouth vanish.

I spoke in my ancient sprit language to all plant life, reassuring the sick plants with a gentle touch of my hand, as I nursed them back to health. The earth spirits guided us around tree roots, under ferns, cracks in rocks, even split, broken tree trunks, which had been struck by lightning. Meanwhile, we both gave and made love to all insects, plants, trees, rocks while we marked the very earth with our feet.

That morning we prepared and cooked our morning meal, naked. We enjoyed looking at each other and touching our bodies as we worked.

Making food had never been just a duty or chore for us. It was a moment to relax, a safe place where we could share stories and make each other feel complete and satisfied.

The pleasing odour of the stew, mixed with small amounts of leeks, onions, parsnips, fennel and parsley, with a dash of wild garlic, slowly brought us around. Our earth spirits continued to entice us by touching our skin, making us feel an unending love for each other.

We began to get too excited and naively talked more to each other about how we had so much to be grateful for; forgetting about any danger in the world.

At that moment, we both became silent, for I was thinking of the Romans and how to kill them. Suddenly, my pleasure turned to fear. Orin picked up on my thoughts.

Yes, my children were important, but my duty was to everyone. I knew Orin was thinking about her first family. The Romans had killed her previous family in Tarraconensis and she was horrified at the thought of her family being killed again. This time, she was prepared to die to save her family.

We tried to forget as much as we could, as we both helped carry out other sweet dishes of bread, honey, walnuts and blackberries.

We blessed our food as we held hands across the table. I leaned over and kissed Orin. We both smiled. The meal was eaten in silence. It was delicious and it seemed a waste to not speak to each other, but our minds were full of ideas and visions of future events.

It was time to leave the dry pond.

It was a sombre moment as the light spirits shook around us. Although our time in the forest was pleasurable and loving. It also felt like we could have used our time more wisely with our families and planning how to save lives.

We did not talk about it, but I felt guilty and selfish again.

Orin and I had finished packing. We had helped each other with our clothes, weapons and armour. We were ready, as we sat on our horses. I looked at Orin. We both did not feel like moving, even though the horses were anxious, as they stomped their hooves, neighing several times, and lurching about with the reins.

"Wait, Tiernan. Just a few more moments, then we can be on our way." She looked around and showed a serene countenance. Her eyes were open wide as she gave me a loving smile.

Orin preferred to ride light for speed and agility. She wore only a leather cuirass and carried many knives on her legs, with one sword strapped to her back.

I wore my green stag chest plate, carried many sized swords for different purposes, spears and knives tucked all over the horse and body, ready for close, heavy combat.

Orin said, "Thank you, Tiernan. It is a beautiful place and I feel we will never return."

I agreed with her in my mind, but did not want to tell her. "It is a beautiful place."

"It's time to go."

I leaned over to kiss her, "You lead."

Orin did not wait for my kiss! She pulled her horse up on its two hind legs, she whelped several times and sped away, with me charging close behind, trying to catch up. With the rush of the wind in our faces, the forest became a blur of green, as we both raced on.

The earth spirits lifted our horses up off the ground, coming down heavily again, as the hooves beat the ground, repeating our flight, as we flew up again, passing over logs, branches, roots and rocks, up and around wide trees as we pushed over young saplings. The animals of the forest cried out, as insects and all plants squawked and bellowed, urging us both on.

It was a race and Orin shouted that I would never catch her. I was right behind her!

At first, I thought it was snow. Then I realized it was not snow, but the light of earth spirits being discharged from all living things. The spirits did not take sides, for they only sought happiness and love. We could both feel the spirits flowing through our bodies, encouraging us on while our horses became stronger and faster.

Behind me, I saw men and women with large, white wings quickly catching up to us. As they got closer, the flapping of their wings moved the air around us. The ripple of air jolted our horses off course, but we regained our balance and direction. The winged creatures now were on each side of us.

Orin shouted, "What are they?"

"Angels! I told you about them in the story about Becan!"

The winged creatures were flying on either side of us. Suddenly, both groups switched sides as their bodies merged within our bodies, seemingly pushing us to race ahead. The horses lifted themselves off the ground, as we were now flying! We both screamed, enjoying the moment! I felt and heard a long euphoric cry of joy, a pure sound was coming uncontrollably from the both of us. The winged angels then left our bodies, flying straight up into the sky; out of sight.

Orin was still in the lead. There was no way I could catch up to her. Beyond her and the trees further ahead, I saw sunlight in a vast open meadow. We had arrived back at Yeshua's farm.

Chapter 46

INNIS AND AINE

The tall trees of the forest were coming to an end. It was dawn. The cleared land of Yeshua's farm was full of light from the sun.

We slowed the horses down as we entered the flat fields. Our horses trotted beside each other, slowly making our way to Yeshua's small stone house. It was a simple farming village, without a name, more a gathering of a few cottages, barns, livestock, a well and a central meeting place.

The market stalls were empty, almost signalling a famine or an impending disaster.

Orin, "Where is everyone?"

I reached back to pull my sword out, looking all around. "I don't know."

"Have the Romans attacked already?"

I saw two, ragged, old figures holding on to each other, walking out into an open area, with a large group of children huddled around them. I sensed that they did not know who we were and were frightened for their own safety.

I shouted and heard a weak reply. I knew that voice and shouted back, "Innis, is that you, Innis?"

Orin, "That must be his wife, Aine beside him."

Then out of the group, our son Caeomhin came running across the land towards us, followed by more children, then all of them broke free, as Innis and Aine gave up as they could not hold all of them all back.

We dismounted, leading our horses and their images became clearer. Innis was very old and had fought bravely with us for years. He had paid the price, as he had lost an arm and had a nasty scar across his mouth, which impeded his speech.

His wife, Aine, reminded me of an older Orin, for despite her age, she remained a beautiful, strong woman with an intense spark in her eye. Their only son was killed in battle by the Romans. They helped others who needed simple tasks completed, and in return they were fed and given shelter. I thought if Orin ever aged, that is how she would look.

I would do anything for them. They were gentle and faithful people, living the ways of the earth spirits.

Orin lifted Caeomhin up and we kissed him. "I am so glad to see you, my sweet boy!"

We both hugged and kissed all of the children, knowing they were alone, away from their mothers and fathers.

I greeted Innis and Aine, as they dropped to one knee. "Innis. Aine. Please get up; you don't have to do that."

Aine, "They've all left. Everyone! Left us here to look after the children."

Orin, "The Romans?"

Innis slowly shook his head, "Nooo." He touched Aine urging her to continue.

Aine became distracted as she saw the children wandering away, moving around, going further away, while running and chasing each other. In a very sharp, firm, voice she shouted. "Children, come back! Sit here down around us, and do not move!"

All the children returned and Caeomhin sat by my feet as he looked up at me. I touched his head and whispered for him to be good.

Aine, "Last night there was a runner from Beaumaris."

I could feel my legs beginning to give way and my breathing tightened in my chest. I saw the terrified look on Orin's face as she spoke fast, "Beaumaris? What news? Egan? Has anything happened?"

Innis shook his weary head as he bleakly moved his lips. I could not tell whether that was good or bad news; I expected bad news, as was my nature. I put my hand on his shoulder for some comfort, as we both seemed to need physical contact.

Aine faced Orin, "Orin, no, it is good news, we think."

"What?"

Aine looked at Innis. Innis moved his only hand for her to continue. "The runner told Brithomar and his warriors that a battle had been won by us in Beaumaris."

I was confused for Beaumaris was an ancient port at the end of Ynys Mon. There was nothing there. I had sent Egan and other warriors on a scouting mission up through the forest following the straits to make sure the Romans were not going to land there and try to outflank us.

I looked at Aine, "What else was said?"

"Nothing."

"What do you mean nothing? A man runs that far and there is no other message?"

Innis nodded and said very clearly, "Eeegaan."

Aine, "Yes. Egan is on his way here?"

Orin, "Here?"

"Not here. He left most of his warriors protecting Beaumaris. He is coming with some warriors to tell you about the battle. When Brithomar heard this, he was angry that no other information was given. I thought he was going to kill the runner, but the runner swore he did not have any other news."

The water was very deep around Beaumaris, especially where the harbour narrowed. Maybe the Romans had tried to attack and were driven off, but I was sure more Romans would be on the way there, after their defeat.

"Egan likely picked a runner in the rear that was not in the battle, so if captured by the Romans he would not have any specific detail that would help them."

Aine, "The runner said that the tribal chiefs should be summoned and should head to the underground winter grove in the copper mine, after midday, today. By that time, Egan should be there."

Orin was relieved and embraced Aine for some time as she kissed her cheeks.

Aine, "What are we to do here, my lady? We are scared for the children. There are only two of us."

I felt a little more confident. It was better than a battle lost; Egan was alive and there was a victory!

I was sure there must be more Romans going to Beaumaris. He was a well-trained Drui warrior like me. I felt we were missing something, and that there must be more to this story. Egan did not ask for reinforcements, or tell us of an impending disaster. He wanted to tell us of the battle, perhaps warn us of the Roman attack strategy against the island.

Egan had not been told of the healing potion; none of the family knew. The final battle was looming and at that moment I thought that I had made the wrong decision not telling him of it. Egan must be told. Orin and I had increased our discussions on this issue lately, especially now for we were in more danger since the Romans had arrived.

We always knew that one day we would have to let Egan know about it and give it to him; it might have to be given to other deserving people, so that the legacy would live on to another generation. Keeping it to ourselves was selfish. The time to tell him was imminent.

Orin once said to me that we should give it to all Britons and Druids. The Romans would never dare attack us on our sacred isle. But Armaigen made me promise that I wouldn't give the potion to all people. He said it would upset the earth-spirit balance. Men would want to become gods and wars would ensue.

Armaigen believed if everyone did not age, then the respect for the spirit world would die.

All spirits would vanish if praise was not given; how could everyone become a sentry for all spirits? Only certain people were benevolent by nature: Orin, Galen and I had been selected. I still felt guilty about giving it to Orin, for Armaigen had died before I met her and I knew I could not live without her. If everyone took the potion, or if it ever got into the wrong hands, then the earth would be ruled for an eternity by many different Empires that only sought material greed and pleasure.

Armaigen was very serious about this; he often told me that our purpose was to give praise to the existence of everything: the trees, the water, every animal, the rocks, the smallest insect and the sun. And in response, those things that the earth gave birth to would naturally heal us one day without the potion. Without us being alive, that day would never come. It would give us the inner wisdom to live our lives in harmony, with all living things even the dirt of the earth that we stand on, or the rocks and worms that live below the earth that never see the sun. Everything is alive and connected.

Orin looked at me then Aine and Innis, "They just can't stay here. It is too dangerous. We don't know what is going to happen."

I looked down at the children and told them not to worry. "You will be in a safe place, soon."

I saw the creased, tired faces of Aine and Innis. It was clear that they had lived through situations like this before: the forlorn look, thin, rounded shoulders and soiled clothes from constant use. I knew that every day they got up and worked hard, without complaining. I felt guilty and remembered the well I had fallen into as a child. I knew that if Armaigen had not come along, I would have died. The earth spirits knew that they had to keep me alive until he came to rescue me.

Why not rescue Aine and Innis?

I motioned to Orin and asked Aine and Innis to follow me away from the children, so they could not hear me speak.

"I am going to tell you of the path to the spirit dry pond."

Orin was shocked, "What?"

"It is safe there and the earth spirits will protect you. All spirits love children. I'm sure they will keep them under control so that they stay close to the cottage. A sleeping spell will be given by the earth spirits to the children tonight, so you can both rest in front of the fire. There is plenty of food, supplies, some weapons and the spirits will replenish anything thing you need without you knowing; you will be warned of any stranger that means you harm. That is, if the spirits do not take care of him first!"

At that moment, I saw the winged creatures that had guided us through the forest; they had all landed on the swaying branches of Armaigen. Aine and Innis looked concerned.

Orin, "They're friendly. Don't worry."

I warned the children to sit down and not move. "Stay! All of you. We're nearly finished."

A few children stood up and pointed; while others started to walk excitedly towards the giant pine tree we called Armaigen. The last of the winged creatures, with colourful wings had landed in Yeshua's nest. He was taller than the rest, powerfully built, as if he were their leader. He moved his large wings blowing a tender, reassuring wind at our faces making our hair move. The children giggled. He did not frighten any of us, for the mere presence of him soothed us as we felt safe and protected.

I asked, "Where is Yeshua?"

Aine, "He left with Brithomar."

The winged creatures began shaking the branches on the tall tree, jumping up and down, until the whole tree rolled and shook. At first, I did not know what they were doing. Pine cones began to fall onto the ground, building a high, dark mound around the tree.

The tall, winged man in Yeshua's nest spoke to me without saying a word out loud, telling me what to do. He told me to collect all the pine cones for safekeeping. Soon there was no pine cones left on the tree.

Soon, the colorful creatures left the tree, falling up into the endless sky. The leader went first and slowly flapped his wings effortlessly, ever upwards into the sun soaked sky. He stopped moving, suspended in air, his wings slowly waving and looked back to make sure everyone was sky-bound, as he shouted to the others, "Follow me! Follow me!"

Like nervous devoted birds, they all left the branches in a gracious, preordained order; all together, following the leader in a single line, as they obeyed without question, vanishing like dark, dotted stars, invisible to us in the light of the day.

I told to the children that they were our friends and needed our help. I told them to find as many baskets as possible and if we ran out of baskets, to use their hands to carry as many pine cones into the big barn until there was no pine cones left on the ground. They were happy for something to do; some turned it into a game, seeing who could get the most and finish first.

As the children were busy, I continued talking. "We will send someone to you when it is safe to leave."

Aine, "What about the pond and the children?"

Orin, "Children can't sink in the pond. In fact, adults who can't swim are held up by the spirits, so it is safe for everyone." She smiled at me.

"There is one last thing." I looked at Orin; she had that difficult, apprehensive look, knowing I was going to say something unusual, that either would surprise her or that she disagreed with. She did not like surprises, and looked at me with a developing concern. I just knew that this would please her and continued.

"Have you heard of the wonder of spirit-coupling?"

Orin gave me a hard stare. She did not know what I was about to say next. I could see that she was ready to dismiss it.

Aine, "I have heard of it, but never seen or been a part of one. I thought it was a man's joke." She laughed. "Isn't that like mating with anyone? I could not do that to my Innis!"

Innis looked shocked and shook his head.

"What I wish to talk about is the goal of spirit-coupling. I can help you and Innis."

Aine, "You can help me? Orin, what is this all this about? I am uncertain what you have in mind. Tiernan, I am old and been barren for years. I love Innis, but look at him. Look at us. Why?"

Orin, "Tiernan?"

"What I am about to say must be kept between ourselves. It is your choice." I paused, so I could get my thoughts straight and allow everyone to hear plainly. "I have a potion that will make you young again. The potion has the strength of the earth spirits to renew you; it is a form of spirit-coupling. It will heal any infirmities due to aging. Innis, it would even help you heal that scar on your face, so that you could speak again."

Innis touched his face, "Ttrouue?"

"Yes. No more pain. You will speak."

"Arrm?" He held up the remaining stub of his arm for me to see.

"I'm afraid it would not heal your arm, but the potion has never been given to a man like you. I can only tell you of what I have seen."

Orin immediately knew what I was planning. She looked at me in agreement; the look of frustration towards me disappeared. She stepped away quietly, taking Aine's arm and stood close to her, speaking softly, "Aine you will be young, able to make love again, have a child. We will give you a supply of the potion and the recipe. Enough for both of you, for years to come, until the child is old enough to look after themselves."

"Then, what?"

"Then you stop, if you wish and the both of you will start aging normally again. Grow old together with your family and grandchildren. Or you might decide to never stop taking the potion."

"You take it?"

"Yes. We feel blessed by the spirits."

Orin smiled compassionately, wiped a tear away from Aine's face; she stood back looking at them as she held hands with Aine and Innis.

Aine and Innis were shocked by their fate; they looked pleased to begin their lives again.

I told them, "You can have many lives."

After I had said this I worried about the impending Roman attack. Nothing was ever certain. I hoped that giving Aine and Innis the potion would not upset the order and the spirit balance of life; Armaigen had warned me to be careful of who took the potion.

Chapter 47

MURIELL

Orin and I sat patiently on our horses, watching Aine lead the children into the forest. Innis stood at the edge of the meadow counting each child as they passed, to make sure they were all there. We felt good that the children would be safe at the dry pond.

I found it hard to believe that the Romans were so close; it was surreal. We had lived in peace on Ynys Mon as long as I could remember. I knew there were too many Romans to fight and thought not in terms of a battle strategy to defeat them, but how to survive somehow.

"Look Tiernan, see Caeoimhin! He is at the end, by Innis."

Caeoimhin did not look back as we saw his small body enter the forest. We knew he was independent and smart, but he was still an innocent child. I looked at Orin and she was sad he was leaving, and at that moment, deep inside, I felt she was angry with her fate.

Innis turned and looked at us, giving one last, long wave before the spirits welcomed him, as he entered the forest.

I looked around at all the empty buildings; even all the chickens were gone. I could not see or hear any birds. The wheat was tall for this time of the year; it would have been a good harvest. The flowers and plants had grown all over Yeshua's small cottage. I hoped Yeshua had secured our potion.

I looked up to the top of Armaigen and thought it was strange and unusual that Yeshua spent so much time up there.

"Tiernan, are you ready?" She became frustrated, for she wanted to leave. "Are you listening?"

I was thinking of Yeshua, when he was a boy. I thought of Yeshua giving Galen a small figure of himself as a grown man: a physician. Wait. A thought was forming in my head. There was a connection; a thread that linked numerous events together. It covered many years. It was so simple and I began to smile. I could not believe I had not thought of it before!

"What are you so happy about? I can't see the humour in our situation."

I pulled the horse around so that I could face Orin. "I have the answer!"

"What answer?"

"I know what to do! It is not the solution we all hoped and prayed for, but it is a start! We must go the large grove, to the stone altar. The answer waits for us!"

"We should go to Brithomar and let him know we are here."

"Trust me, this is more important. We must go! It cannot wait!"

When we arrived at the oak grove, I must have looked and sounded like a madman who had lost control of himself. There were a few Druids and Britons hanging about. I made up some story about the spirits and that I was here to put a spell on the Romans, which was not entirely untrue.

I had no choice but to request, as nicely as I could, for them to leave. I felt bad, for I knew that this ground was sacred and provided comfort to them. I told them to return after midday.

I took off my weapons and piled them at the back of the altar. I was in such a rush that I began to sweat as I was excited to prove my theory. I was turning about in circles, trying to reach back and unhook my breastplate.

"Help me. Please."

"What are you doing?"

"Undo the straps and take this off me!"

As soon as Orin removed it, I ran to the altar and took my strongest knife, chipping away at the joints of the stone slab at the back. Orin saw what I was doing and started at the other end of the slab trying to scrape the seam clear of all material.

"Move your blade about. Try to loosen the stone!"

"I am! What is this all about?"

"There is a large chest in here. It will give us the answer that we seek."

Orin looked at me and kept working, until we felt the stone begin to move a little. It started to rock. We then inserted our swords on one side, then the other, switching our effort back and forth until the rock slid outwards, on an angle, hanging over the edge, as it dropped to the ground.

The chest was huge and we both slowly pulled it, dragging it across the ground. I took my knife and broke the lock. I lifted the top open and there were thousands of small, detailed figures of men, women, children, animals, warriors, trees, ships and buildings. Each figure and carving had been painted and looked so real.

I began to grab desperately, with both hands, all the carvings and place them on top of the altar. Many fell to the ground; there were so many that I became confused at what to do and could not think clearly.

"What are you doing? I don't understand."

I stopped and took a deep breath. I was thankful that Orin had said something. Now that I was certain the chest was here and not disturbed, I felt it was time to tell Orin what I was up to. I knew what I had to do. It was a big task but I needed help with it. She had to know the truth.

"There is something I have not told you."

"Oh, no."

"It's good. Let me start at the beginning. Remember I told you that Yeshua had carved a wooden figure of a physician for Galen when he was sick boy? Galen became that physician and his carving was identical to what Galen would look like as a man."

Orin nodded.

"I took Armaigen's ashes back to his home in Eire. It took me weeks to find the exact house. It was in the County of Kerry. The house was a derelict manor house, which in some ways appeared like a castle. It was in ruins. It sat on a sharp cliff overlooking the sea. There was one high, square tower still intact and a few stone buildings with no roofs or complete walls. As I came closer, I went inside the fragmented inner wall, to the courtyard. The ground was black and bare; it appeared as if there had been a fire. I walked about and on closer examination I found that many timbers were charred and broken. On different parts of the outside walls, smoke had also blackened the stone. The fire had been recent.

I looked for a suitable place for Armaigen's ashes. I noticed that inside the main building, at the back near the tower, the light of a fire. I looked up and saw the smoke coming out of the chimney. I went to the door, not knowing what to expect. The door was answered by a very old man called Eircheard. He asked me in, saying he was expecting me. As I walked into the great room, I saw an old woman sitting on the floor in front of the fire. Her hands and legs were deformed, as well as her curved shoulders. She had lined up around the room wooden carvings of people, animals, trees and buildings, just like we have here in the chest. She was playing with them, talking to them. She was simple-minded and did not notice me come into the room."

"Who were they?"

"Eircheard was the brother of Armaigen. The old woman was Muriell; she is the sister of Armaigen."

"But how can that be?"

"The complete story was told to me by Eircheard. When Armaigen had gone missing down the sink hole, the village thought that he had been murdered by his family. Eventually, the family was forced to move away. Armaigen eventually left the UnderWings and lived secretly in the tower for years, alone. He was a powerful Drui and experienced a prophesy while he was there. He carved and painted thousands of wooden figures and objects of the more important people and event he would

331

have to deal with in his life. He eventually left the house, ready for his pilgrimage. He left behind all of the wooden figures and carvings, as well as hidden instructions about the potion that only his family members and close friends could decipher."

"The parents died and many years after they had moved away, Eircheard and Muriell returned to the house. The coastal village had been destroyed by a storm. There was no one living that knew them. Armaigen was aware that they were coming back and wanted to keep them young. Eircheard showed me the statues of him and Muriell that Armaigen had carved."

"You said they were old?"

"Yes, they were old. Some months before I had arrived, some drunken thieves had set fire to the house. Fortunately, the fire was contained but it destroyed the plants that made the potion. They were dying. I had plenty of seeds and mixtures in my cart and I offered to grow a new garden for them. Until the plants were mature, I gave them enough of the potion to last until the plants were fully grown.

Muriell had not spoken a word to me. Something had captured her attention. She made a sound, mostly created by her inhaling and exhaling quickly. It was a repeated, a guttural shrieking sound, her body shook as she seemed excited about what she was holding. She took the last figure in the long line of figures, crawling over to me. She handed me a carved figure of myself!

Eircheard told me that they had been expecting me. They knew why I was there.

I got down on the floor with Muriell and the next person in the line was Yeshua. I followed the line back as I recognized people in Asia, the Romans and many outspoken villagers. At the beginning of the line were the UnderWings. It was all there, on the floor of the room. There were thousands of carvings! The wooden carvings told the story of Armaigen's life before he had met anyone!"

"What has that got to do with us?"

"Well, Eircheard got up and took me to another room and showed me a large chest.

I knew what it was, as soon as I saw it. He said that this was my chest. Armaigen had carved people, places and events I would meet and travel to in my lifetime." I looked down and touched the top of the chest we had just taken out of the altar. "This chest contains those figures! This is my life!"

Orin was trying to decipher all this information. "But what does it mean for us?"

I bent down picking many carvings off the ground and placed them on the altar again.

"Help me." Orin began helping me take them out of the chest.

I talked as we worked, "You see, we have to line up all wooden carvings of my life. In sequence, from the time I met Armaigen until now. You will see who I have met and the places I have travelled to, even the ones I have not told you about. You should also be able to see yourself and all of our children."

"Our unborn baby?"

"Yes. You should know whether it is a girl or a boy."

Orin giggled, like an excited child. "Can I keep the carvings of our children?"

"Yes. Put them off to the side."

"Where is all this leading to?"

"Don't you see? We can disregard the carvings of the past. We want to line up in order the present: everything that relates to the past four equinoxes. I saw Paulinus today for the first time, including his Commanders, Barrius and Slavious; they should all be in the chest. Likewise, Brithomar, Cathal, the other Chieftains and some of the Britons will be recognizable. We need to place them on the altar, as well as anyone else that I have met recently. Find them. Line them all up and let's see what we have."

"What I am interested in is seeing carvings of people I do not recognize. By the process of elimination, anyone or place I do not recognize has not happened yet."

"I understand. If you don't recognize them, then that means we might live, for Armaigen saw it in his prophesy."

"Exactly."

We worked as fast as we could. My mind was reeling as Orin showed me hundreds, if not thousands of carvings; I either accepted or rejected them. I started to develop a keen eye, as my senses became inflamed. I was re-living my past lives again, through many generations.

I told Orin that I had stayed a while with Eircheard and Muriell. "I took care of the potion garden and made many repairs to the house. As days became weeks, both Eircheard and Muriell became young again, using my potion supply. We had many unforgettable conversations about my life with Armaigen.

Before I left, Muriell asked whether she and her brother could come with me, back to Europa. I told her that it was not possible; she would be safer here. But I told her that I would come back to Eire one day and take her and her brother away.

The top of the altar was becoming full. Rows upon rows of carvings had been precisely placed. There were only a few wooden carvings left at the bottom of the chest. I was beginning to feel worried. We had already found the figures of Paulinus, Barrious and Slavious, but no new unknown carvings of people and places.

Orin reached in and pulled out several men and women. The men held short bows and spears. Some had clubs with stones tied to the end. They all were naked, except for a covering over the middle of their body. They had colourful feathers in their hair and attached to some of their weapons.

Orin handed me one of the two last carvings left in the chest. It looked like a long narrow boat with an identical bow and stern, ending in a flat point. I thought it was likely capable of going in two directions.

These unusual primitive people were at the end of the line. I studied them closely. I had never seen them before; this was a good discovery.

But who were they and how would I meet them?

Orin then completed the line and placed a small baby on the altar. It was a girl.

THE END OF BOOK I

AUTHOR'S NOTE

I have a natural love of history and I enjoy telling a good story.

Missing Earth has an eclectic mix of characters and events that span time. Many characters and events are true. Some liberties have been taken to create and capture the imagination of the reader. This is not an alternative history story. I prefer that it is not given a typical literary category such as 'fantasy'. Our world is too quick to create and label everything; which usually undermines the intended meaning.

However, if I had to select a genre, this story is closely related to 'mystical realism'. A story about real people caught within a transcendent experience.

The main theme of the story is man's search for meaning. Almost everyone in the story is on a quest of some sort. Armaigen and Tiernan explore the world teaching, learning about other cultures while increasing their connection and control over the earth spirits. Yeshua (Jesus) is on a special mission as he tries to reconcile the role his Father has given him. This contrasts for his desire to live and enjoy life as a man. Galen enjoys the love of learning and seeks to increase his knowledge beyond any human living. He is impatient as he waits to save the earth; as foretold in a prophesy when he was a young boy. The Romans find meaning in themselves and their way of life.

As an aside, I find it fascinating that Empires sincerely seek to liberate people for their own benefit of some sort. Even today, without formal empires, there is sometimes little room for the individual to find personal spiritual meaning. But we must keep moving forward and seek some sort of spiritual meaning to our lives, even though many of us find ourselves disabled. Armaigen did warn Tiernan that the Romans are smothering the earth. The earth needs to breathe or all the earth spirits will die.

Spiritualism governs the events and conversations in the story. I am certain that many readers will be uncomfortable on how I described Yeshua living as a man. My purpose was not to undermine him but place him in difficult situations. No harm was intended. I sought to examine the intrinsic questions that he would have considered as a man. I was intrigued to assess what his thoughts might have been and the relationship with his Father; as he makes his decision to enter heaven or stay on earth as a man. I also wanted to answer some questions about Yeshua, that are not written in the New Testament. I described what Yeshua was like as a child. His desire as a man to love and have a family. I also thought it would be interesting for Matthew to visit Galen who is an atheist as he writes his Gospel and meets Picasso, the father of modern cubism.

I enjoyed relating the friendship between Tiernan and Yeshua; as they do not really understand the religious beliefs of each other. Tiernan controls all of nature. Yeshua lives almost in exile never giving up on the position of grace awarded to him by his Father.

Galen, the Greek physician did exist in the 2nd century CE. His real name was Aelius Galenus. His father was Aelius Nicon Galenus and he was an architect. They lived in Pergamon, Greece which is now located in modern Turkey and called Bergama. The Altar of Zeus did exist in Pergamon. Galen did go to Rome and became a famous physician and philosopher. Many of his writings on the anatomy, heart and brain were still followed and considered reliable up to the 15th century CE. The information regarding Nero is true.

In my research, there are references to Armaigen being the father of Druidism in ancient Ireland. Tiernan, Orin and all the other Drui names, including the Briton tribal Chieftain names were created; but not the Briton tribal names. It is difficult to find objective descriptions of the Druids and their religious practices. Most of the writings were written by victorious Roman Generals like Caesar, Claudius, the philosopher Pliny the Elder and Agricola. Agricola eventually became the Governor of Britannia near the end of the 1st century CE. The information is not without prejudice but I sought to balance and enrich the beautiful Drui philosophy of living amongst nature which they must have supported. The Druids were likely the first environmentalists.

Most of the names of places have not been changed. Britannia was divided in many tribal cultures and territories pre-invasion. Please refer to the map of Pre-Roman Britain. In fact, I have taken liberty again at calling most people 'Britons' on the island for expediency. Recent investigations have shown there were many different cultures from within the Empire living in 'Briton' with a variety of physical features. I was tempted to identify the Celtic contribution, which I am sure existed but there is growing information that the word 'Celt' was not used as a national or cultural identity until much later. The same applies to the references to 'Europa' for the Romans did not identify the Empire as a continent but rather combining Empire provinces as 'Gallia' (Aquitania, Lugdunensis, Belgica, Germania) and 'Hispana' (Tarraconensis, Lusitania). Likewise, Ireland has been through many name changes and one of them was Eire. The Romans called Eire Hibernia and I selected Eire. Finally, the ancient island of Ynys Mon, sometimes referred to as Mona is the modern island of Anglesey.

Gaius Suetonius Paulinus did exist. He was a very powerful Roman General that lived during the timeline of the book. He was the first General to cross the Atlas Mountains and was undefeated. Because of his contribution to the Empire he was promoted to Governor of Britannia and given the task of suppressing the tribal rebellions. He gained a ruthless reputation but was admired for his battle tactics and strategy. Britons and Druids did find sanctuary on Ynys Mon from Roman oppression. Barruis, Slavious and Kiefer are fictional names in command of the Roman legions. It is amazing the preparation the Romans found necessary to cross the treacherous straits.

In 61CE, Paulinus did attack Ynys Mon with the intent of killing every Drui and Briton. Boudicca, the famous Iceni woman warrior would prove a problem to the Romans. It would be one of the bloodiest Roman campaigns ever witnessed.

In Book II of the series you will find out what happened!

ABOUT THE AUTHOR

C. H. Byart is a teacher and educator living in Niagara-on-the-Lake, Ontario. He was born in Toronto and spent his childhood in Ontario.

Byart has a Bachelor of Arts with Honours in History and English and a Bachelor of Education from the University of Toronto. He has always loved researching history, visiting ancient sites, studying theology, and spinning stories.

Byart is available for speaking engagements. For more information, please visit his website, www.missingearth.ca, or e-mail him at chbyart@gmail.com.

Shelburne Public Library
201 Owen Sound Street
Shelburne, ON   L9V 3L2

42028619R00200

Made in the USA
Middletown, DE
30 March 2017